Jack [...   ...., taxi driver, Engl.   teacher, and motivational trainer, and is now a full-time writer. Eleven of his novels have been Nebula finalists. *Seeker* won the award in 2007. McDevitt lives in Georgia with his wife Maureen.

Praise for Jack McDevitt:

'You're going to love it even if you think you don't like science fiction. You might even want to drop me a thank-you note for the tip before racing out to your local bookstore to pick up the Jack McDevitt backlist'   *Stephen King*

'A real writer has entered our ranks, and his name is Jack McDevitt'
Michael Bishop, Nebula Award winner

'Why read Jack McDevitt? The question should be: Who among us is such a slow pony that s/he isn't reading McDevitt?'
Harlan Ellison, Hugo and Nebula Award winner

'You should definitely read Jack McDevitt'
Gregory Benford, Nebula and Campbell Award winner

'No one does it better than Jack McDevitt'
Robert J. Sawyer, Hugo, Nebula and Campbell Award winner

Jack McDevitt titles published by Headline:

The Academy (Priscilla Hutchins) Novels
The Engines Of God
Deepsix
Chindi
Omega
Odyssey
Cauldron

The Alex Benedict Novels
A Talent For War
Polaris
Seeker
The Devil's Eye
Echo
Firebird

Jack McDevitt

DEEPSIX

headline

First published in Great Britain in 2013 by
HEADLINE PUBLISHING GROUP

First published in 2001 by Eos Books
An imprint of HarperCollins Publishers

1

Cataloguing in Publication Data is available from the British Library

ISBN 978 1 4722 0321 2

Set in Sabon LT Std by Palimpsest Book Production Limited,
Falkirk, Stirlingshire

Printed and bound in Great Britain by
Clays Ltd, St Ives plc

Headline's policy is to use papers that are natural, renewable and
recyclable products and made from wood grown in sustainable
forests. The logging and manufacturing processes are expected
to conform to the environmental regulations of the country of origin.

HEADLINE PUBLISHING GROUP
An Hachette UK Company
338 Euston Road
London NW1 3BH

www.headline.co.uk
www.hachette.co.uk

FOR WALTER CUIRLE

who continues to provide
the special effects

On that final day, we stood bent against the wind at world's end, and watched the churning hell-lit clouds. Somewhere out there, over the eastern peaks we could no longer see, dawn was breaking. But it was a terrifying dawn, cold and lethal and black.

—GREGORY MACALLISTER, *Deepsix Diary*

Acknowledgments

I'm indebted to John Spencer of the Lowell Observatory for collision data; to science fiction writer Sage Walker for dietary assistance; to Les Johnson of NASA for showing me how it could be done; to Ralph Vicinanza, for timely help; to Eos editor Caitlin Blasdell, who seems to have all the right instincts. To Maureen, for infinite patience. To Sara and Bob Schwager for their work with the manuscript. To Brian A. Hopkins for his suggestions. And special appreciation to Henry Mencken, for a glorious half century.

Prologue

'They went in *there*.' Sherry pointed.

The afternoon was quiet and deadly still. The sun rode in a cloudless sky. It was not, of course, a bright sun. The dusty Quiveras Cloud, within which this system had drifted for three thousand years, prevented that. Randall Nightingale looked around at the trees and the river and the plain behind him, and considered how rare, in this equatorial place, was a summer's day.

In his mind, he replayed the screams. And the staccato sounds of the stinger blasts.

His pilot, Cookie, was checking his weapon. Tatia shook her head, wondering how Cappy could have been so dumb as to wander off. She was redheaded, young, quiet. Her usually congenial expression was bleak.

Andi watched the line of trees the way one might watch a prowling tiger.

Capanelli and his two colleagues had started just after dawn. Sherry explained again. They'd entered the forest despite the prohibition against getting out of sight of the lander. And they hadn't come out.

'But you must have *heard* what happened,' said Nightingale.

1

The three members of the party had been wearing e-suits and talking to each other on the allcom.

She looked embarrassed. 'I went in the washroom. Tess called me when it started to happen.' Tess was the AI. 'When I got out, it was over. There was nothing.' Her lip trembled, and she looked on the edge of hysteria. Tess had recorded a few seconds of screams. And that was all they had.

Nightingale tried calling them, and heard only a carrier wave. 'Okay,' he said. 'Let's go'

'All of us?' asked Andi. She was blond, chunky, usually full of wisecracks. One of the boys. At the moment, she was strictly business.

'Strength in numbers,' he said.

They spread out across the hardscrabble grass, glanced at one another for mutual support, and started toward the tree line. 'There,' Sherry said. 'They went in *there*.'

Nightingale led the way. They proceeded cautiously, drawing together again, weapons at the ready. But these were researchers, not trained military types. To his knowledge, none had ever fired a stinger in anger. Seeing how nervous they were, he wondered whether they didn't have as much to fear from themselves as from the local wildlife.

The sunlight dimmed beneath the canopy, and the air temperature dropped a few degrees. The trees were tall and fleshy, their upper branches tangled in a canopy of vines and large spade-shaped leaves. Thick cactuslike growths were everywhere. The ground was covered with vegetable debris. Overhead, an army of unseen creatures screeched, scratched, ran, and flapped. As was the case in forests everywhere, he knew, the majority of animals would be found living in the canopy and not on the ground.

The e-suit reduced his olfactory sense, but imagination came to his rescue, even in this curious woodland, and he could smell the pines and mint of his native Georgia.

Biney Coldfield, the starship's captain and pilot of the third lander, broke in to inform him she was approaching and would join the search as soon as she was down.

He acknowledged, letting his irritation show in his voice. Capanelli had embarrassed him, ignoring the established guidelines and plunging into an area with such limited visibility. It made them all look like rank amateurs. And had probably gotten him killed.

Nightingale scanned the ground, trying to spot footprints, or any sign Cappy's group might have left in passing. But he saw nothing. At last he turned to the others in his party. 'Do we have a woodsman, by any chance?'

They looked at one another.

'Where were they going?' he asked Sherry.

'Nowhere in particular. Straight ahead, I guess. Following the trail.'

Nightingale sighed. Straight ahead it was.

Something raced up a tree. At first glimpse he thought it resembled a squirrel, but then he saw it had extra legs. It was their first day on Maleiva III.

A couple of birds circled them and settled onto a branch. Redbirds. They looked like cardinals, except that they had long beaks and turquoise crests. The colors clashed.

'Wait a minute,' Sherry said.

'What?' demanded Nightingale.

She raised her hand for quiet. 'There's something behind us.' They whirled as one and weapons came up. In their rear, a tree limb fell. Nightingale backed into something with spines.

Cookie and Tatia went back and looked. 'Nothing here,' they reported.

They moved out again.

There was little space for walking. They were constantly pushing through bushes and fighting their way past brambles. He pointed out a couple of broken stalks that suggested something had come this way.

Then he stepped into a glade and saw them.

All three were lying still. Their force-field envelopes were filled with blood. Their faces were frozen in expressions of terror and agony.

Sherry came out behind him, gasped, and started forward.

He stopped her and held her until she calmed down a bit. The others scanned the trees for the attacker. 'Whatever it was,' said Tatia, 'it's not here now.'

Sherry freed herself from him, approached the bodies, moving progressively more slowly, and finally dropped to her knees beside them. He watched her whisper something. Watched her rock back on her haunches and stare into the trees.

He joined her, put a hand on her shoulder, and stood wordlessly, looking down at the carnage.

Andi came up beside him. She'd been a close friend of Al White's for years. She sighed and began quietly to sob.

Tatia remained at the edge of the glade, glancing first at the bodies and then hardening her gaze and surveying the ring of trees.

Biney, listening from the third lander, broke in: 'What's going on, Randy?'

All the blood was trapped inside the Flickinger fields, so it was difficult to make out details of the wounds. But each of the three looked as if he'd been jabbed, bitten, gouged, whatever, numerous times. The wounds looked small, he thought. The *attacker* had been small. *Attackers*. There had certainly been more than one.

He must have said it aloud. *'Small?'* said Biney. *'How small?'*

'Rat size, maybe. Maybe a little bigger.'

Whatever they had been, they'd succeeded in tearing off a few pieces of meat, although they hadn't been able to eat any of it because they couldn't extract it from the e-suits.

The area had been the scene of a battle. Scorch marks on some of the trees. Pulp blasted away from the soft-bodied vegetation, and a green viscous liquid bleeding out. Several overhead branches were blackened.

'They were shooting up,' said Nightingale.

4

They gathered almost unconsciously into a circle, backs protected, and stared at the trees and the canopy.

'Man-eating squirrels?' said Andi.

Several shrubs were burnt-out. One tree down. But no corpses or other remains of large predators. 'There's no sign of whatever did it.'

'Okay,' Biney said. 'We're just setting down. We'll be there in a few minutes. You might want to head out. Forthwith.'

'Can't leave the bodies. And we don't have enough muscle here to move them.' Cookie was the only full-size male. Nightingale himself was barely as big as Andi, the smallest of the women.

'Okay. Wait for us. We'll be with you as soon as we can.'

A couple more birds settled onto a branch. The ugly cardinals.

'You all right, Andi?' asked Nightingale, putting an arm around her.

'I've been better.'

'I know. I'm sorry. He was a good guy.'

'They were *all* good guys.'

Tatia's head came up. 'Over there,' she said.

Nightingale looked, but saw only trees.

The e-suit tended to dampen sound. He turned it off so he could hear better. The cold bit into him. But something in that direction *was* padding around.

Nightingale's instinct was to get everyone out of the woods. But he couldn't just leave everything. The stinger had a comfortable heft. He glanced at it, felt the hum of power inside the grip. It would bring down a rhino.

He pushed past Tatia. Cookie whispered to him to stay put, but he felt that his position as leader somehow required him to lead. To get out front.

Something moved rapidly, squealing, through the canopy. At ground level, a pair of eyes watched him through heavy shrubbery.

Cookie moved up beside him. 'Lizard, I think, Randy. Wait—'

5

'What?' asked Tatia.

It came out into the open, a long reptilian head with a crest, followed by a thick mud-colored body. It had short legs and nictitating eyes. Its jaws were open, and it was watching Nightingale and Cookie.

'Croc,' said Cookie.

'*Croc?*' Biney's voice.

'Same general order,' said Nightingale. 'More like a small dragon.'

'Is it what killed Cappy?'

'I don't think so.' It was too big. Anyhow, this thing would gore and mangle, Cappy and the others appeared to have numerous puncture wounds.

Its tail rose slowly and fell. He wondered whether it was issuing a challenge.

Nightingale reactivated his e-suit. 'What do you think. Cookie?'

'Don't do anything to provoke it. Don't shoot unless it attacks. Don't make eye contact.'

His heart was pounding.

The dragon snorted, opened its jaws, and showed them a large gullet and lots of razor teeth. It pawed the ground.

'If it takes another step toward us,' said Nightingale quietly, 'take it down.'

The dragon's gaze shifted. It looked above them, toward the upper branches of the trees. Its jaws opened and closed, and a serpentine tongue flicked out. Then it was backing away.

Backing away.

Nightingale followed its gaze.

'What's happening?' asked Cookie.

'I'd swear,' said Nightingale, 'something scared it.'

'You're kidding.'

'I don't think so.' A couple of the furry spiders were chasing each other through the canopy. One leaped across an open space, caught a branch, and hung on for dear life while the branch sank halfway to the ground. There was nothing else up there. Save the redbirds.

Biney was a tall woman, almost as tall as Cookie. She had hard humorless features, a voice loaded with steel, and the easy grace of a linebacker. She might have been attractive if she'd ever loosened up. Ever smiled.

She arrived with the full complement of her team, two men and a woman, all with weapons drawn.

She more or less took over, as if Nightingale no longer existed. And in truth he was pleased to hand over responsibility. This sort of thing was more in her domain than his.

She directed Tatia and Andi to stand guard, and assigned everyone else to construct slings from branches and hanging vines. When the slings were ready they laid them on the ground, placed the bodies within, and began the cumbersome effort of withdrawal.

She gave crisp directions, ordered the march, kept them together. There'd be no wandering off and no idle sight-seeing.

The trees forced them to travel single file. Nightingale was assigned a position at the rear, behind Cookie, who had charge of Cappy's body. It was hard not to stare at the corpse as they walked. The terrified expression of the dead man held him in a kind of tidal lock.

Biney had brought a laser cutter, which she wielded with grim efficiency, slicing away the undergrowth. Nightingale, as the smallest of the men, or possibly because of his position as project director, had been spared the effort of trying to drag one of the slings. When he offered to help, Biney told him on a private channel that he'd be more useful as a lookout.

So he watched the tiny forest denizens, the ubiquitous spiders and redbirds and a dozen other animals. A barrel-shaped creature literally rolled past, apparently oblivious of the presence of the rescue force.

It was an intriguing beast, but there'd be no further investigation on this world. At least not for Nightingale. He knew that

Biney would insist on allowing no one to return to the surface until the incident had been reported to the Academy. And he knew how the Academy would react. They'd have no choice, really.

Come home.

To his right, a half dozen of the big-footed redbirds sat on a branch. There was something in their manner that chilled him.

Their beaks were the right size.

Had it been redbirds the dragon had seen?

Their heads swung as the party passed. The forest grew deadly still.

The trees were *full* of them.

As they walked, birds in their rear took flight, glided beneath the canopy, and descended onto branches ahead. 'It's the redbirds,' he said softly to Biney.

'What?'

'It's the cardinals. Look at them.'

'Those little critters?' Biney could scarcely keep the derision out of her voice.

Nightingale picked out a branch from which four, no, five, of the animals were watching. He sighted on the middle one, set the intensity low since it was such a small creature, and knocked it off its perch.

As if it had been a signal, the redbirds descended on them from a dozen trees. Off to his left, Tatia screamed and fired her weapon. They were like scarlet missiles and they came in from all sides. Stingers crackled and birds exploded. A cactus erupted and burned fiercely. The air was filled with feathers and fire. One of the people who'd come in with Biney, Hal Gilbert, went down.

The stinger was a discriminating weapon. You had to aim it. That meant it wasn't of much use against this kind of attack. But Nightingale used his as well as he could, keeping the trigger depressed, and just swinging it around his head.

Biney's laser was a different matter. He saw it flash through the air, watched whole legions of the redbirds spin wildly and go down. *Down in flames, you sons of bitches.*

8

Other cactuses blew up as the stingers touched them.

Then something ripped into his back. He bit down a scream and fell to his knees, thinking he'd been hit by one of the weapons. But when he reached behind, his fingers closed on a feathery thing, which struggled frantically to get free. He crushed it.

The injury was in an awkward place, near his shoulder blade. He tried to reach it, gave up, and fell down on his back, gaining some relief by pressing it against the ground. He got off a couple more shots when something hit him again. In the neck.

The edges of his vision turned dark, his breathing slowed, and the world began to slip away.

Tatia was bending over him. She smiled when she realized he was awake. 'Glad to see you're back with us, boss.'

They were in the lander. He was on a couch. 'What happened?' he asked.

'Here.' She produced a mug from somewhere. 'Drink this.' Apple cider. It tasted warm and sweet. But his back and neck felt stiff. 'We had to give you a painkiller.'

He tried to look past her. Saw only Cookie. 'Did everybody make it back?'

'All of Biney's people.' She squeezed his arm. 'But not Biney. Not Sherry. And not Andi.' Her voice caught.

'There were *swarms* of the goddam things,' said Cookie. 'We were lucky any of us got out of there.'

'It was horrible.' Tatia shuddered. 'They were *coordinated*. They'd hit us, and back off. Hit us, and back off. They came in waves, came from every direction.'

Cookie nodded solemnly.

Nightingale tried to get up, but the painkiller hadn't taken hold.

'Careful.' She held him in place. 'You got jabbed a couple of times. You were lucky.'

He didn't quite see how he was lucky. And my God, Biney was dead. How was that possible? And the others. Six all told.

It was a disaster.

He tasted the apple cider, let it slide down his throat.

'Will says you'll be okay.' *Will* was Wilbur Keene, who'd been with Biney. He included an M.D. among his credentials, the principal reason he'd been selected for the voyage.

'They followed us all the way back,' Tatia said. 'Kept attacking.'

'The bodies are still out there?'

'We waited until it got dark,' she said. 'Then we were able to recover them.'

'Will says they had venom,' said Cookie. 'Thank God for the e-suits. He says it would have worked on us. Paralyzed us. Sent the nervous system into shock.'

He slept. When he woke again they were getting ready to leave. 'Who's in *Tess*?' he asked. He was talking about Cappy's lander. Its pilot and all its original passengers were dead. But they didn't want to leave it down here.

'Nobody,' said Cookie. 'But it's no problem. After we're on our way, I'll just tell her to come home.' The AI.

The cabin was dark, save for the soft illumination of the instrument panel. Tatia sat silently on the far side, staring into the darkness.

He watched lights blink on outside and lift into the night.

'Okay, folks,' said Cookie. 'Looks like our turn.'

It occurred to Nightingale that Cookie, as the surviving member of the command crew, was now the captain.

The harness, adjusting for his prone position, slipped down over his thighs and shoulders. It was fortunate that it did, because a sudden gust of wind hit them as they started up, rocking the spacecraft.

'Hold on,' said Cookie. Nightingale couldn't see much of what was happening, but the pilot's movements suggested he'd taken manual control. The lander steadied and rose toward the stars.

No one spoke. Nightingale stared at the illuminated instruments. Tatia sat with her head thrown back, her eyes now closed.

The reality of it was hitting home. Andi's absence was a palpable quality, something they could *touch*.

'Tess.' Cookie spoke to the remaining lander. 'Code one one. Accept my voice.'

Nightingale listened to the wind rushing over the wings. Tatia shifted slightly, opened her eyes, and glanced at him. 'How you doing, boss?'

'Pretty good.'

'Will they send another team, do you think?'

He shrugged reflexively and felt his neck pull. It was numb. 'They'll have to, I mean, this is a *living* world, for God's sake. There'll be a settlement here one day.' But there'd be some political fallout, too. For him, responsible for the mission, for its people, there'd be hell to pay.

'Excuse me,' said Cookie. 'Randy, I'm not getting a response from Tess.'

'That's not so good. Are you telling me we have to go back for the lander?'

'Let's see if we can spot what happened.' The displays lit up and Nightingale was looking at a vid record, the woods in daylight. The view from their lander. A flock of redbirds flew across the face of the screen and vanished. People were coming out of the forest. One was being helped, one was being carried. A swarm of the birds ripped into them.

Nightingale saw Remmy, one of Biney's people, covered with blood, holding a hand to his left eye. He was down on one knee, firing away. Biney stood over him, providing as much cover as she could.

He saw himself, cradled in Hal's arms. Cookie appeared in the picture, swinging a branch.

Biney's laser cut everywhere, its white beam slashing through the afternoon. The birds fell to earth whenever it touched them.

'*There,*' said Cookie. The laser grazed *Tess,* scorched her hull, moved up, and sliced off the communication pod. The pod exploded in a shower of sparks.

11

Cookie froze the picture.

'How'd Biney die?' Nightingale asked. 'She was there at the end.'

'She stood outside the airlock and held them off until we got everybody else in.' Cookie was shaking his head. 'We'll have to go back down.'

No. Nightingale did not want anything more to do with this world. Under no circumstances would they go back.

'To get the lander,' said Cookie, mistaking Nightingale's silence for indecision.

'Leave it. Cookie.'

'We can't do that.'

'It's too dangerous. We aren't going to lose anybody else.'

PART ONE
Burbage Point

November 2223

1

The impending collision out there somewhere in the great dark between a gas giant and a world very much like our own has some parallels to the eternal collision between religion and common sense. One is bloated and full of gas, and the other is measurable and solid. One engulfs everything around it, and the other simply provides a place to stand. One is a rogue destroyer that has come in out of the night, and the other is a warm well-lighted place vulnerable to the sainted mobs.

—GREGORY MACALLISTER, *Have Your Money Ready*

They came back to Maleiva III to watch the end of the world.

Researchers had been looking forward to it since its imminence was proclaimed almost twenty years earlier by Jeremy Benchwater Morgan, an ill-tempered combustible astrophysicist who, according to colleagues, had been born old. Even today Morgan is the subject of all kinds of dark rumors, that he had driven one child to tranks and another to suicide, that he'd forced his first wife into an early grave, that he'd relentlessly destroyed careers of persons less talented than he even though he gained nothing by doing so, that he'd consistently taken credit for the work of others. How much of this is true, no one really knows. What *is* on the record, however, is that Morgan had been both hated and feared by his colleagues and apparently by a deranged brother-in-law who made at least two attempts to kill him. When he'd died, finally, of heart failure, his onetime friend and longtime antagonist, Gunther Beekman, commented privately that he had beaten his second wife to the punch. In accordance with his instructions, no memorial was conducted. It was, some said, his last act of vindictiveness, denying his family and associates the satisfaction of staying home.

Because he had done the orbital work and predicted the coming collision, the Academy had given his name to the rogue world that had invaded the Maleiva system. Although that was a gesture required by tradition in any case, many felt that the Academy directors had taken grim pleasure in their action.

Morgan's World approached Jovian dimensions. Its mass was 296 times that of Earth. Diameter at the equator was 131,600 kilometers, at the poles about five percent less. This oblateness resulted from a rotational period of just over nine hours. It had a rocky core a dozen times as massive as the Earth. It was otherwise composed primarily of hydrogen and helium.

It was tilted almost ninety degrees to its own plane of movement, and half as much to the system plane. It was a gray-blue world, its atmosphere apparently placid and untroubled, with neither rings nor satellites.

'Do we know where it came from?' Marcel asked.

Gunther Beckman, small, bearded, overweight, was seated beside him on the bridge. He nodded and brought up a fuzzy patch on the auxiliary display, closed in on it, and enhanced. 'Here's the suspect,' he said. 'It's a section of the Chippewa Cloud, and if we're right, Morgan's been traveling half a billion years.'

In approximately three weeks, on Saturday, December 9, at 1756 hours GMT, the intruder would collide head-on with Maleiva III.

Maleiva was the infant daughter of the senator who'd chaired

16

the science funding committee when the initial survey was done, two decades earlier. There were eleven planets in the system, but only the doomed third world had received a name to go with its Roman numeral: From the beginning they called it *Deepsix*. In the often malicious nature of things, it was also one of the very few worlds known to harbor *life*. Even though locked in a three-thousand-year-old ice age, it would have made, in time, an exquisite new outpost for the human race.

'The collision here is only the beginning of the process,' Beekman said. 'We can't predict precisely what's going to happen afterward, but within a few thousand years Morgan will have made a complete shambles of this system.' He leaned back, folded his hands behind his head, and adopted an expression of complacency. 'It's going to be an interesting show to watch.'

Beekman was the head of the Morgan Project, a planetologist who had twice won the Nobel, a lifelong bachelor, and a onetime New York State chess champion. He routinely referred to the coming Event as 'the collision,' but Marcel was struck by the relative sizes of the two worlds. It would most certainly *not* be a collision. Deepsix would fall into Morgan's clouds, like a coin casually dropped into a pool.

'Why doesn't it have any moons?' he asked Beekman.

Beekman considered the question. 'Probably all part of the same catastrophe. Whatever ejected it from its home system would have taken off all the enhancements. We may see something like that here in a few centuries.'

'In what way?'

'Morgan's going to stay in the neighborhood. At least for a while. It's going into a highly unstable orbit.' He brought up a graphic of Maleiva and its planetary system. One gas giant was so close to the sun that it was actually skimming through the corona. The rest of the system resembled Earth's own, terrestrial worlds in close, gas giants farther out. There was even an asteroid belt, where a world had failed to form because of the nearby presence of a jovian. 'It'll eventually mangle everything,' he said, sounding almost wistful. 'Some of these worlds will get dragged out of their orbits into new ones, which will be irregular and probably unstable. One or two may spiral into the sun. Others will get ejected from the system altogether.'

'Not a place,' said Marcel, 'where you'd want to invest in real estate.'

'I wouldn't think,' agreed Beekman.

Marcel Clairveau was captain of the *Wendy Jay,* which was carrying the Morgan research team that would observe the collision, record its effects, and return to write papers on energy expansion, gravity waves, and God knew what else. There were forty-five of them, physicists, cosmologists, planetologists, climatologists, and a dozen other kinds of specialists. They were a picked group, the leading people in their respective fields.

'How long's it going to take? Before things settle down again?'

'Oh, hell. I don't know, Marcel. There are too many variables. It may never really stabilize. In the sense you're thinking.'

A river of stars crossed the sky, expanding into the North American Nebula. Vast dust clouds were illuminated by far-off Deneb, a white supergiant sixty thousand times as luminous as Sol. More stars were forming in the dust clouds, but they would not ignite for another million years or so.

Marcel looked down on Deepsix.

It could have been an Earth.

They were on the daylight side, over the southern hemisphere. Snowfields covered the continents from the poles to within two or three hundred kilometers of the equator. The oceans were full of drifting ice.

Frigid conditions had prevailed for three thousand years, since Maleiva and its family of planets plowed into the Quiveras, one of the local dust clouds. They had not yet come out the other side, wouldn't for another eight centuries. The dust filtered the sunlight, and the worlds had cooled. Had there been a civilization on Deepsix, it would not have lived.

The climatologists believed that below fifteen degrees south

18

latitude, and above fifteen degrees north, the snow never melted. Had not melted in these thirty centuries. That wasn't necessarily a long time, as such things went. Earth itself had gone through ice ages of similar duration.

Large land animals had survived. They sighted herds moving through the plains and forests of the equatorial area, which at present formed a green strip across two of the continents. There was also occasional movement out on the glaciers. But along the equatorial strip, a multitude of creatures had hung on.

Beekman got up, took a deep breath, rinsed his coffee cup, clapped Marcel on the shoulder, and *beamed*. 'Have to get ready,' he said, starting for the door. 'I believe the witching hour has arrived.'

When he was gone, Marcel allowed himself a long smile. The host of scientific leaders riding on *Wendy* had given way to unalloyed enthusiasm. On the way out they'd run and rerun simulations of the Event, discussed its potential for establishing this or that view of energy exchange or chronal consequences or gravity wave punctuation. They argued over what they might finally learn about the structure and composition of gas giants, and about the nature of collisions. They expected to get a better handle on long-standing puzzles, like the tilt of Uranus or the unexplained large iron content of worlds like Erasmus in the Vega system and Mercury at home. And the most important implication: It would be their only opportunity to see directly inside a terrestrial planet. They had special sensors for that, because the eruption of energy, during the final spasm, would be blinding.

'It's going to begin to break up *here*,' they'd said, one or another, over and over, pointing at the time line, 'and the core will be exposed *here*. My God, can you imagine what that'll *look* like?'

The common wisdom was that one could not be a good researcher if one had completely outgrown childhood. If that was so, Marcel knew he had good people along. They were kids who'd come to watch a show. And however they tried to disguise the reality of that, pretending that this was first and foremost a

19

fact-gathering mission, nobody was fooling anybody. They were off on a lark, cashing in the real reward that came from lives of accomplishment. They'd broken into the structure of space, mapped the outer limits of the universe, solved most of the enigmas associated with time, and now they were going to sit back and enjoy the biggest wreck of which anyone had ever heard.

And Marcel was pleased to be along. It was the assignment of a lifetime.

NCA *Wendy Jay* was the oldest operating vessel in the Academy fleet. Its keel had been laid almost a half century before, and its interior decor consequently possessed a quaintness that gave one a sense of stepping into another age.

Its passengers were watching Morgan through a battery of telescopes and sensors, some mounted on the ship's hull, others on satellite. In every available space throughout the vessel, researchers were peering down into misty blue-gray depths that fell away forever. Gigantic lightning bolts flickered across the face of the world. Occasional meteors raced down the sky, trailing light, vanishing into the clouds.

They gauged its magnetic field, which was two-thirds as strong as Jupiter's, and they recorded the squeals and shrieks of its radio output.

The mood remained festive, and the physicists and planetologists wandered the passageways, visiting one another's quarters, hanging out in the operations center, visiting the bridge, pouring drinks in the workout room. When Marcel strolled down to *Wendy*'s project control, he encountered half a dozen of them gathered around a screen, and when they saw him they raised their glasses to him.

It was a pleasant feeling, to be toasted by the crème de la crème. Not bad for a kid who'd resisted schools and books for years. One teacher had taken him aside when he was fourteen and suggested he might as well apply for the dole then. Get in line early, she'd advised.

When they'd finished the Morgan observations, they moved over to Maleiva III and began the process of inserting probes and positioning satellites. The intention, as Chiang Harmon explained it, was to 'take the temperature of the victim, and to listen to its heartbeat, throughout its final days.' The team wanted to get every possible physical detail on file. They would establish Maleiva Ill's density and record the fluctuations of its albedo. They would watch the shifting tides. They would examine the depth and composition of its core, analyze the atmospheric mix, and record the air pressure. They would chart its hurricanes and its tornadoes, and they would measure the increasing intensity of the quakes that would eventually shatter the planet.

At breakfast during their first full day in orbit around Deepsix, Beekman announced to everyone in the dining room, and by the PA to the rest, that the correlation of hydrogen to helium, 80.6 to 14.1, matched perfectly with that of Morgan's suspected home star. So now they knew with near certainty where it had been born.

Everyone applauded, and somebody suggested in a deliberately slurred voice that the occasion called for another toast. The noise turned to laughter and Beekman passed around the apple juice. They were in fact a sober lot.

Marcel Clairveau wanted to get a job in management but expected to spend the rest of his life piloting superluminals for the Academy. Prior to that, he'd worked for Kosmik, Inc., shuttling personnel and supplies out to Quraqua, which Kosmik was terraforming. But he hadn't liked the people running the organization, who were both autocratic and incompetent. When it reached a point at which he was embarrassed to reveal for whom he worked, he'd resigned, done a brief stint as an instructor at Overflight, had seen an opportunity with the Academy, and had taken it.

Marcel was a Parisian, although he'd begun life on Pinnacle. He had been the second child born on an extrasolar planet. The first, a girl, also born on Pinnacle, had received all kinds of gifts, up to and including a free education.

'Let it be a lesson,' his father had been fond of telling him. 'Nobody remembers who Columbus's first mate was. Always go for the top job.'

It had been a running joke between them, but Marcel had seen the wisdom in the remark, and now a variation of it hung over the desk in his quarters. *Jump in or sit down.* Not very poetic, but it reminded him to leave nothing to chance.

His father had been disappointed with the aimlessness of his adolescent years, and he'd died while Marcel was still adrift, undoubtedly convinced his wayward offspring would do nothing substantial with his life. He'd put Marcel into a small college at Lyon, where they specialized in recalcitrant students. And they'd introduced him to Voltaire.

It might have been his father's unexpected death, or Voltaire, or a math instructor in his sophomore year who unfailingly believed in him (for reasons Marcel never understood), or Valerié Guischard, who had told him point-blank she would not allow herself to become involved with a man with no future. Whatever had caused it, Marcel had decided to conquer the world.

He hadn't quite achieved that, but he was captain of a super-luminal. He'd been too late to capture Valerié, but he knew no woman would ever again walk away from him because he had nothing to offer.

Starships, however, had turned out to be less romantic than he'd expected. His life, even with the Academy, had devolved into hauling passengers and freight from world to world with monotonous regularity. He'd hoped to pilot the survey ships that went out beyond the bubble, that went to places no one had ever seen before, like the *Taliaferro*, which had come out twenty-one years ago and found Morgan. *That* was the kind of life he wanted. But those were compact ships, and the pilots also tended to be part of the working crew. They were astrophysicists, exobiologists, climatologists, people who could carry their weight during a mission. Marcel could run the ship and in a pinch repair the coffeemaker. He was a skilled technician, one of the few pilots who could do major repairs under way. That skill counted for a great deal, but it was one more reason why the Academy liked him on flights that carried large numbers of passengers.

Marcel had found himself living a curiously uneventful life.

Until Morgan.

Because the collision would be a head-on, a kind of cosmic train wreck, Maleiva III was not yet feeling the gravitational effects of the approaching giant. Nor was it yet more than a bright star in her skies. 'Nothing much will change down there,' Beekman predicted, 'until the last forty hours or so. Then' – he rubbed his hands with anticipation – 'Katie bar the door.'

They were over the night side. Filmy clouds floated below them, limned by starlight. Here and there they could see oceans or snow-covered landmasses.

The *Wendy Jay* was moving east in low orbit. It was early morning again aboard ship, but a substantial number of the researchers were up, crowded around the screens. They ate snacks and drank an endless supply of coffee in front of the displays, watching the sky brighten as the ship approached the terminator.

Marcel's crew consisted of two people. Mira Amelia was his technical specialist, and Kellie Collier was copilot. Kellie had taken the bridge when he went to bed. But sleeping had been difficult. There was too much excitement on the ship, and he hadn't dozed off until almost one. He woke again several hours later, tossed and turned for a while, gave it up, and decided to shower and dress. He'd developed a kind of morbid interest in the approaching fireworks. The realization irritated him because he'd always thought of himself as superior to those who gape at accidents.

He'd tried to convince himself that he was simply showing a scientific interest. But there was more to it than that. There was something that ran deep into the bone with the knowledge that an entire planetload of living things was going about their normal routines while disaster approached.

He turned on his monitor and picked up one of the feeds from project control. The screen filled with the endless arc of the ocean. A snow squall floated uncertainly off one edge of the cloud cover.

They were over snowcapped mountains, which in the distance subsided into an endless white plain.

It wasn't possible to *see* the Quiveras dust cloud. Even on the superluminal, they needed detectors to tell them it was there. Yet its effect had been profound. Take it away, and Maleiva III would have been a tropical world.

They were passing over a triangle-shaped continent, the largest on the planet. Vast mountain ranges dominated the northern and western coasts, and several chains of peaks formed an irregular central spine. The landmass stretched from about ten degrees north latitude almost to the south pole. Its southern limits were of course not visible to the naked eye because it simply connected with the mass of antarctic ice. Abel Kinder, one of the climatologists on board, had told him that even in normal times there was probably an ice bridge to the cap.

He found Beekman sitting in his accustomed chair on the bridge, chatting with Kellie and drinking coffee. They were looking down as the last of the mountains passed out of the picture. A herd of animals moved deliberately across the plain.

'What are they?' Marcel asked.

Beekman shrugged. 'Fur-bearing something-or-others,' he said. 'The local equivalent of reindeer. Except with white fur. Did you want me to bring up the archives?'

It wasn't necessary. Marcel had just been making conversation. He knew that the animals on Deepsix were by and large variations on well-established forms. They had all the usual organs, brains, circulatory systems, a tendency toward symmetry. A lot of exoskeletons here. Heavy bone on both sides of the wrapper. Most plants used chlorophyll.

Insects on Deepsix ranged all the way up to beasts the size of a German Shepherd.

Detail was lacking because, as the whole world knew, the Nightingale expedition nineteen years ago had been attacked by local wildlife on its first day. No one had been on the ground since. Research had been limited to satellite observations.

'It's a pleasant enough world,' said Beekman. 'It would have made a good prospect for your old bosses.'

He meant Kosmik, Inc., whose Planetary Construction Division selected and terraformed worlds for use as human outposts. 'Too cold,' said Marcel. 'The place is a refrigerator.'

'Actually it's not bad near the equator. And in any case it's only temporary. Another few centuries and it would have been away from the dust and everything would have gone back to normal.'

'I don't think my old bosses were much at taking the long view.'

Beekman shrugged. 'There aren't that many suitable worlds available, Marcel. Actually, I think Deepsix would have been rather a nice place to take over.'

The plains turned to forest and then to more peaks. Then they were out over the sea again.

Chiang Harmon called from project control to announce that the last of the general-purpose probes had been launched. In the background, Marcel heard laughter. And someone said, 'Gloriamundi.'

'What's going on?' asked Beekman.

'They're naming the continents,' said Chiang.

Marcel was puzzled. 'Why bother? It isn't going to be here that long.'

'Maybe that's why' said Kellie. Kellie was dark-skinned, attractive, something of a scholar. She was the only person Marcel knew who actually read poetry for entertainment. 'You'll have a map when it's over. Seems as if we ought to have some names to put on it.'

Marcel and Beekman strolled over to project control to watch. Half the staff was there, shouting suggestions and arguing. One by one, Chiang was putting locations onscreen, not only continents but oceans and inland seas, mountain ranges and rivers, islands and capes.

The triangular continent over which they'd just passed became Transitoria. The others had already been named. They were Endtime, Gloriamundi, and Northern and Southern Tempus.

The great northern ocean they called the Coraggio. The others became the Nirvana, the Majestic, and the Arcane. The body of water that separated Transitoria from the two Tempi (which were connected by a narrow neck of land) became the Misty Sea

They continued with Cape Farewell and Bad News Bay, which pushed far down into northwestern Transitoria; and with Lookout Rock and the Black Coast and the Mournful Mountains.

In time they filled the map, lost interest, and drifted away. But not before Marcel had noticed a change in mood. It was difficult to single out precisely what had happened, even to be certain it wasn't his imagination. But the researchers had grown more somber, the laughter more restrained, and they seemed more inclined to stay together.

Marcel usually wasn't all that comfortable with Academy researchers. They tended to be caught up in their specialties, and they sometimes behaved as if anyone not interested in, say, the rate at which time runs in an intense gravity field is just not someone worth knowing. It wasn't deliberate, and by and large they tried to be sociable. But few of them were capable of hiding their feelings. Even the women seemed generally parochial.

Consequently, most evenings he retired early to his quarters and wandered through the ship's library. But this had been a riveting day, the first full day on station. The researchers were celebrating, and he did not want to miss any of it. Consequently he stayed until the last of them had put their dishes and glasses in the collector and gone, and then he sat studying Chiang's map.

It was not difficult to imagine Maleiva III as a human world. Port Umbrage established at the tip of Gloriamundi. The Irresolute Canal piercing the Tempi.

Even then he was not sleepy. After a while he went back to the bridge. The ship's AI was running things, and he got bored looking at the endless glaciers and oceans below, so he brought up a political thriller that he'd started the previous evening. He heard people moving about in the passageways. That was unusual, considering the hour, but he assigned it to the general electricity of the day.

He was a half hour into the book when his link chimed. 'Marcel?' Beekman's voice.

'Yes, Gunther?'

'I'm back in project control. If you've a moment, we have something on-screen you might want to see.'

There were about a dozen people gathered in front of several monitors. The same picture was on all of them: a forest with deep snow and something among the trees that looked like walls. It was hard to make out.

'We're at full mag,' said Beekman.

Marcel made a face at the screen, as though it would clarify the image. 'What is it?' he asked.

'We're not sure. But it looks like—'

'—A *building*.' Mira Amelia moved in close. '*Somebody's down there.*'

'It might just be filtered sunlight. An illusion.'

They all stared at the monitor.

'I think it's artificial,' said Beekman.

2

Extraterrestrial archeology sounds glamorous because its perpetrators dig up transistor radios used by creatures who've been gone a quarter million years. Therefore, it carries an aura of mystery and romance. But if we ever succeed in outrunning the radio waves, so we can mine their broadcasts, we'll undoubtedly discover that they, like ourselves, were a population of dunces. That melancholy probability tends to undercut the glamour.

—GREGORY MACALLISTER, *Reflections of a Barefoot Journalist*

Inside the e-suit, Priscilla Hutchins caught her breath as she gazed around the interior of the reconstructed temple. Late-afternoon sunlight slanted through stained windows in the transepts, along the upper galleries, and in the central tower. A stone dais occupied the place where one might usually look for an altar.

Eight massive columns supported the stone roof. Benches far too high for Hutch to use comfortably were placed strategically throughout the nave for the benefit of worshipers. They were wooden and had no backs. The design was for creatures which lacked posteriors, in the human sense. The faithful would have

29

used the benches by balancing their thoraxes on them, and gripping them with modified mandibles.

Hutch studied the image above the altar. It had six appendages and vaguely insectile features. But the eyes very much resembled those of a squid. Stone rays, representing beams of light, radiated from its upper limbs.

This, the experts believed, was intended to be a depiction of the Almighty, the creator of the world. The Goddess.

The figure was female, although how the team had reached that conclusion escaped Hutch. It had a snout and fangs and antennas whose precise function still eluded the researchers. Each of its four upper limbs had six curved digits. The lower pair had evolved into feet, of a sort, and were enclosed in sandals.

The skull was bare save for a cap that covered the scalp and angled down over a pair of earholes. It wore a jacket secured with a sash, and trousers that looked like jodhpurs. The midlimbs were shrunken.

'Vestigial?' asked Hutch.

'Probably.' Mark Chernowski was sipping a cold beer. He took a long moment to taste it, then tapped an index finger against his lips. 'Had evolution continued, they'd no doubt have lost them.'

Despite the odd features and the curious anatomy, the Almighty retained the customary splendor one always found in the inhabitants of the heavens. Each of the four intelligent species they'd encountered, as well as their own, had depicted its assorted deities in its own image, as well as in a few others. On Pinnacle, where for a long time the physical appearance of the inhabitants had not been known, it had been difficult to sort out which representation was also that of the dominant species. But inevitably everyone succeeded in capturing the dignity of divine power.

Hutch could not help noting that the more somber qualities and moods were somehow translatable in stone from one culture to another. Even when the representations were utterly alien.

They moved closer to the altar. There were several other carved figures, some of which were animals. Hutch could see, however, that the creatures were mythical, that they could never have developed on a terrestrial world. Some had wings inadequate to lifting the owner. Others had heads that did not match the trunks. But all were rendered in a manner that suggested religious significance. One bore a vague resemblance to a tortoise, and Chernowski explained that it symbolized sacred wisdom. A serpentine figure was believed to represent the divine presence throughout the world.

'How do we know these things?' she asked. 'Plainfield told me that we still can't read any of the script.'

Chernowski refilled his mug, glanced at her to see whether she'd changed her mind and would share some of the brew, and smiled politely when she declined. 'We can deduce quite a lot from the context in which the images are traditionally placed. Although questions and doubts certainly remain. Does the turtle represent the god of wisdom? Or is it just a symbol of the divine attribute? Or, for that matter, is it just a piece of art from a previous era that no one took seriously in any other sense?'

'You mean this place might have been just an art museum?'

Chernowski laughed. 'Possibly,' he said.

The reconstruction had been raised a few kilometers away from the site of the original structure, in order to preserve the ruins.

Some pieces were quite striking. Especially, she thought, the winged beings. 'Yes.' He followed her gaze. 'Flight capability does add a certain panache, does it not?' He looked up at a creature that bore a close resemblance to an eagle. It was carved of black stone. Its wings were spread and its talons extended. 'This one is curious,' he said. 'As far as we can determine, this world never had eagles. Or anything remotely like an eagle.'

She studied it for a long minute.

'It often appears on the shoulder of the Almighty,' he continued, 'and is closely associated with her. Much as the dove is with the Christian deity.'

It was getting late, and they retreated to the rear of the nave.

Hutch took a last look. It was the first time she'd seen the temple since its completion. 'Magnificent,' she said.

The rover was waiting outside. She looked at it, looked up at the temple, compelling in its austerity and simplicity. 'It's several hundred thousand years ago, Mark,' she said. 'A few things might have changed since then. Maybe they had eagles in the old days. How would you know?'

They climbed in and started back toward the hopelessly mundane mission headquarters, little more than a collection of beige panels just west of the original ruins.

'It's possible,' he admitted. 'Although we've got a pretty good fossil record. But it's of no consequence. Better to agree with Plato that there are certain forms that nature prefers, even though we may not see them in the flesh.' He got up and stretched.

'What do *you* think happened to the natives?' she asked. 'Why'd they die off?' Pinnacle's dominant race was long gone. Almost three-quarters of a million years gone.

Chernowski shook his head. He was tall and angular, with white hair and dark eyes. He'd spent half his life on this world and had made arrangements to be buried here when the time came. If he was fortunate, he was fond of telling visitors, he'd be the first. 'Who knows?' he said. 'They got old, probably. Species *get* old, just like individuals. We know their population was falling drastically toward the end.'

'How do you know that?'

'We can date the cities. There were fewer of them during the later years.'

'I'm impressed,' she said.

Chernowski smiled and accepted the compliment as his due.

Hutch looked out the window at the handful of collapsed stones that comprised all that remained of the original temple. 'How much of it was extrapolation?' she asked. 'Of what we just saw?'

The vehicle settled to the ground and they climbed out. 'We know pretty much what the temple looked like. We're not exactly sure about all the details, but it's close. As to the statuary, we've recovered enough bits and pieces here and elsewhere to make informed guesses. I suspect if the natives could return, they'd feel quite at home in our model.'

The archeological effort on Pinnacle was almost thirty years old. There were currently more than two thousand research and support personnel scattered across several dozen sites.

Pinnacle was still a living world, of course, but it was of minimal interest to exobiologists. Its various creatures had been cataloged, its pure electrical life-forms had been analyzed, and the only work that remained now was data collection. There would be no more surprises, and no more breakthroughs.

But there was still a great deal of fascination with the prime species. The temple-builders had spread to all five continents; the ruins of their cities had been found everywhere except in the extremes at the ice caps. But they were gone to oblivion. They were by far the earliest civilization known by humans. And despite Chernowski's boasts, not one member of their species was known by name. Not even, she thought, the name of their prime deity.

Hutch thanked him for the tour and returned to the rover. She stood a few moments, half in and half out of the vehicle, gazing at the circle of antique stones, wondering how much of the temple she'd seen had come out of the imaginations of Chernowski's designers.

The e-suit fitted itself to her like a garment, save at the face, where it formed a hard oval shell, allowing her to speak and breathe comfortably. It afforded protection against extremes of temperature and radiation, and also countered air pressure within the body so that she could function in a vacuum. It felt rather like wearing a bodysuit of loose-fitting soft cloth. Power was derived from weak-force particles, and consequently the suit could maintain itself indefinitely.

When the temple had stood on this spot, the climate had been far more hospitable, and the surrounding lands had supported a thriving agricultural society. Later, the town and the temple had been sacked and burned, but the place had risen again, had risen several times from assaults, and eventually became, according to the experts, a seat of empire.

And then it had gone down permanently into the dust.

Her commlink vibrated. 'Hutch? We're ready to go.' That was Toni Hamner, one of her passengers. At the moment Toni was directing the loading crew.

A couple of Chernowski's people were lifting an engraved stone out of a pit. 'On my way,' she said.

She set down minutes later beside the lander. Another rover was on the ground, from which packing cases were being loaded. The cases contained artifacts, almost exclusively pieces of the temple, protected by foam. 'We've got some ceramics to take back,' said Toni. 'Including a statue.'

'A *statue*? Of whom?'

She laughed. 'No one has any idea. But it's in good condition.'

There were two loaders. One was looking at the shipping labels. 'Cups,' he said. 'You believe *that*? After all this time?'

'John's new,' said Toni. 'It's fired clay,' she told him. 'Do it right, and it'll last forever.' She was lithe, olive-skinned, happy-go-lucky. Hutch had brought her out from Sol four years before, with her husband. Rumor had it that she'd been maybe a bit *too* happy-go-lucky. *He* gave it up and wanted to go home, while Toni made it clear she intended to stay indefinitely. She was a power-flow expert, with an opportunity to show what she could do. Her time at Pinnacle, where she had an opportunity to design and implement her own systems without undue supervision, was priceless.

Apparently Toni had considered the husband expendable.

The cases were heavy, and it was essential to balance the load. Hutch showed them where she wanted everything, and then climbed into the cabin. Her other three passengers were already seated.

One of them was Tom Scolari, an ADP specialist whom she'd known for years. Scolari introduced her to Embry Desjardain, a physician ending her tour, and Randy Nightingale, with whom she had a passing acquaintance. Nightingale had been a surprise, a late addition to her manifest. The flight home, she explained, would last thirty-one days. Not that they didn't already know.

She sat down, pressed the commlink, and informed the transport officer that she was ready to go.

His voice crackled over the circuit. 'You're clear,' he said. 'It was nice having you here. Hutch. Will you be coming back this way soon?'

'Next two trips are to Nok.' Nok was the only world they'd found with a functioning civilization. Its inhabitants had just begun to put electricity to work. But they were constantly waging major wars. They were a quarrelsome lot, given to repression, intolerant of original ideas. They believed they were alone in the universe (when they thought about it at all), and even their scientific community refused to credit the possibility that other worlds might be inhabited. It was a curious business, because humans walked among them, clothed in lightbenders, which rendered them invisible.

Hutch wondered why the civilization on Pinnacle, dead these hundreds of thousands of years, should be so much more interesting than the Noks.

Toni took a last look at the artifacts to be sure they were secured. Then she said good-bye to the two loaders and took her seat.

Hutch started the spike, and while the system built energy she recited the safety procedures for them. Spike technology allowed her to manipulate the weight of the lander in a relatively light (i.e., planetary) gravity field from its actual value down to about two percent. She instructed her passengers to remain in their seats until advised otherwise, make no effort to release the harness until the harness itself disengaged, attempt no sudden movements once the red light went on, and so forth.

'All right,' she said. 'Here we go.'

The harnesses settled around their shoulders and locked them in. She rotated the thrusters to a down angle and fired them. The vehicle began to rise. She eased back on the yoke, and the lander lifted gently into the air.

She turned it over to the AI, informed her passengers they could switch off their e-suits if they desired, and shut her own down.

The excavation site had already become indistinguishable from the brown sands surrounding it.

The *Harold Wildside* had exquisite accommodations. Hutch had seen several major changes during the twenty-odd years she'd been piloting the Academy's superluminals, the most significant of which had been the development of artificial gravity. But it was also true that Academy people now traveled well. Not in luxury, perhaps, but current accommodations had come a long way since the early days, when everything had been bargain-basement.

The extra infusion of money into the space sciences had largely resulted from the discovery of the Omega clouds, those curious and lethal objects that drifted out of galactic center in eight-thousand-year cycles and which seemed programmed to assault technological civilizations. What they really assaulted, of course, was straight lines and right angles on structures large enough to draw their attention. Which was to say, shapes that did not appear in nature. Since their discovery two decades before, architectural styles had changed dramatically. The curve was now a basic feature everywhere. Bridges, buildings, spaceports, whatever an architect put his hand to, were designed with sweep and arc. When the Omega clouds arrived in the vicinity of Earth – they were expected in about a thousand years – they would find little to trigger them.

The entities had ignited a long debate: Were they natural objects, an evolutionary form perhaps that the galaxy used to protect itself against sentient life? Or were they the product of a diabolical intelligence of incredible engineering capability? No one knew, but the notion that the universe might be out to get the human race had caused some rethinking among the various major religions.

The temple in the desert had been rounded, without any architectural right angles. Hutch wondered whether it signified that the problem was ancient.

The lander settled into its bay on board *Wildside*. Hutch waited for her panel to turn green. When it did, she opened the airlock. 'Nice to have you folks along,' she said. 'Quarters are on the top deck. Look for your name. Kitchen's at the rear. If you want to change, shower, whatever, before we leave, you have time. We won't be getting under way for another hour.'

Embry Desjardain had long dark hair and chiseled cheekbones. There was something in her eyes that made it easy to believe she was a surgeon. She'd done three years at Pinnacle, which was one more than a standard tour for medical personnel. 'I enjoyed myself,' she explained to Hutch. 'No hypochondriacs out here.'

Tom Scolari was medium height, redheaded, laughed a lot, and told Hutch he was going home because his father had become ill, his mother was already disabled, and they just needed somebody around the house. 'Just as well,' he continued with a straight face, 'there's a shortage of women on Pinnacle.'

He made it a point to shake Nightingale's hand. 'Aren't you,' he said, 'the same Nightingale who was out to Deepsix a few years ago?'

Nightingale confessed that he was, commented that it would be good to get home, and opened a book.

While waiting for *Wildside*'s orbit to bring it into alignment with her departure vector, Hutch ran her preflight check, talked to an old friend on Skyhawk, Pinnacle's space station, and read through the incoming traffic.

There were some interesting items: the TransGalactic cruise ship *Evening Star* was on its way to Maleiva with fifteen hundred tourists to watch the big collision. The Event would also be broadcast live by Universal News Network, although the transmission would be a few days late arriving on Earth. Separatists in Wyoming had gone on another shooting spree, and another round of violence had broken out in Jerusalem.

The *Star* was the biggest in a proposed series of cruise vessels. A couple of years ago a smaller ship had taken passengers out to the black hole at Golem Point. They'd not expected much interest. As the joke went, there's not much to see at a black hole. But subscriptions had overwhelmed the ticket office, and suddenly deep-space marvels had become big business and a new industry was born.

The Maleiva story reminded her of Randy Nightingale's connection with that system. He'd lost his future and his reputation during the ill-fated mission nineteen years ago. Now the place was in the news again, and she wondered whether that had anything to do with his sudden decision to go home.

Bill asked permission to fire up the engines. '*It's time,*' he added. The onboard AI for all Academy superluminals was named for William R. Dolbry, who was not the designer, but the first captain to be brought home by the onboard system. Dolbry had suffered a cardiac arrest while ferrying an executive yacht and four frightened passengers on a self-reliance voyage eighty light-years out.

Bill's image (which was not Dolbry's) revealed a man who would have been right out of central casting for a president or chairman. His face was rounded, his eyes quite serious, and he wore a well-manicured gray beard. His designers had been careful not to allow him to establish too great a degree of presence, because they didn't want captains automatically resigning their judgment to him. Illusions could be overwhelming, and AIs still lacked the human capacity to make decisions in real-world situations.

'Go ahead, Bill,' she said.

Wildside was carrying a substantial cargo of ceramics and clay tablets. Altogether, they'd brought up eleven loads, and if the ship vas a trifle light on passengers, the cargo more than compensated.

Replicas of the cups and bowls, she knew, would turn up later in the Academy gift shop. She would have liked very much to have an original. But the stuff was worth its mass in titanium. And then some.

Pity.

'Okay, folks,' she told the PA, 'we're going to start accelerating in three minutes. Please be sure you're locked down somewhere. And check in when it's done.'

It would be a long haul back to Earth, but Hutch was used to it. She'd discovered that most of her passengers inevitably found they shared a community of interests. There was an endless supply of entertainment available, and the voyages invariably became vacations. She knew of cases in which people who had made this kind of flight together were still holding annual reunions years later. She recalled instances in which passengers had fallen in love, marriages had disintegrated, a scientific breakthrough had been made, and a nearly nonstop orgy had been conducted.

Marcel was amused. 'I understood there was nothing intelligent down there. Didn't they specify that on the profile?'

They were back in project control, surrounded by Beekman's technicians and analysts. Beekman himself heaved a long sigh. 'You know how surveys are,' he said. 'And keep in mind that *this* survey team got run off pretty quick.'

'Okay.' Marcel grinned. He'd have enjoyed being there to watch the reaction of top management when this news came in. *I say, we seem to have had a bit of an oversight on Deepsix.* 'When you're ready to transmit your report, Gunny, let me know.'

Beekman went below and, within twenty minutes, was on the circuit. 'We went back over the recordings, Marcel,' he said. 'Take a look at *this.*'

A snowfield clicked onto his display. Taken by the satellites, it seemed ordinary enough, a landscape of rolling hills and occasional patches of forest. On the desolate side, but the whole world was desolate. 'What am I looking for?'

'There,' said one of the researchers, a blond young man whose name was Arvin, or Ervin, or something like that.

A shadow.

A *building*. No doubt this time.

'Where is this?' he asked.

'Northern Transitoria. A few hundred kilometers south of the coast.'

It was a spire. A *tower*.

They magnified it for him. It appeared to be made from stone blocks. He saw a scattering of windows. 'How high is it?'

'About three stories. Probably another three below the snow line.'

He stared at it. The tower and the snow. It looked like a cold, solitary, forbidding place.

'It doesn't look lived in,' said Arvin.

Marcel agreed with the assessment. It looked old, and the surrounding snow was undisturbed.

'I don't think there's any glass in the windows,' said someone else.

A map appeared with the location marked. It was south of the ocean they'd called Coraggio. Not far from Bad News Bay.

Well named, he thought. 'What's under the snow?' Beekman nodded to someone off-screen. A network of lines appeared. Houses. Streets. Central parks, maybe. An avenue or possibly a onetime watercourse curving through the middle of the pattern. *Watercourse* probably, because it was possible to make out a couple of straight lines that looked like bridges. 'It's *big*,' he said.

Beekman nodded. 'It would have supported a population of probably twenty thousand. But it's *small* in the sense that the roads and buildings are scaled down. We figure the streets are only a couple of meters wide. That's narrow by anybody's standards. And here's something else.' He used a marker to indicate a thick line that seemed to circle the network. 'This looks like a wall.'

'Fortifications,' said Marcel.

'I'd think so. And that *kind* of fortification means pretechnological.' He looked uncomfortable. 'I wish we had an expert here.'

The tower appeared to be connected to the wall. 'Nothing else visible above the snow?'

'No. Everything else is buried.'

He'd suspected the wall they'd found yesterday to be a freak of nature, an illusion perhaps. But *this* – 'It makes five of us now,' said Marcel. Five places where sentience had appeared. 'Any structures anywhere else on the planet, Gunther?'

'Nothing other than the wall, so far. We've started looking. I'm sure there *will* be.' He tugged distractedly at his beard. 'Marcel, we'll have to send a team down. Find out who they are. Or were.'

'Can't,' said Marcel.

The project director met his eyes. Beekman lowered his voice so that there would not appear to be a disagreement. 'This is a special circumstance. I'll sign a release from any instructions or policies that preclude you from acting. But we *have* to go down and take a closer look.'

'I'd love to help, Gunny,' said Marcel, 'but I meant *can't*. We don't have a lander.'

Beekman's jaw literally dropped. 'That can't be right,' he said. 'You have three of them down in the shuttle bay.'

'Those are *shuttles*. Ship to ship. But they can't operate in an atmosphere.'

'You're *sure*?' He was visibly dismayed. 'We've got to be able to do *something*.'

'I don't know what,' said Marcel. 'Report it. Let Gomez worry about it.'

'How could we not have a lander?'

'We don't carry dead mass. Landers are heavy. This operation, we weren't supposed to have any use for one.'

Beekman snorted. 'Who decided that? Well, never mind. I guess we've all learned something about preparedness.'

41

'You don't have anyone qualified to conduct an investigation anyhow,' said Marcel.

'*Qualified?*' Beekman looked like a man facing a world of idiots. 'You're talking about poking around in an old building. Look for writing on the wall and take some pictures. Maybe find a couple of pots. What kind of qualifications do you need?'

Marcel grinned. 'You'd break all the pots.'

'Okay, let the Academy know. Tell them to send out another ship, if they want. But they'll have to hurry.'

'They will *that*,' said Marcel. He knew there wouldn't be time for a second mission to reach them from Earth. They'd have to divert somebody.

3

It surprises me that courage and valor have not been bred out of the human race. These are qualities that traditionally lead to an early demise. They are therefore not conducive to passing one's genes along. Rather it is the people who faint under pressure who tend to father the next generation.

—GREGORY MACALLISTER, *'Straight and Narrow'*,
Reminiscences

Hutch was not looking forward to spending the next few weeks locked up inside *Wildside* with Randall Nightingale. He took his meals with the other passengers, and occasionally wandered into the common room. But he had little to say, and he inevitably looked ill at ease. He was small in stature, thin, gray, only a couple of centimeters taller than the diminutive Hutch.

It was an unfortunate circumstance for a reclusive man. The run between Quraqua and Earth usually carried upward of twenty passengers. Had that been the present situation, he could have retreated easily into his cabin and no one would have noticed. But they only had *four*. Five, counting the pilot. And so he'd felt pressure and was doing his best to participate.

But his best served only to create an atmosphere that was both tentative and cautious. Laughter flowed out of the room when he appeared and everyone struggled to find things to talk about.

The biosystem on Pinnacle was, after six billion years, far and away the oldest one known. Nightingale had been there for the better part of a decade, reconstructing its history. Most of the theoretical work was said to be done, and therefore she understood why Nightingale would be going home. But nevertheless it seemed coincidental that he should choose just this moment.

In an effort to satisfy her curiosity, she'd looked for an opportunity to speak with him alone. When it arose, she casually wondered whether someone in his family had taken ill.

'No,' he'd said. 'Everyone's doing fine.' But he volunteered nothing more. Didn't even ask why she'd inquired.

Hutch smiled and suggested she'd been concerned because his name had appeared unexpectedly on the passenger manifest. She hadn't realized he was coming until just a few hours before departure.

He replied with a shrug. 'It was a last-minute decision.'

'Well, I'm glad everybody's okay.'

After the conversation, if one could call it that, she'd gone to the bridge and pulled up the files on the Nightingale mission.

The Maleiva system had been initially surveyed by the *James P. Taliaferro* twenty-one years ago. Its results had excited the scientific community for two reasons: Maleiva III was a *living* world, and it was going to collide with a rogue gas giant. The expedition under Nightingale had been assembled and dispatched with fanfare and some controversy.

Others, seemingly better qualified, had competed for the opportunity to lead the mission. Nightingale was chosen because he was energetic, the Academy said. A man of exquisite judgment. If he had no experience in exploring a biosystem whose outlines were only vaguely understood, neither had any of the other candidates. And if he was younger than some that the establishment would have preferred to see nominated, he was also, as it happened, married to the commissioner's daughter.

44

But the mission had been a disaster, and the responsibility had been laid directly on Nightingale's shoulders.

It was possible that what happened to him at Maleiva III might have happened to anyone. But as she read some of the attacks made on his judgment and on his leadership, on thinly veiled suggestions that he was a coward, she wondered that he hadn't retreated to a mountaintop and dropped out of sight.

No one ever got used to the gray mists of the hyper lanes, where superluminals seemed only to drift forward at a remarkably casual rate. Travelers watching from the scopes felt as if they were moving through heavy fog at a few kilometers per hour.

Wildside slid quietly through the haze, and Hutch could easily imagine that she was somewhere northeast of, say, Newfoundland, gliding over the Atlantic, waiting for foghorns to sound. She'd set the ship's screens, which masqueraded as windows, to display a series of mountain vistas, urban views, or whatever the passengers thought they'd like. Seated in the common room, she was looking out over London, as if from an airship cabin. It was broad daylight, early afternoon, midwinter. Snow was falling.

They were in the sixth day of passage.

'What's really out there?' asked Scolari, who had joined her for lunch.

'Nothing,' she said.

He canted his head. 'Must be *something*?'

'Not a thing. Other than the fog.'

'Where's *the fog* come from?'

'Hydrogen and helium. A few assorted gases. It's our universe in a disorganized, and cold, state.'

'How'd it happen?' he asked.

She shrugged. 'Nothing big ever formed. It has something to do with the gravity differential. Physicists will tell you the real question is why *we* have planets and stars.'

'Gravity's different here?'

They were both eating fruit dishes. Hutch's was pineapple and

45

banana with a slice of cheese on rye. She munched at it, took a moment to contemplate the taste, and nodded. 'The setting's lower, much weaker, than in *our* universe. So nothing forms. You want to see what it looks like?'

'Sure.'

Hutch directed Bill to put the outside view from the forward scope on the screen.

London blinked off and was replaced by the mist.

Scolari watched it for a minute or so and shook his head. 'It almost looks as if you could get out and walk faster than this.'

'If you had something to walk on.'

'Hutch,' he said, 'I understand sensors don't work here either.'

'That's true.'

'So you really don't know that there's nothing out there. Nothing in front of us.'

'It's not supposed to be possible,' she said. 'Solid objects don't form here.'

'What about other ships?'

She could see he wasn't worried. Scolari didn't seem to worry much about anything. But everyone was mystified by hyper travel. Especially by the perceived slowness. And by the illusion of shadows in the mist. Those came from the ship's own lights. 'According to theory,' she said, delivering the answer she'd given many times before, 'we have our own unique route. We create a fold when we enter, and the fold goes away when we leave. A collision with another ship, or even a *meeting* with one, isn't supposed to be possible.'

Nightingale came in, ordered something from the autoserver, and sat down with them. 'Interesting view,' he said.

'We can change it.'

'No, please.' He looked fascinated. 'It's fine.'

She glanced at Scolari, who bit into an apple. 'I love gothic stuff,' he said.

But the conversation more or less died right there.

46

'Do you plan to return to Pinnacle, Randy?' Hutch eventually asked. 'Or will you be going on another assignment?'

'I'm retiring,' he said, in a tone that suggested it should have been obvious.

They both congratulated him.

'I've bought a seaside place in Scotland,' he continued.

'*Scotland.*' Hutch was impressed. 'What will you be doing there?'

'It's tucked away on a remote coastline,' he said. 'I *like* remote.'

'What will you do with your time?' persisted Scolari.

He poured himself a cup of coffee. 'I think, for the first year, absolutely *nothing.*'

Scolari nodded. 'Must be nice.' He commented that he'd lined up a teaching post at the University of Texas, went on for a bit about how good it would be to see his folks again after all these years. And then asked a question that made Hutch wince: 'Randy, do you have any plans to write your memoirs?'

It was of course a minefield. Scolari undoubtedly knew that Nightingale was a celebrity of sorts, but probably didn't have the details.

'No.' Nightingale stiffened. 'I don't think many people would find *my* life very exciting.'

Hutch knew from experience that she and her passengers would form a tight bond. Or they'd come to dislike one another intensely. Small groups in long flights always developed one of those two behavior patterns. Some years ago, a sociologist had been aboard to study the phenomenon and had given his name to it. The Cable Effect. She expected to see this one divide in two, with Nightingale on one side and everyone else bonded on the other.

The voyage so far had been short on entertainment and long on conversation. They'd forgone the games and VRs with which passengers usually entertained themselves, and instead had simply talked a lot.

There'd already been some personal admissions. That was always an indication that passengers were coming together, but it usually took several weeks. Embry confessed the third night out that she was seriously considering giving up medicine. Couldn't stand people constantly complaining to her about how they felt. 'The world is full of hypochondriacs,' she'd said. 'Being a doctor isn't at all the way most people think it is.'

'My mother was a hypochondriac,' said Toni.

'So was mine. So I should have known before I went to medical school.'

'Why'd you go?' asked Hutch.

'My father was a doctor. And my grandmother. It was sort of expected.'

'So what'll you do if you give it up?'

'There's always research,' suggested Scolari.

'No. Truth is, I'm just not interested. I'm bored with it.'

Toni Hamner, despite Hutch's initial impressions, turned out to be a romantic. 'I went to Pinnacle because it was so *different*. I wanted to *travel*.'

'You did *that*?' said Embry.

'And I loved it. Walking through places built by something that wasn't *human*. Built hundreds of thousands of years ago. *That's* archeology.'

'So why are you going home?' asked Scolari.

'My tour was up.'

'You could have renewed,' said Hutch. 'They're paying bonuses to have people stay on.'

'I know. I'd already done a one-year extension. I'm ready to do something else.'

'Uh-huh,' said Embry. 'That sounds like a family.'

Toni laughed. 'At least checking out the prospects.'

Scolari nodded. 'None on Pinnacle?'

She thought it over. 'It isn't that there aren't some interesting men out there. In fact, there were a lot of guys. But they tend to be married to the business. Women are more or less perceived as strictly entertainment value.'

She never mentioned her ex.

Only Nightingale had not revealed himself, and now they sat, gazing at the eternal fog while he said, yes, he wished his life was interesting enough that people would want to read about it. And he said it with such conviction that she wondered whether he actually believed it.

Scolari went back to the foggy outdoors. 'Does anyone,' he asked, 'have any idea about the architecture of this place? How big is it out there?'

'As I understand it,' Hutch said, 'that question has no—'

Bill's message light began to blink.

'. . . no relevance,' she finished. 'Go ahead, Bill.'

'Hutch,' he said, *'we have a transmission from the Academy.'*

'On-screen, Bill.'

Embry walked in as the fog blinked off and the message appeared:

TO: *NCA* HAROLD WILDSIDE
FROM: DIRECTOR OF OPERATIONS
SUBJECT: COURSE CHANCE

HUTCHINS. WENDY HAS FOUND RUINS ON DEEPSIX. DIVERT IMMEDIATELY. GET PICTURES. ARTIFACTS. WHATEVER YOU CAN. ESSENTIAL WE HAVE DETAILS ON ORIGINAL INHABITANTS. NO ONE ELSE WITHIN RANGE. YOU ARE APPOINTED ARCHEOLOGIST FOR THE DURATION. COLLISION WITH MORGAN IMMINENT. AS YOU KNOW. TAKE NO CHANCES.

GOMEZ

It had been a mistake. Hutch should have taken the transmission privately. She stole a glance at Nightingale but could read nothing in his face.

'Uh,' said Scolari, 'how far out of the way is that?'

'About five days, Tom. One way.'

The chime sounded for Nightingale's meal. 'I don't think I'm anxious to go,' Nightingale said.

Hell. She didn't really have a choice. They'd sent her a directive. She couldn't argue it, if only because a round-trip transmission would take several days. She'd been around long enough to know that ruins on a world thought uninhabited was a major find. And they were handing it to her. Had she been alone, she'd have been delighted. 'I'm going to have to do this,' she said, finally. 'I'm sorry for the inconvenience. In the past, when something like this has happened, the Academy has compensated passengers for lost time.'

Nightingale closed his eyes and she heard him exhale. 'I assume they'll charter another ship for us.'

'I don't think there'd be much point unless there's something nearby. If they have to send one from home, it'll take almost five weeks to arrive. By then, the project will be long over, and we'll be on our way back anyway.'

'I'm tempted to sue,' Nightingale persisted.

That was an empty threat. Potential travel diversions and inconveniences were written into everyone's contract. 'Do whatever you think best,' she said quietly. 'My best estimate for the total delay is about three weeks.'

Nightingale put down his knife and fork with great deliberation. 'Outstanding.' He got up and left the room.

Embry wasn't happy either. 'It's ridiculous,' she said.

'I'm sorry.' Hutch tried a smile. 'These things happen.'

Scolari rolled his eyes and slumped back in his chair. 'Hutch,' he said, 'you can't do this to me. I've got a week booked in the Swiss Alps. With old friends.'

'Tom.' She allowed herself to look uncomfortable. 'I'm sorry, but I think you're going to have to reschedule.'

He stared right through her.

Hutch was by now striving to control her own temper. 'Look,' she said, 'you've both been around the organization long enough. You know what this kind of discovery means. And you also know that they haven't given me an option. Please complain where it'll do some good. Write it, and I'll be happy to send it.'

Toni, when she was told, sighed. 'Not my idea of a fun time,' she said. 'But I can live with it.'

Within an hour Hutch had realigned their flight path, and they were bound for Maleiva.

She kept out of the way for the balance of the day. If it couldn't be said that the congenial mood of the first few days returned, it was also true that the anger and resentment dissipated quickly. By morning, everyone had more or less made peace with the new situation. Embry admitted that the opportunity to watch a planetary collision might be worth the inconvenience. As to Scolari, he might have begun to realize that he was, after all, the lone young male with two attractive passengers.

Hutch judged the time was right to take the next step.

All except Nightingale were in the common room during the late morning. Toni and Embry were playing chess while Scolari and Hutch debated ethical problems served to them by Bill. The immediate issue was whether it was proper to pass on to others as certain a doubtful religious stance on the grounds that belief made for a more secure psychological existence. Hutch watched for the chess game to finish, then called for everyone's attention.

'Usually,' she told her passengers, 'there's a boatload of people on these flights, and half of them are archeologists. Does anyone have an archeological background?'

Nobody did.

'When we get to Deepsix,' she said, 'I'll be going down to the surface. Just to look around, see what can be seen, and maybe collect some artifacts. If anyone else would like to go, I could use some volunteers. The work's easy enough.' She drew herself up to her full height. They looked at one another, then gazed at the ceiling or the walls.

Embry shook her head no. 'Thanks anyhow,' she said. 'I'll

watch from here. Hutch, that's the place where they lost a landing party back near the turn of the century. Eaten, as I recall.' She picked up her queen and studied it. 'I'm sorry. I really am. But I have no stake in this. If there was something here they wanted to look at, they had twenty years to do it. Now at the last minute they want *us* to go down and take care of their business. Typical.'

'I'm sorry, Hutch,' said Scolari, 'but I feel the same way. Bureaucratic screwup, and they expect us to run out there and put our lives on the line.' He looked past her, not wanting to meet her eyes. 'It's just not reasonable.'

'Okay,' she said. 'I understand. I'd probably feel the same way.'

'You're supposed to take pictures,' Toni said. 'Do you have a scan?'

Hutch had a case of them, stocked in the supply compartment. *That* at least wouldn't be a problem.

Toni pushed back in her chair. She was watching Hutch carefully, but keeping her expression blank. Finally, she smiled. 'I'll go,' she said.

Hutch suspected that, had one of the others volunteered, she would have found a reason to stay behind. 'There's no pressure, Toni.'

'Doesn't matter. My grandkids'll ask me about this one day. I wouldn't want to have to say I stayed up here and watched it from the dining room.'

The remark earned her a pointed glance from Embry.

As was his custom, Nightingale retired early to his quarters. He knew that the others were more comfortable in his absence, and he was sorry about that. But the truth was that the small talk bored him. He spent his days working on the book that he hoped would one day be perceived as his magnum opus: *Quraqua and Earth: The Evolution of Intelligence.* It was one of the supreme ironies that humans had traced the forces that had produced extraterrestrial intelligence in the known instances, but had not yet satisfactorily applied the lessons to their own species. At least until *he* had appeared on the scene.

He was content to spend his evenings with Harcourt and DiAlva, his great predecessors, rather than listen to the endless chatter that passed for conversation in the common room.

The people he was traveling with were simply not bright, and time was precious. He was coming to a fuller appreciation of that melancholy reality as the years slipped by. One doesn't live forever.

Tonight, though, he was too distracted to think of anything other than Deepsix. Maleiva III. The world with no future. *Do you have any plans to write your memoirs?* Scolari's intent had been uncertain. Had he been laughing at Nightingale? It was the sort of question asked of him again and again, with increasing regularity, as the Event approached, and people remembered. *Aren't you the Nightingale who lost six people?*

He would have liked some rum. But he knew from hard experience that when he got like this, he'd drink too much.

Soon it would be over. Once back on solid ground, he'd retire to the villa his agent had bought for him. It was situated on a promontory, out of the way, off a private road. No visitors. No neighbors. No one left to answer to.

If he'd been smart, he'd have gotten off Pinnacle years ago, before it all came front and center again. But he'd let it go, thinking that since he was no longer involved, people would have forgotten him. Forgotten he was ever there.

Aren't you the Nightingale who botched the first mission so thoroughly that we never went back?

He had no close friends, but he was not sure why that was. Consequently, there'd never been anyone with whom to share his considerable professional success. And now, in this increasingly sterile environment, he found himself reflecting more intensely on his life, and sensing that if indeed it was a journey he hadn't gone anywhere.

Now, with the return of Maleiva III to the news, with the increase of public interest in everything that had to do with the doomed world, his situation was proceeding rapidly downhill. He had even considered changing his name when he got home. But there were serious complications to doing that. The paperwork involved was daunting. No, it should be sufficient just to keep himself out of the directories. He'd already made one mistake, telling these people where he was going, that he was headed for Scotland.

He'd established a code. Any money due him, any formal transactions, anyone trying to reach him for any reason, would get filed in the code box. Then he could respond, or not, as he pleased. No one would know where he was. And if he was careful, no one near Banff, where he proposed to settle, would know *who* he was.

Aren't you the Nightingale who fainted?

On that terrible day, the creatures had ripped into him. The e-suit had been of limited protection, had not stopped the attack, but had prevented the little sons of bitches from injecting their poison. Nevertheless, the beaks had gone into soft flesh. His neck, though physically all right, had never really healed. Some psychic scar that wouldn't go away and the doctors couldn't cure.

Anyone would have done the same thing he did.

Well, maybe not anyone. But he hadn't been afraid, any more than anybody else. And he hadn't run, hadn't abandoned anyone. He *had* tried.

The luxury liner *Evening Star* was carrying fifteen hundred passengers who expected to party through the collision. One of these was the internationally famous Gregory MacAllister, editor, commentator, observer of the human condition. MacAllister prided himself on maintaining a sense of proper humility. On hunting expeditions, he carried his own weapons. He always made it a point with his associates to behave as if they were equals. He was unfailingly polite to the waves of ordinary persons with whom he came in contact, the waiters and physicians and ship captains of the world. Occasionally he made joking references to peasants, but everyone understood they were indeed only jokes.

He was a major political force, and the discoverer of a dozen of the brightest lights on the literary scene. He was ex-officio director of the Chicago Society, a political and literary think tank. He was also on the board of governors of the Baltimore Lexicography Institute, and the editor emeritus of *Premier*. He was an influential member of several philanthropic societies, although he persisted in describing poor people publicly as incompetent and lazy. He had played a major role in hiring the lawyers who'd taken the Brantley School Board to court in the Genesis Trial. He liked to think of himself as the world's only practicing destroyer of mountebanks, frauds, college professors, and bishops.

He had reluctantly agreed to travel on the *Evening Star*. Not that he wasn't excited by the prospect of watching entire worlds collide, but that the whole activity seemed somehow a trifle proletarian. It was the sort of thing done by people who lacked a set of substantive values. Like going to a public beach. Or a football game.

But he had consented, admitting finally to his own curiosity and to an opportunity to be able to say that he'd been there when this particular piece of history was made. Furthermore, it allowed him to demonstrate his solidarity with ordinary folks. Even if these ordinary folks tended to own large tracts of real estate along the Cape and inshore on the Hudson.

After all, a little planet-smashing might be fun, and might even provide material for a few rambles about the transience of life and the uncertainty of material advantage. Not that he was against material advantage. The only people he knew of who would have leveled material advantage so that no one had any were of course those who had none to start with.

His decision to attend had also been influenced by the passenger list, which included many of the political and industrial leaders of the period.

Although he would never have admitted it, MacAllister was impressed by the amenities of the giant ship. His stateroom was more cramped than he would have preferred. But that was to be expected. It was nonetheless comfortable, and the decor suggested a restrained good taste rather than the polished superficial luxury one usually found aboard the big superluminal liners.

He enjoyed wandering through the maze of dining rooms, bars, and lounges. Several areas had been converted into virtual verandas, from which when the time came, the passengers would be able to watch the Event.

Although MacAllister had originally planned to spend much of his time working, he took instead to holding court in a bistro called The Navigator on the starboard side, upper deck. It overflowed each evening with notables and admirers, usually second-level political types, their advisers, journalists, a few CEOs, and some writers. All were anxious to be associated with him, to be seen as his friends. On his first night out, he'd been invited to dine at the captain's table. Not quite settled in yet, he'd declined.

If MacAllister had enemies who would not have been sad to see him left somewhere in the Maleiva system, preferably on the doomed planet, he knew that the world at large perceived him as a knight-errant, righting wrongs, puncturing buffooneries, and generally enlisted in the front rank of those who were striving to keep the planet safe for common sense.

He enjoyed a reputation as a brilliant analyst and, even more important, as a model of integrity. He sided neither with progressive nor conservative. He could not be bought. And he could not be fooled.

Women offered themselves to him. He took some, although he acted with discretion, assuring himself first that there was no possibility of an enraged husband turning up. He harbored a great affection for the opposite sex, although he understood, during an age of weak males, that women belonged in kitchens and in beds.

That they were happiest in those locations, and that once everyone got around to recognizing that simple truth, life would become better for all.

Midway through the voyage, he heard the report that artificial structures had been found on Deepsix and commented on it in the journal he'd kept all his life:

We've known about Maleiva III and the coming collision for twenty-odd years, he wrote, *and suddenly, with a few weeks left, they discover that unfortunate world has had a history. Now, of course, there will be some advanced finger-pointing to determine which rascals are responsible for having overlooked the detail. It will, of course, turn out to be the fault of the pilot of the Taliaferro, who is safely dead. And they'll find that the failure to check the satellite data at home can be laid to a grade-three clerk. It'll be an entertaining show to watch.*

There is now no time to inspect this culture, which is about to be lost. An entire species will be wiped out, and there will be no one alive who knows anything about them other than that several meters of stone once stuck out of a snowbank.

Maybe in the end it's all any of us can expect.

ARCHIVE

TO: NCA HAROLD WILDSIDE
FROM: DIRECTOR OF OPERATIONS
SUBJECT: DEEPSIX PROJECT

HUTCHINS, BE ADVISED PRESENCE OF PREDATORS ON DEEPSIX. ORIGINAL PROJECT RECORDS SUGGESTS EXTREME CAUTION. I AM INFORMED THAT THE REIGNING EXPERT ON THE SUBJECT, RANDALL NIGHTINGALE, IS ON BOARD YOUR SHIP. TAKE HIM WITH YOU WHEN YOU GO DOWN.

GOMEZ

TO: *NCA* WENDY JAY
FROM: DIRECTOR OF OPERATIONS
SUBJECT: ARCHEOLOCICAL SITES

ATTN: GUNTHER BEEKMAN. WE HAVE DIVERTED WILDSIDE TO ESTABLISH ARCHEOLOGICAL INSPECTION TEAM ON DEEPSIX. PRISCILLA HUTCHINS WILL LEAD EFFORT. REQUEST YOU AND CAPT. CLAIRVEAU RENDER EVERY ASSISTANCE.

GOMEZ

4

At the critical moment of a critical mission, when his people most needed him, Randall Nightingale fainted dead away. He was rescued by Sabina Coldfield, and dragged to safety by that estimable woman at the cost of her own life. Everyone now seems shocked that the mission failed, and that no further attempt will be made to examine the mosquitoes and marsh grass of Maleiva III. They say it costs too much, but they're talking about money. It does cost too much. It costs people like Coldfield, who was worth a dozen Nightingales.

—GREGORY MACALLISTER, *'Straight and Narrow'*,
Reminiscences

Marcel no longer believed the inhabitants of Deepsix were long dead. Or maybe dead at all.

'I think you might be right,' said Kellie. She buried her chin in her palm and stared at the screen. They were examining visuals taken earlier in the day.

When this mission was completed, Marcel would certify Kellie Collier as fully qualified for her own command. She was only twenty-eight, young for that kind of responsibility, but she was all business, and he saw no point requiring her to sit second seat anymore. Especially with star travel beginning to boom. There were a multitude of superluminals out there begging for command officers, commercial carriers and private yachts and executive and corporate vessels. Not to mention the recent expansion of the Patrol, which had been fueled by the losses last year of the *Marigold* and the *Rancocas,* with their crews. The former had simply disintegrated as it prepared to jump into hyperspace; its crew had made it into the lifepods but had exhausted their air supply while waiting for a dilatory Patrol to respond. The *Rancocas* had suffered a power failure and gone adrift. Communications had failed, and no one had noticed until it was too late.

As people moved out to the newly terraformed worlds, where land was unlimited, the public was demanding a commitment to safety. Consequently the Patrol had entered an era of expansion. It was hard to know how far a young hotshot like Collier might go.

Kellie was studying the foothills of one of the mountain ranges in central Transitoria. 'I don't think there's any question about it,' she said. 'It's a *road*. Or it used to be.'

Marcel thought she was seeing what she wanted to see. 'It's overgrown.' He sat down beside her. 'Hard to tell. It might be an old riverbed.'

'Look over here. It goes uphill. That was never a watercourse.' She squinted at the screen. 'But I'd say it's been a long time since anyone used it.'

They had, during the five days that had passed since the first discovery, seen widely scattered evidence of habitation. More than that, they'd seen the remnants of cities on three continents. The cities were long dead, buried, crushed beneath glaciers. It also appeared they had been preindustrial. Further elucidation would have to wait until Hutchins arrived and took her team down for a close look. But there were no structures that could be said to *dominate* the surrounding landscape, and the snow wasn't so deep as to bury major engineering work. There were no bridges, no dams, no skyscrapers, no signs of construction on a large scale.

Just here and there a fragment in the snow. A rooftop, a post, a pier.

On an island they'd named Freezover, there was a ring of stones. A cart waited in the middle of a barren field near Bad News Bay, near the place at which Nightingale's mission had come to grief; and an object that might have been a plow had been sighted at Cape Chagrin in the Tempis.

But the road—

It was approximately thirty kilometers long, and they could trace it from its beginnings in a river valley, crosscountry along the boundary of a small lake, onto a rise at the foot of one of the mountains. (Kellie was right: It could not be a watercourse.) It disappeared briefly into a tangle of forest before emerging again near the ocean.

The road ran past the base of one of the taller mountains. It towered almost seven thousand meters over the forest. Its northern side was sheared away, creating an unbroken drop from the cloud-shrouded summit down onto a gradual slope. When the sunlight hit the rock wall at dawn, they detected a cobalt tint, and so they called it Mt. Blue.

'The sightseer route,' said Marcel. Kellie shrugged. 'Maybe. I wish we could go down and look.'

'The *Wildside* should be able to settle things when it gets here.'

She folded her arms and let him see she was about to ask for something. Instead: 'It's lucky there was an archeologist within range.'

'Hutch?' Marcel allowed himself a smile. 'She's no archeologist. Actually, she's in our line of work.'

'A pilot?'

'Yeah. I guess she's all they had. But she's been down on some sites.'

Kellie nodded, stood, and looked at him carefully. 'You think she'd let *me* go down with her?'

'If you asked, she probably would. Probably be glad to get the help. The real question is whether *I'd* allow it.'

Kellie was attractive, tall, with dark bedroom eyes, sleek black skin, and soft shoulder-length hair. Marcel knew that she found no difficulty having her way with men, and that she tried not to use her charms on him. Bad form, she'd told him once. But it came as natural to her as breathing. Her eyelids fluttered and she contrived to gaze up at him even though he was still seated. 'Marcel, they said we should render all assistance.'

'I don't think they meant personnel.'

She held him in her gaze. 'I'd like very much to go. You don't really need me here.'

Marcel considered it. 'The lander's probably going to fill up with the science people,' he said. 'We'll have to give them priority.'

'Okay.' She nodded. 'That's not unreasonable. But if there's room . . .'

Marcel was uneasy. He knew Hutch, not well, but enough to trust her. The experts weren't sure when Deepsix would start coming apart. And there was dangerous animal life down there. Still, Kellie was a grown woman, and he could see no reason to refuse the request. 'I'll check with her, see what she says.'

Beekman was lost in thought when Marcel took a seat beside him. He was frowning, his gaze turned inward, his brow wrinkled. Then he jerked into awareness and looked unsteadily at the captain. 'Marcel,' he said, 'I have a question for you.'

'All right.' They were in project control.

'If there's really something, *somebody*, down there capable of building a house or laying a road, should we be thinking about a rescue operation?'

'Marcel had been thinking about little else, but he could see no practical way to approach the problem. How did one rescue aliens? *Wildside* only has one lander,' he said. 'That's it. How many do you think we could bring off? Where would we put them? How do you think they'd react to a bunch of cowboys rolling in and trying to round them up?'

'But if there are intelligent creatures down there, it seems as if we'd have a moral obligation to try to save a few. Don't you think?'

'How much experience have you with ET life-forms?' asked Marcel.

Beekman shook his head. 'Not much, really.'

'They might be people-eaters.'

'That's unlikely. We're talking about something that makes roads.' Beekman looked seriously uncomfortable. 'I know the lander's small, and we've got only one. But we could take a few. It's what the Academy would want us to do.' He was wearing a gray vest, which he pulled tightly about him as if he were cold. 'How many *does* it hold? The *Wildside* lander?'

Marcel asked Bill. The numbers popped up on the screen. Eleven plus a pilot. 'Maybe we should wait until we're confronted by the problem,' he said.

Beekman nodded slowly. 'I suppose.'

'Taking off a handful,' pursued Marcel, 'might not be a kind act. We'd be rescuing them so they could watch their world die.' He shook his head. 'It would be dangerous. We'd have no way of knowing what they would do when we walked up and said hello. We wouldn't be able to communicate. And then there's the gene pool.'

Beekman heaved himself out of his chair and went over to the wallscreen, which looked down on towering cumulus and cold blue seas. 'We could probably synthesize the genes. Give them a chance to continue.' He stared at Deepsix.

'It's not our call,' said Marcel. 'The Academy knows what we've found. If they want us to do a rescue operation, let them tell us so.'

During the next couple of days, there were other discoveries: a collapsed structure that might have been a storage building along a river in Northern Tempus, a wooden palisade hidden in a forest, an abandoned boat frozen in the ice at Port Umbrage. The boat, lying on its side, was about twelve meters long, and it had masts.

But its proportions suggested the mariners had been considerably smaller than humans. 'Looks like a galley,' said Mira. 'You can even see a cabin in the rear.'

Chiang Harmon agreed. 'It would be small for one of us, but it's there. How old's the ice?'

'Probably been there since the beginning.' She was referring to the system's encounter with the Quiveras Cloud. Port Umbrage, they believed, had been frozen solid three thousand years ago, and had never thawed. It was in the far northern latitudes on the east coast of Gloriamundi.

'What else can we conclude about the boat?' Beekman asked.

'Prow looks like a sea serpent,' said Chiang. 'Little bit of a Viking flavor.'

'You know,' said Mira, 'I hadn't noticed *that*. But you're right. They have art.'

Art was important to Mira. Working on an Academy vessel, she understood that a civilization's art was what defined it. In more personal terms, it was *why* one lived at all. One worked in order to make the time to enjoy the finer pleasures. She'd confided to Marcel that Beekman's people, with few exceptions, were 'quite parochial,' and were so consumed chasing down the details of the physical world that most had never learned to enjoy themselves. She considered herself a Sybarite in the highest sense of the word.

She was one of the older persons on board. Mira had, in her own phrase, crashed through middle age and come out the other side. She was nevertheless willowy, attractive, precise. One of those very fortunate women who seem unaffected by passing years.

'They *had* art,' Beekman corrected.

'If we could get a close look at it,' said Chiang, 'we might be able to figure out what *they* looked like. What we really need is to see it up close.'

Mira nodded. 'Next time,' she said, 'we need to make sure we have a lander with us.' She sounded as if she thought somebody had blundered, and she was looking directly at Beekman.

Later, Pete Reshevsky, a mathematician from Oslo, complained that he couldn't see what all the fuss was about. 'There's nothing down there except ruins,' he said. 'And it's pretty obvious that whatever was here, they were pretty primitive. So we don't really have anything to learn from them.' Reshevsky was small, sharp-nosed, muscular. A man who spent about half his time in the gym. His smile seldom reached his dark eyes. 'We'd be better off,' he continued, 'if everyone would stick to business and try to keep in mind why we're here.'

In the morning *Wildside* arrived. '*Its captain wants to speak with you,*' Bill told Marcel.

Marcel liked Priscilla Hutchins. He'd worked with her on occasion, and had found her competent and easygoing. She'd become something of a legend twenty years ago when she'd piloted the expedition that discovered the Omega clouds.

Marcel had envied her that mission. He'd been working for Kosmik, Inc., at the time, making the long run out to Quraqua every few months. That had been a spirit-killing experience. The money was good, and he'd been ambitious, looking for promotion into the hierarchy. Hutchins had been little more than a kid when it all happened, but the incident had glamorized piloting for the general public and persuaded Marcel that he'd had enough posting back and forth to nowhere. Within months, he'd resigned from Kosmik and signed on with the Academy.

He was pleased to have Hutch in the neighborhood. It was a curious coincidence that the woman who'd played a major, if indirect, role in shaping his own career, should arrive at this moment. If he was going to be called upon to make decisions regarding the possible existence of aliens, it would be helpful to have her input.

'Put her through,' he said.

She was just barely tall enough to have met the minimum standards for a license. She had dark eyes, black hair cut short, animated features that were capable of lighting up a room when she chose. She greeted him with a broad smile. 'Marcel,' she said, 'good to see you again. I understand you've hit the jackpot.'

'More or less. Do you think they'll give me a bonus?'

'The usual, I suspect.'

'How much do you know?'

'Only that there's evidence of habitation. A tower. Are any of them still alive down there?'

'We haven't seen anybody.' He brought her up to date. 'The cities we know about are here and over here; there've been indications of inhabitants in *these* half dozen places.' He used graphics to specify. 'Biggest of the cities is in Southern Tempus.' He showed her. It was deep under a glacier. He didn't think she'd be able to cut through to it in the time available.

How much time *was* available?

'The actual collision will occur around dinnertime, December 9. We expect the planet itself will begin breaking apart about forty hours earlier.' It was late Saturday evening, November 25. 'But we can't really be certain. You won't want to push your luck.'

'What do we know about the natives?'

'Not much. They were small. About the size of five-year-olds, looks like. And we have evidence they were on four of the continents.'

'Where do you suggest we set down?'

'The tower's as good as anyplace. It looks as if you can get right in with a minimum of digging. But there *is* a downside: The area's directly on a fault line.'

She hesitated. 'You think it'll be all right for a few days?'

'Don't know. Nobody here wants to take responsibility for *that* kind of guess.'

'Show me where it is.'

'It's in northern Transitoria—'

'Where?'

Marcel directed Bill to post a chart.

She looked at it, nodded, and asked about the Event. 'What precisely is going to happen? And when?'

'All right. Gunther – that's Gunther Beekman, the head of mission – tells me conditions should remain relatively stable until the breakup begins. Once that starts, though, the end will come quickly. So you'll want to get out early. I'd suggest a week early. Don't monkey around with this. Get in, get your artifacts, get out.

'You'll probably experience quakes, major storms, stuff like that, early on. When Deepsix gets inside something called the Turner Horizon, the atmosphere will be ripped off, the oceans torn out, and the crust will turn to oatmeal. All pretty much within a few hours. The core will be all that's left by the time it plunks into the soup. Just a chunk of iron.'

Her eyes came back to him. 'Okay. I guess we won't want to dawdle.'

'Do you expect to stay and watch it? The collision?'

'Now that I'm here? Sure. If my passengers don't scream too loudly.'

For a long moment neither spoke. 'It's good to see you again, Hutch,' he said. It had been almost two years. She'd been coming in from Pinnacle, about to dock, and he was on his way out with a survey team. They'd talked a few minutes over the system, as they were doing now.

But they hadn't been physically in the same room for twice as long. They'd attended a navigation seminar at home on the Wheel. He'd been drawn to her, had spent part of an evening at a dinner party with her. But conditions had never been right. They'd always been going in opposite directions.

She was looking at pictures, 'It's not much of a tower, is it?' It was circular, made of stone, with eight windows, each at a different level, facing a different direction. It stood twelve meters high. But the sensors had indicated another fifteen meters down to its base below ground, where it appeared to be connected to the interior of the city wall. There was a possibility they could use it to get directly into the city.

Marcel had propped two pictures of it on his console. One was a close-up. The other depicted the tower in all its isolation.

'When are you planning to start?' he asked.

She canted her head. 'Soon as we can pack the sandwiches.'

'Hutch, my number one would like to go down with you.'

She looked pleased. 'Sure. If he wants, we'll be glad to have him.'

'He's a *she*. Name's Kellie Collier. She's good. Be a big help if you run into trouble.'

'I can use her. You don't have any archeologists on board, I don't guess?'

'No. I've got a boatload of mathematicians, physicists, climatologists.'

Hutch nodded. 'How about an industrial-sized laser?'

He laughed. 'Wish I did.'

'Okay. It was worth a try.'

'Hutch, one other thing.'

'Yes?'

'As I'm sure you know, we don't have a lander. If you get in trouble, I can't come after you.'

'I know. Have no fear, I plan to be very careful.'

'Good. And do me a favor while you're down there?'

'Sure.'

'Keep a channel open. So I can listen to what's going on.'

Hutch had put off informing Nightingale that Gomez thought it would be a good idea if he accompanied the landing party. She doubted he'd want to go, and was even less persuaded he'd be of use if he did. But at the moment she, Toni, and Kellie Collier were the entire team. She was going to need a couple of volunteers to stand guard and help carry out the artifacts. If they were able to find any artifacts.

She thoroughly disliked this part of her job. They were calling on her to do something she knew little about, and she'd been around Academy politics long enough to know that Gomez would get credit for anything that came off successfully, and Hutch's name would be forever blackened by any failure.

Like the loss of Richard Wald twenty years ago.

Wald had been a preeminent archeologist whom Hutch had piloted to Quraqua. During a long test of wills with a group of terraformers, Wald had been lost to a tidal wave. That episode had become legendary. Wald had stayed too long at an underwater site on that world, had stayed even while the wave approached, and in the end Hutch had been unable to lift him safely away. Some people had blamed her for the misfortune, claiming that she was the only one who had a clear view of events, and that she'd waited too long to warn him.

She wondered whether Nightingale was another instance of the Academy's tendency to find scapegoats.

It was time to get it over with. She finished talking with Marcel, stopped by the common room for a sandwich, and then strolled down to Nightingale's quarters and knocked on the door.

He opened up and looked surprised. 'Hello, Hutch,' he said. 'Come in.' He'd been working at his computer. An image of Deepsix floated on the wallscreen. She glanced at it, at its blue seas, its cloud masses, its vast ice-covered continents. 'Beautiful world,' she said.

He nodded. 'Cold world. They all look good from orbit.'

'Randy, I'm sorry about the delay getting home.'

'Hutch.' His eyes fixed hers. 'You didn't come here to go on about flight schedules. What can I do for you?'

She handed him a copy of the transmission. He read it, looked at her, dropped his eyes again to the paper, looked up. 'This is what *Gomez* wants,' he said. 'What *you* want?'

She'd expected him to decline without hesitation. 'I'd be pleased if you came. I can use some help.'

'Who else is going?'

'First officer from *Wendy*.'

'That's it?'

'And Toni.'

'You understand, despite what Gomez thinks, I have no special knowledge. I know the place is dangerous, but *any* living world is dangerous. You don't need me to tell you that. And I'm not an archeologist.'

'I know.'

'If anyone were to ask my advice, Hutch, I'd say forget it. Stay away from the place.'

'I don't have that option.'

'I know. You still want me?'

'Yes. If you'll come, I'd like very much to have you.'

Marcel was surprised to discover how little interest in going down to the surface existed among his passengers. The general consensus seemed to be that if it were true there were natives of one sort or another on Deepsix, it was hard to see the significance of the fact. Nobody really cared. The culture was clearly primitive, and therefore there would be nothing to learn.

He understood that exocology, that branch of the sciences which concerned itself with the social structures of alien societies, wasn't part of their specialty, but he thought nonetheless they'd want to be on the ground for a major scientific find. A few came forward, commented that they wished they could go down, but then, when he offered to ask Hutch, backed off. Just too much to do. Experiments to set up. Otherwise, I'd go in a minute. You understand.

Only Chiang Harmon volunteered. And Marcel suspected he wanted to go because Kellie was going.

Theoretically, the ground mission should be simple. Just land, get pictures and samples, and come back. If natives show up, get pictures of them, too. Hutch hadn't brought up the thorny issue of attempting to rescue any inhabitants, so he was going to let it lie. He decided that if locals appeared, and they indicated they wanted help, then he would try to provide it. Otherwise, he would simply let it go. It was a decision that kept him awake at night, but it seemed the only practical approach.

There was another aspect to the mission that worried him. He knew how the scientific mind worked. Hutch's team would get

70

down there, they'd be looking at a new marvel, and they'd inevitably discover things that would be hard to explain. And they'd want to get the last possible artifact, the last possible answer, and he had no trouble imagining Deepsix gliding toward its unhappy conclusion while he pleaded with Hutch to get off the surface, and she continually reassured him that she would. That she needed only another hour.

Of course Hutch didn't officially possess a scientific mind. And she'd stated she planned to be away with time to spare. So why not take her at her word?

On the *Evening Star*, Gregory MacAllister had just excused himself for the evening and left The Navigator, headed for his quarters, when a young woman approached and asked if she might speak with him briefly. He recognized her as having been present in the bistro during the evening's discussion on the postmodernist movement in Russian theater. She'd been seated toward the rear, and had contributed nothing, but had remained attentive throughout.

That the woman was extraordinarily attractive cut no ice with him. MacAllister never had trouble collecting beautiful women. But he could be impressed by a person's ability to concentrate, which always implied talent.

He was no respecter of money or position, nor could he be won over by charm or by that series of affectations known as charisma. During his sixty-odd years, he had found there were as many louts in the patrician classes as there were ignoramuses farther down the social spectrum. He liked to believe that only intellect engaged him, although he was inclined to assess intellect as a direct corollary of an individual's regard for MacAllister's opinions.

'My name is Casey Hayes,' she said. She fumbled in a jacket pocket and produced a press card. 'I'm with Inter-web.'

MacAllister allowed his eyes to drift momentarily shut. A journalist.

She was tall, with fashion-model features, and lush brown hair brushed back in the current style. She wore gray slacks and a dark jacket with a diamond stud. No ordinary journalist, this one, he decided.

'What can I do for you?' he asked, noncommittally.

'Mr MacAllister, have you been listening to the reports out of the Maleiva system?'

'Regarding the ruins? Yes, I've been keeping up with them. Of course.'

He had slowed his pace but not stopped. She fell into step beside him. 'It occurred to me,' she said, 'that this is precisely the sort of event that would interest you. A solitary tower in a faraway place.'

'Really?' Journalists always saw in him a potential story, and they were perfectly willing to fabricate whatever circumstance might dictate to get him to talk. There was just no knowing when MacAllister might say something outrageous and shock the public sensibility, or perhaps offend a whole bloc of people. Like last year's remark at Notre Dame, where he was receiving an award, that anyone who truly wished to develop tolerance toward other human beings should start by casting aside any and all religious affiliation. When challenged by one of the other guests, he had asked innocently whether anyone could name a single person put to death or driven from his home by an atheist over theological matters. Had the individual been fully functional, MacAllister had thought, he would have questioned the editor's own celebrated intolerance.

But thank God these people were never quick on their feet.

'Yes,' she continued. 'I've been a reader of yours ever since college.' She launched into a short dissertation on the wonderfulness of his work, and he was inclined to let her go on. But it was late and he was tired. So he encouraged her to come to the point.

'On Maleiva III,' she said, 'we're looking at a lost civilization. Maybe some of them are even still alive.' She beamed a smile intended to sweep his resistance into the night. 'What were they like, do you think? How long had they been there? Does this kind of climax suggest that their entire history, everything they've ever accomplished, is really of no consequence?'

'Young lady,' he began.

'Casey.'

'Young lady, how on earth would I know? For that matter, why would I care?'

'Mr MacAllister, I've read *Reflections of a Barefoot Journalist*.'

He was surprised. *Barefoot* was a collection of essays from his early days, jabbing every social stupidity from breast worship to the timorousness of husbands. But it also contained a long essay defending the bizarre notion, originally promulgated by Rousseau, that there was much to be learned from those untouched by the decadent influence of civilization. That of course was before he'd grasped the truth, that decadence was rather an appealing state. 'None of it applies,' he said. 'The fact that somebody lived on Deepsix who knew how to pile stones on top of one another scarcely seems to be of any significance. Especially since they *and* the stones are about to go to a happier world.'

She looked at him and he saw determination in her eyes. 'Mr MacAllister, you must be wondering why I stopped you.'

'Not really.'

'I'd like very much—'

'To do an interview with me.'

'Yes. As a matter of fact, I would. If you could spare the time.'

He'd been a young journalist himself once. Long ago. And it *was* hard to refuse this particular woman. Why was that? Was he being compromised by his wiring? 'About what?' he asked.

'I'd just like to do a general conversation. You can talk about whatever pleases you. Although since we're both here for the Event, that would undoubtedly come up.'

He thought about demanding the questions in advance. But he wouldn't want to have it get about that one of the world's most spontaneous thinkers had to have everything up front. 'Tell me, uh . . .' He hesitated, his mind blank. 'What did you say your name was, again?'

73

'Casey Hayes.'

'Tell me, Casey, how do you happen to be on this flight? Did you have some sort of foreknowledge about this?'

She tilted her head and gazed steadily back at him. He decided he liked her. She seemed intelligent for a woman journalist.

'Why, no,' she said. 'In fact, I'm not supposed to be working at all. The ticket was a birthday gift from my parents.'

'Congratulations,' he said. 'You're very lucky to have such parents.'

'Thank you. I'll confess I thought that the prospect of watching worlds crash into one another had considerable possibility for a story. If I could get the right angle.'

'Let us see if you've done so, Casey. How did you plan to approach the matter?'

'By finding one of the world's most brilliant editors and presenting his reactions to the public.'

The woman had no shame.

She gazed steadily at him. He thought he saw the glitter of a promise, of a suggestion for a reward down the road, but ascribed it to the same male software that rooted him in place, that prevented his precipitate retreat to his quarters. 'Maybe,' she continued, 'we could talk over lunch tomorrow, if you're free? The Topdeck is quite nice.'

The Topdeck was the most posh eating spot on the vessel. Leather and silver. Candles. Bach on the piano. Very baroque. 'Doesn't seem quite right,' he said.

'All right.' She was all compliance. 'Where would *you* suggest?'

'I put it to you, as an alert journalist. If you were going to interview someone on the significance of the *Titanic*, or the *Rancocas*, where would you propose to hold the conversation?'

She looked blank. 'I'm not sure,' she said.

'Since both have been recovered and, to a degree, reconstructed, surely nothing would serve as effectively as one of the forward staterooms.'

'Oh,' she said. And again: 'Oh! You mean go down to the surface.'

Did he mean *that*? But yes, why not? History of a sort was about to be made. It wouldn't hurt his reputation to be present at the nexus. He might be able to put the appropriate interpretation to events. The world's uplifters, sentimentalists, and moralists would be in rare form during these next few days, drawing what lessons they could from the death of a sentient species. *(How* sentient, of course, would never become an issue.) There would be the usual references to the event as a warning from the Almighty. It occurred to him that if any of those unfortunate creatures were actually found, there would be a heart-wrenching outcry for some sort of desperate rescue effort, presumably from the decks of the *Evening Star.*

Why not indeed?

'Yes,' he said. 'If we want to talk about Deepsix, then Deepsix is the place we should go.'

She was hesitant. 'I don't see how we can arrange it,' she said. 'Are they sending any tours down?'

He laughed. 'No. But I'm sure it can be managed. We have a couple of days yet. I'll see what I can do.'

When he got back to his stateroom, MacAllister locked the door and sank into a chair.

The journalist reminded him of Sara.

Not physically. The angles of Sara's face were softer, Sara's hair was several shades darker, Sara's bearing not quite so imperial. They were both about the same size and weight, but once you got beyond that, it was hard to see a physical similarity.

Yet it was there.

The eyes, maybe. But Sara's were green, Casey's blue. Nonetheless, he recognized the steady gaze, and maybe something in her expression, in the way her smile played at the corners of her mouth or the way her voice softened when she thought she could work her will no other way.

Or maybe his imagination had simply run wild, because he was on a flight that was going to become memorable, and he would have liked very much to share it with Sara.

After spending twenty years relentlessly attacking marriage as an institution for the mentally deficient of both sexes, an evolutionary trap, he had met her one evening during a presentation to a group of young journalists. She'd invited *him* to dinner because she was working on an assignment and it required an interview with him. He was at the time perhaps America's best-known misogynist. The grand passion always wears out, he'd maintained. He'd set its maximum limit at one year, three months, eleven days.

With Sara, he never got a chance to test his figures. Eight months after he'd met her, three weeks after the wedding, she'd died in a freak boating accident. He hadn't been there, had been in his office working on *Premier* when it happened.

It was a long time ago now. Yet no day ever passed that he did not think of her.

Sara had lived in many moods, somber and delighted, pensive and full of laughter. Her last name had been Dingle, and she used to tell people that the only reason she'd consented to marry him was to effect the name change. It had, she said, always been an embarrassment.

He couldn't have said why, but that was the Sara whose spirit occupied his stateroom at the moment.

Stupid. He was getting old.

He collected a strawberry clipper from the autobar and called up the library catalog. There was a new novel by Ramsey Taggart that he'd been wanting to look at. Taggart was one of his discoveries, but he'd begun coasting. MacAllister had spoken with him, shown him where he was going wrong. Nevertheless the last book, a dreary adultery-in-the-mountains melodrama, had shown no improvement. If the trend continued in this latest book, MacAllister would have no choice but to take him to task more formally. In public.

He thought through the conversation with Casey, because it seemed to him he was missing something. He was not one to put himself to trouble on behalf of others, and yet he'd volunteered to do an on-site interview that would seriously inconvenience him. Why had he done that?

Gradually, it occurred to him that he *wanted* to go down to the surface of Maleiva III. To walk among its ruins and let its great age surround him. To soak the sense of oncoming disaster into his blood. What would it be like to stand on the surface of that doomed world and watch the giant rushing down?

To manage things, he would have to win over the assistance of Erik Nicholson.

Nicholson was the captain of the *Evening Star*, a small man, both in physical stature and in spirit. He was, for example, quite proud of his position, and strutted about like a turkey. He spoke in a manner that was simultaneously distant and weak, as if he were delivering divine instructions from the mountaintop and hoping you'd believe him.

MacAllister was scheduled to join the captain for dinner next evening. That would serve as an opportunity to draw him into a private conversation and get the ball rolling. The trick would be to find a reason strong enough to persuade him it would be in his interest to send the ship's lander to the surface. With MacAllister in it.

The book came up and he started on it. Once or twice, though, he glanced around the room to reassure himself he was really alone.

5

All the important things that ever happened to me occurred while I was going someplace else.

—GREGORY MACALLISTER, *Notes from Babylon*

Wendy's shuttle delivered two passengers, the additions to the ground survey team, to *Wildside*. Hutch met them in the bay, where they traded introductions.

Kellie Collier was a head taller than Hutch and wore a standard blue-trimmed white *Wendy Jay* jumpsuit. She shook Hutch's hand warmly and said how pleased she was to be included.

Chiang Harmon's Asian ancestors revealed themselves in the shape of his eyes but nowhere else that she could see. His hair was brown, he was big-boned and broad-shouldered, and he seemed a trifle clumsy. Hutch decided on the spot she liked him. She also recognized that he had more than a professional interest in Kellie.

'Either of you ever been down on a frontier world before?' she asked.

Kellie had. Although she confessed she'd never traveled anywhere beyond the bases and outposts. 'No place where there might have been trouble,' she admitted.

On the other hand, she knew how to use a stinger.

'We don't have any stingers on board,' said Hutch.

Her eyebrows rose. 'You're going down onto a potentially lethal world without weapons?'

Hutch showed her a cutter.

'What is it?' she asked.

Hutch turned it on. A blade of white light appeared. 'Laser' she said. 'Cut through anything.'

'I don't think I'd want to let the local gators get that close.'

'Sorry' said Hutch. 'They're all we have. We have to make do.'

They had half a dozen on board. They were probably a notch or two more efficient than the cutter Biney Coldfield had used to fight off the cardinals. They were a basic tool for archeologists, but in the right hands they also made an effective weapon. But Hutch was unsure whether her volunteers were people to whom she was willing to entrust the weapons. If they weren't, she decided, she shouldn't take them along.

She'd given long consideration to the wildlife hazards on Deepsix. There'd be no repetition of the earlier mistakes. She'd put together a set of operational requirements that everyone would adhere to without exception. She gave each of them a copy, and insisted they read and sign it before the discussion went any farther. Any deviation, she explained, would result in the offender's being shipped back into orbit. Posthaste.

Did everyone understand?

Everyone did.

She showed them around *Wildside*. They found Scolari and Embry in the common room, where Chiang asked whether they were going down to the surface, too. When they replied that they weren't, both looking uncomfortable and a shade indignant, Kellie glanced at Hutch, and it was impossible to miss the judgment she'd just made.

'Why not?' Kellie asked innocently. 'It's the chance of a lifetime.'

'I'm not an archeologist,' said Scolari defensively. 'And to be honest, I think it's a damn-fool thing to do. That place down there is full of wild animals, and it's going to start breaking up at any time. I don't plan to be there when it happens. Not for the sake of a few pots.'

Embry smiled coolly and let it go.

Hutch would have preferred more young males in the group, because she hoped they would be cutting engraved stones out of walls and hauling them back to the lander. Gravity on Deepsix was .92 Earth normal, and .89 Pinnacle, which was the level to which Toni was accustomed. It would help somewhat, but they might still have use for some muscle.

Nightingale joined them, and they did another round of introductions, and then took time for a training session. Hutch explained the importance of getting pictures of whatever they might find, and of taking measurements and mapping where everything was. 'We do all that,' she said, 'before we touch anything.'

She described the hazards, not only from predators, but simply from moving around in an ancient building. 'Be careful. Floors will give way; overheads will cave in. Sharp objects won't penetrate your suit, but they can still punch holes in *you*.' She invited Nightingale to speak about his experience. He was understandably reticent, but he advised them not to underestimate anything. 'The predators on Deepsix have had an extra couple of billion years to evolve. They have very sharp teeth and some of them look innocuous. Trust nothing.'

She handed out the cutters and talked about how they would be used and where things could go wrong. She watched while they practiced, and required each to demonstrate proficiency. 'Be careful in close quarters, if it comes to it. The cutter is almost certainly more dangerous than anything we're going to meet.'

Nightingale met that remark with a frown. But he said nothing.

She dismissed the rest of the team and ran a short course for Chiang in wearing the e-suit. The others were experienced with working inside a Flickinger field.

They joined Scolari and Embry for dinner. Whatever tension might have existed seemed to have dissolved. Embry even made a point of taking Hutch aside and apologizing. 'I hope you don't think this is personal,' she said. 'My objection is to management. If they hadn't had a chance to do this earlier and get it right—'

'I understand,' Hutch said.

The lander was loaded and ready to go. Hutch opened the cargo hatch and turned to face her four passengers. 'We've stowed rations for ten days,' she said. 'That's more than we'll need. Temperature is a few degrees below zero Celsius at noon near the tower. Atmosphere is breathable, but the mix has a little more nitrogen than you're used to. Breathe enough of it and you'll start feeling detached and lazy. So we'll leave the e-suits on when we're outside. There's no known problem with biohazards.

'I want to reemphasize that nobody wanders off on his or her own.' She looked around, made eye contact with each of them to make sure her meaning was clear, and to assure herself they would comply. She was prepared to refuse passage to anyone who looked amused. But they all nodded.

'A day on Deepsix is a bit over nineteen hours long. We'll be landing near the tower in the middle of the night, and we'll stay with the lander until sunrise. After that we'll play it by ear.

'Incidentally, we'll be going down on snow. We don't think it's very deep because it's close to the equator, but there's no way to know for sure.' She looked at Nightingale. 'Randy, anything to add?'

He stood up. 'I just want to underline what Hutch said. Be careful. Protect one another's backs. We don't want to leave anybody down there.' His voice sounded a bit strained.

'I tend to *ask* people to do things,' Hutch continued, 'rather than tell them. Habits are hard to break. But I'll expect immediate compliance with any request.

'You'll have a vest that you should put on *after* you activate the e-suit. You can put tools, sandwiches, anything you like, in

82

the vest. Keep the cutter *in* the vest and never put it in a trouser or shirt pocket. The reason is simple: If you need it and it's *inside* the suit, you won't be able to get to it. Furthermore, if you figure out a way to get your fingers around it, and you activate it inside the suit, you'll be limping for a long time to come.

'Any questions?'

There were none.

Hutch checked the time. 'We're going to launch in eight minutes. In case anybody wants to use the washroom.'

If the experts were right, they had twelve standard days before breakup would begin, which meant they really had about a week before conditions would become unduly dangerous on the surface. So her intention was to move with dispatch.

Kellie's enthusiasm caught hold of the others, and they carried it into the lander. Everyone was excited, and even Nightingale seemed to have shed his dark mood.

Somebody applauded when she launched. A half hour later they dropped into a blizzard, and emerged finally into gloomy, overcast skies at an altitude of four thousand meters. The landscape below was utterly dark. The sensors provided glimpses of rolling hills and broad plains marked by occasional forest. Several large clearings might have been frozen lakes. The ocean, the Coraggio, lay a couple of hundred kilometers north, behind a wall of mountains.

The lander possessed dual-purpose jet/rocket engines, to enable it to maneuver in space, or to function as an aircraft. It was an exceedingly flexible vehicle, owing largely to its spike technology, which was the heart of its lift capability, allowing it to hover, to land in any reasonably flat space, and to leave the atmosphere without the necessity of hauling along vast amounts of its hydrogen fuel.

Power for all systems was supplied by a Bussard–Ligon direct-conversion reactor.

Hutch listened to her volunteers talking about how anxious

they were to get into the tower, and she wondered about her own responsibility bringing them down. She couldn't do the work alone, yet she had the sense that only Nightingale understood the dangers. She had never before led people into a hazardous situation. She had seen what Nightingale's errors had cost, what they'd done to *him* personally, and she wondered why she was taking so large a risk. What the hell did she know about keeping people alive in what Kellie had accurately described as a lethal environment? She thought seriously about calling the whole thing off, returning to *Wildside*, and sending her resignation to Gomez.

But if she did that no one would ever know who had built the tower.

Hutch picked the structure up on her sensors and put it on-screen. It was a night-light image, brighter than it would be in normal optics. Nevertheless it looked old, dark, abandoned. *Haunted.*

She was descending almost vertically, using the spike and guide jets, coming in cautiously. Her instruments did not reveal whether the snow-covered surface would be firm enough to support the spacecraft.

She'd left the storm behind, but there were still a few flakes blowing past the windscreen. Otherwise, the night was calm, with only a breath of wind. Outside air temperature read −31°C. Here and there stars were visible through the partly cloudy skies.

Hutch turned on the landing lights.

Kellie was seated beside her, her dark features illuminated in the glow of the instrument panel. Watching her, Hutch became aware of a precaution left untaken. 'Kellie's our alternate pilot,' she said. 'In the event something unexpected happens and I become . . .' She hesitated. '. . . kaput, Kellie will take over. Will succeed to command.'

Kellie glanced in her direction, but said nothing.

'I'm sure nothing'll happen,' Hutch added.

The ground surrounding the tower was flat, bleak, and empty. There was a scattering of hills on the western horizon, a patch of woods, and a couple of solitary trees.

'I'll set down as close to it as I can,' she said.

The snow seemed to run on forever, losing itself finally in the dark. There was, she thought, a lot to be said for having a moon.

The lander rocked gently, and the tower, cold and dark, reached up toward them.

Hutch might have used the AI to make the landing, but she preferred to fly on her own in this type of circumstance. If something unexpected happened, she didn't want to be at risk while the AI thought about an appropriate course of action.

She lowered the treads. The snow cover looked undisturbed.

It was hard to believe an entire city lay below that smooth white surface.

She took a moment to visualize its dimensions. The wall to which the tower might or might not be attached went off *that* way under the snow for a kilometer and a half, then turned north, angled back and forth a bit, and eventually returned to the tower, which was at the southwest corner of the fortification.

The city had apparently lain at the top of a low hill.

The lander sank through the night.

'Easy,' said Kellie, her voice so low that Hutch suspected she wasn't supposed to hear it.

Hutch kept the nose up, cut back on the spike, and reached for the ground the way a person might descend into a dark room.

Wind blew up around them, and she could almost *feel* a draft come through the hull. She phased back the power, allowing the lander's weight to ease down. The cabin was silent.

They touched the snow.

She let the vehicle settle and cut power. A few flakes fell on the windscreen.

'Good show,' said Nightingale.

'Hutch, you down?' It was Marcel's voice.

'On target,' she said.

During her career, Hutch had walked on probably twenty worlds and moons. This was the fifth time she'd landed on a world about which little was known, the first during which she'd been in charge.

They were twenty meters from the tower.

Hutch turned the lander's lights on it. Pocked and beaten by long winters, it was circular, not more than three stories high. Although she was thinking in human terms. It wasn't wide: She could walk around it in a minute.

There were eight windows, all at different levels, each looking in a different direction. The lowest would permit easy access. The top of the tower was circled by twin ring cornices projecting just above the uppermost window. A convex roof capped the structure.

She activated her e-suit and felt the familiar push away from the seat and the back of the chair as if a cushion of air had formed around her. Kellie ran a radio check with her and nodded. Okay. She pulled on a utility vest and asked Toni to pass up the microscan from the backseat. She clipped it on and put a cutter into a pocket.

'What are you going to do?' asked Nightingale. He looked worried.

'Historic moment. It's worth preserving.' She popped the inner airlock hatch, set the cabin air pressure to match the outside level, and got out of her seat. 'Everybody please get into your e-suit. Set the breather for conversion mode.' That would allow the system to work off the environment so they didn't have to wear air tanks.

Kellie passed out the Flickinger generators. They attached them to their belts and activated the suits. The converters kicked in and commenced moving air.

'Mine won't work,' said Toni.

Kellie looked at it, made an adjustment, and reset it. 'Try it now.'

The field whispered on and Toni held up a thumb.

'Okay.'

'I thought,' said Chiang, 'we were going to wait until morning.'

'We are. Chiang, I'd like you to come stand in the airlock.'

'Okay,' he said, joining her. And after a moment: 'Why?'

'In case of screwups, surprises, whatever.' She checked the time. 'We're about two hours from sunup. Soon as we have light, we'll go into the building.'

'Nothing's going to sneak up on us out there,' Chiang said. 'Why don't we just take a look now?'

'When we have daylight.' She trained the sensors to do a sweep along a patch of forest. It was the only place she could see where a predator might hide. Other than the tower itself.

Green lights flashed, and the outer hatch opened. 'Anything moves out there,' she said, 'I want to know about it.' She climbed out onto the ladder.

Chiang produced a lantern and played its beam across the snow. 'Looks like Christmas.'

Hutch climbed down, tested the ground, and sank in about halfway up her shins. The field kept her feet warm and dry. 'Snow's a bit soft,' she said.

'So I see.'

The tower loomed over her. Morgan was a bright green star in the western sky, where its brilliance washed out even Deneb. It was 84 million kilometers away, and the two worlds were rushing toward each other at a combined velocity of just under seventy kilometers per second.

The tower itself was singularly dull. A pile of stone blocks and not much more. She took its picture. Took it again.

She kept an eye on the line of trees. Somebody, Nightingale, she thought, undiplomatically asked whether Kellie knew how to fly the lander.

Hutch heard no response. Kellie, she suspected, had answered with a glance.

She faced the spacecraft, providing the scan with a good look, gave it a moment to adjust to the lighting, and took the lander's picture also.

'That's good,' said Kellie. 'Come on back now.'

There was still a picture she wanted, one she would hang in whatever future quarters she might occupy. She moved to the far side of the vehicle, got far enough back until she had both the nose of the spacecraft, its *Wildside* designator, and the tower, all in the frame. 'Perfect,' she said.

Dawn broke gray and listless.

The sun was larger than Sol. But it seemed dusty and not quite tangible, almost as if it were one of those solar illusions called sun dogs one sees from North America's Great Plains.

Deepsix had a rotational period of nineteen hours, six minutes, eleven seconds. It was a few million kilometers closer to its sun than Earth was to Sol, but Maleiva was older and cooler.

There was snow on the tower roof. Hutch wondered who had lived in the building, how long ago, where they had gone.

It was possible that the tower marked the site of a climactic battle, or a place where opposing forces had come together to establish an alliance. A Plato might have conducted discussions on this hillside, in warmer times. Or a Solon laid out a system of laws.

Who knew? And no one ever would, except for what little she could salvage.

They descended from the lander, checked their gear, and began trudging through the snow toward the ground-floor window. The merest whisper of wind was audible around the tower. The snow was crusted, and it crunched loudly underfoot, breaking the general stillness.

Two birds appeared in the distance, well out to the northwest. Nightingale turned to look at Hutch, and a chill passed down her spine. But he said nothing.

The birds were flying in great slow circles, wings out, riding the air currents.

The ground-level window had a frame, in which remained a few shards of what might once have been glass. Inside the building they saw a room, utterly bare save for some wooden sticks and debris.

Through an open doorway, a narrow wooden staircase ascended

between beams into the ceiling. The steps were close together, far too close to accommodate human feet.

Hutch set her scan to record everything, hung it around her neck, and climbed through the frame. There was just enough clearance for her head. The floor seemed solid. Beneath a layer of snow and earth, it was constructed of planks. She examined a plaster wall, stained and crumbling, punched full of holes. Several sets of shelves had been built into it.

The ceiling was low, not quite two meters. Not enough to allow even Hutch to stand up straight.

She looked into the other room, the one with the stairway, and saw a third chamber.

The stairway apparently rose to the top of the tower. And down several levels to the bottom. It was made of wood.

Hutch signaled the others to come in.

Chiang pushed on the ceiling. Dust drifted down.

The chambers above and below also had one window each. They appeared identical to the one at ground level, save that the windows were in different locations.

They climbed to the room above, and then to the level above that. They were all scrunching down to avoid hitting their heads. 'Marcel was right about these folks.' grumbled Kellie. 'They were a little on the short side.'

After the initial inspection they went back to the lander and Hutch distributed gear: luminous cable and chalk to mark off areas where finds were made; bars and lamps, compressed air dusters, whatever else she'd been able to think of. Find anything unusual, she told them, call me. And almost *anything* you find will be unusual.

As the day brightened, they spread out through the tower. There were eight levels above ground. They counted six more going down. The topmost space consisted of a single chamber with a surprisingly high ceiling, enough to allow everyone except Chiang to stand upright. There was a hook up there, and they found two objects on the floor: one that might once have been a piece of chain, and a smashed wooden tripod.

'What do you think?' asked Toni.

'Maybe,' said Kellie, 'it was used to sharpen axes. See, you could put a stone in here.'

They found at each level a charred niche that must have been a fireplace. In addition, at the bottom of the structure, a door opened out to the north. Into the interior of the city. It was closed, warped, and it wouldn't budge. They decided to finish examining the building before taking it down.

The rooms were empty, save for a chair arm that one would have described as a child's furnishing, a flat piece of wood that might once have been a tabletop, a few rags, a shoe, and some other debris so far corrupted that it was impossible to know what it might once have been.

The shoe was quite small, designed for the foot of an elf.

But the tabletop became a discovery.

'It's engraved,' said Chiang.

The engravings were worn, so much so that little could be made out. Hutch couldn't even be sure whether the symbols were intended to be representative of actual objects, whether they were geometrical figures, pictographs, or letters.

The tripod had also been carved. Decorated. But these, too, had faded beyond any hope of recovery. They were examining it when Marcel's voice broke into her thoughts. 'We just got a report back from the Academy. I thought you'd be interested in knowing they've named your city.'

'Really? What?'

'Burbage Point.'

'They named it for *Burbage*!' He was the senator who was eternally holding up the Academy as an example of mismanaged funds.

'I guess.'

'My God. Maybe they're trying to send him a message.'

'Not that bunch. They think they're ingratiating themselves.'

'Anything else, Marcel?'

'Yes. The analysts have been looking at the scans for the cities.

We've located nine now, most under heavy ice, *all* under something. And they all have defensive ramparts, by the way. Walls.'

'That locks it.'

'Yep. Primitive civilization. There *is* one exception, one without a palisade, but that's on an island. Incidentally, they're naming all these places for people they think can give them money, or get money *for* them. We now have Blitzberg, Korman City, Campbellville . . .'

'You're not serious.'

He laughed. 'You ever know me to kid around?'

Nightingale's eyes caught hers, and she knew exactly what he was thinking: *And these nitwits have us down here risking our necks.*

'Marcel,' she said, 'any more information about Burbage Point?'

'A little. It looks as if there were some wars. Somebody took the city at one point and pulled the walls down. Apparently left only the tower standing.'

'What's our position vis-à-vis the city? We've got a door at the bottom of the building, leading out toward the north. Any idea what we'll see when we go through it?'

'Probably just ice.'

'Okay. We'll let you know how it turns out.'

'I'm listening to every word, Hutch. We've redirected a couple of the satellites, so we won't lose you when we're over the horizon.'

'All right.' Not that it would do the landing party any good if it got into serious trouble.

They'd brought the pieces of chain and the ax sharpener down to the lower levels to bag and tag. Kellie was writing the description of where the pieces had been found and was about to seal the wrapper on the tripod when Chiang asked to see it.

He studied it for a moment, held the bottom of the one complete leg against the floor, looked up the staircase to the top of the tower. 'You know,' he said, 'we might be in an observatory.'

'How do you mean?' asked Toni.

'I'd bet my foot the roof used to open.'

Kellie looked from the tripod to Chiang, puzzled. 'You mean you think *this* thing supported a *telescope?*'

'It's possible,' he said.

Toni grinned at Kellie. 'And *you* said it was an axe sharpener.'

Kellie laughed and her eyes sparkled. 'I could still be right. They might have opened the roof to man the battlements.'

Hutch looked at it. 'It seems too small,' she said. 'The eyepiece would be down at your hips.'

Chiang aimed a thumb at the ceiling. 'Don't forget who lived here.'

They trooped back up to the top level. There *was* a break down the middle of the ceiling. A separation. They dug around in the dirt and vegetable debris that covered the floor and found a small metal plate and an object that might have been a sidebar.

'You might be right,' said Hutch, trying to imagine a tiny astronomer with a tiny telescope peering through an open roof. 'It would mean,' she said, 'they had some knowledge of optics.'

6

Show me a man of unflinching rectitude and I'll show you a man who hasn't been offered his price. And it's a good thing for the progress of the species. Throughout our long and sorry history it has been men who supposed themselves to be exemplars of integrity who have done all the damage. Every crusade, whether for decent literary standards or to cover women's bodies or to free the holy land, has been launched, endorsed, and enthusiastically perpetrated by men of character.

—GREGORY MACALLISTER, *'Advice for Politicians',*
Down from the Mountain

'Mr MacAllister.' Captain Nicholson rested his elbows on the arms of his chair and pressed his fingertips together. 'I'd like very much to oblige you. You know that.'

'Of course, Captain.'

'But I simply cannot do it. There are safety considerations. And in any case it would be a violation of company policy.' He showed MacAllister his palms, signifying his helplessness in the matter.

'I understand,' said MacAllister. 'But it *is* a pity. After all, how often does an event like this occur?'

The captain's gold-flecked brown eyes reflected a degree of uncertainty. He obviously did not want to offend the influential editor. But if MacAllister pressed his request, Nicholson would be pushed into a no-win situation.

MacAllister didn't want that.

They were in the captain's reception room, sipping Bordeaux, munching finger sandwiches. A private brunch. The bulkheads were appointed with brass and leather, a few leather-bound books occupied shelves on either side of the room, and electric candles supplemented a pair of lamps. A schematic of the *Evening Star* occupied an entire bulkhead, and the Starswirl logo of TransGalactic Lines looked down from above a virtual fireplace.

They sat in padded chairs, angled toward each other. 'I completely understand your reluctance,' MacAllister said in a matter-of-fact I'd-feel-exactly-the-same-way manner. 'And I can see you're not one to be easily intimidated.'

Nicholson modestly signaled his agreement with the proposition. There was much about the captain that was cautious. Conservative. MacAllister guessed that he had a reliable exec and a good AI tucked away somewhere to take over and run things in the event a nonroutine decision had to be made. It seemed likely that Nicholson had gained his position by influence, had possibly married into it, or was the son of someone important.

'No,' the captain said, 'it's quite so, Mr MacAllister. We do have an obligation to abide by the rules. I know you of all people would understand that.'

MacAllister kept a straight face. *Me* of all people? 'Of course, Captain. I couldn't agree with you more.' He used a tone designed to ease the sudden tension. 'It *is* unfortunate, though, to let an opportunity of this nature slide.'

'What opportunity is that?' asked Nicholson.

'Well . . .' He shook his head, sipped his wine, and waved the subject off. 'It's of no consequence. Although my guess is that it would be quite a coup.'

'*What* would be quite a coup, Mr MacAllister?'

'Deepsix is about to pass into legend, Erik. May I call you Erik?' MacAllister's tone warmed.

'Yes. Of course.' Nicholson softened, pleased to go on first name terms with his celebrated guest. 'Of course, Gregory.'

'After next week, Maleiva III will be gone forever. People will be talking about this cruise, and wondering about that world's ruins, for decades, and possibly centuries, to come. And' – he looked wistfully at a spot over Nicholson's left shoulder – 'pieces of those ruins are lying around down on the ground, waiting to be picked up.' He drained the glass and set it on a side table. 'A few of those pieces, on display here on the *Star*, would be an invaluable asset.'

'In what way?'

'They would generate a great deal of publicity. Relics from a lost civilization. Exhibited on the ship that recovered them. What a testament to the *Evening Star* and its captain. And to TransGalactic. I'd expect you could anticipate a great deal of gratitude from your employers.'

Nicholson made a sound halfway between a snort and a laugh. 'Not likely,' he said. 'Baxter and the rest of those people are too wrapped up in themselves to appreciate that kind of acquisition.'

'Maybe.'

'Still . . .' The captain grew thoughtful. 'It would be nice.'

'It would be very easy to do.' MacAllister saw that he had judged his man correctly. Nicholson was not greedy for money. A suggestion that he pirate some artifacts for himself would have gone nowhere. But the notion that upper management might see their way to appreciate him a bit more. Ah, yes. That was working nicely.

The captain fingered his glass. 'I wouldn't want you to misunderstand me, Gregory. I abide strictly by the policies and procedures laid down for the safe operation of this vessel.'

'As any competent commanding officer would.' MacAllister

refilled both glasses. 'Erik, I'm sure you have certain prerogatives, conditions which in your judgment allow you to interpret procedures in a manner that would benefit TransGalactic's passengers, and the corporation itself.'

'Yes,' he admitted, 'that's certainly true.'

MacAllister gazed admiringly at the ship's schematic and let his companion consider the situation.

'You really think,' said Nicholson, 'that stuff is just lying around on the ground?'

'Oh, I've no doubt. Just pick it up and cart it off. That's all it would take. And I ask you, when that world is gone, gone forever beyond any power to recall, what do you suppose, say, an idol from a Maleivan chapel would be worth?'

'Oh, yes. I'd think so. You're quite right on that score.'

MacAllister could see him wrestling with his fear of getting in trouble. 'This would seem to be your opportunity, Erik.'

'You don't think the archeological team that's down there now would object?'

'I can't imagine why they would. As I understand it, they've only got one lander. How much can you haul away in one lander?' He tried to look thoughtful. 'There's an excellent place down on deck, near the pool, that would serve nicely as a museum.'

'The hyper wing.' It was an area currently given over to displaying the ship's various propulsion systems, especially the FTL drive. 'Yes,' he said. 'It *is* tempting.'

'If you wanted to do it,' said MacAllister, 'I'd be willing to go along. Cover the story. Give it some credential, so to speak.'

'You mean you'd write one of your commentaries?'

'I'd do that, if you like.'

'We could put the artifacts—'

'In the museum.'

'Stage a ceremony. Would you be willing to participate? Possibly say a few words?'

'I'd be honored, Erik.'

Nicholson nodded sagely. To himself, more than to MacAllister.

'Let me think about it, Gregory. If there's a way to manage it, we'll go ahead.'

Marcel kept the speaker on so he could follow what was happening on the surface. That gave him access to all conversations that took place on the allcom. The transmissions were relayed out of the lander either directly to *Wendy* or to one of the commsats.

He was uncomfortable. Living worlds were unpredictable places, and this one especially, as it drew closer to Morgan. But they should be relatively safe for the present. Beekman was certain that gravitational effects from the giant planet would not be felt until late in the process because the collision would be direct, like two vehicles hitting each other head-on. No gradual spiraling in here.

He'd been listening while Hutch and her people prowled through the tower, watching the images being transmitted back by the microscan Hutch wore on her vest. The place wasn't much to look at, just bare walls and floors covered with snow and dust.

They'd cut a hole in the tower wall at ground level to preclude having to climb through the window. Hutch had posted Chiang by the newly made door to watch for signs of potential predators. She then stationed Toni at the window in the astronomer's perch, with the same responsibility.

Meantime she, Kellie, and Nightingale were trying to cut through the door on the bottom level. They weren't talking much at the moment, but he could hear the hiss of the laser working on stone.

Beekman came in, looked at him, frowned, and sat down. 'Marcel,' he said, 'are you all right?'

'Sure. Why?'

'You don't look happy.'

Kellie's startled voice came over the speaker: *'Look out with that thing, Randy.'*

Marcel folded his arms across his chest in a defensive posture. 'Somebody's going to get killed down there,' he said. 'If I had my way, we'd just write the damned thing off and let it go.'

Beekman had always maintained an exceedingly low opinion of the competence of Academy management. Marcel expected him to make an observation in that direction. Instead, he remarked that Marcel was probably correct, that the ground team was unlikely to find anything useful in so short a time, and that it was indeed dangerous.

'*Okay.*' Hutch's voice. '*That should do it. Give it a minute and we'll see if we can break it loose.*'

'You know,' Beekman said, 'you might remind her that they should be more careful.'

'She knows who she's working with.' He folded his hands behind his head. 'I'd rather not become a nuisance.'

'What if something happens?'

'We'll let management worry about it.'

Kellie's voice: '*Okay, throw some more snow on it.*'

'I'd feel better,' said Beekman, 'if we had a bona fide archeologist down there.'

Marcel didn't agree. 'We're probably safer with Kellie and Hutch. They might not get all the details right, but I'd rather have them in charge if trouble starts.'

'*Still won't open,*' said Nightingale.

'*Let me try.*'

'How big's the door?' asked Beekman.

'A little more than a meter high. Everything's on a small scale.'

'*I don't think we cut all the way through.*'

Beekman leaned down and fingered the SEND key.

'What are you going to tell them?' asked Marcel.

'To be careful.'

'I'm not sure they'll be receptive to gratuitous advice. They've already threatened to cut me off.'

Another laser ignited.

'*Stay with it.*' Nightingale's voice. '*Here. Get it here.*'

It went on for several more minutes. At one point Hutch cautioned someone to relax. Take it easy. We'll get through. Then

Marcel heard the sound of scraping stone and some grunts. And finally cries of satisfaction.

When things got quiet again he switched over to his private channel with Hutch. 'What have you got?' he asked.

'Used to be a passageway,' she told him. 'It's just a lot of ice and dirt now. I'm not even sure where the walls are.'

Beekman got coffee for them and began to describe how preparations for the collision were going. Much of the detail was boring, but Beekman inevitably became so enthusiastic when he started talking about the Event, that Marcel pretended more interest in the details of the observations than he really felt. In fact, he didn't understand fine points like gravity wave fluctuations, and didn't much care how the planetary magnetic fields were affected. But he nodded at the right times and tried to look surprised when Beekman seemed to be springing some new piece of breakthrough data on him.

Then Hutch's voice interrupted the flow. 'Marcel, are you still there?'

'I'm here. What have you got?'

'I think we're into the Astronomer's private quarters. They're in pretty good shape. Looks like a suite of rooms. With *cabinets*—' She stopped a moment to caution one of the others to use care.

'*Cabinets?* What's in them?'

'They've been cleaned out. But they're in decent condition. And they've got symbols carved into them.'

'Good,' said Marcel. 'That's important, right?'

'Yes,' she said. 'That's important.'

As he had with Beekman, he tried to sound enthusiastic. 'Anything else there?'

'A *couch*. You believe that? For a little guy. *You* wouldn't be able to use it, but a ten-year-old could.'

It was less than dazzling news. 'Anything more?'

'A table. Pretty badly smashed, though. And another door. In back.'

He heard Kellie's voice: '*Hutch, look at this.*'

'Can we have more light?'

'*I'll be damned,*' said Nightingale.

Beekman frowned with impatience. But while they waited to hear what was happening, the AI broke in. '*Marcel? I'm sorry to interrupt, but we have an anomaly.*'

'What is it. Bill?'

'*Strange object adrift.*'

'On-screen, please.'

Marcel couldn't make it out. It looked like a long pin. *Very* long. It extended from one side of the screen to the other. And apparently beyond.

'Bill, what *is* this thing? What are its dimensions?'

'*I am unable to determine its function. It's three thousand kilometers long. Roughly.*'

'Three thousand klicks,' said Beekman. 'That can't be right.'

'*Actually, three thousand two hundred seventy-seven, Gunther.*'

Marcel made a face and pushed back in his chair. 'That's one odd-looking puppy, Gunny.' It was long enough to reach from the tip of Maine down through Miami and well out into the Atlantic.

'*Its diameter is seven and a fraction meters.*'

'Well,' the planetologist said, 'seven meters across and three thousand kilometers long.' He looked at Marcel and shook his head. 'That's not possible.'

'Are you sure, Bill?' Marcel asked. 'We don't think those kinds of dimensions can happen.'

'*I'll recheck the results of the scan.*'

'Please do.'

'Bring it up to full mag,' said Marcel. 'Let's see a piece of it up close.'

Bill complied. It consisted, not of a single very long barrel, but of a series of parallel shafts. They could see between the shafts, see the night sky beyond.

'*The dimensions are correct as reported,*' said Bill.

Marcel frowned. 'So what is it, Gunther? What's it do?'

'Don't know.'

'Bill, is it a *ship* of some sort?'

'*I do not see how it could be, Marcel. But this is not a type of object with which I have any experience.*'

'Is this typical of the entire construct?'

'*This is typical,*' said Bill. '*The shafts are solid. They are connected at regular intervals by braces. A few cables are adrift at one end, and an asteroid is attached to the other.*'

An asteroid. 'Bill, is it doing anything? The construct?'

'*There is no sign of activity.*'

'You reading any energy output? Any evidence of internal power?'

'*Negative.*'

Beekman was staring at the image. 'I just can't figure it, Marcel. Object that long. It shouldn't hold together. Stresses would *have* to break it up.'

'Wouldn't that depend on what it was made from?'

'Sure. But something like this would have to be pretty strong stuff. Diamond, maybe. I don't know. It's not my field.'

'*Range is sixty-two thousand kilometers, increasing. It appears to be in orbit around Maleiva III.*'

'What do you think?' asked Marcel. 'Want to chase it down?'

'Hell, yes. Let's go take a look.'

Marcel gave instructions to Bill, and let Hutch know what they were doing. 'It sounds,' she told him, 'as if there's more to Deepsix than the Academy thinks.'

'A *lot* more, apparently. You sure that place down there looks preindustrial?'

'It's all stone, mortar, and planks. Right out of the Middle Ages.'

'Okay,' he said. 'By the way, it sounded as if Kellie found something a couple of minutes ago. But we got distracted.'

Hutch nodded. 'I don't think what we have is quite as interesting as your *pole*. But it looks like an armored vest. It was in one of the cabinet drawers.' She turned toward it so he could see it. Like everything else, it was in miniature. It would have been secured from behind, and was designed apparently to protect as low as the groin. It was severely corroded.

Toni Hamner hated to admit to herself that she was bored, but it was true. She'd expected the expedition to be exciting. But she should have known it wouldn't work out that way: She'd been around the archeologists at Pinnacle and knew how deadly dull excavations could be. This, she'd thought, would be different. This time she would be with the first people in the door. She'd be there when the discoveries got made. But so far it had been just a lot of digging and dredging out of debris. Now, standing guard in the entrance to the tower, looking out across that flat dreary plain, she yearned for it to be over.

A flight of birds passed overhead. They were brown, with long beaks, flying in formation. For a few seconds they filled the sky, and then they were gone, headed southwest.

She let her mind drift back to the brief shipboard romance she'd been enjoying with Tom Scolari. She hadn't thought highly of Scolari in the beginning, but she'd begun to change her mind and was actually getting quite caught up with him when they'd come here and she'd watched him turn his back on Hutch. That seemed to her to be mean-spirited. Or cowardly. She couldn't decide which.

She was anxious to get home. To see old friends and restart her life. To see a few live shows. Go to an expensive restaurant again. (How long had it been?)

Below, the digging went on.

Hutch was taking a break when Marcel called to tell her how difficult it was to explain the presence of the construct. Could she keep an eye open for anything that indicated the inhabitants were more advanced than we were giving them credit for? She would, but she knew they'd find nothing high-tech near the tower.

They'd opened a passageway behind the Astronomer's apartment, and were now engaged in widening it. The work went slowly. Hutch had brought containers and digging implements so that they weren't entirely dependent on the lasers, which were dangerous in the close confines of the corridor. They had to remove the rock, dirt, and ice, which entailed a lot of crawling around.

It was only possible for one person at a time to dig in the passageway. A second carried away the debris, dragging it back through the Astronomer's apartment. A third picked it up there, hauled it through the connecting corridor and into the bottom of the tower, where he, or she, sorted through it looking for anything of value. They found a few shards, a knife, a broken shaft with a blade insert, and a couple of pieces of stone with engraved symbols. In time, as the bottom chamber began to fill up with detritus, they started carrying it up to the next level.

Eventually, they brought in a collapsible worktable and set it up in the ground-level room. A plan of the site was hastily put together, and the locations of the artifacts were recorded thereon. The artifacts themselves were brought to the table to be tagged and bagged.

The cabinet they'd found in the Astronomer's apartment was made of wood. It had inlays and metal hinges, a door pull and some fasteners. It also contained several scrolls, too far gone to risk trying to unroll. They put them in separate bags, and sealed them.

'I can't see that it matters much,' said Nightingale. 'Nobody'll ever be able to read any of that.'

Hutch set the bags carefully off to one side. 'You'd be surprised what they can do,' she said.

At midafternoon, Chiang, Hutch, and Toni went back down into the tunnel. Kellie was posted topside, and Nightingale stood guard at the tower entrance. He'd been there only a few minutes when a *thing* came out of a patch of trees several hundred meters to the south. It was on two legs, and it had feline grace and a feline appearance. Nightingale, who'd been standing out in the sunlight, scrambled inside. The cat stood for perhaps a minute looking toward the tower. Toward *him*. He wasn't sure whether it had seen him. But when it started walking casually in his direction, he alerted everyone. Within minutes, they were all in the doorway.

It was moving across the plain as if it had nothing whatever to fear. 'King of the hill,' whispered Chiang, setting his cutter up a couple of notches.

The creature was considerably taller than a human male and maybe twice the mass. It was a model of muscles and grace.

'What do we do, boss?' asked Chiang.

Right, thought Hutch. *Remind me I'm in charge.*

It continued striding toward them, throwing a quick and unconcerned glance at the lander.

Effective laser range was about five meters. They'd be able to smell its breath. 'Randy,' she said, 'you know anything about this critter?'

'Nothing whatever.' Nightingale was standing well away from the entrance. 'I'll tell you this, though. It's a cat. And cats are pretty much the same wherever you find them.'

'Which means what?' asked Chiang.

'Anything smaller than *they* are, they eat.'

Marcel broke in: 'Shoot it, Hutch. As soon as it gets close.'

She didn't have the option of firing a warning shot, because the cutter didn't produce a *bang*, or anything akin to it. Not that this thing looked as if it would be scared off by a loud noise.

She was suddenly getting advice from everyone: *'Be careful.' 'Look out.' 'Don't let it get too close.'*

She picked up some profanity from Nightingale.

There came a moment when it paused perceptibly, when its muscles tightened, when its weight shifted slightly. It had seen her.

'Hutch' Marcel again. 'What's happening?'

No point hiding. 'Stay out of sight,' she told the others. And she stepped out in full view of the creature.

The lips curled back, revealing more teeth. It came forward again. Hutch raised the weapon and leveled it.

'*Shoot, for God's sake!*' said Nightingale.

Hutch told him to be quiet. The cat's eyes brushed hers. She broke the connection, looked off to one side.

She wanted to see a sign that it was in fact hostile. She wished it would drop down on all fours and charge. Or simply pick up its pace. Or raise its claws.

It did none of these things. It just kept coming. And Hutch suspected it had no experience with weapons. It saw nothing she could do to harm it.

She turned the cutter on the stone side of the building, activated the beam, scorched the rock, and brought the weapon level again.

The creature stopped.

Chiang stepped out beside her.

It stood for several moments, uncertain.

Hutch took a step forward,

It began to back away.

'It's no dummy,' said Chiang.

It angled off behind the lander, and it kept the vehicle between itself and the tower while it retreated back into the patch of woods from which it had come.

It was a short day, of course, less than ten hours from dawn to dusk. Nobody was hungry when the sun went down, and, other than Nightingale, they wanted to stay with the job. Hutch brought them out of the tower anyhow.

It had grown dark when they logged in their most recent finds. These consisted mostly of vases and utensils and a few tiny hunting knives. There was also an armchair and a pack that seemed to be full of fabric.

They took the pack out to the lander cabin and secured everything else in the cargo bay. Then they called it a day and climbed inside.

Hutch opened the bag and took out a small faded blue cloak.

It was ribbed, with a ring and chain at the top to fasten the collar. In its own time, it might have been a deep purple. Now it was too washed-out to be sure. The cloth was brittle, and a small piece of it broke off in her hands. She passed the garment to Kellie, who bagged it.

Next was a shirt.

And a robe.

Both were cut down the sides, presumably to accommodate limbs, but what those limbs might have looked like, or even how many there might have been, was impossible to know.

They found leggings.

And a pair of boots.

The boots were disproportionately wide. 'Duckfeet,' said Kellie.

Many of the garments sported decorations, sunbursts and diamond-shapes, representations apparently of flowers and trees, and various arcane symbols.

They were delighted. Even Nightingale seemed to loosen up and find occasional reason to smile. They inventoried and packed everything, including the bag itself.

'Not a bad day's work,' said Toni, with a satisfied smirk.

Hutch agreed. First day down, they'd done pretty well.

The lander had a washroom about the size of a closet. It wasn't convenient, but it would be adequate to their needs.

One by one, they retreated into its cozy confines to wash up and change clothes. There was a fair amount of grumbling during the process, especially from Chiang and Kellie, neither of whom could move easily inside it. Both eventually gave up and got dressed in the rear of the cabin.

Hutch broke out the reddimeals. They had a choice among pork, chicken, fish cakes, hamburger steak, Sauerbraten. The meals came with salads and snacks.

She produced two candles, lit them, and killed the lights. Then she set out five glasses and a bottle of Avignon Blue. She uncorked it and filled the glasses. 'To *us?*' she said.

They drank the second round to the owner of the bag who'd been thoughtful enough to leave it behind for them.

When they'd finished and were sitting quietly in the candlelight, Hutch congratulated them for what they'd accomplished. 'It'll be a short night,' she said. 'Dawn comes early here. But we can sleep a bit late if we need to.

'Tomorrow, I want to change the emphasis of the search. The Academy will like what we've gotten so far. But time's limited. What we really need is to find something that'll shed some light on who these people were. On their history.'

'How do we do that?' asked Toni.

'Look for engravings. Something with pictures on it. Writing. Symbols. Pictographs.

'We probably won't find much in the way of documents on paper, or paperlike materials. We have the scrolls that somebody *might* be able to do something with, but what we really want is stuff that's clearly legible. Check pottery for symbols or pictures. Anything like that, we—' A queasy sensation blossomed in her stomach, something she couldn't quite get hold of. The candles flickered.

'What was that?' asked Toni.

They looked at one another.

Tremor.

She switched to Marcel's private channel. 'I think,' she told him, 'we just experienced a minor quake.'

'Everybody okay?' he asked.

'Yeah. It wasn't much. But it's not a good sign.'

'We have sensors on the ground. I'll check them, see what they say.'

'You were right,' Marcel told her a few minutes later. 'It was a 2.1.'

'How strong is that?'

'Barely perceptible.'

'Scares birds,' she said.

'Yeah. I suppose.'

107

'I thought we weren't supposed to feel anything until the last day or so.'

'I don't think I ever said *that*, Hutch. But I *did* warn you that the tower area is not stable. You're sitting right on top of a fissure. The experts up here are telling me that it's not a good place to be with Morgan coming.'

'Morgan's still pretty far.'

'Not far enough. It's *massive*. Think *Jupiter.*'

'All right. We'll be careful.'

'Maybe you should leave. Get out of Dodge.'

'If it gets serious, we'll do that.'

'I think it *is* serious. How about going to one of the other sites?'

'Where do you suggest?'

'Any of the cities.'

'Which one's accessible?'

He paused. 'Well, what do you mean by *accessible?*'

'That we don't have to cut through ten or twenty meters of ice to get to it.'

'I don't know anywhere you can walk in the front door. But even if you have to do some digging, they'll be safer.'

'But probably not after the couple of days we'll need to get into one of them.' Everyone else in the cabin had become intensely interested. 'We won't take any chances. Marcel. Okay? If things start to go downhill, we'll clear out.'

When she signed off, Chiang leaned toward her. 'I was at the University of Tokyo for a few years,' he said. 'Lamps used to swing all the time. It really doesn't have to amount to something.' He wore a cheerful short-sleeved blue team jersey stenciled *Miami Hurricanes*. 'We'll be okay,' he said.

They talked the problem over. How important was the tower and its contents? Hutch knew that a professional archeologist would have told them it was priceless. But she confessed there was really no way to know.

In the end they compromised. They'd spend one more day there. Then find someplace safer to work.

A wind kicked up. The sky was full of stars and the snowscape sparkled.

Chiang found it difficult to sleep, knowing Kellie was so close. Just the seat in front of him. But he hadn't realized she was awake until he heard her moving. He leaned forward and touched her elbow. 'You okay?' he asked.

She angled her seat so she could see him. Her eyes were dark and lovely. Her hair fell down around her collar, and he ached to take it, take *her*, in his arms. 'The quake's not good,' she said, looking toward the tower. 'That thing could come down on our heads.'

'Sorry you came?'

'Wouldn't have missed it.' Her eyes came back to him. 'On the other hand . . .' She took a deep breath and he tried not to stare at her breasts. And whatever she was going to say was left unfinished.

7

Women were intended by their Maker to be cheerleaders. One has only to examine their anatomy and their disposition to recognize that melancholy fact. So long as they, and we, keep this rockbound truth firmly in mind, the sexes will perform their joint functions with admirable proficiency.

—GREGORY MACALLISTER, 'Night Thoughts', Notes from Babylon

Wendy was still two hours away from the object, but they were close enough to have good visuals, which were displayed in various aspects across a bank of screens in project control. The area was crowded with Beekman's people, clustered in front of the monitors and hunched over consoles.

The object had turned out to be an assembly of *fifteen* individual shafts, connected by bands set at regular intervals of about eighty kilometers. Eight shafts were on the perimeter, six in an inner ring, and one in the center. They were of identical dimensions, each with a diameter of about three-quarters of a meter, each long enough to stretch from New York to Seattle. There was considerable space between them, so Marcel could see through the assembly, could detect stars on the far side.

111

A rocky asteroid was attached to one end, webbed in by a net. The overall effect, Marcel thought, was of a lollipop with a stick that projected into the next county.

The end opposite the asteroid just stopped. A few lines trailed out of it, like dangling cables. Marcel noticed that the fifteen cylinders were cut off cleanly, suggesting the object had not broken away from some larger structure, but rather had been released.

'Impossible thing,' said Beekman, who was delighted with the find. 'Far too much mass for so narrow a body.'

'Is it really that big a deal?' asked Marcel. 'I mean, it's in *space*. It doesn't weigh anything.'

'Doesn't matter. It still has mass. A lot of it along the length of the assembly.'

Marcel was studying the configuration: The asteroid was up, the lower end of the assembly was pointed directly at Deepsix.

Beekman followed his eyes. 'At least its position is about what we'd expect.'

'Stable orbit?'

'Oh, yes. It could have been there for thousands of years. Except—'

'What?'

He delivered a puzzled grunt. 'It just shouldn't hold together. I'll be interested in seeing what the thing's made of.'

John Drummond, a young mathematician from Oxford, looked up from a screen, '*Impossibilium,*' he said.

Marcel, fascinated, watched the image. It was so long they couldn't put the entire thing on a single screen without shrinking the assembly to invisibility. One of the technicians put it up across a bank of five monitors, the lollipop head on the far left, and the long thin line of the supporting pole stretching all the way over to the far right-hand screen. 'So it's not a ship of any kind, right?' he asked.

'Oh, no,' said Beekman. 'It's certainly not a ship.' He shook his head emphatically. 'No way it could be a ship.'

'So what is it? A dock?' asked Marcel. 'Maybe a refueling

112

station?' They homed in on one of the braces. It appeared to be a simple block of metal, two meters thick, supporting all fifteen shafts in their positions. 'Where do you think it came from?'

Beekman shook his head. 'Deepsix. Where else *could* it have come from?'

'But there's no indication they ever had technology remotely like this.'

'We really haven't seen anything yet, Marcel. The technology may be under the ice. Kellie's tower might be very old. Thousands of years. *We* didn't look very advanced a few centuries ago either.'

Marcel couldn't bring himself to believe that all evidence of a high-tech civilization could just *disappear.*

Beekman sighed. 'The evidence is right outside, Marcel.' He tried to rub away a headache. 'We don't have any answers yet. Let's just be patient.' He looked at the screens and then glanced at Drummond. An exchange of some sort took place between them.

'It's probably a counterweight,' Drummond said. He was about average size and generally uncoordinated, a thin young man with prematurely receding hair. He seemed to have had trouble adjusting to low gravity. But he'd come to *Wendy* with a reputation for genius.

'Counterweight?' said Marcel. 'Counterweight for *what*?'

'A skyhook.' Beekman glanced at Drummond, who nodded agreement. 'There's not much else it could have been.'

'You mean an elevator from the ground to L.E.O.?'

'Not Earth orbit, obviously. But yes, I'd say that's exactly what it was.'

Marcel saw several smiles. 'I was under the impression there was no point putting up a skyhook. I mean, we've got spike technology. We can *float* vehicles into orbit. Why go to all the trouble—' He stopped. 'Oh.'

'Sure,' said Beekman. 'Whoever built this thing doesn't have the spike. They've got some other stuff, though, that we don't. *We* could never make one of these. Not one that would hold together.'

113

'Okay,' said Marcel. 'What you're telling me, if I understand this correctly, is that this is the part of the skyhook that sticks out into space and balances the section that reaches to the ground, right?'

'Yes.'

'That brings up a question.'

'Yes, it does,' said Beekman. 'Where's the rest of the skyhook?' He shrugged. 'Remove the counterweight, and everything else falls down.'

'Wouldn't we have seen it if that had happened?'

'I'd think so.'

'Maybe they cut it loose near the bottom of the elevator. If that happened—'

'Most of it would get yanked out into space and drift off.'

'So there could be another piece of this thing out here somewhere.'

'Could be. Yes.'

'But what we're saying is that it was put up and then taken down?'

'Or fell down.'

They retired into the project director's office, and Beekman waved him to a chair. A large globe of Deepsix stood in one corner.

'It's crazy,' said Marcel. 'You can't hide a skyhook. Up or down.'

'Maybe the pieces that collapsed are under the glaciers,' Beekman said. 'We really can't see much of the surface.' He zeroed in on the equator and began to turn the globe. 'Although it would have to be along here somewhere. Along the equator where we *can* see the ground.'

They called up pictures of Maleiva III and began looking. For the most part, the equator crossed open ocean. It touched a few islands in the Coraggio east of Transitoria, rounded the globe without any land in sight, passed through Northern Tempus, leaped the Misty Sea, and returned to Transitoria a couple hundred kilometers south of Burbage Point. The tower.

'Here,' said Beekman, indicating the archipelago, 'or *here*.' The Transitorian west coast.

'Why?' asked Marcel.

'Big mountains in both places. You want the highest base you can get. So you put it on top of a mountain.'

'But a structure like that would be *big*.'

'Oh, yes.'

'So where is it?' Marcel looked at both sites, the archipelago, where several enormous mountains stood atop islands that appeared to be volcanic. And the coastal range, which featured a chain of giants with cloud-covered peaks.

'I don't know.' Beekman held out his hands.

'Tell me,' said Marcel. 'If you had a skyhook, and something happened to it, so it collapsed, which way would it fall?'

The project director smiled. *'Down.'*

'No. I'm serious. Would it fall toward the west?'

'There'd be a tendency in that direction. But the kind of structure we're talking about, thousands of kilometers of elevator shaft and God knows what else. Mostly it would just come down.' Someone was knocking. Beekman kept talking while he opened the door and invited Drummond inside. 'If it were here, in Transitoria, the base could be hidden on one of these peaks under the clouds. But that still doesn't explain where the wreckage got to. It should be scattered across the landscape.'

Marcel looked at Drummond. 'Maybe not,' Drummond said. 'Suppose you wanted to *take* it down. With minimum damage to the terrain below. What do you do?'

'I have no idea, John,' Beekman said. 'But I'd think we would want to separate the shaft at a point where the longest possible section would get hauled *up* by the counterweight. What's left—'

'Falls west—'

'—into the ocean.' Beekman drummed his fingers on the tabletop. 'It's possible. If you've got a hell of a good engineer. But why would someone deliberately *take* it down? I mean, that thing's got to be an architectural nightmare to put up in the first place.'

'Maybe they developed the spike and didn't need it anymore. Maybe it was becoming a hazard. I'd think one of those things would need a lot of maintenance.'

'Well.' Beekman shrugged. 'There are a number of mountains in that range. We'll have an orbiter in the area in a bit. Why don't we run some scans and see what we can see.'

MEMO FOR THE CAPTAIN
11/26 1427 hours
From Bill

The cruise ship Evening Star *transited from hyperspace four minutes ago. It has set course for Maleiva III and will arrive in orbit in approximately two hours.*

People boarding cruise liners usually did so via standard GTOs, Ground-to-Orbit vehicles that employed the spike for lift and standard chemical thrusters for velocity. The *Star*'s onboard lander was a luxury vehicle, seldom used, maintained primarily to accommodate VIPs who had commercial or political reasons for shunning the more public modes of transportation.

It resembled a large penguin. It had a black-and-white hull with retractable white wings. The nose was blunt, almost boxy, with *Evening Star* emblazoned in black script below the TransGalactic Starswirl. The interior was leather and brass. It had a small autobar and a pullout worktable so that riders could shuffle papers or relax as they wished.

After making arrangements to send the shuttle down, Nicholson had become concerned that some of his other passengers would learn about the flight and demand places on board. He had consequently impressed on MacAllister that he was to say nothing to anyone. The news that he wished to take another journalist along had been unsettling, but Nicholson had been caught by then, committed, and wanted to do nothing to upset his illustrious guest. This was not the first time the old editor had discovered the

116

advantage of his reputation for volcanic outbursts against those who, for whatever reason, had incurred his wrath. Consequently he and Casey remained, aside from the pilot, the only persons aboard.

The pilot's name was Cole Wetherai. He was a taciturn man who would have made a successful funeral director. He had morose eyes and a long nose and long pale fingers that fluttered across the controls as if they were an organ keyboard. He gave preflight instructions and information in a stentorian tone: 'Please be seated.' 'You will wish to check the status board above your seat before attempting to move around the cabin.' 'We want you to enjoy your excursion; please feel free to ask if there is anything you need.' He informed them also that it would be early morning local time when they arrived.

Casey looked dazzled, and MacAllister wondered whether it was a condition brought on by the chance to visit a world a few days before it was to end, or by his own presence. He waited until she was inside, then climbed in and sat down beside her.

'Have you ever been down on another world before, Mr MacAllister?' she asked.

He hadn't. Had never seen a point to it. He perceived himself as the end product of three billion years of evolution, specifically designed for the Earth, and that was where he was inclined to stay. 'I expect,' he told her, 'that this will be the only visit I ever make to alien soil.'

She *had,* as it turned out. She'd been to Pinnacle and Quraqua, and to Quraqua's airless moon, with its enigmatic city on the plain. Doing features, she explained.

The pilot closed the hatches. Interior lights came on. He spent about a minute hunched over his control board, then reached up and threw a couple of switches on an overhead panel. 'We are depressurizing the bay,' he said. 'We'll be ready to depart in just a couple of minutes.'

The vehicle rose slightly.

'I appreciate your doing this,' Casey told him.

He smiled benevolently. MacAllister liked doing things for people. And there was nothing quite so gratifying as the appreciation of a young person to whom he was lending the luster of his name. 'To be honest, Casey,' he said, 'I'm glad you asked. Without your initiative, I'd have spent most of the next week in The Navigator.'

The lander's motors whined and began to pulse steadily.

She smiled. MacAllister had made a career of attacking women in print, as he had attacked college professors, preachers, farmers, left-wing editorial writers, and assorted other do-gooders and champions of the downtrodden. Women, he'd argued, were possessed of an impossible anatomy, top-heavy and off-balance. They could not walk without jiggling and rolling, and consequently it was quite impossible for men of sense to take even the brightest of them seriously.

Many women perceived him as that most dangerous kind of character: an articulate and persuasive demagogue. He knew that, but accepted it as the price he had to pay for saying the things that everyone else knew to be true, but which they denied, even to themselves. To a degree, his literary reputation protected him from the rage that surely would have fallen on the head of a lesser man. It demonstrated to him the intellectual bankruptcy of both sexes. Here, after all, was this sweet young thing, beaming and smiling at him, hoping to improve her career through his auspices, and quite willing to overlook a substantial series of ill-tempered remarks on his side, should he choose to make them, simply because they would provide excellent copy. *There is a perfectly good reason, my dear, why the downtrodden are trodden down. If they deserved better, they would* have *better.*

The bay doors opened.

'We'll lose all sense of gravity after we launch,' said the pilot.

Harnesses swung down and locked them in. The interior lights blinked and went out. Then they sank back into their seats and began to move through the night. MacAllister twisted around and looked back at the great bulk of the *Evening Star.*

Lights blazed fore and aft. An antenna mounted just beyond the launch pod rotated slowly.

The power and majesty of the great liner was somehow lost when it was in dock. He'd not been all that impressed when he'd boarded her back at the Wheel. But out here the *Star* was in her element, afloat among strange constellations beneath a sun that wasn't quite the right color, above a world whose icy continents bore unfamiliar shapes. This view alone, he decided, was worth the side trip.

'Did I tell you,' said Casey, 'I'm checked out to pilot these things?' She looked pleased with herself.

That fact caught MacAllister's respect. Deep space seemed to be her journalistic specialty. Acquiring a pilot's skills told him she was serious. 'Excellent' he said. He turned away from the view, glanced at her, then looked out again at the shimmering atmosphere below. 'So how did you manage *that*?'

'My father owns a yacht.'

'Ah.' He recognized the family name. 'Your father's *Desmond* Hayes.'

'Yes.' She clamped her teeth together as if she'd been caught in a faux pas. And he understood: rich man's daughter trying to make it on her own.

Desmond Hayes was the founder of Lifelong Enterprises, which had funded numerous biotech advances, and was one of the major forces behind recent life-extending breakthroughs. He was notoriously wealthy, had a taste for power, and talked often of running for political office. He was seldom seen without a beautiful young woman on his arm. A ridiculous figure, on the whole.

'Well,' MacAllister said, 'it's always a good idea to have a backup pilot.'

They were over clumps of cumulus now, bright in the starlight. MacAllister heard and felt the beginnings of atmospheric resistance. He brought up the autobar menu. They were well stocked. 'How about a drink, Casey?'

'That *sounds* like a good idea,' she said. 'A *mint driver* would be nice, if they have one.'

He punched it in, handed it over to her, and made a hot rum for himself. 'Wetherai,' he said, 'let's take a look at the countryside before we set down.'

It proved to be a singularly uninviting landscape, mostly just snow and ice. The narrow equatorial belt provided dense forest along its southern edge, open country to the northeast, and low rolling hills and occasional patches of trees near the tower.

At dawn, they cruised over a shoreline dominated by enormous peaks. 'This is the northern coast,' Wetherai explained. Several strips of beach presented themselves. In all, it was a magnificent seascape.

They continued their exploration while the sun rose higher, until finally MacAllister informed Wetherai they'd seen enough. 'Let's go talk to the people at the tower,' he said.

The pilot brought them back toward the south, and thirty minutes later they descended toward Burbage Point. A few trees rose out of the snow.

'Dismal place,' she said.

But MacAllister liked it. There was something majestic in the desolation.

Despite the short night, they were up early and back in the tower immediately after sunrise. Hutch, Nightingale, and Kellie returned to the tunnel to recommence digging, while Chiang took over guard duty at the entrance and Toni went up to the roof.

This second sunrise on the new world was bright and enticing. The snow glittered in the hard cold light. The trees from which the cat had appeared glowed green and purple, and a sprinkling of white clouds drifted through the sky.

They'd been working only ten minutes when Kellie found a few half-legible symbols on one of the walls.

She recorded them with the microscan, and they decided to try to salvage the images themselves. But when they used the lasers to remove the segment of wall, it crumbled. 'There's a technique for this,' Hutch grumbled, 'but I don't know what it is.'

Marcel broke in on the private channel. 'Hutch?'

'I'm here. What've you got?'

'We think it's a skyhook.'

'You're kidding.'

'You think I could make this up?'

'Hold on. I'm going to put you on the allcom, and I want you to tell everybody.' She switched him over.

He repeated the news, and Nightingale announced himself stunned.

'What does Gunther think?' asked Kellie.

'It's *Gunther's* conclusion. Hell, what do *I* know about this stuff? But I'll give him this: I can't imagine what *else* it could be.'

'That means,' said Hutch, 'this place isn't representative at all. We've wandered into a remote site that didn't keep up with the rest of the world.'

'Looks like it. But there's no evidence of technological civilization *anywhere* on the surface.'

'They had an ice age,' said Hutch. 'It got covered.'

'We don't think even an ice age would completely erase all signs of an advanced culture. There'd be *towers*. *Real* towers, not that debacle you have. Maybe they'd get knocked over, but we'd still be able to see they'd been there. There'd be dams, harbor construction, all sorts of things. Concrete doesn't go away.'

'What's going to happen to it?' asked Kellie. 'The skyhook?'

'In about a week it'll go down with Deepsix.'

'So where does that leave us?' asked Hutch. 'Are we wasting our time here?'

She heard Marcel sigh. 'I don't know anything about archeology,' he said. 'We've forwarded everything we have to the Academy, and to the archeologists at Nok. They're considerably closer, and maybe we'll get some suggestions back from them.'

'There's something else here,' said Kellie. She'd uncovered a metal bar.

'Hold on, Marcel.' Hutch moved into position to give *Wendy* a good look.

Kellie tried to brush the dirt away. 'Careful,' Hutch said. 'It looks sharp.'

Nightingale dug a dart out of the frozen clay. Feather stalks remained at its base.

The bar was attached to a crosspiece. And the crosspiece became a rack. The rack was stocked with tubes.

They were narrow and about two-thirds of a meter long. Hutch picked one up and examined it by torchlight. It was hollow, made of light wood. Brittle now, of course. One end was narrowed and had a fitting that might have been a mouthpiece.

'You thinking what I am?' asked Kellie.

'Yep. It's a blowgun.'

They found a second dart.

And a couple of javelins.

'Stone heads,' Hutch said.

And small. A half meter long.

They also found some shields. These were made of iron and had been covered with animal skins, which fell apart when they touched them.

'Blowguns and skyhooks,' said Marcel. 'An interesting world.'

'About the skyhook—' said Nightingale.

'Yes?'

'If they actually had one at one time, part of it would still be here somewhere, right? I mean, that would *have* to be a big structure. And it has to be on the equator, so it's not under the ice somewhere.'

'We're way ahead of you, Randy. We think the base might have been in a mountain chain along the coast a few hundred kilometers southwest of where you are. We're waiting for satellites to get into position to do a scan.'

'The west coast,' she said.

'Right. Some of the peaks in that area seem to have permanent clouds over them. If we find something, you'll want to take a run over there yourself. We might be looking at the ultimate dig site.'

They carried the blowguns, the javelins, and several darts up to ground level. Outside, the wind had blown up again, and snow had begun to fall. They had no bags of sufficient size for the rack, so they cut the plastic in strips and wrapped it as best they could. But when they tried to move it to the lander, the wind caught the plastic and almost ripped it out of their hands. 'Bendo and Klopp,' said Nightingale, referring to a currently popular comedy team that specialized in pratfalls.

Hutch nodded. 'I guess. Let's leave it here until things calm down.'

They took a break. Kellie and Nightingale went back to the lander for a few minutes, and Hutch hoisted herself onto the table to rest. Spending all day bent over in tunnels, endlessly scraping, sweeping, and digging, was *not* her game.

Toni broke in on the allcom: 'Hutch, we've got company.'

'*Company?*' She signaled to Chiang, who was standing in the doorway, and drew her cutter. It was, she assumed, the cat.

'Lander coming in,' said Toni.

Hutch opened her channel to Marcel. 'Who else is out here?'

'A cruise ship,' he said. 'Just arrived this morning.'

'Well, it looks as if they're sending down tourists.'

'What?'

'You got it. They must be crazy.'

'Don't know anything about it. I'll contact their captain.'

She was getting another signal. 'I'll get back to you, Marcel.' She punched in the new caller. 'Go ahead.'

'Ground party, this is the pilot of the *Evening Star* lander. We would like to set down in the area.'

'Not a good idea,' said Hutch. 'It's dangerous here. There are wild animals.'

There was no response for almost half a minute. Then: 'We accept responsibility for everyone who is on board.'

'What's going on?' she asked. 'Why are you here?'

'I'm carrying two journalists who would like to visit the tower.'

'I don't believe this,' she said. 'The tower is dangerous, too. It could fall down at any time.'

123

There was a new voice, a baritone with perfect diction: 'We've been warned. It's on record. So you need not concern yourself further.'

'May I ask who's speaking?'

'Gregory MacAllister,' he said. 'I'm a passenger on the *Evening Star*.' He implied a *merely* at the beginning of the sentence, which in turn suggested modesty by someone who was in fact a great deal more than merely a passenger.

Hutch wondered if this would turn out to be *the* Gregory MacAllister. 'I don't think you understand,' she said. 'We are formally designated an archeological site. You're in violation of the law if you land.'

'What section of the code would that be, ma'am?'

Damned if she knew. There *was* such a law. But she had no idea where to find it.

'Then I think we'll have to continue as is.'

She switched to another channel. 'Bill, tie me in to the *Evening Star*. Get me a command channel if you have one.'

Bill replied with an electronic murmur and then told her none was available. *'There's only one main link,'* he said.

'Put me through.'

She listened to a series of clicks and a chime. Then: 'The Evening Star *welcomes you to first-class accommodations on voyages throughout the known universe.'* The voice was female. *'We feature luxurious cabins, a wide range of international cuisines, leading entertainers, three casinos, and special accommodations for parties. How may we serve you?'*

'My name's Hutchins,' she said. 'I'm with the landing party at the dig. I'd like to speak with someone in command, please.'

'I'm fully authorized to respond to all requests and complaints, Ms. Hutchins. I'd be pleased to help you.'

'I want to talk to the captain.'

'Perhaps if you explained your purpose in making this request—'

'Your captain has put some of his passengers in danger. Would you please put me through to him?'

There was a pause, then barely audible voices. Finally: 'This is the duty officer. Who are you again?' A human being this time. A male.

'I'm Priscilla Hutchins. The archeological project director on Deepsix. We have a team on the ground. You people have sent down some tourists. And I wanted you to know that there are hazards.'

'We have tourists on the surface?'

'Yes, you do.'

'I see.' A pause. 'What kind of hazards?'

'They could be eaten.'

Still another delay. Then: 'Do you have some sort of authority I should be aware of?'

'Look. Your passengers are approaching a protected archeological site. Moreover, it's an earthquake zone, and somebody could get killed. Please recall them. Or send them somewhere else.'

'Just a minute, please.'

He clicked off the circuit.

The lander pilot came back: 'Ms. Hutchins, we are going to set down near the tower. Since it seems to be snowing, and I assume visibility isn't any better on the ground, please clear your people away for the moment.'

'They're directly overhead,' said Kellie.

Hutch called everyone into the tower. 'Stay inside until they're on the ground,' she said. Then she switched back to the lander. 'Are you still there, pilot?'

'I'm still here.'

'Our people are out of the way. You're clear to come in. If you must.'

'Thank you.'

Marcel came back on: 'Hutch.'

'Yeah, what'd they tell you?'

'You know who's on board?'

'Gregory MacAllister.'

'Do you know who he is?'

Now she did. This was Gregory the Great. Self-appointed

champion of common sense who'd made a fortune attacking the pompous and the arrogant, or, depending on whom you listened to, simply those less gifted than he. Years before she'd been in a graduate seminar with a historian whose chief claim to fame was that he'd once been publicly chastised by MacAllister. He'd even put an account of the assault up on the screen and stood beside it grinning as if he'd touched greatness. 'Yes,' she said. 'The only person on the planet who could bring church and science together. They both hope he dies.'

'That's *him*. And I hope he's not listening.'

'What am I supposed to do with him?'

'Hutch, management would not want you to offend him. My guess is that it'll be your job if you do.'

'How about if I just feed him to the big cat?'

'Pardon?'

'Let it go.'

'I think it would be a good idea to treat him well. Let him look at whatever he wants to. It won't hurt anything. And don't let him fall on his head.'

The snow had grown heavier and become so thick MacAllister didn't see anything until moments before they touched down. He got a glimpse of the other lander, and of the tower beyond, and then they were on the ground, so softly he barely felt the impact. Wetherai had the personality of a pinecone, but there was no question he was a competent pilot.

The man himself turned around in his seat and studied them momentarily with those sad eyes. 'How long,' he asked, 'did you folks plan on being here?'

'Not long,' said MacAllister. 'An hour or so.'

The snow was already piling up on the windscreen.

'Okay I have a few things to take care of. Make sure you activate your e-suit before you go out, and we want you to keep it on the entire time you're here. You can breathe the local air if necessary, but the mix isn't quite right.

'The captain also directed me to ask you both to be careful. There've been wild animal sightings.'

'We know that,' said MacAllister.

'Good. There's a great deal of paperwork involved if we lose either of you.' He said it without a trace of irony.

'Thank you,' said Casey.

They went through the airlock and climbed down out of the spacecraft into the storm. 'To do the interview correctly,' MacAllister said, 'we're going to want to wait until it subsides.' Ordinarily, heavy weather provided great atmosphere for interviews. But in this case the tower was the star of the show, and people needed to be able to see it. 'Wetherai, how long before this blizzard lets up?'

The pilot appeared in the hatch. 'I don't know, sir. We don't have a weather report.'

'Seems as if it might be a good idea to get one.'

'Won't be one for this area,' he said seriously. He looked around, shook his head, and came down the ladder.

The archeologists' lander was dead ahead. It was smaller than the *Star*'s vehicle, and sleeker. More businesslike.

A woman materialized out of the driving snow. She wore a blue-and-white jumpsuit and he knew from the way she walked it was Hutchins. She was trim, built like a boy, and came up almost to his shoulders. Her black hair was cut short, and she looked unfriendly. But he shrugged it away in his usual forgiving manner, recognizing anger as a natural trait exhibited by females who didn't get their way.

'You're the mission commander, I take it?' he asked, extending his hand.

She shook it perfunctorily. 'I'm Hutchins,' she said.

He introduced Casey and Wetherai.

'Why don't we talk inside?' Hutchins turned on her heel and marched off.

Delightful.

They clumped through the snow. MacAllister studied the tower while he tried to get used to the e-suit. He should have been cold, but wasn't. His feet, clad in leisure shoes, sank into the drifts. But they stayed warm.

The tower loomed up through the storm. At home, it would have been no more than a pile of rock. Here, amidst all this desolation, it was magnificent. But the Philistines had punched a hole in the wall. 'Pity you chose to do that,' he told Hutchins.

'It made egress considerably easier.'

'I quite understand.' He did, of course. And yet this tower had obviously stood a long time. It should have been possible to show it a bit more respect. 'I don't suppose we have any idea how old it is?'

'Not yet,' she said. 'We don't have an onboard facility for dating. It'll take a while.'

The storm caused him to speak more loudly than necessary. He was having a hard time getting used to the radio. Hutchins asked him to lower his voice. He did and focused on trying to *keep* it down. 'And there's nothing else?' he asked. 'No other ruins?'

'There are some scattered around the planet. And there's a city buried down there.' She pointed at the ground.

'*Really?*' He tried to imagine it, a town with houses and parks and probably a jail under the ice. 'Incredible,' he said.

'Watch your head.' She led him through the entrance they had made. He ducked and followed her into a low-roofed chamber with a table on which were piled some cups and darts. He had to stay bent over.

'Tight fit,' he said. The small-gauge stairways caught his eye. 'The inhabitants were, what, – elves?'

'Apparently about that size.'

'What have you learned about them so far?' He wandered over to the table and reached for one of the cups, but she asked him, if he would, to avoid handling them. 'Forgive me,' he said. 'So what can you tell me about them?'

'We know they favored blowguns.'

128

He smiled back at her. 'Primitives.'

Hutchins's people drifted in to meet him. They struck him as by and large a forgettable lot. The other two women were reasonably attractive. There was one young male with a trace of Asian ancestry. And he recognized the second male but couldn't immediately place him. He was an elderly, bookish-looking individual, with a weak chin and a fussy mustache. And he was in fact staring at MacAllister with some irritation.

Hutchins did the introductions. And the mystery went away. 'Randall Nightingale,' she said.

Ah. Nightingale. The man who fainted. The man carried relatively uninjured out of battle by a woman. MacAllister frowned and pretended to study his features. 'Do I know you from somewhere?' he asked with benign dignity.

'Yes,' said Nightingale. 'Indeed you do.'

'You're . . .'

'I was the director of the original project, Mr MacAllister. Twenty years or so ago.'

'So you were.' MacAllister was not without compassion, and he let Nightingale see that he felt a degree of sympathy. 'I *am* sorry how that turned out. It must have been hard on you.'

Hutchins must have sensed the gathering storm. She moved in close.

MacAllister turned to his companion. 'Casey, you know *Randall* Nightingale. A legendary figure.'

Nightingale took an aggressive step forward, but Hutchins put an arm around his shoulder. *Little woman,* he thought. *And a little man.* But Nightingale wisely allowed himself to be restrained. 'I haven't forgotten you, MacAllister,' he said.

MacAllister smiled politely. 'There, sir, as you can see, you had the advantage of me.'

Hutchins drew him away and turned him over to the Asian. Something passed between them, and he coaxed Nightingale out of the chamber and down the child's staircase.

'What was that about?' asked Casey.

'Man didn't like to read about himself.' MacAllister turned back to Hutchins. 'I'm sorry about that,' he said. 'I didn't expect to find *him* here.'

'It's okay. Let's just try to keep it peaceful.'

'Madam,' he said, 'you need to tell that to your own people. But I'll certainly try to stay out of everyone's way. Now, can I persuade you to show us around the site a bit?'

'All right,' she said. 'I guess it can't do any harm. But there's really not much to see.'

'How long have you been on the ground, if you don't mind my asking?'

'This is our second day.'

'Do we know anything at *all* about the natives, the creatures, who built it? Other than the blowguns?'

Hutchins told him what they had learned: The natives were of course preindustrial, fought organized wars, and had a form of writing. She offered to take him to the top of the tower. 'Tell me what's up there, and I'll decide,' he said.

She described the chamber and the levered ceiling which apparently had opened up. And she added their idea that the natives might have owned a telescope.

'Optics?' he said. 'That doesn't seem to fit with blowguns.'

'That's our feeling. I hope we'll get some answers during the course of the day.'

MacAllister saw no point making the climb. Instead they descended into the lower chambers, and Hutchins showed him a fireplace and some chair fragments.

Near the bottom of the tower they looked into a tunnel. 'This is where we're working now,' she said.

The tunnel was too small to accommodate him. Even had it not been, he would have stayed out of it. 'So what's back there?' he asked.

'It's where we found the blowguns. It looks as if there was an armory. But what we're really interested in is finding writing samples and maybe some engraved pictures. Or possibly sculpture.

Something that'll tell us what they looked like. We'd like to answer *your* question, Mr MacAllister.'

'Of course.' MacAllister looked around at the blank walls. 'We must have some idea of their appearance. For example, surely the staircase is designed for a bipedal creature?'

'Surely,' she said. 'We're pretty sure they had four limbs. Walked upright. That's about the extent of what we know.'

'When do you expect to be able to determine the age of this place?'

'After we get some of the pieces back to a lab. Until then everything is guesswork.'

Wetherai was still standing by the chair fragments, trying to catch Hutchins's attention. 'Yes?' she said.

'May I ask whether you're finished with these?'

'Yes,' she said. 'We've already stowed a complete armchair in the lander.'

'Good.' He looked pleased. 'Thank you.' And while she watched, clearly surprised, he gathered the fragments, a beam, and a piece of material that might once have been drapery. And he carried everything up the staircase.

'The ship hopes to salvage a few pieces,' MacAllister explained. His back was beginning to hurt from all the bending. 'Anything that might interest the more historically minded passengers.'

She showed no reaction. 'I can't see that it'll do any harm.'

'Thank you,' said MacAllister. 'And if there's nothing we missed' – he turned to Casey – 'this might be a good time to go outside and, if the weather will allow, do our interview.'

8

The results of archeological enterprise at home are predictable within a set of parameters, because we know the general course of history. Its off-world cousin is a different breed of cat altogether. Anybody who's going to dig up furniture on Sirius II or Rigel XVII better leave his assumptions at the door.

—GREGORY MACALLISTER, 'Sites and Sounds', The
Grand Tour

It was the first time in his adult life that Nightingale had seriously considered assaulting someone. That he had resisted the impulse, that he had not taken a swing at the smirking, self-satisfied son of a bitch, was a result not of Hutch's restraining hand or of any reluctance over attacking somebody considerably more than twice his size. It had been rather his sense of the impropriety of violence that had shut him down.

Nightingale had grown up with a code. One did not make a scene. One retained dignity under all circumstances. If an opponent was to be attacked, it was done with a smile and a cutting phrase. Unfortunately, he hadn't been able to come up with the cutting phrase.

133

Now, working in the tunnel with Toni and Chiang, he was embarrassed by his outburst. He had not gotten it right, had not come *close* to getting it right. But he *had*, by God, confronted MacAllister, and that at least had relieved part of the burden he'd been carrying all these years.

MacAllister had written an account of the original expedition, titled 'Straight and Narrow,' as the lead editorial for *Premier*. It had appeared shortly after Nightingale's return, when the investigation was still going on, and it had laid the blame for failure at *his* door, had charged him with mismanaging the landings, and had concluded by branding him as a helpless coward because he'd fainted after being wounded. The article in fact made light of his wounds. 'Scratches,' MacAllister had remonstrated, as though he'd been there.

It had branded him publicly and, in his view, had caused the examining board to render a verdict against him, and to shut down plans for future expeditions. *We need to put Maleiva III behind us,* one of the commissioner's reps had told him after the commissioner herself had cut off all contact. Didn't want to be seen with him.

'Straight and Narrow' had appeared again, six years ago, in a collection of MacAllister's memoirs. A fresh attack. And the man had pretended not to know him.

'You okay?' asked Chiang.

They were working to clear the chamber where they'd found the blowguns, the area they now called the armory. But he realized he had stopped in the middle of the effort and was staring off somewhere. 'Yeah,' he said. 'I'm fine.'

Toni and Chiang were both watching him. They'd asked on the way down what had caused his outburst, and he'd put them off. How could he possibly tell them? But it galled him that MacAllister, glib, irresponsible, that judge of all mankind, had been within reach, and that he had been impotent. What a pathetic creature he must have appeared.

John Drummond had made his reputation within a year of receiving his doctorate by devising the equations named for him, which had provided a major step forward in understanding galactic evolution. But he'd done nothing of note during the decade that had passed since that time. Now, at thirty-five, he was approaching the age at which he could be expected to begin tottering. Physicists and mathematicians traditionally make their mark early on. Genius is limited to the very young.

He'd adjusted to the realities, and had been prepared to spend the balance of his career on the periphery, criticizing the results of his betters. His reputation was secure, and even if he did nothing else notable, he still had the satisfaction of knowing that, during his early twenties, he'd outpaced damned near everybody else on the planet.

Despite that sense of his own contributions, he could not help feeling overawed in the presence of people like Beekman and al-Kabhar, who were known and respected everywhere they went. Drummond inevitably detected a note of condescension in his treatment by his peers. He suspected they perceived him as someone who, in the end, had to be regarded as a disappointment, who had not quite lived up to the promise of the early years.

He had consequently become somewhat defensive. His profession had passed him by, and he suspected that his selection to join the Deepsix mission had been a political choice. He had been simply too big a name to leave off the invitation list. It would have been better, he sometimes thought, to have been a mediocrity from the start, to have been perceived as a man of limited promise, than to have raised such hopes in others and in himself, and gone on to disappoint them all.

Like Chiang, he was also attracted to Kellie Collier, although he'd never made any sort of advance. He drank coffee with her when the opportunity permitted, spent what time with her that he could. But he feared rejection, and he detected in her manner that she would not take him seriously as a desirable male.

He was not entirely surprised when Beekman invited him into his office to ask whether he wanted to join the team that would inspect the artifact they'd found orbiting Maleiva III. It was an offer most of his colleagues would have coveted, and his reputation may have left the project director with little choice. But Drummond wasn't anxious to embrace the honor, because it seemed to mean he would have to leave the ship. And the idea of going outside frankly scared him.

'That's very good of you, Gunther.' He loved using the great man's first name.

'Think nothing of it. You deserve the honor.'

'But the others—'

'—will understand. You've earned this assignment, John. Congratulations.'

Drummond was thinking about the void.

'You *do* want to participate, don't you?'

'Yes. Of course I do. I just thought that the more senior members should have the privilege.' His heart had begun to pound. He knew spacewalking was supposed to be simple. You just wore air tanks and a belt and magnetic shoes. And comfortable clothing. They emphasized comfortable clothing. He didn't like heights, but everything he'd read about work in the vacuum indicated that wasn't a problem either.

Before the offer had come, before he'd thought it out, he'd made the mistake of telling several of his colleagues how he'd like to cross to the assembly, to touch it and walk on it. He knew that if he refused the offer, no matter what reason he gave, it would get out.

'Do you know how to use a cutter?' Beekman asked.

'Of course.' Punch the stud and don't point it at your foot.

'Okay. Good. We'll be leaving in two hours. Meet in front of the cargo bay airlock. On C Deck.'

'Gunther,' he said, 'I've never worn an e-suit.'

'Neither have I.' Beekman laughed. 'I suspect we'll be learning together.' Then, abruptly, the conversation was over. The office door opened. Beekman had picked up a pen. 'Oh, by the way,'

136

he said without looking up, 'the captain says if you want to eat, you should do it now, and keep it light. Best not to have a fresh meal in your stomach when we go out.'

Drummond closed his eyes and wondered whether he could get away with claiming to be ill.

Marcel regretted having allowed Kellie to travel down to the surface. Had she been available, she would have accompanied the inspection team over to the assembly, and he could have held himself in reserve for an emergency. Or for a less arduous afternoon.

He didn't like taking Beekman's people outside. None of them had ever before gone through an airlock in flight. There was in fact little that could go wrong. The Flickinger field was quite safe. But it still made him uncomfortable.

At Beekman's request, Marcel had brought *Wendy* to the Maleiva III end of the assembly, the section most distant from the asteroid and closest to the planet. There, they could see quite clearly that it had been detached from a larger construct. The terminal ends of the shafts had latches and connectors.

He matched course, speed, and alignment so they maintained a constant relative position. That was crucial, not only because having the airlock within a couple of meters of the assembly was convenient, but because the sight of the two objects moving in relation to one another would almost certainly sicken his embryo spacewalkers. The only problem was that the two globes currently in the sky, Deepsix and the sun, would be in apparent motion. Enough to make you dizzy if you weren't used to it.

'Don't look at them,' he advised his team. 'You've got a bona fide alien artifact out there, unlike anything we've ever seen before. Concentrate on *that*.'

Beekman had chosen two people, a man and a woman, to go out with him. Both were young, and both were celebrated members of his science team. The woman, Carla Stepan, had done some pioneering work in light propagation. Appropriate, Marcel thought. She was herself a luminous creature.

Drummond's reputation was known to all. But the man himself was something of a mystery. Quiet, reserved, a bit bashful. An odd choice, the captain thought.

He demonstrated how to use the e-suit. The Flickinger field had several advantages over the pressure suits of the previous century, principal among them being that it couldn't be punctured.

But someone could get so caught up in the drama of the moment that he accidentally released his tether. And the field itself wasn't entirely foolproof. It was possible with a little imagination to screw up the antiradiation shielding and fry. Or make adjustments to the oxygen-nitrogen mix and thereby render oneself incompetent or maybe dead. Consequently, Marcel insisted they were all to keep their fingers off the control unit once it had been set.

Marcel had suggested to Beekman that he, Beekman, not go. The planetologist had told him he worried too much.

Theoretically, his medical record was fine, or he wouldn't be on board. But he never really looked well. His pale complexion might have been emphasized by the black beard. But he seemed to get out of breath easily, he wheezed occasionally, and the slightest exertion brought color to his cheeks. Marcel had the authority to prevent his going, but this was Gunther's show, and the captain couldn't bring himself to deny the man an experience that promised to be the supreme moment of his professional career.

'Everybody ready?' Marcel asked. They were all standing by the airlock, Beekman and Carla obviously anxious to get started, John Drummond looking reluctant. He checked their breathers and activated their suits. Carla had some experience with cutters, so he'd assigned one to her, and he took one himself. They strapped on wristlamps. He handed out vests and waited while they put them on. Each vest was equipped with a springlock so that a tether could be connected.

Marcel also strapped on a go-pack.

They did a radio check and went into the airlock. Marcel initiated the cycle. The inner hatch closed, and the lock began to depressurize. Beekman and Carla seemed fine. But Drummond began breathing more deeply than normal.

'Relax, John,' Marcel told him on a private channel. 'There's nothing to this.'

'It might be the wrong time to bring this up,' Drummond said, 'but I have this thing about *heights*.'

'Everybody has a thing about heights. Don't worry about it. I know this is hard to believe, but you won't notice it at all.'

Carla saw what was happening and flashed an encouraging smile. She spoke to Drummond, but Marcel couldn't hear what she said. Drummond nodded and looked better. Not much, but a little.

The go lamps went on, and the outer hatch irised open. They looked across a couple of meters of empty space at the cluster of parallel shafts. They were lunar gray, gritty, occasionally pocked. As thick individually, thought Marcel, as an elephant's leg. From the perspective of the airlock, they might have been fifteen entirely separate pipes, water pipes perhaps, coming to an abrupt end a few meters to their right; but on the left they stretched into infinity. And somehow they were perfectly equidistant, apparently separated and maintained by an invisible force.

'Incredible,' said Drummond, leaning forward slightly and looking both ways.

There were no markings, no decoration, no bolts or sheaths or ridges. Simply fifteen tubes, arranged symmetrically, eight on the outer perimeter, six midway, and the single central shaft.

Marcel attached a flex tether to a clip on the hull and motioned the project director forward. 'All yours, Gunther,' he said.

Beekman advanced to the hatch, never taking his eyes off the long gray shafts. He put his head out and drew in his breath. 'My God,' he said.

Marcel clipped the tether to his vest. 'It'll pay out as you go, or retract as you need.'

'How long is it?'

'Twenty meters.'

'I meant, to the brace.'

There were braces along the entire length of the assembly. The nearest was – 'Almost fifty kilometers away.'

Beekman shook his head. 'If someone else had reported such a thing,' he said, 'I would have refused to believe it.' He put his feet on the outer lip of the airlock. 'I think I'm ready.'

'Okay. Be careful. When I tell you, just push off. Don't try to jump, or I'll have to come after you.' Marcel looked back at the others. 'If anybody *does* contrive to drift away, I'll take care of the rescue. In the meantime, everyone else is to stay put. Okay?'

Okay.

'Go,' he told Beekman.

Beekman hunched his shoulders. He was wearing a pair of white slacks and a green sweatshirt with the name of his university, *Berlin,* stenciled on it. He looked, Marcel thought, appropriately dashing. And quite happy. Ecstatic, in fact.

He leaned forward, gave himself a slight push, and cried out in sheer joy as he launched. They watched him drift awkwardly across the narrow space, one leg straight, one bent at the knee, rather like a runner caught in midstride.

Marcel stood in the hatch, letting the tether slide across his palm until he was sure Beekman wasn't traveling too fast. The project director reached out for the nearest shaft, collided with it, wrapped his arms around it, and shouted something in German. 'Marcel,' he continued, 'I owe you a dinner.'

'I want it in writing,' Marcel said.

Beekman loosened his grip, found another shaft for his feet, settled down, and waved.

Carla moved up to take her turn.

Beekman and his team clambered around on the assembly while Marcel stood guard. Carla took pictures and Drummond collected sensor readings. Beekman was talking, describing what he was seeing, and taking various gauges and sensors out of his vest to answer questions for the people inside. Yes, it was magnetic. No, it did not seem to vibrate when low-frequency sound waves were applied.

Carla produced the cutter and conferred with Beekman. Marcel couldn't overhear the conversation, but they were obviously looking for the right place from which to remove a sample. The surface had no features. The only distinguishing marks that they'd been able to see, either from the scanners or up close, were the encircling bands. And none of those was visible from here.

They made up their minds, and Carla steadied herself, took aim at one of the shafts, and brought the laser to bear.

'Careful,' Marcel advised her. The field wouldn't protect her if she made a mistake.

'I will be,' she said.

She switched on the cutter, the beam flashed, and the view fields in all four suits darkened.

She began to work. They were going to take off the last two meters of one of the outside shafts.

Drummond had put his instruments away and was simply holding on. He appeared to be examining the assembly very carefully, keeping his eyes away from the void. Marcel left the airlock, went over, and joined him. 'How you doing?' he asked privately.

'I guess I'm a little wobbly.'

'It's all right,' he said. 'It happens. You want to go back inside?'

'No.' Drummond shook his head but kept his gaze on the assembly.

'You'll feel better in a bit. When you're ready to go back, I'll go with you.'

He mumbled something. Marcel only caught '. . . damn fool.'

'Maybe not. You might just be a little more sensible than the rest of us.'

Drummond managed a smile, still looking at the metal. 'Marcel,' he said, 'maybe I *ought* to go back over there before I become a problem.'

'Whatever happens, John, you won't be a problem. Everything's under control.'

'Okay.'

Drummond did not want to make the jump. Even though there was no gravity, Marcel suspected his senses were relating to the proximity of the *Wendy Jay,* using that to determine what was up and down. He had maintained a position which, related to the ship, kept his head *up*. Now he was being asked to cross that terrible void again. People who claim there's no sense of altitude in space, Marcel thought, have never been there. He reached out to place an arm gently on his shoulder, but Drummond drew away.

'Thanks,' Drummond said. 'I can manage.'

'It has plenty of juice,' said Carla, admiring her laser. From Drummond's perspective, she was upside down. His eyes closed tight.

She had already sliced halfway through her target shaft. Beekman was hanging on the edge of it to make sure it didn't drift away when she'd completed the job.

Drummond's eyes opened, and he looked back at the airlock as if it were a half klick away. Its light spilled out into the vacuum.

'I thought there'd be more resistance,' Carla said.

'You're okay,' Marcel told Drummond. 'Can I make a suggestion?'

Drummond's breathing was becoming ragged, but he didn't reply.

'Close your eyes, John. And let me take you over.' *Wendy* hovered only two meters away. Bill was keeping the ship perfectly still in relation to the artifact. But Marcel was aware of Deepsix climbing slowly but steadily up the sky.

'Something wrong, John?' Beekman's voice.

'No,' said Marcel. 'We're fine.'

'John?' Carla this time, sounding worried. 'You okay?'

'Yes.' His voice was tight and angry. He looked at Marcel. 'Yeah. Please get me away from here.'

Marcel put an arm gently around his waist. This time Drummond didn't pull away. 'Tell me when you're ready,' he said.

Drummond stiffened and closed his eyes. 'Just give me a minute.' But it was too late. Marcel, without waiting, anxious to end the suspense, pushed them forward, off the shaft. They floated toward the open hatch and the light.

'We'll be there in a second, John.'

By then the others were watching. Carla's laser went out, and she asked whether she could help. Marcel saw that Beekman was shifting his posture, preparing to join them. 'Stay put, Gunny,' he said. 'We're okay.'

'What happened, Marcel?' he asked.

'A little motion sickness, I think. Nothing serious. Happens all the time.'

Drummond struggled briefly and they bumped into the hull. But he got one hand on the hatch and pulled himself into the airlock. Marcel let him do it on his own. When John was safely on board he climbed in beside him. 'Damned coward,' Drummond said.

They were inside the ship's artificial gravity field. Marcel sat down on the bench. 'You're being a little hard on yourself.'

Drummond just stared back out of bleak eyes.

'Listen.' Marcel sat back and relaxed. 'There are very few people who would have done what you did. Most wouldn't have gone out there at all, feeling the way you must have.' He looked at the assembly, and the stars beyond. 'You want me to shut the hatch and we'll go inside?'

He shook his head. 'No,' he said. 'Can't do that. They're still out there.'

Beekman and Carla returned a few minutes later with their prize. They negotiated it carefully into the airlock, into the half-gee gravity field that was normal for ships in flight. (Maintaining full Earth normal would have consumed too much power.) The piece was as long as Marcel was high. They expected it to be quite heavy inside the ship.

Instead, a look of bewilderment formed on Carla's features. She signaled Beekman to let go and easily hefted the object herself. '*Impossibilium* is the right word,' she said. 'It weighs next to nothing.'

Beekman stared. 'They're pretty good engineers, aren't they?'

'Yes,' she said.

'Because of the weight?' Marcel asked.

Drummond was almost breathing normally again. He wanted to speak, and Beekman gave him the floor.

'The problem,' he said, summoning each word as if it were Greek, 'with this kind of construction . . .' He stopped to take another breath. 'Problem is that you have too much mass distributed over such an extreme length.'

He glanced at Beekman, who nodded.

'The strength of the structure at any given point isn't enough to support the strain put on it. Think of the, ah, Starlite Center in Chicago and imagine you had to build it from cardboard.'

'It'd collapse,' Marcel said.

'Exactly right,' said Carla. 'The kinds of building materials we have now, applied to *this* kind of structure' – she nodded toward the airlock door, toward the assembly – 'equate to cardboard. If we tried to make one of these, its own mass would crumple it.'

Beekman picked up the thread. 'If you're going to erect something as big as the Starlite, you want two qualities in your building materials.'

144

'Strength,' said Marcel.

'And light weight,' finished Carla. She glanced at the sample. 'We know it's strong because the assembly holds together. And now we know at least part of the reason it holds together. It doesn't have much mass.'

They closed up. Minutes later green lamps blinked, and the inner hatch opened. They shut off their suits and came out of the airlock.

'So what's next?' asked Marcel.

Beekman looked pleased. 'We analyze it. Find out how they did it.'

For August Canyon, Deepsix was aptly named. His flight to that unhappy world as pool representative for the various press services, to do a feature that was of only marginal interest to the general public, signaled beyond any doubt management's view of his future. Is there a labor strike in Siberia? Send Canyon. Did they find water on the far side of the Moon? Get Canyon up there to do the interviews.

'It isn't that bad,' said Emma Constantine, his producer and the only other soul aboard the *Edward J. Zwick* other than the pilot.

'Why isn't it?' he demanded. He'd been simmering during the entire five weeks of the outbound flight, saying none of the things that were on his mind. But he was tired of being cooped up, tired of spending his time on virtual beaches while other people his age were doing solid investigative journalism, chasing down corruption in London, sex in Washington, stupidity in Paris.

'It'll be a good feature,' she said. 'Worlds collide. That's big stuff, if we handle it right.'

'It *would* be,' he said, 'if we had somebody to interview.' Canyon had all the credentials – graduate of Harvard, experience with Washington Online and later Sam Brewster. Brewster was an extraordinarily effective muckraker, and Canyon had been with him a year and a half, just long enough for Brewster to recognize he lacked a muckraker's stomach while Canyon alienated every power center in the capital. After their less than amicable parting, he'd been lucky to catch on with *Toledo Express*.

'We've got a whole *boatload* of scientists to talk to.'

'Right. You ever try to get a physicist to say something people are remotely interested in hearing?'

'We've done it, on occasion.'

'Sure we have. Cube theory. Gravity waves. Force vituperations. That's pretty hot stuff.'

'I think that's force *correlations*.'

He took a deep breath. 'As if it mattered. What we need is a good politician. Somebody to take a stand against planetary wrecks.'

'Look,' she said. 'Stop feeling sorry for yourself. We've got a database on these people.'

'I know,' he said. 'Tasker's on *Wendy*, and he'll talk, but that's the problem. He talks forever.'

'We can *edit* if we have to. Listen, Augie, we're here and we have to make the best of it. This isn't the assignment I'd have chosen either. But there's going to be a lot more interest in this than you think.'

'Why would *that* be?'

'Because worlds don't crash into each other every day.' She was frowning, maybe regretting not the assignment, but her partner. 'Because there are *ruins* on Deepsix.'

'But no sign of a *civilization*. Do you think anybody's going to care that a pile of stones goes down with everything else?'

'Augie, who built the pile?'

'I doubt that the people they're sending down there are going to have time to find out.'

She smiled benignly. 'That's exactly my point. Look, forget *Wendy*. This is a world that's been racked up. Ice age for three thousand years. No sign of cities. That means if anybody's left,

146

it's savages. Savages are relentlessly dull. But vanished civilizations? That's *news*. The people we want to interview are on the ground, poking around the tower. Not in the starship. Figure out where to go with *that* side of the story, and we're in business.'

He let his head drop back in his chair and stared at the ceiling. 'You know, Emma,' he said, 'sometimes I really hate this job.'

9

Archeology is a career for the terminally weak-minded. An archeologist is a trash collector with a degree.

—GREGORY MACALLISTER, *'Career Night'*,
Ports of Call

Wendy proceeded in a leisurely manner along the entire length of the assembly. They took pictures, although every section looked like every other section, counted the bands (thirty-nine altogether) that secured the shafts to each other, and arrived at last at the asteroid.

A rock rather than a chunk of iron, it was almost a perfect sphere. A metallic net was wrapped around it, securing it to the assembly by means of a rectangular plate. The plate, several meters thick, had rounded edges and corners.

The extreme length of the assembly tended to diminish the apparent size of the asteroid, until one drew near. It was in fact more than a kilometer in diameter.

Marcel and Beekman watched from project control as they approached. Beekman looked disappointed, and Marcel, wondering how he could possibly be out of sorts at such a supreme moment, asked what was wrong.

'I'd hoped,' he replied, 'to find something that would give us an idea who put it here. What its purpose was. I thought maybe there'd be a control station at one end or the other. *Something.*'

Marcel put a hand on his shoulder. 'People leaving stuff like this around the neighborhood should include a manual.'

'I'm serious.'

'I know.' Stupid remark.

They went outside again, just the two of them, and inspected the asteroid. They floated above the rockscape, using Marcel's go-pack to get around.

Much of the net was concealed by a layer of dust. The metal links appeared to be made of the same material as the shafts. They were only a couple of centimeters thick and were linked with crosspieces at lengths of about three-quarters of a meter.

They stopped to examine the connecting plate and were pleasantly surprised to discover a series of engraved symbols. All the characters were joined, in the manner of cursive writing. 'Eventually,' Beekman said, 'I'd like to take this inside. Take it home with us.'

It was *big*. Marcel measured it with his eye and concluded it wouldn't fit through the cargo airlock. 'We might have to cut it in half,' he said.

'Whatever's necessary—' They drifted above it and looked back the way they'd come, down the long straight line of the assembly toward the heart of Deepsix.

They took samples of everything, of the rock and the dust, of the net, of the plate. When they were finished they went back inside and had some coffee. It was after 2:00 A.M. ship time, November 27.

Beekman suggested the unknown architects had developed quantum technology, and the skyhook had simply become obsolete. Marcel was too tired to care. But just as he was getting ready to head for his quarters, Bill broke in: *'Captain, we now have the satellite scans you requested of the coastal mountain range.'*

'Okay, Bill.' Ordinarily he'd have asked to look. But not at this hour. 'Anything interesting?'

'There is a structure of substantial dimensions on one of the peaks.'

The door opened almost at the first touch of the laser. Beyond lay shelved walls and a vaulted ceiling. Hutch played her light over a bare wooden table. Shadowy figures looked back out of alcoves.

'Bingo,' said Toni.

Statues. There were six alcoves, and at one time there had been six figures. Five lay broken and scattered in the dust that covered the floor. One remained.

The survivor resembled a falcon. But it stood upright, in a vest and trousers that suggested pantaloons. A medallion of illegible design hung about its neck. It reminded Hutch of Horus. 'You think that's what they looked like?' she asked.

'Maybe,' said Nightingale. 'It would fit. Little creatures, descended from birds.'

Whatever might once have filled the shelves was gone.

She flashed pictures to *Wendy*. Hutch half expected to hear from Marcel, but it was early morning on the ship. In the interests of diplomacy, she also sent a picture to MacAllister, who was having brunch in the *Star* lander.

He took it rather calmly, she thought, but made it a point to thank her and ask that he be kept informed. The manner of it implied that he thought it trivial.

The room, she suspected, had been a study. Or perhaps a library.

Nightingale agreed. 'I wish we could read their scrolls.'

Indeed. What would a history not be worth?

The other figures had apparently all been representations of the falcon, in various poses. They gathered up the pieces, packed each of the six separately to the extent they were able, took them out to the lander, and stowed them in the cargo hold.

The snow had stopped and by late morning the last clouds cleared away. The environment was now suitable, MacAllister judged, for the interview.

Wetherai had loaded several pieces of the doll-like furniture, a couple of cabinets, a chair, and a table into the cargo section. Everything was badly decomposed, but that didn't really matter. TransGalactic could process the stuff easily enough and make them look as if they were antiques in exquisitely restored condition. The details wouldn't matter as long as some part of the original remained.

Wetherai had even made off with a *javelin*. It had an iron tip, and MacAllister wondered whether it had ever actually been used in combat. He tried to visualize hawks in trousers flying about trying to stab each other with these pea-stickers. The only thing more absurd than someone else's civilization, he thought, is someone else's religious views.

Casey had brought a couple of folding chairs along and had planned to sit out in the open with him while they talked, with the tower as a backdrop. Or possibly even sit *inside* the tower.

'The atmosphere's all wrong for any of that,' he told her. 'We don't want to be outside. Either in the building or in the snow.'

'Why not?'

'It looks *cold*, Casey.'

'What does the audience care?'

'If *we* look cold, your audience will not get caught up in the conversation.'

'You're kidding.'

'I'm quite serious.'

'But they'll know we're inside e-suits.'

'What do *they* know about e-suits? Only what they see in the sims. They'll see the snow; they'll see you and me sitting there in shirtsleeves. They *won't* see the e-suit. It doesn't look cozy.'

'I want *cozy*?'

'Absolutely.'

She sighed. 'All right. So what do we do? Sit in the lander?'

'Correct. Roughing it, but not too rough.'

She gave him a tolerant smile, and he knew what she was thinking. They were too far from the tower. In fact, the tower was partially hidden behind the other spacecraft. 'I'll get Wetherai to move us closer.'

'I've a better idea,' said MacAllister. Two of the women, Hutchins and Toni What's-Her-Name, were carrying a table out to their spacecraft. He studied Hutchins and realized that her problem was that she had no sense of humor. She was certainly not the sort of woman one would want to have around on a long-term basis. Took herself far too seriously, and seemed utterly unaware that she was a lightweight.

The table was big, and they were struggling. He excused himself, got down out of the vehicle, walked over and magnanimously asked if he could help. Hutchins glanced suspiciously at him. 'Yes,' she said finally. 'If you'd like.'

It was a rectangular table, so old it was impossible to be sure what the original composition material might have been. It was large, considering the scale of the other furniture, and probably would have seated twelve of the natives. A decorative geometry that might have represented leaves and flowers was carved into its sides.

Casey joined the party and lent a hand.

The cargo section was so full there was a question whether it would fit, but after some rearranging they got it in.

'Thanks,' Hutchins said. 'That turned out to be heavier than it looked.'

'Glad to help.'

She looked at him and smiled. 'Was there something you wanted to ask me?'

Not a complete dummy, he decided. 'As a matter of fact, I could use your assistance. Casey and I are going to record an interview. I was wondering if you'd allow us the use of your lander.'

'In what way?' She looked at him, looked at the cargo bay

153

loaded with artifacts, and showed him she didn't much approve. 'What did you have in mind?'

'Just sit in it and talk. It's warm and out of the snow, but we still get the atmosphere of the dig. And a perfect view of the tower.'

'You can't close it up,' she said.

He guessed that she meant they could not seal off the cabin and repressurize it. 'We don't need to. The audience won't know the difference.'

She shrugged. 'You can have an hour. After that we'll need it back.'

'That's good. Thank you very much.'

She turned away. Ridiculous woman.

They climbed into the cabin, and Casey removed her link, tied a microscan into it, put it on a tray, and aimed it at her subject. She set up two more in strategic locations.

There were artifacts in the rear of the cabin, which would provide additional atmosphere. MacAllister placed himself so that a weapons rack was behind him, and the tower was visible through his window. Casey was moving things out of the way in order to get shots from different angles.

Something large and dark rose out of the trees to the west, flapped in a large uncertain circle, and descended again. Clumsy creature, whatever it was. *Yes,* he thought, *let's have Armageddon for this cold world and all its living freight.*

Hutch had turned away from MacAllister and was standing at the tower entrance talking to Nightingale when Chiang came on the circuit. 'Hutch,' he said, 'we might have something else.'

'What?' she asked. 'What is it?'

'Looks like an inscription. It's in pieces, but it's writing of a sort. We've also broken through into an open corridor.'

'Where are you?'

'Back of the library.'

'I'm on my way.'

She descended staircases and entered the tunnels, crossed the armory, and kept going until she saw lights. Toni and Chiang were examining a wall covered with symbols.

Toni looked up, waved, and moved off to one side to provide Hutch a clear view. The wall had partially collapsed, and several large pieces lay on the ground. But it was covered with lines of engraved characters, almost all quite legible.

'Lovely,' said Hutch.

They were not pictographs, and there was a limited number of individual symbols, suggesting she was indeed looking at an alphabet. Furthermore, the text was divided into sections.

Paragraphs.

There was an ethereal quality about the script. It reminded her of Arabic, with its curves and flow. 'You've got pictures?' she asked.

Toni patted her microscan. 'Everything.'

Several sections of the script, at the top, were more prominent than the text that followed. 'They might be names,' suggested Chiang.

'Maybe. It could be a commemorative of some sort. Heroes. Here's who they were, and there's what they did.'

'You really think so' asked Toni.

'Who knows?' said Hutch. 'It could be anything.'

The beam from Toni's torch fell on a shard, a piece of pottery. 'We really need time to excavate,' Hutch said. And to move out into the city, to find the kinds of tools these people used, to unearth their houses, dig up more icons. Maybe get the answers to such basic questions as whether they used beasts of burden, how long their life spans were, what kind of gods they worshiped. 'Okay,' she continued. 'Let's get this stuff upstairs, then we'll come back and see what else we've got.'

They cut the central section out of the wall. Chiang tried to move it, but it was too heavy to handle in the confined quarters. 'Let it be for now,' said Hutch. 'We'll figure it out later.'

He nodded, picked up a couple of the fragments, and headed

back. Toni collected two more, leaving Hutch to try to gather together the smaller pieces.

Nightingale stood in the tower entry and tried to turn his mind to other things. He couldn't help glancing up every few minutes at the *Wildside* cabin, where MacAllister sat in his officious manner, gesturing and making pronouncements. Suddenly, the great man turned in his seat and looked directly at him, He got up, moved through the cabin, climbed down onto the ground, and started in his direction. Nightingale braced himself for a fight.

'Nightingale,' he said as soon as he'd gotten close, 'I wonder if I could ask a favor?'

Nightingale glared at him. 'What do you want?'

'We're going to be using this whole area as a background. Could I persuade you to stay out of sight? It works better if there's a complete sense of desolation.'

Casey snapped the recorder back on, smiled nervously at him, and resumed the interview: 'In a week, Mr MacAllister, Deepsix won't even exist anymore. It's cold and bleak, and that stone tower behind you is apparently the only building in this entire world. What brings you to this forlorn place?'

'Morbid curiosity, Casey.'

'No, seriously.'

'I'm never anything *but* serious. Why else would *anybody* come here? I'd be the last one to want to sound morose, but loss is the one constant we all have to deal with. It's the price of living. We lose parents, friends, relatives. We lose the place we grew up in, and we lose the whole circle of our acquaintances. We spend ungodly amounts of time wondering whatever happened to former teachers and lovers and scoutmasters.

'Here, we're losing a *world*. It's an event absolutely unique in human experience. An entire planet, which we now know has harbored intelligence of a sort and which still serves as a refuge for life, is going to end. Completely and finally. After these next few days, there will exist nothing of it other than what we can carry off.'

She nodded, telling him what he already knew, that this was good stuff. 'You had an opportunity,' she said, 'to tour the tower earlier today. What were your impressions? What about it did you find significant?'

MacAllister glanced meaningfully toward the structure. 'We know that whoever built it left a telescope behind, as if to say to us, *we also wanted the stars.*

'But they're lost, Casey. They probably had their own versions of Homer and Moses, Jesus and Shakespeare, Newton and Quirt. We saw the blowguns, and we know they built walls around their cities, so we can assume they fought wars. They must have had their Alexandrian campaigns, their Napoleon and Nelson, their civil wars. Now, everything they ever cared about is to be lost forever. That's a disaster of quintessential proportions. And I think it's worth coming to see. Don't you?'

'I suppose you're right, Mr MacAllister. Do you think anything like this could happen to *us*?'

He laughed. 'I'd like to think so.'

'Surely you're joking.'

'I'd be pleased to believe that when the time comes for us to make our exit, we will do so as gracefully as the inhabitants of *this* world. I mean, the blowguns tell us all we need to know about them. They were undoubtedly every bit as perfidious, conniving, hypocritical, and ignorant as our own brothers and sisters. But it's all covered up. The disaster gives them dignity they did not otherwise earn. Everybody looks good at his funeral.

'We're not even sure what they looked like. Consequently, we'll remember them with a kind of halo shining over their ears. People will speak of the Maleivans in hushed voices, and with great respect. I predict that some fool in Congress or in the Council will want to erect a monument in their honor. When in fact the only thing we can be sure they achieved was that they made it to oblivion without getting caught in the act.'

157

During the course of his life, Nightingale couldn't recall having ever *hated* anyone. Other than MacAllister. In the moment that the editor had asked Nightingale to step inside the tower, he had searched his mind for the correct riposte, the cutting remark that would slice this walking pomposity into his component parts.

But nothing had come to mind. *You buffoon,* he might have said, and MacAllister would have flicked him away. *Windbag. Poseur.*

The pilot of the *Star* lander walked past him with another pile of sticks. 'Chair,' he said.

'Okay.'

'Hutch said I could have it.'

'Okay.'

In the end he had meekly complied with the request and stood away from the scan's line of sight. But he really couldn't do his job properly, stowed inside the tower, couldn't see everything he needed to, especially couldn't see the strip of trees from which the biped cat had emerged. So he came out every few minutes, in a small act of defiance, walked about for a bit, and then retired back inside.

He was following the conversations in the tunnels. Toni, hauling chunks of inscribed stone to the surface, announced that she'd found a coin. 'What kind?' Nightingale asked, excited. 'What's on it?'

He was standing outside watching the trees. Watching Wetherai.

'Just a minute.' she said.

And while he waited, the ground moved.

It rolled beneath him. MacAllister and the woman in the lander stopped talking and turned to stare at him. Wetherai paused midway between the tower and his own spacecraft and stood with the chair held absurdly over his head.

The earth shrugged and threw Nightingale flat into the snow. He heard frightened cries on the allcom, watched the *Wildside* lander begin to lean over on one tread until the tread collapsed. The earth shook again, briefly. The ground and the sky seemed to be waiting. More was coming; he knew damned well more was coming.

He thought about retreating into the tower. But that would be stupid. *Why put rocks over his head?* Instead he moved out away from it, but had gone only a few steps when another shock hit. *Big* one this time. He went down again. A ripple ran across the landscape. The snow broke apart under Wetherai's feet. The pilot tried to run, absurdly still holding the chair. The ground ripped open and he fell in. *Disappeared.* His lander tilted, and it, too, slid into the hole.

All this was accomplished in an eerie silence. If Wetherai had protested, screamed, called for help, he'd been off-channel. Now a roar broke over Nightingale's ears, like an ocean crashing into a rocky headland, and the world continued to tremble. The earth shook and quieted. And shook again. An enormous stone block slammed into the snow a few meters away. He looked up, saw that it had broken off the roof, saw also that the tower had begun to lean to one side.

The hole into which Wetherai and his lander had fallen widened. *Gaped.* It was becoming a chasm.

MacAllister was sitting in the *Wildside* lander staring at him, or maybe at the tower, with his eyes wide. *Now,* thought Nightingale with a sense of grim satisfaction, *let's see how it goes with* you.

Marcel came on the link and was demanding to know what was happening. Chiang reported collapsing walls. A cloud of dust rolled out of the tower. Hutch was on the all-com telling everyone to get outside.

Kellie, who'd been on the upper level, climbed through a window, saw him, and dropped to the ground. It was a long fall but she seemed unhurt. 'Did they come up yet?' she asked.

Hutch was still on the link, saying something. He needed a moment to make it out.

'Randy, you there?'

'I'm here,' he said. 'I'm with Kellie.' Just then Chiang staggered out through the entrance.

'Over here,' Kellie told him.

Nightingale caught a glimpse of their lander. It had taken off, was in the air, trying to get away from the quake. 'MacAllister's stealing the lander,' he said.

'Talk to me later. Where's Toni?'

'Don't know. Still inside.'

'How about Chiang?'

'Chiang's here. He's with us.'

'Toni?' said Hutch.

Nothing.

'Toni!'

Still no answer.

'Isn't she below with you?' Chiang asked her.

'She was headed topside.'

Nightingale was knocked down again at the same moment that he heard a distant explosion.

Hutch was still calling Toni's name.

As she moved through the tunnel with her artifacts, Toni was acutely aware of the considerable weight of rock, dirt, and ice overhead. Given her choice, she'd have taken permanent guard duty, preferably at the top of the tower.

She was on her hands and knees, the slabs slung in a pack around her shoulders, thinking about Scolari. He was alone in *Wildside* with Embry. She had no reason to be jealous, but she felt a stab anyhow. It was hard to imagine that they had not been together these last couple of nights.

She was trying to decide how much responsibility Hutch bore for her loss when the quake came.

The floor shook. Dust rained down on her, the room sagged, and a crossbeam crashed down directly in front of her. The room continued to tremble, and she threw herself flat out and put her hands over her head. Her lamp went out. She tried crawling past

160

the fallen beam but the room kept moving, tilting, and then a terrible grinding began above her. The overhead grated and rasped and screeched. Something cracked, loud and hard, like a tree broken in two. Or a backbone.

A weight fell on her, driving the air from her lungs, pinning her to the floor. A darkness, deeper and blacker than that in the chamber, rushed through her. She couldn't move, couldn't breathe, couldn't call anyone.

Somewhere, she heard a voice. Hutch's, she thought, but she couldn't make out what she was saying.

Her last thought was that all her plans, her new career, Scolari, her return home, the child she hoped one day to bear, none of it was going to happen.

She wasn't even going to get off this goddam world.

Hutch was crawling through the dark when Nightingale came on the circuit. 'I think we've got some bad news out here,' he said.

'What?' she asked, bracing herself.

MacAllister watched with horror as first Wetherai and then the *Star* spacecraft disappeared into the chasm that had opened, that was *still* opening, like a vast pair of jaws. Wetherai had frozen, not knowing which way to run, had slipped and gone to his knees, and the crevice had come after him like a tiger after a deer while he futilely jabbed that pathetic pile of sticks at it as if to fend it off. He was still jabbing, falling backward, when it took him and, in quick succession, took the lander.

Their own vehicle was shaking itself to pieces. He looked at Casey, and her eyes were wide with fear.

The ground beside them broke open, and the lander began to sink. The hatch, which was not shut, swung wide, and MacAllister stared down into a chasm.

Got to get out. They would die if they stayed where they were. But the only exit was through the hatch, which hung out over the hole.

He searched for something he could use to knock out a window. Casey read his mind and shook her head. 'They're not breakable,' she cried.

A door in the rear of the cabin led through to the cargo locker, but *he'd* never fit. The angle kept getting more pronounced. They were sliding into the chasm. MacAllister leaned hard to his right, in the opposite direction, pushed against his chair arm, as if that might slow the process.

'My God, Casey.' His voice squeaked. 'Get us out of here.'

'*Me?*' Her face was pale. 'What do you expect *me* to do?'

'You said you could fly these damned things.'

'I said I had some experience with *landers*. *This* is a *bus*.'

'*Do* it. Try it, for God's sake, or—'

She got up and climbed into the pilot's seat, taking care not to look toward the hatch.

'Use the autopilot,' MacAllister urged. 'Just tell it to take off.'

'It doesn't know who I am,' she said. 'It has to be reset to respond to me.'

'Then reset it.' They were sliding.

'That takes *time*.' She blurted the words.

'Casey—'

'I *know*. Don't you think I know?' She was bent over the control board.

He was pushing hard, trying to get as far as he could from the airlock. 'Do something!'

'I have to figure out how to disengage the autopilot.'

'Maybe it's that thing over there.' He pointed to a yellow switch.

'This is going to go a whole lot better if you don't talk too much just now. I'll . . .' She pressed a stud, apparently having found what she was looking for.

MacAllister heard a few electronic bleeps, then the soft rumble of power somewhere beneath the seat. The restraints locked him down, and he gripped the chair arms and closed his eyes.

The seat lifted, and the spacecraft seemed to begin righting itself. Locked behind squeezed-shut eyelids, he couldn't be sure what was happening and was afraid to look. He was regretting the stupidity that had brought him down to this despicable place. His life for a pile of rubble.

Gravity flowed away, and the lander began to rise. 'Good, Casey,' he said, speaking from his long experience that one should encourage people when they're doing what you desperately want them to do. As if she might otherwise crash the spacecraft.

He slowly opened his eyes. She was moving a yoke, pulling it back, slowly, cautiously, and he saw that she was every bit as terrified as he was. The ground was several meters below, dropping away. Thank God.

They rose over the crevice. It appeared still to be widening. Great mounds of earth and snow were crashing into it.

The vehicle dipped suddenly, and Casey fought for control.

'You're doing fine,' MacAllister pleaded. 'Beautiful.'

'Please shut up,' she snapped.

He wished she sounded more confident. He wished she would head for the north, where there was plenty of space, *worlds* of space, of quiet flat plain, and just set it down. It seemed easy enough. She'd already done the hard part. Yet she continued to wrestle with the yoke and the engine made odd noises and they spurted across the sky and then she slowed them down and a sudden wind hammered at them.

'Is something wrong?' he asked.

The vehicle lurched. Dropped. Soared. 'The spike,' she said through clenched teeth. 'It's different from the system I trained on.'

'Just take your time.'

'Need to use the thrusters,' she said.

'Can you do it?'

'If I can figure out how to aim them.'

MacAllister caught a glimpse of Nightingale kneeling in the snow, watching. *Lucky bastard*, he thought. *Luck of the draw. The crevice opens under us instead of under* him. *In the end, survival goes not to the fit, but to the fortunate. It explains a lot about the way Darwin really works.*

At that moment the thrusters roared on. The seat came up and hit MacAllister in the rear. The ground blurred beneath him, and Casey yelped and began frantically doing things to the console. He decided that his Darwinian thought would be his last, and composed himself for the inevitable. Dead in a spacecraft accident on a distant world. But not in the canyon, at least. Not buried.

They raced over the ground toward a line of hills in the north-west, and it occurred to him that they would not be able to take him back for proper disposal. Because the madwoman at the controls was about to wreck the lander. And nobody was going to volunteer to come down from orbit to pick up the pieces.

The spacecraft was trying to turn over, and it didn't look as if Casey had any idea what she was doing. The roar of the thrusters filled the cabin and then suddenly the thunder was gone. She must have found the cutoff switch and she'd now be looking for whatever constituted the brakes.

The hills were coming up fast, and the only sounds were the wind whipping over the fuselage and the frantic pleas of his pilot.

'*Come on, you son of a bitch.*'

She yanked back on the yoke. The slopes rolled beneath them. Beyond the land flattened. The spacecraft, having apparently spent all forward energy, and having somehow lost the levitating power of the spike, began to fall.

'Damn,' said Casey.

MacAllister squeezed the arms of his chair, and they slammed into the ground. The impact jarred his neck, snapped his head back, twisted his spine. But the damned thing hadn't blown up. Casey slumped in her harness. He started to release his restraints, heard an explosion in back and smelled smoke.

He climbed out of his seat and noted that they'd never closed the hatch. Just as well. Save him the trouble of opening it.

The seats were crushed together, and he had to struggle to get to Casey. She was covered with blood, and her head lolled back. A massive bruise was forming on her jaw, and her eyes had rolled up into her head. Another blast rocked the lander. Flames began to lick up around the windows.

He released her from her harness and backed out through the airlock, half carrying, half dragging her. They were just clear when it erupted into a fireball.

Nightingale watched the thick pall of smoke rising from behind the cluster of hills to the northwest. He wasn't aware of the true significance of the last minute until he heard Kellie's voice on the circuit.

'Marcel,' she said, 'I think we just lost both landers.'

10

Faith has its price. When misfortune strikes the true believer, he assumes he has done something to deserve punishment, but isn't quite certain what. The realist, recognizing that he lives in a Darwinian universe, is simply grateful to have made it to another sunset.

—GREGORY MACALLISTER, *Preface to James Clark: 'The Complete Works'*

Hours to breakup (est): 255

'*Both landers?*' Marcel was horrified. 'When?'

'Just now.'

'For God's sake, Kellie, how could *that* happen?'

'The *Star*'s boat fell into a hole. Ours went down behind a hill and exploded. Randy and I are on our way over there now. But there's a lot of smoke.'

'Who was in the lander?'

'MacAllister and the woman he came down with. Both passengers from the *Star*. They must have tried to get clear, but I don't think whoever was flying knew what they were doing.'

'Anybody else hurt?'

'Their pilot's gone, too. I'm sure he's dead. Fell into the same hole as his lander.'

Marcel stared openmouthed at Bill's image, which was watching from the overhead monitor. Nobody from either of the Academy ships had been hurt. But it sounded as if it had been a clean sweep for the *Evening Star*. What the hell were those people doing down there in the first place?

'Okay,' he said. 'I'll let Captain Nicholson know. And I'll arrange to get another lander out here. Keep me informed.'

'Will do, Marcel. We're on our way out now to the crash site.'

Marcel signed off and massaged his forehead. 'Bill,' he said, 'who's close enough to get here in time?'

'I'll *check*,' the AI said. '*Should be somebody.*'

Huddled in the tunnel. Hutch had a more immediate problem. The roof had fallen in and blocked her exit. Nevertheless, the implication left her chilled. '*Both* of them? Well, that's sure good news.' She played her lamp beam against the rock, rafters, and dirt that sealed the passageway. 'I hate to add to your problems,' she said, 'but I could use a little help myself.'

'Chiang should be there any minute.'

One dead. Maybe three or four.

'Kellie,' she said, 'call Marcel. Tell him what happened. We're going to need another lander.'

'I've already done that. He's working on it. Told me not to worry.'

'Uh-oh. I always get nervous when people tell me that.'

'Have no fear.'

'Hutch.' Chiang's voice. 'How're you doing?'

'As well as could be expected. I'm not hurt.'

'Did you want us to hang on until you get out?' asked Kellie.

'No. Leave Chiang. But do what you can for MacAllister and the woman. And Kellie . . .'

'Yes?'

'Try to salvage the lander. I don't need to tell you how

168

helpful that would be.' She switched back to Chiang. 'Where are you?'

'I'm in the far passageway, near the armory.'

'No sign of Toni?'

'Not yet.'

She felt cold.

'I'll start digging,' he said.

'Be careful. It Probably wouldn't take much to bring more of this place down.'

'Okay.'

'I'll start from this end.'

'It's going to take a while,' he said.

'At your leisure, Chiang. I'm not going anywhere.'

She heard his laser ignite. Hutch put her lamp down and got to work.

MacAllister had no idea what to do. He shut off Casey's suit and tried to revive her, but she didn't respond. Thirty meters away, the lander lay in the snow, scorched, crumpled, burning, and leaking black smoke.

He surveyed the place where they'd come down: flat barren hills, a few trees, some brush. He felt terribly alone. Where was that idiot woman who wanted to run everything? Now that he could use her, she was nowhere to be seen.

He contemplated the odds against a quake hitting just as he was doing the interview, and considered not for the first time whether the universe was indeed malicious.

They had crossed a line of hills, so he could no longer see the tower. He sat helplessly, cradling Casey's body, feeling responsible, wondering how he could ever have been so stupid as to leave the safety of his stateroom on the *Star*.

He was immensely relieved to see two figures come out of a defile. One was the woman they called Kellie. The other was Nightingale. They paused and looked his way. He waved. They waved back and started toward him, trying to hurry through deep snow.

'Mr MacAllister.' Kellie's voice in his earphones. 'Are you all right?'

'Casey's not breathing,' he said.

They struggled up to his side and Kellie sank into the snow beside him. She felt for a heartbeat, then for a pulse.

'Anything?' MacAllister asked.

Kellie shook her head. 'I don't think so.' They worked on her for a while, taking turns.

'Looks as if we wrecked your lander,' MacAllister said.

'What happened?' asked Nightingale. 'Don't you know how to fly it?'

'I wasn't the pilot,' he said. 'Casey was. I don't have any experience with these things.'

'What went wrong?'

'She wasn't used to it. It was too big. Or something.' He looked down at her limp, broken form. 'She was out here on a birthday gift. From her parents.'

After a while they gave up. Kellie sighed and laid Casey's head gently in the snow and walked silently over to the wrecked spacecraft. She circled it a couple of times, and they heard her banging on something on the far side.

'What do you think?' asked Nightingale nervously.

She reappeared from behind the tail. 'It's scrap. We'll want to see what we can salvage.'

MacAllister tried to read her eyes, to see whether she was worried. But her expression was masked. 'We'd better inform whoever's in charge,' he said.

'It's been done.'

He was weary, exhausted, frightened. He'd brought two people with him, and both were dead.

MacAllister had trained himself over the years to avoid indulging in guilt. You have to beat your conscience into submission, he'd once written, because the conscience isn't really a part of you. It's programming introduced at an early age by a church or a government or a social group with its own agenda. Avoid sex. Respect authority. Accept responsibility for things that go wrong even when events are out of your control.

Well, earthquakes are goddam well outside my control.

Bill's bearded features reflected the general concern. '*Yes, Marcel?*' he asked. '*What can I do?*'

'Inform the *Star*, personal for the captain, that there's been an earthquake at the site. Ask him to call me.'

'*I will get right on it.*'

'Tell him also that his lander was wrecked. Ask him if he has another on board.'

'*Marcel, our data banks indicate the* Star *carries only a single lander.*'

'Ask him anyhow. Maybe there's been a mistake somewhere. Meantime, do a survey. I need to know who's within six days' travel time. The closer the better. Anybody with a lander.' Most vessels did not carry landers. There was usually no need, because ports were all equipped to provide transportation to and from orbit. Routinely, only research flights to frontier areas in which a landing was contemplated, or cruise ships, which occasionally scheduled sight-seeing tours in remote locations, made room for one.

Beekman came in. 'I heard,' he said. Several others entered behind him. 'Are Kellie and Chiang okay?'

'As far as we know. But we're going to bring them home. The ground mission is over.'

'I concur,' Beekman said.

Marcel was angry, frustrated, weary. 'How much time do we have to get them off?'

Beekman glanced at the calendar. 'They should be reasonably safe until the end of the week. After that, it's anybody's guess.'

Marcel tried to call Hutch on the private channel. But he couldn't even pick up a carrier wave.

'Is she still in the tower?' asked Beekman.

'Yes. Last I heard.'

'*Marcel.*' It was the AI. '*I'm sorry to break in, but your message to the* Star *has been delivered. And I can find only one ship with a lander within the required range. The* Athena Boardman. *It's owned by—*'

'I know who owns it,' said Marcel. The *Boardman* was part of the Kosmik fleet, a vessel he had piloted himself on occasion when he worked for the government-subsidized terraformer during the early years of his career. 'How far are they?'

'*They can be here in four days. And we have an incoming from the* Star. *Captain Nicholson wants to speak with you on the cobalt channel.*'

Encrypted. 'Set it up, Bill.'

'Who died?' asked Beekman. 'Do we have any names?'

'Two that we know of. The pilot of the *Star's* lander. And a young woman passenger. Maybe more. I don't know yet.' Marcel had been scribbling in his notebook. 'Bill.'

'*Yes, Marcel.*'

'Send a four-bell message to the *Boardman*: "*Wendy Jay* is declaring an emergency. We have people stranded on Deepsix vulnerable to impending Morgan event. Require your lander and your assistance to perform rescue. Time presses. Request you proceed immediately. Clairveau." Standard closing. Give them our coordinates.'

'*Okay, Marcel. And I have Captain Nicholson on the circuit.*'

Marcel asked those who'd accompanied Beekman to withdraw, and closed the door. Then he told the AI to proceed. Nicholson's image appeared on-screen. He looked scared. 'Captain Clairveau,' he said. 'How bad is it?'

'It's bad,' said Marcel.

Nicholson spotted Beekman and hesitated.

'Professor Beekman,' said Marcel, 'is the director of the Morgan Project, and he is the soul of discretion. One of his people is down there, too. As are several others.'

Nicholson nodded. Muscles worked in his cheeks. 'What exactly happened?'

Marcel told him.

He lost all of his color, and his eyes slid shut. 'God help us,' he said. For a long moment he was silent. Then: 'Forgive me, but did you say *both* landers have been destroyed?'

'Yes. That's why I asked whether you might have an extra one available.'

It was hard to believe he could have gone even whiter, but he did. 'You mean you don't have a backup vehicle?'

'We didn't have a lander at all. Captain. Hutchins used the one from *Wildside*.'

'I see.' He nodded and seemed to be having trouble breathing. Marcel thought for a moment that a stroke might be imminent. 'Okay,' he said finally. '*We* don't have one either, so we're going to have to get help.'

'We've already done that. The *Boardman*'s only a few days away.'

'Thank God.' He was trembling. 'You *will* let me know when you hear more?'

'Of course.'

'Hutch, I found her.'

Chiang sounded grim and her heart sank. Hutch sat propped against a wall, tired, trying to catch her breath. Her air was beginning to get stale.

'She's dead,' he said softly. 'Looks as if she was killed outright. I don't think she suffered.'

Hutch squeezed her eyes shut.

'Hutch, you reading me?'

She killed her transmitter until she could get control of her voice. 'Yes.' Another long silence. 'Can you get her free?'

'I'll need a couple of minutes. You doing okay?'

'Yeah. I'm fine.'

'Kellie tells me she's been trying to reach you.'

'Signal's not getting through. What's the situation?'

'I'll relay it. After Kellie's done, Marcel wants to talk to you, too.'

Kellie sounded frightened. 'The woman passenger's dead,' she said. 'MacAllister's okay.'

'How about the lander?'

'Wrecked.'

'No chance at all?'

'None.'

Three dead. And the rest stranded. My God. 'Okay' she said. 'We're talking about the *Wildside* boat, right?'

'Yes.'

'What about the other one? The one that fell in the chasm?'

'Haven't looked.'

'We'll want to look. Maybe we got lucky.'

'Hutch,' Kellie said, 'how are *you* doing?'

'I'll be fine as soon as I see daylight again. You know about Toni?'

'Chiang told me. I'm sorry.'

'We all are.'

After a while, Chiang got on again: 'I've got Toni out, and I'm cutting into *your* wall. Stay as far away from it as you can.'

'Okay. I'm clear.'

'Putting Marcel on.'

'Thanks.'

Marcel tried to sound encouraging. 'Chiang tells me he'll have you out in a few minutes. You're not hurt, are you?'

'No.' She looked around at the rubble.

'The *Boardman*'s nearby. Should be here in a few days.'

'That the best we can do? A few *days?*'

'Yes. Sorry. It's all we have.' And lucky to have that, his voice told her. 'Hang in there, Hutch. We'll have you all off as soon as we can.'

Bill came back: '*I have some mail for you. Did you want to see it?*'

'Sure.' What better time? 'Go ahead.'

'*Hello, Priscilla. This is Charlie Ito.*'

She projected his image into the center of the chamber. This was a man who looked as if he'd enjoy collecting taxes. He had an unctuous smile and was vaguely familiar. *'You remember we met at your aunt Ellen's birthday party last spring. You might recall that at the time you mentioned how you'd like one day to move to Cape Cod. As it happens, an incredible deal came up yesterday, and I thought of you right away. We have a luxury seaside home that just came on the market. And I know what you're thinking, but bear with me a moment—'*

She went to the next message.

'Hi, Priscilla.'

It was her mother. Bright, beautiful. And as always, arriving with impeccable timing.

'I'm looking forward to seeing you again when you get home. It would be nice if we could take a few days and maybe go to the mountains. Just us girls. Let me know if that's okay, and I'll reserve a cabin.

'I know you don't like my bringing up men, but your uncle Karl recently introduced me to the most gorgeous young architect. I'd say he has a brilliant future—'

She tried again:

Hi, Hutch.

This one was audio only. Audio transmissions were less expensive.

'I know it's been a while since we've talked, but I just heard you were on Wildside *when it got diverted to Deepsix.'* It was from Frank Carson, an archeologist with whom she'd been through a lot in what now seemed another lifetime. *'Sounds as if you're in on the action again. I envy you. I'd give anything to be with you. We're still digging into Beta Pac, and beginning finally to translate some of the local languages. But you don't care about that, right now. I just wanted you to know I was thinking about you. You're a lucky woman.'*

She managed a smile.

'Ms. Hutchinson.'

Another audio only. With a deep baritone this time.

175

'You might remember we met at the United Pilots Association Conference last year. My name's Harvey Hutchins – that's right, same as yours, which is how we got talking. Anyhow, I'm a program manager for Centauri Transport. We're looking for experienced pilots. We haul supplies and personnel throughout the web. I can guarantee you challenging work, a generous signing bonus, and a wide range of fringe benefits. The openings won't last long, but I can get you in if you like—'

And a young woman with a cloying Boston accent:

'Hello, Ms. Hutchins, I represent the Northeastern University Alumni Fund-Raising Committee, and we wanted to ask for your help again this year—'

There were a few more, all more or less impersonal, all from people who knew her just well enough to evade the antijunk filters that never seemed to work anyhow.

There was nothing from any of the occasional men in her life. Times like this, she wondered if her charm had failed altogether. But she understood that nobody was anxious to accept a relationship with a woman who was never home. It was a lonely existence. And maybe pulling out after this was over wasn't a bad idea. Go home and get herself a normal life.

She could hear Chiang getting close. Then light broke into the tunnel.

She helped him collect Toni's body and get it up into the tower. The twenty minutes or so they spent doing that, moving her through the narrow passageways, trying not to drop her, struggling up those irritating dwarf staircases, were possibly the longest twenty minutes of her life. The e-suit was still on, so the body still felt warm and alive. She kept looking down at her, imagining Toni's eyes, behind her lids, watching her accusingly. *You brought me here . . .*

She was trembling when they finally got her up to ground level, took her outside, and laid her in the sunlight.

*

MacAllister lifted Casey in his arms, and they started back. Kellie had rummaged through the burnt-out lander, collecting whatever was left that might be useful: some clothes, a few snacks, and an extra cutter. The reddimeals were fried, so they'd have to survive on donuts for the time being.

They tried to divide the load, although only MacAllister was strong enough to handle Casey. The others attempted to spell him occasionally, but they stumbled along with the body until his patience gave way and he insisted on taking care of her himself. So he carried her and they simply took frequent breaks and moved at his pace. Chiang met them about halfway, after which he and MacAllister took turns.

When they got back to the tower, they found Hutch sitting stone-faced by Toni. They laid Casey beside her.

'What about the *Star* boat?' Kellie asked her. 'Did you look for it?'

She nodded. Kellie saw no hope in her expression. After a minute, she walked out to the chasm.

The lander hadn't fallen far. Only about fifteen meters. It was wedged between the rock walls, over a long drop to a snow-filled bottom. There was no trace of Wetherai.

Eliot Penkavic was captain of the *Athena Boardman,* outbound for Quraqua, hauling solar mirrors, DNA samples of over eleven thousand species of fish, birds, plants, grasses, and trees; and of more than thirty thousand assorted insect types. He had a full manifest of equipment for the ongoing effort to terraform Quraqua, and sixty-four experts and technicians of various stripes. He was three days away from his destination when the distress call arrived from the *Wendy Jay.*

It was not a side trip he wanted to make. But the code of conduct, *and* the law, was quite clear. When an emergency was formally declared, when lives were reported in jeopardy, vessels were *compelled* to assist. After several weeks on *Boardman,* no one was going to be happy about his extending the flight by another nine days or so. Especially Ian Helm, who was going out to the new world to take over as director of operations.

He checked his database, looking for another ship that could go in and bail out the Academy group. There were a couple in the area that could get there, but nobody with a lander. Except the *Boardman*.

Unfortunate.

How could the nitwits possibly have gotten themselves into such a situation?

He wrote out his reply, and then read it to the AI: *Sit tight. Cavalry coming.* Boardman *will be there in four days, six hours. Penkavic.*

'*I think that sums things up nicely, sir,*' said the AI.

'As do I, Eve. Send it.'

'*It is done, Captain.*'

'Good.' Penkavic pushed himself out of his chair. 'Now for the hard part.'

'*Explaining it to Dr Helm?*'

'Precisely.'

11

Living well is a high-wire act without a net. It is a matter of locating one's proper place and balancing it against the programming imposed by society. We're surrounded by the wrecks of those who have crashed, the reformers, the upright, the various militants and the true believers who think the rest of us need their guidance.

—GREGORY MACALLISTER, *'The Best Revenge', Lost at Moonbase*

Hours to breakup (est): 252

'*Marcel,*' said the AI, '*we have a response from the* Boardman. *They say they understand our problem and are on their way.*'

Marcel breathed an audible sigh of relief.

'*They anticipate arrival in four days and six hours.*'

He informed Hutch, who tried to conceal the fact that she'd been holding her breath. Then he called the *Star.* Nicholson, who'd been delighted to hear that MacAllister was still alive, raised a fist in an unlikely gesture of exultant thanksgiving at this second piece of good news. He notified Beekman, so he could announce it to his people. When that had been done, he passed the word to the two passengers waiting on *Wildside.* He spoke to a woman,

179

who commented that she was delighted help was on the way, that they'd been very lucky, and that she'd been against the mission from the start. She implied that Marcel was at least partly responsible for a situation that had clearly gotten out of hand.

Captain Nicholson reached for another trank and watched his wallscreen convert itself into a hologram of a woodland scene. Thank God that at least there'd be no more deaths. Maleiva was remote from the travel lanes, and it could easily have turned out that nothing would have been close enough to come to their rescue.

Of course the damage already done was enough to ruin him. A dead passenger and a dead crewman. A wrecked lander. On a flight that violated regulations. How would he ever explain it?

It was the darkest moment in a life that had been relatively free of trouble and disappointment. But he knew that regardless of what happened now, he could not survive. He'd be hauled before a disciplinary panel, where it would be made quite plain to him and to the world what a scoundrel he was. He would be reprimanded, and he would be terminated. In the full glow of the worldwide media.

Subsequently, he could expect to be sued, held liable for any damages accruing to the families of the two victims, and for the loss of the lander. He might even be prosecuted. Not that TransGalactic would hunger and thirst after justice, but they could be expected to take every opportunity to disassociate themselves from him in an atmosphere rife with legal action.

How could he have been so dumb?

Scarcely three minutes had passed after his conversation with Clairveau when word came from the duty officer that the surviving passenger, Mr MacAllister, desired to speak with him.

The transmission came in, audio only. 'You know what's happened here?' the great man asked.

Here was the person responsible for the captain's plight. *You'll be able to set up a small shrine to a lost world,* he'd said. *People*

will love it. Management will admire your foresight. Your audacity.
'Yes, I've heard.' He tried to keep his tone level. 'Are you all right. Mr MacAllister?'

'Fine, thank you.' He seemed subdued. The charming arrogance that had informed his manner was gone. 'I assume you're in some difficulty as a result of this – incident.'

'I don't expect any explanation I can offer will satisfy my superiors.'

'No, I thought not. I wanted to apologize. Captain.'

'Yes. Of course. Thank you.'

'It never occurred to me that anything like this could happen.'

'Nor to me. Captain Clairveau informs me you are temporarily stranded.'

'Yes. I'm afraid so. Until the rescue vehicle gets here.'

'It's on its way. Now, I hesitate to ask, but there's something you can do for me.'

'I understand, Captain. There's no need for any of us to go publicly into the details of this unfortunate business.'

'Yes. Precisely.' Nicholson hesitated. There was always the possibility that someone somewhere was listening. Maybe even recording the conversation. He had no secure channel with MacAllister. 'That's probably best.'

When he'd signed off, the captain retired to his quarters and contemplated the dress uniform jacket he traditionally wore to meals with the passengers.

There might be a way.

He could delete the pertinent log entry and declare the flight unauthorized. That would leave Wetherai responsible.

That was not exactly to his taste, and it did not play well to his self-image. But Wetherai was dead and couldn't be harmed by any conclusion a board of inquiry might draw. Moreover, the only other living party to the conspiracy had given his word not to reveal what he knew. And he would be motivated to keep that word, since he, too, could become legally liable should the truth get out. No one else was in a position to deny

181

that Wetherai had taken the lander down on his own. All that would be necessary was to agree on a story explaining how MacAllister and Hayes came to be on board. And that was child's play.

Maybe, he thought, he could come out of this unscathed after all.

MacAllister's associates would never have accused him of possessing an overbearing conscience. Disagree with the great man on literary standards or on a matter of historical interpretation, and one was likely to find his or her judgment and taste questioned and possibly his or her native intelligence held up to ridicule in full view of the general public. He took particular delight in neutralizing those who desperately needed to be neutralized, those overblown, self-important, arrogant half-wits who were always running about dictating behavior, morals, and theology to everyone else. And he never looked back.

Yet he stood a long time at the edge of the chasm, staring down at the *Evening Star's* crippled lander, thinking about the dead pilot, who had struck him as not particularly bright; and about Casey, who'd been too young to develop whatever talent she might have had. That they were dead was not directly due to any fault of his. But he understood clearly that had he not given in to the dark impulse that had prompted him to want to visit this godforsaken place, they would be alive. It would be an exaggeration to suggest he contemplated, even for a moment, throwing himself in. But it was true that for the first time in his adult existence, he questioned whether the world was better for his being in it.

The lander was wedged tight. Below it, the chasm fell away probably another hundred meters. It was a long way down. Heaps of snow lay at the bottom, if indeed it *was* the bottom. And somewhere down there, beyond reach, Wetherai had come to rest.

He was still staring when he became aware that someone was speaking to him.

Hutchins.

'Mr MacAllister,' she said, 'are you okay?'

'Yes.' He straightened a bit. 'I'm fine.'

There was no way to preserve the bodies, and after a series of conferences among Nicholson, Marcel, and Hutch, it was agreed that Toni and Casey be buried on the plain where they died.

They picked a spot about thirty meters to one side of the tower, cleared away the snow, and dug two graves. An armed party consisting of Chiang, MacAllister, and Kellie trekked to the patch of forest, cut down a couple of trees, and fashioned two makeshift coffins.

Meantime, Hutch and Nightingale collected background information from the ships. They cut three slabs of rock from the tower walls to serve as markers and engraved them. They wrapped the bodies in plastic brought originally for the artifacts. By then night had fallen, and their colleagues had returned. They stored the coffins inside the tower, posted a guard, built a fire, and slept in the open.

There was a ghostly quality to it all. Ordinarily, Flickinger fields were invisible, but they tended to reflect light in the 6100-6400 angstrom range. Orange and red. So they all developed a mild glow whose gradations varied with the intensity of the flames. When occasionally the fire flared, golden auras became visible, providing a flavor of the angelic. Or of the demonic, if one preferred. In either case, Hutch hoped it would be more than enough to keep whatever creatures might haunt the neighborhood at a respectful distance.

She took the first watch. They were well away from the tower, to ensure that the guard, equipped with night goggles, had a good view in all directions. Nothing moved in that vast wasteland, and after two hours she wearily turned the duty over to Nightingale and curled up in a snowbank.

But she couldn't sleep, and for a time she watched him pacing nervously around the camp. It was snowing lightly, and the sky was overcast.

It had been a mistake to bring him. Even the news that help was on the way had failed to cheer him measurably. While the others had collectively taken a deep breath, and Hutch herself had shed the pall of concern that came with knowing it could easily have gone the other way, Nightingale had seemed not to react. 'Good,' he'd said. 'Thank God.' But his tone had been flat, as if it didn't really make much difference.

Nightingale wasn't young, and the next few days, with no food, were going to be difficult. She wondered how he'd hold up. Wondered how any of them would hold up. They had nobody, as far as she knew, with the kind of background they were going to need to make themselves reasonably comfortable. They had only the donuts and a few other assorted snacks. But hell, how hungry could they get in four days? If necessary, maybe they could nibble on leaves. It would be just a matter of putting something into their stomachs.

Nightingale stood in the glare of the fire, scanning the area. He seemed discouraged. Part of that obviously stemmed from the casualties they'd taken, and she wondered whether he was shocked by their loss, or whether he was sensing a kind of parallel with his earlier experience on this world. She also knew he had no confidence in her. He hadn't said anything overt, but she could read his feelings in his eyes. Especially since their situation had turned difficult. Who are you, his attitude asked, to be making decisions? What's your degree? Your level of expertise in these matters? You're not even an archeologist.

A mild tremor rolled through the night. It was barely discernible, but she wondered whether it wouldn't be a good idea to head out somewhere tomorrow. Get a reading from Marcel and make for a safer place.

Nightingale knelt close to Chiang and brushed snow away from his converter. They were in no danger even if the device *did* become buried, of course. If the air flow into the Flickinger field were cut off, an alarm would sound.

Hutch's heat exchanger put out a barely audible hum as it

warmed the envelope of air circulating inside her suit. She heard it change tone and looked at her link. The outside temperature was fifteen below. A fairly constant wind was blowing out of the northwest, and the snow was getting heavier.

Four and a quarter days until help came. It wasn't exactly a hardship situation. The e-suits would protect them from the cold, but it would occasionally be necessary to shut them off, when eating or performing other basic functions. They'd established a privacy area behind the tower. It wasn't very private, though, because Hutch insisted no one go back there without an escort. MacAllister, who had often remonstrated against the foolishness of puritanical ideals, seemed particularly upset by the arrangement. If one had to use the facility during the night, it was necessary to wake one of the others. It was not a circumstance that would help morale, he pointed out.

'Getting eaten,' Hutch told him, 'does nothing for morale either.'

In the morning, under lowering skies, they held a farewell ceremony. Kellie recorded it for the next of kin.

Toni had been a Universalist. Wetherai a Methodist. And Casey was not known to be affiliated with any religious group.

Hutch spoke for Toni, a difficult assignment because Universalists did not believe in mantras or formal prayers. One always spoke from the heart. They all mourned the loss of one so young, she said. Nothing they could recover from the site would be worth the price they'd paid. She added that she personally would always remember Toni, who had refused to allow her to come alone to the tower.

Captain Nicholson, using VR, performed the ceremony for Wetherai. He spoke of selfless service, dedication to duty, a willingness always to put forth extra effort. Hutch concluded that Nicholson and his officer were strangers, and it seemed to her particularly painful that the man had died with no one present who knew him as a human being. His first name, she'd discovered, was Cole. She wished, at least, that they could have recovered his body.

The marker for Toni read *Faithful Unto Death*. Wetherai's might easily have read *Buried by Strangers*.

MacAllister surprised her by asking to speak for Casey.

'I knew her only brirfly,' he said. 'She seems to have been an honest woman in an honest profession. Maybe no more need be said. Like Toni Hamner, she was only at the beginning of her life. I will miss her.'

He stared down at the marker, which at his suggestion had been engraved with only her name and dates, and the single word *Journalist*.

When they were finished, they put the two coffins in the graves and replaced the soil.

'Wait a minute,' said Helm. 'Tell me again what we're going to do?'

'Five people are stranded on the surface of Maleiva III. It's the world that's going to—'

'I know about Maleiva III. Why are *we* going there?'

'To rescue them,' Penkavic said.

A chessboard was set up on his desk. Helm sat behind the black pieces, but his cold blue eyes had locked on Penkavic. He ran long fingers through thick gray hair and nodded, not to the captain, he thought, but to some inner compulsion of his own.

They were in Helm's private quarters. The tabletop that supported the chessboard was buried under disks, notes, schematics, printouts. 'Why is that *our* concern?' he asked, keeping his tone polite. As if he was honestly curious. 'We're, what, several days away, aren't we?'

'Yes, sir.'

Helm was Kosmik's chief engineer and director of the terraforming project at Quraqua. 'So why do they need us?'

'They need the lander. They don't have any way of getting their people off the surface.'

'What happened to *their* lander?'

'It got wrecked. In a quake.'

'That seems shortsighted.'

'I don't know the details. In any case, we've already jumped out of hyper. We're maneuvering onto a new heading, and as soon as we have it we'll make the jump again. The sooner we—'

'Wait just a minute. We're carrying a full load of equipment, supplies, people. All needed at Quraqua. We have constraints on when we have to get there. Eliot. We can't just go wandering around the region.'

'I understand that, sir. But there's nobody else available to do this.'

Helm's tone suggested a gentle uncle trying to reason with an adolescent. 'Surely that can't be.'

'I checked it, sir. We're the only ship close enough. The only one with a lander.'

'Look, Eliot.' He got up, walked around the table, sat down on it, and pointed to a chair. Penkavic stayed on his feet. 'We can't just hold up the cargo. Or the people.' He leaned forward and looked at the captain. 'Tell me, if we were to do this, make the run, how late would we be getting into Quraqua?'

'About nine days.'

'About nine days.' Helm's face grew rigid. 'You have any idea what that would cost?'

'Yes, sir. But I didn't think that was a consideration.'

'Come on, Eliot, it's *always* a consideration.'

'What I know,' Penkavic said, striving to keep his anger under control, 'is that the law, and our own regulations, require us to provide assistance to anyone in distress. We can't just ignore it. People will die.'

'Do you think the Academy will reimburse us for what this will cost?'

'No,' he said. 'Probably not.'

'Then maybe we should consider our options.'

'We don't have any options, Dr Helm.'

Helm stared at him for a long moment. 'No,' he said, 'I suppose not. All right, Eliot. Let's go off and rescue these damned fools. Maybe we'll get some decent press out of it.'

After they'd finished the memorial, they trekked back to the *Wildside* lander and tried to salvage what they could of the artifacts. The tables and chairs were scorched, reduced to rubbish; the scrolls had burned; the pottery had melted. They couldn't even find the pack and the garments it had contained. A couple of blowguns, some darts, and a javelin were all that had survived.

Listlessly they returned to the tower and cleaned and bagged the few remaining artifacts.

MacAllister glowered the whole time, and when Chiang asked him what was wrong, he looked over at Hutch with genuine anger. 'The bottom line,' he said, 'is that this is *all* just trash. It's *old* trash, but that doesn't change what it is.'

Hutch overheard, and in fact he'd obviously intended that she should. It was more than she could take. 'You have too many opinions, MacAllister,' she told him. 'I've read some of your stuff. You've a talent with the language, but most of the time you don't know what you're talking about.'

He'd looked at her with infinite patience. Poor woman.

They inventoried their new set of artifacts, weapons, pieces of cloth that had once been clothing, cabinets, chairs, and tables, and set them aside to wait for the rescue vehicle.

'What do we do about food?' MacAllister asked suddenly.

'We'll have to run it down,' said Chiang. 'Anybody here a hunter?'

MacAllister nodded. 'I am. But not with *this*.' He glanced down at his cutter. 'Anyhow, I don't know whether anybody's noticed or not, but there seems to be a distinct lack of game in the neighborhood. Moreover, there might not even be anything here we *can* eat.'

'I doubt,' said Nightingale, 'that the local wildlife would supply nutrition. We never ran any tests, but at least it would fill our bellies. Provided there are no toxins or other problems.'

'Good,' said MacAllister. 'When we catch one of them, you can sample it.'

'Maybe there's an easier way,' said Hutch.

Kellie's dark eyes narrowed. 'To do *what*?' she asked. 'Find a better guinea pig?'

'The *Star* lander isn't too deep. It might be possible to go down there and retrieve the reddimeals. They'd help get us through until the *Boardman* arrives.'

'Not worth it,' said Kellie. 'We're better off trying the local menu.'

'I doubt it,' growled MacAllister.

'Hutch,' said Marcel, 'it's not your fault. You have to pull yourself together.' They were on the private channel.

'You know, Marcel, it just never . . .' Her voice was shaking and she had to stop to collect herself. '. . . It just never occurred to me that anything like this could happen.' He could hear her breathing. 'I didn't ask for this. I'm a pilot. They've got me making life-and-death decisions.'

'Hutch.' He made his voice as gentle as he could. 'You were trying to do what you were directed to do. Everybody with you is an adult. They knew what *you* knew. It wasn't just your decision.'

'I could have canceled it after the first tremor. Put everybody in the boat and gone back to *Wildside*. That's what I should have done.'

'And if we all had hindsight up front, everybody'd be a millionaire.'

She was quiet.

'Hutch, listen to me. They're going to need you until we get through this. You have to stop feeling sorry for yourself.'

'*Sorry for myself?* You think that's what it is?'

'Yeah. That's exactly what it is. Your job right now is to keep your people safe until we can get them back here. You can't do anything about Toni. But you *can* see that nothing happens to anyone else.'

She broke the connection, and he took a deep breath. He understood she'd been through a horrific experience, but he had expected more of her somehow. Had the conversation continued, he'd been prepared to suggest she retire in favor of Kellie. He wondered whether he shouldn't call her back and advise her to do just that.

But, no. Not yet. If everything went well, it was just a matter of biding their time until help came. He left the bridge and wandered down to project control, where a couple of technicians were trying to analyze the impossibilium.

Bill's image formed on a nearby screen. *'Marcel? You have a text message.'*

Wendy was lingering in the area of the assembly, although Marcel would have preferred to return to orbit to be as close as possible to the stranded team. But he was helpless to do anything other than watch, so he'd indulged the researchers and granted their wish to stay near the giant artifact. They hovered within a few meters, while every instrument the ship possessed poked, scanned, and probed the shafts.

They lacked the laboratory facilities to do extensive evaluation of the onboard samples, but they were trying to determine melting and boiling points, specific heat and thermal conductivity, density, Young's modulus, bulk and shear modulus. They wanted to define yield and ultimate strength, electrical conductivity and magnetic permeability at varying temperatures, currents, and frequencies. They wanted to know how quickly sound moved through it, and compile an index of refraction over a range of frequencies. Beekman and his people had begun to put together a stress and strain graph. It didn't mean much to Marcel, but the researchers took turns gaping at the results.

'On-screen.'

TO: *NCA* WENDY JAY
FROM: *NCK* ATHENA BOARDMAN
SUBJECT: STATUS REPORT

FOR CAPT CLAIRVEAU. WE ARE ON SCHEDULE, MINUTES FROM MAKING OUR JUMP. ONBOARD

LANDER WILL BE PRIMED AND READY TO GO.
MARCEL, YOU OWE ME.

'*Is there a reply?*'
'Tell him I'll buy him lunch.'

12

Nothing kills the appetite quite as effectively as a death sentence.

—GREGORY MACALLISTER, *'In Defense of the Godly',*
The Incomplete MacAllister

Hours to breakup (est): 252

It was almost 1800 hours, forty-two minutes since they'd made the jump into transdimensional space, when Penkavic ordered an inspection of the lander and retired to his quarters. He had just arrived when Eve, *Boardman*'s AI, reported all in order.

The ship had begun to quiet. Many of his passengers had retired for the night. The common room had pretty much emptied out, and only two or three remained in the various planning or leisure areas. A small group of technicians and climate specialists were engaged in a role-playing game in the Green Room, a contest which would probably continue well into the morning. Several biologists were still in project control arguing about stocking procedures, and a few individuals were gathered in the relatively intimate Apollo Porch, where they could look out at the stars.

Penkavic was more rattled by his confrontation with Helm than he cared to admit to himself. It wasn't just that he'd offended one of the most powerful people in the corporation. He had, after all, done the right thing, and kept both himself and Helm out of trouble. But there was a quality to Corporate's chief engineer that unsettled Penkavic, inducing a reaction that went far beyond concern over what he might or might not do to damage the captain's career. It was hard to pin down. Helm did not seem especially threatening or intimidating, but he invariably induced a sense that he and he alone understood the correct and reasonable course. In his presence, Penkavic inexplicably wanted very much to please him. Even when he disagreed strongly with the older man's conclusions.

He climbed out of his uniform, showered, and slipped into bed. But the lights had just died when Eve's voice filtered through the room. *'Captain, we have a problem.'*

He sat up. 'What's wrong, Eve?'

'The lander is preparing to launch.'

'Stop it.' He threw the sheet aside, put his feet on the deck, and waited for her response.

'I can't. I'm locked out.'

He called for lights and threw on a robe. 'Go to the red circuit,' he told her. 'Shut it down. Shut everything down in the launch bay if you have to.'

He was out the door, headed for the lower deck.

'Negative,' she said. *'Lander is sealing.'*

She put a visual on a wallscreen. He watched the vehicle rotate, saw the bay doors open. 'Who's doing it?' he demanded.

'I can't tell if there is a deliberate agency at work. There seems to be a partial breakdown in Delta comm.' In Eve's ability to communicate with the various automated systems.

He watched the lights in the launch bay brighten and dim, as they routinely did at the start of an operation, and then the lander floated out into the gray mist.

Penkavic now made the history books. In the only known instance in which a commercial starship attempted to maneuver in hyperspace, he banked to port, tried to calculate the location of the lander, and made an effort at intercept.

He had to work manually because Eve's condition had not stabilized. Jack Castor, his copilot, was already on duty.

He put Castor on the sensors despite his protests that they would not work.

They tried them anyhow. Short-range, long-range, pinpoint, and shotgun. It didn't matter; all returns were negative. There seemed to be nothing out there but empty space. Optical visibility was limited to a couple of hundred meters, and attempts to activate the lander AI failed.

No one knew how to pinpoint a position in transdimensional space. Because the only other physical object in the field was the lander, and they did not know where it was, the notion of *position* became meaningless.

Eve came back up. *'The disturbance seems to have abated,'* she said.

'Can you tell where the problem originated?' Castor asked.

Not that the answer mattered. Penkavic knew who had arranged it.

'Lambda.'

The backup mission control.

Helm was dressed and waiting for him.

'Do you have any idea what you've done?' demanded Penkavic.

'I'm aware.' he said. His eyes were hooded. He seemed unusually pensive. 'I know exactly what I've done.'

'You've condemned those people. We were the only way they had of getting clear.'

'Eliot.' He nodded, agreeing with the accusation. 'I wish there had been another way. But the Quraqua operation can't afford a nine-day delay. Some of the material we have on board is time-sensitive. Extremely so. As are two critical operations that depend on our making a prompt delivery. The company would have been hit very hard. *Very* hard. It would have cost millions, at the very least. God knows how many ongoing efforts would have to be restarted. If we had gone off to the rescue, nobody at Corporate would have thanked us, believe me.'

'I don't really care—'

'*I* do, Eliot. And so would you, if you knew the people involved, how hard they've worked to turn Quraqua into a second Earth. What the stakes are. These idiots got themselves into their situation, and they're just going to have to get themselves *out*.' He seemed to be studying the chessboard. Penkavic noticed the position had not changed. 'God help me, I wish it could have been otherwise.'

Penkavic stared at him.

'You'd have done the same thing,' Helm persisted, 'if you'd had my responsibilities. Known what I know.'

'I don't think so,' said Penkavic.

'Eliot.' The kindly uncle showed up again. 'Your investigation will uncover a defective switch in the central system and a cross-connected R-box in Lambda. You'll want to find both promptly and replace them so that the problem with the AI does not recur. Unfortunately, the launch was triggered when a signal intended to shut down the mess for the night was misrouted through the bad switch to the launch system. Because the R-box activated almost simultaneously, Eve was effectively locked off for several minutes and was unable to stop the sequence. An unfortunate accident. One in a million. But quite comprehensible. Responsibility will be laid on the AIs that run the inspection programs back at the Wheel, or possibly on design glitches. In any case, no one here need be blamed.'

For a long time, neither man spoke.

'Unless you insist.'

Penkavic sat down and tried to resist his inclination to look the other way.

'You have a choice to make now,' Helm continued. 'You can

accuse me, and log what you know. Or you can forget this conversation ever happened, and the incident will remain what it presently is, a piece of bad luck. I'd remind you there's always a price to be paid for progress. And that there's nothing to be gained by sending anyone to a hanging.' His fingers touched the crown of the black queen. He lifted her, moved her diagonally across the board, and settled her behind a protecting knight. 'I'm in your hands, Eliot.'

'*Incoming traffic, Marcel.*'

'On-screen, Bill.'

'*You're not going to like it,*' the AI added.

TO: *NCA* WENDY JAY
FROM: *NCK* ATHENA BOARDMAN
SUBJECT: LANDER DIFFICULTIES

MARCEL: REGRET TO REPORT THAT SYSTEMS BREAKDOWN RESULTED IN UNCONTROLLED LAUNCH OF LANDER DURING HYPERFLIGHT. ALL ATTEMPTS AT RECOVERY FAILED. NO CHOICE BUT CONTINUE TO QURAQUA. REGRET UNABLE ASSIST YOU. ELIOT.

Marcel was reading the message a second or third time when Beekman broke in: 'How the hell do you accidentally launch a lander?'

'I don't know.' A chill was expanding at the pit of Marcel's stomach.

'And they don't have a spare?'

'No.'

He could hear Beekman's slight wheeze. 'There must be some-body else.'

'There isn't. We checked.' The room had gone quiet.

'So what do we do now?'

Marcel couldn't see there was anything they *could* do.

'I don't think we should try it,' said Kellie. 'What if you get inside the damned thing and it decides to go the rest of the way into the chasm?'

They were looking down on the *Star* lander. It was wedged sideways, starboard side up. The hull was gouged, and the cabin roof was hammered in. One wing was bent, one of the jets looked misaligned. And both landing treads had been broken off.

Hutch thought the descent *looked* more dangerous than it was. Her link tingled, and Marcel's voice whispered her name. 'I'm here,' she said. 'How're we doing?'

'Not so well, I'm afraid.'

She read it in his voice, knew what he would say before it went any farther. 'What happened?'

'*Boardman*. They accidentally launched the lander in hyperflight.'

'They lost it.'

'Yes.'

Hutch saw the others watching her. 'How the hell could *that* happen?'

'Don't know.'

'What is it?' asked Kellie.

They all looked scared. Even MacAllister. She switched the conversation onto the allcom. 'Nobody else in the area?'

'No. Nobody.'

'What about the Patrol?'

'Not even remotely close.'

'No private vessels? A corporate yacht, maybe?'

'No, Hutch. Nothing with a lander.' She listened to him breathing. 'I'm sorry.'

'What happened?' asked Nightingale.

'We haven't given up,' Marcel said.

'I don't suppose that means you've thought of something else.'

'Not yet.'

'What happened?' Nightingale demanded, louder this time. The question hung there.

'What now?'

Hutch wasn't sure who'd spoken. They stood on the brink of the chasm, staring down, while the implications settled around their shoulders.

MacAllister looked into the sky, as if to locate *Wendy*. 'Captain Clairveau. Are you listening?'

A brief delay. Then: 'I'm here, Mr MacAllister.'

'What's our course of action now?' he asked. 'What do we do?'

'I don't know yet. I haven't had a chance—'

'—to analyze the situation.' MacAllister could summon the tones of an angry god. He did so. 'As I understand our status, rescue would seem to be out of the question. Impossible. Am I correct?'

'It would appear so.'

'Am I correct?'

'Yes.' Hesitantly.

'Then do us a common courtesy, Captain: The situation here has deteriorated severely. You'll make it easier on all of us if you confine yourself to the facts and refrain from cheerleading.'

Marcel was silent.

And MacAllister was right. Hutch was crushed by the finality of events. 'Marcel,' she said, 'we're going to sign off for a bit.'

'Okay.' But she didn't hear the distant click and knew he was still on the circuit. 'I'll be here,' he said at last. 'If I can help.'

He signed off.

Chiang kicked some snow into the chasm. 'We could all just jump in,' he said. 'End it.'

'Save the gallows humor,' said Kellie.

'I wasn't trying to be funny.' He folded his arms, and for an unsettling moment Hutch thought he really was considering it. She started cautiously in his direction, but Kellie got there first, took his arm, and pulled him away from the edge. He laughed. 'Although,' he said, 'I can't see where it makes much difference.'

Hutch changed her tone, implying they were now getting to

serious business. 'How much time do we have left?' she asked. 'Anybody know?'

'Impact occurs December 9,' said Kellie. 'At 5:56 P.M. Zulu.' Ship time.

MacAllister glanced at his watch. 'What kind of time are we talking?'

'Zulu,' Nightingale sneered. 'Orbital. Greenwich Mean. The time on your watch.'

It was just after midnight on the twenty-eighth. At the tower, it was a couple of hours after sunrise.

'But the place will begin to break up,' said Nightingale, 'a day or so before the collision.'

'Pity.' MacAllister shook his head. 'We have front-row seats for the most spectacular extravaganza in history, and we won't be here at showtime.'

Chiang did not look amused. 'Something to consider,' he said. 'Do we have a way to make a painless exit? When the time comes?'

MacAllister pushed his hands down into his vest pockets. 'What about tranks?'

'It's a little premature to be talking like that,' said Hutch.

'Is it really?' MacAllister looked down at her from a considerable height. 'Well, let's all be sure to keep our spirits up. Wouldn't want anything less, would we?'

'That's enough, MacAllister,' she said. 'Try not to get hysterical.'

'You know,' Nightingale said, 'if you hadn't panicked and tried to get clear with the lander, maybe none of this would have happened.' He let them see he was enjoying himself.

'Look, the lander was about to go into the ditch. We tried to save it.'

'You tried to save your fat ass—'

Hutch broke in and got between them. 'Gentlemen, this isn't going to help.'

'Sure it is,' said Nightingale. 'There's something to be said for truth. That's what *you* always say, isn't it, *Mac*'? It doesn't matter who gets hurt; let's just get the truth out on the table. The truth is, you tried to run. The other lander was already gone, and *you*—'

'That's enough. Randy.' She used the most threatening tone she could summon.

He glared at her and turned away.

'What *is* it with you two?' Hutch asked, looking at MacAllister.

The editor shrugged. 'He objects to something I wrote a long time ago.'

'MacAllister,' she said, 'you have friends everywhere.'

'Even at World's End. I guess so.'

Nightingale stood, looking out over the abyss. The others hunkered down in the snow. Nobody said much. Hutch pulled her knees close and propped her chin on it.

Nightingale pushed his hands into his vest pockets. The wind had already blown a covering of snow over the graves. Chiang took Kellie's arm and asked if she was okay. MacAllister glanced at the time every couple of minutes, as if he had a pressing appointment.

Hutch withdrew into her own black thoughts until Nightingale's voice brought her out of it. 'There might still be a way to get to orbit,' he said.

She looked at him bleakly. One did not walk off a planetary surface. 'How?'

'There's a lander on the ground. Not far from here, I don't think.'

'*Tess!*' said MacAllister.

Nightingale nodded. 'That's good,' he said. 'You remember after all.'

'I remember that you left one of the landers behind. But that's twenty years ago.'

'I didn't say there was transportation. I said *there might be a way*.' He was moving snow around with his foot, pushing it over the edge into the chasm 'It sure as hell beats jumping in there.'

Hutch felt a rush of hope. Any kind of chance looked pretty good at the moment. 'You said *not far*, Randy. *How* far?'

'I'm not sure. Southwest of here. Probably about two hundred kilometers. We were a little bit north of the equator.'

Twenty years. Kellie shook her head. 'The fuel will be long gone,' she said.

MacAllister looked from Kellie to Hutch to Nightingale, hoping someone would say something encouraging.

Hutch obliged. 'Maybe not.' she said. 'Marcel, we need you.'

It took a few moments, but he came on-line. 'What can I do for you, Hutch?'

'Do you have access to the schematics for *Tess*? The lander that got left behind in the original expedition?'

She could hear him relaying the question to Bill. Then he was back. 'I'm looking at them,' he said.

'What kind of reactor was it equipped with?'

'Direct-conversion Bussard–Ligon.'

'Okay.' Her spirits rose. 'There might be a chance at that.'

'I see where you're headed,' said Marcel.

Kellie was puzzled. 'I still don't understand where we'd get fuel for it.'

'Think about it a minute,' said Hutch. 'Most landers are designed for the sole purpose of getting from orbit to surface. Up and down. Moving supplies and people between a ground base and a ship. The landers used in planetary exploration, though, like the one we came down in, or like *Tess*, are different: They were intended to get around on the ground. You take it down, and you keep it with you. It helps in the exploration, and you don't have to run it back and forth to orbit every few flights to refuel.'

Kellie was starting to show interest.

'That's why they carry the Bussard–Ligon,' continued Hutch.

'Which means what?' asked MacAllister.

'Their jets burn hydrogen, like all landers. The reactor maintains the ship's normal power levels. It keeps batteries charged, powers the capacitors, keeps the lights on.'

'And?'

'It can also be used to separate hydrogen from oxygen to produce fuel.'

MacAllister's face lit up. 'You're saying it can make jet fuel?'

'All we'll need is some water,' said Hutch. 'Yes. That's exactly what it can do.'

'There was a river nearby,' said Nightingale.

'Well, how about that,' said MacAllister. 'We finally get lucky.'

Nightingale allowed his contempt for MacAllister's ignorance to show. 'Landing sites for exobiologists,' he said, 'were often near water. On beaches, near lakes, and so on. It's where animals congregate.'

'And pilots are trained to use them,' added Hutch, 'whenever they can. So they can keep the tanks topped off.'

'So how do we get the reactor running?' asked Nightingale. 'What fuels *it*?'

'Boron,' said Hutch.

That induced a worried look. 'Where do we get boron?'

'There should be a supply in the lander. There'd *have* to be.'

'How much would we need?' asked Nightingale.

She held thumb and index finger a few centimeters apart. 'Not much at all. I'd think a couple of tablespoons will be more than sufficient to get us up and running. We'll check the specifics later.'

MacAllister clapped his palms together. 'Then we're in business,' he said. 'All we have to do is head over to the other lander, and we're out of here.' He turned to Chiang. 'I have to tell you. Chiang, I was worried there for a minute.'

'Well,' said Hutch, 'we're not exactly out of the soup. The jets will give us *some* power, enough to get around down here. But—'

'They won't be enough,' said Kellie. 'to get us off-world. For that we need the spike.'

'The problem we can expect,' said Hutch, 'is that after all these years the capacitors will be degraded. *Seriously* degraded. We need the capacitors at full capability to run the spike.'

'You mean,' asked MacAllister. 'we can't use it to get into orbit?'

'That's correct.'

'Then what have we been talking about?'

Hutch gazed down at the *Star* lander. 'What we need,' she said, 'is a fresh set of capacitors. Any idea where we might find them?'

The engine compartment of the *Wildside* lander had been thoroughly fried. But the *Evening Star*'s boat was a different story. It lay wedged in the chasm like a giant black-and-white insect. 'Marcel,' Hutch said, 'this thing's *big*. How much do the capacitors weigh?'

There was a long pause. Then: 'Uh-oh.'

'Give me the uh-oh.'

'*On Deepsix, 43.4 kilograms. Each.*' Damned near as heavy as *she* was.

It wouldn't be practical to haul them overland. 'We'll pull them out,' she said, 'and leave them in the tower. Come back for them after we get *Tess* up and running.'

'That won't work, will it?' asked Beekman. 'Can you operate the lander without capacitors?'

'Once we convert the water, sure. We just won't have much lift capability.'

Marcel broke in: 'Good news, folks. We've located *Tess*.'

'How far?'

'Looks like 175 kilometers, give or take. We figure you've got about twelve days to get there. Maybe eleven. Eleven *Maleivan* days.' Eleven nineteen-hour days.

'That doesn't sound far,' said MacAllister. 'A couple of us ought to be able to cover that in short order.'

'It wouldn't be a good idea to stay here alone,' said Hutch.

'Why not? I can't walk 175 kilometers.'

'You stay here, you'll probably get eaten.'

He looked uncomfortable. 'Leave me a weapon.'

'When are you going to sleep?'

'We've got plenty of time,' said Chiang, helpfully. 'You'll be able to make it.'

'Think about the big cat,' said Nightingale.

'Okay,' he said. 'Point taken.'

She turned her attention to the chasm. 'If that's settled, let's collect the capacitors and get on the road.'

The capacitor compartments looked accessible. It was just a matter of climbing down to them.

'There's another possibility,' said MacAllister. 'How about trying to *fly* it out?'

'It's jammed in *sideways*,' said Hutch.

'You've got an AI. It's not as if anybody would have to be on board when you made the effort.'

Kellie's expression implied that she agreed.

It *was* conceivable. If it wasn't wedged too tight, the thrusters might break it loose. Maybe they could bring it out, land it in front of the tower, climb in, and go home.

But it *did* look *tight*. *Had* to be tight.

The ship's prow was angled down about ten degrees.

MacAllister saw her reluctance. 'Why not?' he persisted. 'If we can make it work, nobody has to risk his – or *her* – life climbing down and prying open engine compartments.' The use of the feminine pronoun was pointed. He was reminding her who was in charge and who, therefore, should take any such risk.

'What it would probably do,' said Hutch, 'is rip the roof off the cabin.'

'What's to lose? If we can't get it out, we don't care whether the cabin's secure, do we?'

Kellie shook her head. 'Fireball time,' she said. 'Crunch the cabin, split the fuel tanks, everything goes up. Including the capacitors.'

'Even if we try to *ease* it out?' said Nightingale.

'We can try it,' said Hutch finally. She got the *Evening Star* duty officer on the circuit, and told him what they wanted to do.

'You sure?' he asked.

'No,' she said. And then: 'Yes. We need your assistance.'

The duty officer spoke to the lander AI: 'Glory, can you hear me?'

'I hear you, Mark.'

'What is your status?'

The AI ran off a series of numbers and conditions. On the whole, Hutch thought, the damage might not be as serious as it looked. There was some broken circuitry, which meant control problems. Maybe they could replace them with parts from the other lander. Maybe they could fly it over to *Tess* and use the two to make a fully functioning spacecraft.

The AI reported that thrusters were okay, and there was lift. 'Although there seem to be balancing problems.'

'That's because it's on its side,' said Kellie.

The vehicle weighed probably eight metric tons.

'Glory,' said the duty officer, 'the next voice you hear will belong to Priscilla Hutchins. I want you to code her. Do what she says.'

'I will comply, Mark.'

'Go ahead, Hutch,' he said. 'She's all yours.'

'Glory, this is Priscilla Hutchins.'

'Hello, Priscilla.'

'I want you to engage the lifters and raise the nose until I tell you to stop.'

They heard metal grind against the chasm wall. Snow broke loose and fell to the bottom. A piece of rock let go, and the lander slipped deeper into the trench.

'Glory, stop,' she said.

'Priscilla, I do not have freedom of movement.'

'Try firing the rockets' said MacAllister. 'That should break it loose.'

'Break it, period,' said Kellie. She leaned over and looked down. 'We could try to cut away some of the rock.'

Nightingale made a face. 'It would just slip down farther. If it changes its position, we might lose access to the capacitors.'

He was right. The best chance lay in the original idea: Collect the capacitors, then get the other lander. But it would have been so good, so *elegant*, to ease the spacecraft out into the open.

Chiang must have seen the hesitation in her face. 'It's your field of expertise. Hutch. Call it.'

MacAllister looked to heaven. 'God help us, we're in the hands of the experts. I think you ought to direct the AI to pour it on, stake everything on one roll of the dice. Get it over with.'

Below the spacecraft, the walls dropped away, gradually narrowing until they sliced down into the snow. Anyone falling would become a permanent feature of the crevice.

'No,' she said. 'Glory's our ticket out of here. We need to take care of her.'

'I'll make the climb,' said Chiang.

She could see he was uncomfortable with the idea. Hutch herself had no love for precipices. But MacAllister was right: It was her responsibility, which she'd have happily ducked had Chiang looked a bit more confident. 'It's okay,' she said, trying to put steel into her voice. 'I'll do it.'

She hoped someone, possibly Kellie, would try to argue her out of it. Chiang nodded, relieved. Was she sure? he asked.

'Yeah,' she said.

Kellie tossed a rock over the side and watched until it dropped silently into the snow at the bottom. 'That's a long way down, Hutch.'

Thanks, Kellie. I really needed that. But she bit down on the comment.

Nightingale studied the situation. 'We'll just lower you and bring you back up,' he said. 'No way you can fall. You'll be safe as long as the lander doesn't give way at the wrong time.'

'That should reassure her,' said MacAllister.

Hutch began by asking the duty officer to confirm that she retained verbal control over the AI. While she was doing that, Kellie and Nightingale retreated to the tower and returned with two long pieces of cable. Hutch tied one around her waist and handed it to Chiang. She kept the other one looped and gave it to Kellie. 'Toss it down when I tell you,' she said.

Marcel broke in. 'Be careful.'

MacAllister surprised her. He looked genuinely worried, but she wondered whether he was afraid she'd fall into the pit before retrieving the capacitors. 'I don't think this is a good idea, Priscilla. There's no need. Just tell the AI to put the throttle to it.'

She was touched. 'Just hang on to me,' she told him.

There was no nearby tree or other solid object around which to secure the line. So Chiang and MacAllister drove a couple of stakes into the ground. When they'd finished and gotten set up, Hutch took a deep breath, backed out over the rim, felt the emptiness beneath her, and smiled diffidently at Kellie.

Kellie gave her a thumbs-up.

She knew how the professionals did it, bracing their feet against the face of the rock and walking down. But she couldn't quite balance herself that well and instead simply dropped into a sitting position at the edge and eased herself over. 'Okay, guys,' she said. 'Lower away.'

They complied and she kept her eyes on the wall, which was earth-colored and rough and pebbly. Kellie was watching her and passing instructions and encouragement back and forth. *'Okay, Hutch, you're doing fine.'*

'Hold it, she's got an abutment to deal with.'

Trails of snow and pebbles broke loose and poured into the canyon.

There were no handholds. She realized belatedly that she should have looped the cable around her thighs instead of just connecting it to her belt and harness. It was dragging up on her, trying to pull her belt up under her vest. The Flickinger field did not provide sufficient resistance.

'You okay, Hutch?' Kellie asked.

'I'm fine. Keep going.'

She maintained a stranglehold on the cable, gripping it so tightly that her muscles began to hurt. She told herself to relax, and checked cautiously to see where the lander was, trying to keep her eyes away from the abyss. Occasional clumps of snow and earth spilled down on her.

Kellie and Nightingale were both looking over the edge now, and she wished they'd be more careful. Last thing she needed would be to have one of them land in her lap, but when she complained, both seemed surprised.

'Just a little more.' Kellie told the line handlers.

The lander was directly beneath her, and she reached down with her left foot, got nothing, wiggled around in the belt, tried again, and touched metal. She was delighted to discover that it did not drop lower as she eased her weight onto it. 'Okay,' she said. 'I'm on board.'

Safety line or not, she felt better kneeling rather than standing on the spacecraft. Despite its boxy appearance, the hull was adequately cycloid and aerodynamic. Wherever she touched it, it seemed to curve around away from her. She perched on the starboard side and gazed through the cabin windows. The door between the cargo hold and the cabin hung open. Two pieces of luggage had fallen out of the bins and lay against the downside bulkhead.

First things first: She worked her way to the communication pod, opened it, and removed as many of the parts as would come out. She also took the connectors and put everything in her vest.

The fuselage narrowed toward the tail. She moved cautiously in that direction, toward the capacitor compartments.

There was one on either side of the spacecraft, about halfway back. From her perspective, one faced up, the other down. She went after the easy one first. 'Glory,' she said, 'can you hear me?'

'I hear you, Priscilla.'

'Call me Hutch. And if you will, open the starboard compartment.'

The panel popped open. The capacitor didn't look at all like the capacitors in her own lander. It was wide, silver and brown, and flattened. Hers was a dark blue box. She considered whether it would fit in *Tess*'s compartment, and concluded it would not. But that needn't be a problem. If necessary, the installation could be done by putting them in the backseat and wiring them in.

'Glory,' she said, 'release the capacitor.'

She heard a soft click. The unit came loose. 'Okay, Kellie,' she said, 'send the other line down.'

Kellie got it to her after several tries. Hutch tied it securely around the capacitor, knotted it, and looked up. Kellie waved.

Hutch put the assorted spare parts from the comm pod into a bag and attached it also to the line. 'Okay,' she said. 'Take it up.'

They began to pull. Hutch assisted, and the line lifted the capacitor out of its compartment and hauled it clear of the spacecraft. Kellie leaned out, trying to keep it away from the face of the cliff so it wouldn't get damaged. It swung back and forth while it rose, and then it disappeared over the crest. A moment later the line dropped back in her direction. She gathered it in.

She was just moving back into her crouch when the spacecraft dropped a few centimeters. It wasn't much, but her heart stopped. Everyone asked what had happened and whether she was okay. 'Yes,' she said, trying to sound composed. 'Going below.'

She slipped off the fuselage and dangled at the end of her line. 'Lower away,' she said. 'Not too fast.'

'Tell us when,' said Kellie.

'A little more.' She descended past the hull until she could see the port side. The down side.

'Glory,' she said, 'is the remaining capacitor secure in its compartment?'

'*Yes, it is, Hutch.*'

'Open the compartment.'

Pause. '*I can't. Hutch. It doesn't respond.*'

'Okay. I'm going to try it manually.' She popped a panel, found the lever, and pulled on it. But it had too much give. 'Not working,' she said. 'Kellie.'

'Yes.'

'There's a bar back in the tower. Have somebody get it for me.'

Kellie kept talking to her, telling her that the capacitor looked good, that everything was under control, while somebody tracked the tool down. Finally, MacAllister broke in: 'We've got it.' And a minute later they were lowering the bar.

She caught it and went back to work.

The capacitor compartment was suspended over her head. She looked up at it and tried to insert the bar under the lip of the metal.

'Toward the top,' said Glory. *'The problem's near the top.'*

It was difficult to work without a perch, to get any leverage on the bar when she had no place to plant her feet.

'How are you making out?' asked Chiang.

The bar was heavy. Her arms quickly got tired, and once she almost dropped it. The compartment door was jammed tight.

'Okay' she said.

She struggled on. Chiang said he thought it was taking too long and they should pull her up and let him try.

'He thinks' said Kellie, 'we need more muscle down there.'

'He's probably right.' Hutch slid the bar into her vest and took a minute to rest her arms. Despite her boyish dimensions, she was, like all women, somewhat top-heavy, and she had to fight a tendency to turn turtle. 'Let's stay with this a bit,' she said. 'If I can't get it, I'll be happy to give Chiang a shot.'

Her vest was cutting off the blood in her armpits. She changed position, retrieved the tool, and tried again. She worked with increasing desperation and finally got the bar inside the compartment. She pulled down, pushed it in farther, and pulled again. Something gave, and the door popped open. The capacitor hung immediately overhead.

'I've got it,' she said. She secured the bar to her belt, reached up into the compartment, felt around, and estimated she had a reasonable amount of clearance. She tied the line around the front and rear of the capacitor and secured it.

'Okay,' she said. 'Take up the slack. But not too tight.'

They complied. She got out from under the compartment. 'Glory,' she said.

'Yes, Hutch?'

'Release the capacitor.'

It dropped out of the compartment and swung back and forth in a long arc. But the line held, and her knots held. To her immense relief it did *not* fall to the bottom of the canyon.

After they'd recovered the second capacitor, she resisted the temptation to get out of the chasm and instead pushed up through the airlock into the spacecraft.

She salvaged as many reddimeals as she could, breakfasts, lunches, and dinners packed in self-heating containers. They weren't exactly food off the griddle, but for something to eat on the trail in an alien place, they were going to look pretty good. She picked up some coffee packs, found two bottles of wine, and some sandwiches and fruit from the refrigerator. The galley supplied unbreakable dishes, utensils, and mugs. She paused in front of the water tank. *That* was something they were going to need at the far end of the journey. She removed it, emptied it, folded it up, and put it in her vest.

There were other useful items: towels, washcloths, toothbrushes, soap, an extra e-suit, a lantern, a pair of *Evening Star* jumpsuits, more cable, two backpacks, and a medkit.

The lander slipped a few more centimeters.

She packed everything into plastic bags and they hauled them up. Kellie was urging her not to press her luck.

'Coming now,' Hutch said.

And then Glory's voice: *'Hutch?'*

'Yes, Glory.'

'Are you leaving now?'

'Yes.'

212

'You won't be back?'

'No, Glory. I won't be back.'

'Would you shut me off?'

The capacitors were marked with the manufacturer's name, *Daigleton Industries,* the date of manufacture, which was the previous year, and the Daigleton logo, a stylized atom.

They put them on the worktable and threw canvas over them, and MacAllister opened a private channel to Hutch. 'Maybe we should leave a couple of people here to make sure they're still here when we get back.'

'Who's going to take them?' she asked.

'What about the cat?'

'I can't imagine what it would do with them.' She adjusted the canvas. 'No, we're safer together. If this place is as dangerous as Randy thinks it is, we shouldn't leave anybody here.'

'Congratulations, Hutch. Outstanding job.' Marcel sounded delighted, relieved, wiped out. Had he really been following all that?

'Thanks, Marcel. We've got a bunch of survivors here.'

'I see that. By the way, we have a message for you from the Academy.'

'Read it,' she said.

'The subject is "Aliens on Deepsix." It says: *Priscilla, you are directed to make every effort to rescue whatever inhabitants of Deepsix you can find. Humanity requires no less of us.* It's signed by the commissioner.'

MacAllister snorted. 'Gomez thinks she's writing for the ages. "Humanity requires. . . ." Poor boob. They'll be laughing at her for a thousand years.'

PART TWO
Overland

13

One of the sure signs of a moron is that he, or she, babbles about the glories of the wilderness. Moonlight. Cool crisp air. The wind in the trees. Flights of birds overhead. Be assured these people always do it virtual. That way one drags no mud into the house.

—GREGORY MACALLISTER, 'Boy Scouts and Other Aberrations', Editor at Large

Hours to breakup (est): 240

They melted snow, boiled the water, and drank it down. There'd been water in the lander, but there had been no practical way to retrieve it. MacAllister predicted they'd all break out in hives by dinner. He added, more seriously, that they'd better start learning how to hunt. They estimated that they had a six-day food supply. 'That means,' he added, 'we'll be traveling on empty stomachs when we get to *Tess*.'

Their destination lay south-southwest, but they couldn't immediately proceed in that direction because they had no way to cross the crevice that now divided the landscape as far as they could see.

They made snowshoes and put all their gear and food into

217

sample bags and the two backpacks Hutch had salvaged from the lander. Hutch provided MacAllister with a cutter and showed him how to use it. Then they took a last look at the tower and the capacitors and struck off across the plain.

'You'll be out of the snow in a day or two,' Marcel told them. That was good news. Once they had solid earth underfoot they'd be able to move more quickly. But it was a struggle for the two older men right from the beginning. Nightingale developed a blister after they'd gone about a kilometer. Hutch treated it with ointment from the medkit. Within another hour, MacAllister was limping and grumbling.

Their first challenge was to find a way across the chasm. They walked along the northern edge, moving slowly so the two could keep up. Hutch wondered whether MacAllister had been right, that he and Nightingale should have been left behind to take their chances.

At a patch of forest, they called a halt and fashioned walking staffs for everyone. 'Don't need it,' protested Kellie.

'Use it anyhow' Hutch insisted. 'It's good for you.'

Nightingale took his gratefully. MacAllister manfully swallowed his discomfort and smiled. 'We all look good with staffs.' he said. 'Adds a certain panache.'

They traveled well into the afternoon before they were able to get around the crevice. Gradually it closed, and the plain was solid again. They turned southwest.

Aside from bird sightings, all of which Nightingale treated with barely muted alarm, they encountered their first full-size native beast shortly afterward. It was about the size of a moose, shaggy, with white fur and unsettling blue eyes that gazed steadily at them with, Hutch thought, cool intelligence. For all that, it did not look particularly ferocious. Its snout was shoved into an icy stream, and it did not straighten up as they approached.

They drew their weapons nonetheless, switched on the power, and spread out.

It looked at each of them in turn, studying Hutch with special

218

attention as if it recognized that she was directing the small party.

Hutch glanced at the worried faces and unsteady hands of her comrades, concluded she was in as much danger from them as from the creature, and moved out of MacAllister's line of fire.

As the last of them were passing, it startled them by rearing up onto its hind legs. A collar of hard bone rose around its neck. The collar ended in two long spikes, one flanking either jaw. The creature had a wide mouth full of shark's teeth and a permanent grin that reminded Hutch of an alligator.

'That thing's all dental work,' whispered MacAllister.

It inspected Nightingale and showed him its teeth. Nightingale froze.

Armored ridges protected the animal's underside and its back. Its claws looked like daggers.

'Stay cool,' said Hutch. The exobiologist stood absolutely still, his eyes wide. She slowly inserted herself between him and the creature. It swung its long jaws her way, looked back at Nightingale, and hesitated.

'We're not in its food chain,' said Chiang.

MacAllister snorted. 'By the time it discovers that, somebody's going to have a decided limp.'

It looked at them, waiting perhaps for a hostile act.

The drawback of the cutter was its limited range. Notched up to full power, it had little effect beyond a few meters. MacAllister leveled his weapon and his thumb hovered over the punch pad. He was going to shoot.

'No.' Hutch kept her eyes on the creature. 'Don't do it, MacAllister. Everybody back away.'

'Why don't we just kill it while we can?' the editor insisted.

'Slowly,' said Hutch.

MacAllister frowned at her. 'It's a mistake.'

Hutch made her voice cold. 'Do what I say.'

The animal watched and after a few moments appeared to lose interest. It dropped back onto all fours and recommenced drinking.

After they'd gotten to what appeared to be a safe distance, Kellie let out her breath. 'Shoo' she said quietly.

Nightingale thought he'd gotten through the experience pretty well. He felt he'd stood his ground, and believed he was ready to use his weapon if need be. He found it hard, however, to control his trembling afterward.

'You all right?' Kellie asked him.

He nodded and tried a smile. 'I'm fine,' he said.

They had no compass. Marcel followed their progress from *Wendy* and occasionally issued course corrections. The landscape remained unfailingly bleak, cold, and desolate. By late in the day they were seeing more hills. Occasional flocks of birds appeared overhead.

Nightingale was not in anything resembling the kind of physical condition required for this sort of effort. Everything he owned *hurt*. There was, however, consolation in the knowledge that MacAllister was having an even harder time. Hutch, who was certainly aware that she was encumbered by two people who preferred taxis wherever they went, continued to call frequent breaks.

The other four talked constantly. Chiang and the two women seemed to have accepted MacAllister in spite of his abrasiveness. Nightingale was once again hampered by his natural shyness and defensiveness. He tried to make acute observations, throw in occasional witty remarks, but it didn't work. Nobody really seemed to listen to him. He was the outsider, and gradually he withdrew and concentrated his efforts simply on trying to keep up.

It should have been different. After all, they were the only five human beings on the planet. That fact alone should have bound them together, should have prevented the development of factions and militated against the exclusion of any single member.

It was unfair, especially in light of the fact he'd given them their one chance at survival.

By sundown, he was limping badly and was being actively assisted by Kellie. They'd arrived in a glade, and Hutch called a halt. Nightingale eased himself gratefully to the ground, killed his field, pulled off his shoes, and rubbed his soles. By God it felt good.

He applied more of the salve from the medkit. Warmth spread through his feet, and then a general sense of relief.

The others fell quiet.

And something moved in the shrubbery.

There was a scramble for weapons.

The thing looked like a big scorpion, a scorpion the size of a child's wagon. It had a pair of antennas, which swept them in a kind of rhythm. Mandibles clicked audibly. The tail was shorter by far, and bisected. It had eight legs.

'Stay still' said Hutch.

It didn't matter. At the same moment, the creature charged Chiang. Chiang fell over backward, firing wildly. Hutch and Kellie burned it simultaneously. The thing let go a high keening sound, changed direction, and went for Hutch. They caught it again, and the scorpion crashed into a rock, rolled over, and lay on its back with its legs moving weakly.

'That's the biggest bug I've ever seen,' Chiang said, getting to his feet.

MacAllister examined his cutter. 'It's a good weapon.' he said. 'Will it run down? How much energy does it have?'

'It'll recharge on its own,' said Hutch. 'Just like your suit. But yes, there *are* limits. Don't play with it.'

It wasn't a scorpion, of course. There were major differences, other than size and the tail, which mounted no stinger. The narrowing between cephalothorax and abdomen wasn't correct. The eyes were wrong. The segmenting was unique. Its chelae were smaller. The head was more heavily armored. Not for the first time, Nightingale mourned the lost opportunity to examine this world's biology.

There had been some thought of stopping there for the night, but they now agreed unanimously that it would be a good idea to move on.

Nightingale had not been able to get used to the shortened days. When they finally made camp, an hour later, he was bone weary and half-starved. They were in light forest, on the crest of a long, gently curving ridge. It had gotten dark. Overhead the superluminals moved serenely among the constellations, and he would have given much to be aboard one of them. Nevertheless, he was, by God, keeping up.

They broke out the reddimeals.

Nobody was dressed for this kind of weather. The heaviest garment anyone wore was probably MacAllister's black sweater. The two women were in jumpsuits. Chiang had only a light pullover shirt and a pair of shorts. And Nightingale's slacks and casual shirt were designed for a far more balmy climate. None of this would have mattered much were it not that they had to shut off the e-suits to eat.

They collected some wood and built a fire. When it was up and burning steadily, they keyed the reddimeal containers, which cooked the food. Then, at a kind of prearranged signal, they got as close to the fire as they could, shut off the suits, and gobbled chicken, beef, and whatever else showed up in the dinners. Everything tasted good that night.

Kellie made coffee. Nightingale swallowed everything down and, as quickly as he could, buttoned up again. He hated having to gulp his food when he was so hungry. But it was just too cold to linger over it.

They held a council of war, and agreed it was time to think about testing some of the local food supply, in order to conserve the reddimeals. If they discovered the native stuff was inedible, they would have to resort to rationing. There should be some game in the woods, and Kellie suggested to everyone's horror that the scorpions might make a food source. If any more showed up.

No one wanted to discuss it further.

They asked Nightingale, the resident expert. Did he know what they could expect to find? Was the local food edible?

'No idea,' he said. 'Nobody knows. We terminated the mission too quickly, and what we learned was inconclusive. Deepsix biology uses levo sugars and not dextro. So that's okay. They use DNA to make proteins, which is good. You might get some nutrition, but I doubt it. You have at least an equal chance of being poisoned. The fact is we have a supply of reddimeals, and we're only talking about a few days.

'What I mean is . . .' He paused, then plunged ahead: 'We don't have to worry about subsisting indefinitely. What we're really interested in is satisfying our appetites. We could ration, go on half meals. But that's not going to help old guys trying to walk long distances. There's no real way we can be sure about toxins or allergens; if there's, say, a poison, our immune system may not even recognize it, or if it did, it might have no defense against it. I think we're reasonably safe, but I can't guarantee it.'

Hutch nodded, called Embry on *Wildside*, and asked for advice.

'Best would be not to go near anything local,' she said.

'That'll give us some very hungry people.'

Embry wasted no time becoming irritated. 'Better hungry than dead.'

There was a long silence. 'If you really have to do this,' she continued, 'have someone sample the stuff first. A very small sample. *Very* small. Give it some time. A half hour, at least. If he doesn't throw up, or get diarrhea—'

'Or fall over,' said MacAllister.

'—or fall over, you're in business.' Embry took a deep breath. 'Hutch,' she said, 'I feel guilty about the way things turned out.'

'It's okay. You didn't cause the quake.'

223

'Still . . . Well, anyhow, I wanted to wish you luck. Anything I can do, I'm here.'

'I know.'

They'd covered eleven kilometers that first day. Not bad, considering they'd gotten a late start, had to detour around the crevice, and were walking through snow.

They had, of course, no bedding. Nightingale made himself as comfortable as he could, lay back in the firelight, and wondered if his body would ever feel right again.

They decided to forget trying to divide the nineteen-hour days into standard temporal terminology, because nobody was ever quite sure what nine o'clock actually meant. Instead they thought in terms of dusk and dawn, noon and midnight. There were roughly nine hours of darkness, which they divided into four watches. Midnight came when Morgan's World rose.

Nightingale unstrapped his oxygen converter and laid it beside him, where it would continue to work, without pressing into his shoulders. He slept for a while, woke, noticed that the fire had burned down, heard someone throw a fresh branch onto it, slept some more, and eventually found himself gazing up at the stars.

Morgan had moved over into the west. It was framed within a stellar rectangle. A couple of stars lined up under the rectangle, providing it with a stand or stem. To primitive people, he thought, it would have become a constellation. A flower, perhaps. Or a tree. Or a cup.

Morgan. It was a commonplace name for a world-killer.

It glittered through the branches, the brightest star in the sky.

Clouds were approaching from the west. By the time Chiang knelt beside him and told him the watch was his, the only visible light was the fire.

He checked his cutter and put on the night goggles. They'd stopped atop a ridge where they could see for kilometers in all directions. Tomorrow they'd cross a narrow basin and begin a long uphill climb into dense forest.

A few flakes drifted onto his arm.

Nightingale glanced over at the sleepers. MacAllister had punched up a mound of snow to serve as a pillow. Kellie seemed to be dreaming, and he judged by her expression that it was not altogether unpleasant. He suspected Hutch was awake, but she lay unmoving, with her face in shadow. Chiang was still trying to get comfortable.

Ordinarily, he would have hated the guard duty assignment. Nightingale liked to keep his mind active. Time not spent in a book or doing research or attempting to solve a problem was time wasted. He had no interest hanging about in a wilderness for two hours peering into the dark. But that night, he stood atop the ridge, watching the snow come down. And he enjoyed the simple fact that he was alive and conscious.

Marcel brought *Wendy* back to Deepsix. He felt better if he could stay closer to the people on the ground. They were just completing their first orbit when Beekman came onto the bridge. 'Marcel,' he said, 'we've finished the analysis of the material we took from the artifact.'

'And . . .?'

'They're enhanced carbon nanotubes.'

Which are what?'

'Precisely the sort of material you'd want to have if you were building a skyhook. They're extremely light and have incredible tensile strength.' Beekman lowered himself into a chair and accepted some coffee. 'We'll be taking back a whole new technology. Probably revolutionize the construction industry.' He looked quizzically at the captain. 'What's wrong?'

'I don't like the plan to get our people off the ground.'

'Why?'

'There are too many things that can go wrong. *Tess* may not fly. They may not even get there in time. There may be some incompatibility between the capacitors and the onboard spike. Another quake could bury the damned things beyond recovery.'

225

'I don't know what we can do to change any of that.'

'I'd like a backup option.'

Beekman smiled patiently. 'Of course you would. Wouldn't we all? What do you suggest?'

'The ship going to Quraqua. The *Boardman*. It's big, loaded with construction equipment. Mostly stuff they're going to use to put together the ground stations. I looked at the manifest. It has hundreds of kilometers of cable.' Marcel laid emphasis on the last word, expecting Beekman to see immediately where he was headed.

'Go on,' Beekman said, showing no reaction.

'Okay. If we were to get some of the cable off the *Boardman*, and tie together about four hundred kilometers of it, we could attach one end to a shuttle.'

'And crash the shuttle,' finished Beekman.

'Right. We take it down as far as it'll go, which would be within a couple of kilometers of the surface before we'd lose it. It crashes. But the cable's down. On the ground.'

'And we use it to haul them out.'

Marcel thought it seemed too simple. 'It won't work?'

'No.'

'Gunther, why not?'

'How much does the cable weigh?'

'I don't know.'

'All right. Say it's on the order of three kilograms per meter. That's not very heavy.'

'Okay.'

'That means one kilometer of the cable would weigh in at about three metric tons.'

Marcel sighed.

'That's *one* kilometer. And this thing is going to stretch down from orbit? Three hundred kilometers, you say?'

He did the math in his head. The cable would have to be able to support roughly nine hundred metric tons.

'You see the problem. Marcel.'

226

'How about if we went for lighter material? Maybe hemp rope? They've got hemp on board.'

Beekman made a noise in his throat. 'I doubt the tensile strength of rope would be very high. How much do you think a piece one meter long would weigh?'

So they sat, drinking coffee, staring at one another. Once they called down and talked to Nightingale, whom Marcel knew to be the security watch. Any problems? What time did you expect to leave in the morning? How's everybody holding up?

That last question was designed to elicit a comment from Nightingale on his own physical condition, as well. But he only said they were fine.

Marcel noticed that he was beginning to feel disconnected from those on the ground. As if they were somehow already lost.

14

Walking through these woods, filled with the creatures of an alternate biosystem, constitutes an unusual emotional experience. They are all extinct, or shall be within a very few days. The sum total of six billion years of evolution is about to be erased, leaving nothing behind. Not so much as a tail feather.

And good riddance, I say.

—GREGORY MACALLISTER, *Deepsix Diary*

Hours to breakup (est): 226

All the sunrises on Deepsix were oppressive. The sky was inevitably slate, and a storm was either happening or seemed imminent.

Kellie Collier stood atop the ridge, surveying the woods and plains around her. In all that wilderness, nothing moved save a pair of wings so high and far as to present no detail to the naked eye. Through binoculars, she judged it to be not a bird at all. It had fur and teeth, a duckbill skull, and a long, serpentine tail. As she watched, it descended into a patch of trees and emerged moments later with something wriggling in its claws.

She turned toward the southwest. The land sloped downhill

and rose again gradually and then almost precipitously toward a long spine. The spine extended from one horizon to the other. It was going to be a difficult climb with Nightingale and the great man in tow. The wind tugged at her, trying to blow her off the ridge. Reminding her that they had ground to cover and that time was short.

Hutch lay quietly near the fire, and Kellie saw that her eyes were open. 'How we doing?' she asked softly.

'Time to go,' said Kellie.

She nodded. 'Let's give them a little longer.'

'I'm not sure we shouldn't push a bit harder.'

'It won't help us,' Hutch said, 'if they start breaking down.' MacAllister snored peacefully with his head pillowed against one of the packs; Nightingale lay near the fire, his shoes off to one side.

Kellie sat down beside her. 'We've a long way to go,' she said.

'We'll make it' said Hutch. 'As long as no one collapses.' She looked into the fire. 'I don't want to leave anybody behind.'

'We could come back later for them.'

'If they aren't eaten first. You really think either of those guys could stay alive on his own?'

'One of us could stay with them.'

Hutch shook her head. 'We're safer keeping our firepower concentrated. If we split up, we are absolutely going to lose somebody else.' She took a deep breath and looked at Kellie. 'We'll stay together as long as we can. And if we get behind, we'll do what we have to.'

Kellie liked to think of herself as the last of the fighter pilots. She'd begun her career as a combat aviator for the Peacekeepers. When the Peacekeepers became effectively obsolete (as they did every half century or so), when the latest round of civil wars had been fought and the dictators put to bed, she'd learned to fly spacecraft and transferred to the Patrol. But the job had been surprisingly routine. The Patrol simply didn't go anywhere. They *patrolled*. When people drank too much or neglected their maintenance or got careless, Kellie and her colleagues had shown up to rescue whoever was left.

But she never really traveled. A zone was assigned and she just went round and round, visiting the same eight or nine stations over and over. And during those years, she'd watched the Academy's superluminals coming in from places that no one had names for yet. Or from conducting surveys of the Omega clouds. Or from examining the space-twisting properties of neutron stars and black holes.

She'd lasted less than a year before giving it up to interview for a pilot's job with the Academy. The money was about half as much, the ships were more spartan, the fringe benefits barely existed. But the people with whom she traveled tended to have wider interests than the Patrol crews. And she loved the work.

That morning, though, she was having second thoughts. As MacAllister would have put it, there was something to be said for boredom.

Nightingale sat up, looked around, and sighed. 'Love the accommodations,' he said. He struggled to his feet. 'Back in a minute.'

She woke Chiang. 'Duty calls,' she said. 'Go with him.'

Chiang made a face, took a moment to figure out what he was being asked to do, got up, and trailed along behind the older man. Nobody went anywhere alone. The designated commode was halfway down the back side of the hill, in a gully. There was just enough ground in the way to provide a modicum of privacy.

Kellie filled a pot with snow and put it on the fire.

MacAllister rolled over and looked up at her. 'What time's the tour start?' he asked.

'Sooner the better,' said Kellie.

Hutch rubbed her eyes, closed them again, and looked at the gray sky. 'Another glorious morning on Deepsix.' She took a deep breath and let it out slowly. Then she fished for her cup and toothbrush.

Off to the east, something was moving. Kellie raised her binoculars and looked out across a stretch of grassland downslope. A herd of fur-bearing animals was approaching. They were big, lumbering creatures, with trunks and tusks. Their heads were extraordinarily ugly, much in the manner of rhinos. She watched them veer off and disappear into a wall of forest, but she could hear them for a long time after.

They disposed of another round of reddimeals. Kellie had bacon, eggs, and fried apples. She washed everything down with coffee.

'While we're on the trail,' said Hutch, 'let's see what we can hunt up for lunch.'

'Right.' MacAllister raised his coffee. 'I suspect we're all anxious to taste the local fare.' Kellie wondered if he could ask for the correct time without sounding cynical.

They trekked down the south slope, into and out of patches of trees, crossed a stream at the bottom, and started up the far side. Occasional furry creatures, the local equivalent of squirrels, showed themselves, as well as a few larger animals that looked as if they might serve for a meal. If anybody could get close enough to use a cutter. But the creatures kept their distance. 'We need a weapon that'll work at long range,' said Chiang.

Hutch asked whether anybody had experience with a bow and arrow.

Nobody did.

They crossed the valley and started uphill, up the long increasingly steep slope Kellie had studied from the crest of her ridge the night before. The snow became soft, and the walking grew more difficult. Nightingale's blisters got worse, and MacAllister struggled and grumbled. Hutch called a break.

The sun was directly overhead and they were still about an hour below the summit. A few donuts remained, which they divided. Mac insisted he was feeling fine and thought they should get going. Nightingale agreed, although he was obviously in some discomfort, and they set off.

They reached the crest and discovered that the land dipped sharply and then started uphill again, but at a more moderate angle. MacAllister observed that the entire planet seemed to run uphill.

They pressed on for another hour before they stopped, built a fire, and made coffee. 'We can feed anyone who's hungry,' Hutch said. But a nineteen-hour day was short, and lunch followed hard on breakfast. Consequently no one was anxious for an undue delay. 'We'll eat an early dinner,' she promised.

During the afternoon march Nightingale said that he was cold.

Hutch checked his gear and saw that his powerpak was failing. She replaced it with one of the units she'd pried out of the lander.

A freak thunderstorm broke over them, eliciting an observation by MacAllister that lightning wasn't supposed to occur at low temperatures.

That brought a response from Marcel: 'Some of our people here say it's a result of Morgan's approach. It translates into unusually severe high- and low-pressure areas. Consequently, you get screwy weather.'

They walked through a steady downpour while thunderbolts boomed overhead. The rain hissed into the snow, which turned to slush. The e-suits kept them dry, and they trudged on.

Nightingale seemed distracted, self-absorbed, remote. While they walked, his eyes were rarely focused. His gaze was directed inward, and when Kellie spoke to him, he invariably asked her to repeat herself.

He remained walled off from the others, resisting everybody's efforts at small talk. He did not snap at anyone, showed no sign of anger. But it was as though he walked alone through those frozen forests.

She began to notice that the lamp on his commlink was constantly glowing. She could see he wasn't talking with any of the others. Someone on *Wendy*, perhaps?

It gave rise to a suspicion. 'Randy?' she said, using a private channel.

He looked up at her and came back from someplace far away. 'Yes, Kellie? Did you say something?'

'Could I ask what you're listening to?'

'Right now? Bergdorf's *Agronomy on Quraqua*.' He looked over at her and smiled. 'Might as well make the time count.'

As she'd guessed, he was tied in to one of the ships' libraries. 'Yes,' she said. 'I know what you mean. But it might be a good idea if you shut it down. It's dangerous to do what you're doing.'

'Why is that?' He became defensive.

'Because there may be critters in the area who will mistake you for a hamburger. We've got five pairs of eyes, and we need them all. You don't want to be thinking about other things while we're moving through tiger country.'

'Kellie,' he said, 'it's not a problem. I can listen and watch—'

'Randy. Please do what I'm asking you to.'

'Or you'll blow the whistle on me?'

'Or I'll make off with your staff.'

He sighed visibly, a man of culture put upon by the barbarians of the world. She stayed with him until he showed her his thumb and pressed it to his commlink. The lamp went out. 'Okay?' he asked. 'Satisfied?'

Kellie could see Hutch talking, too. She glanced around at the others. You always knew who was conversing with whom because people inevitably look at one another during a conversation. But Chiang and MacAllister were not using their links. That probably meant Hutch was talking to Marcel.

She missed Marcel.

Kellie had not realized how much she enjoyed the company of the tall Frenchman. She'd thought he had looked at her with a touch of envy when she'd asked to make the descent to the surface.

At the moment they'd be having late night snacks on *Wendy*. She would have given a great deal to join him at his table, to listen to him talk about the elegance of Dupré and Proust.

After a while, the rainstorms blew off, and the sun broke

through. But it was only momentary. More clouds were building in the west.

They were buffeted by rain and sleet for most of the rest of the day. Although the e-suits kept them warm and dry, a constant wind made progress difficult, and the rain tended to smear vision. In addition, Hutch knew from long experience there was a psychological factor: When the weather was cold and wet, and your eyes made it clear you were wearing no more than a jump suit, that you should be shivering and miserable, it was difficult to be entirely comfortable. It was called the McMurtrie Effect.

They cleared a ridge and finally started downhill, but the descent was steep, and they had literally to *lower* MacAllister from one perch to level ground. They came at last to a river. It looked deep, but the current appeared placid.

'How're we doing for time?' Kellie asked.

Progress reports came regularly from Marcel, but they were directed to Hutch. 'Thirteen so far today,' she said.

Kellie frowned. Not great. But it was enough.

'Everybody here can swim?' asked Hutch.

Surprisingly, only Chiang lacked the skill.

The river was wide, and it looked deep in midstream. Thick twisted foliage hung down along both banks. They surveyed the area, looking for a local alligator-equivalent, but saw nothing.

'We still don't know what's in the water,' said Nightingale. 'I suggest we build a raft.'

'Don't have time,' said Hutch. If there was anything in the river, there was a good chance that the e-suits would prevent their being perceived as prey. There would, after all, be no scent.

'I don't think you should rely too heavily on that,' said Nightingale.

Hutch waded in until she was hip deep. Then they waited. Her heart pounded, but she tried to look calm. She watched the river and the banks for any sudden movement. But nothing came for her, and she felt more confident with each passing minute. When they were at last convinced it was safe, they found a dead limb Chiang could cling to and pushed off. MacAllister turned out to be an accomplished swimmer. Chiang said nothing while they towed him across, but Hutch saw that he felt humiliated. It would have been less difficult for him, she realized, had Kellie not been there. She was pleased to see that Kellie was also aware of the situation and made a point of staying close to him. She caught an amused smile from MacAllister, who seemed to miss none of the undercurrents among his companions.

They arrived on the far side in good order and resumed their march. Eventually the country turned uphill again. Chiang, who had been leading, fell toward the rear. Kellie moved up beside him and took him again to the front. She said something to him on a private channel.

He was replying when a snowbank rose, roared, and charged. Hutch saw only talons and green eyes and long, curved teeth while she fumbled for her laser, got it into her hand, lost the grip, then dropped it.

Kellie, directly in the thing's path, went down and tried to scramble out of the way. MacAllister seemed to have forgotten about his cutter. Instead, he raised his staff and brought it down on the creature's skull. The thing spat and growled and a cutter beam flashed close to Hutch's face. The growling went high-pitched, then stopped. When Hutch stumbled to her feet, helped by Nightingale, it lay twitching. Its head was half severed, and a red-brown viscous liquid pumped out onto the snow. Its dead eyes continued to watch her.

It was about the size of a bear. Chiang was standing off to one side, his cutter held straight out. He saw Hutch, nodded, shut it off, and lowered it.

Hutch checked her parts. Everything seemed to be there, 'I never saw it,' she said, patting MacAllister's shoulder. 'Hell of a job with the staff.'

Kellie embraced Chiang and kissed his cheek.

'What was it?' Chiang asked.

'Dinner,' said Hutch. 'If all goes well.'

They sliced off gobs of meat and wrapped them in plastic bags.

Toward the end of the afternoon, they topped the last rise, and the land began a long gentle decline. The storms had cleared off, and they had, for the first time since leaving the tower, a bright cheerful sky. They kept on until sundown, and Kellie urged that they continue. But the pace was too much for Mac and Nightingale, so Hutch called a halt near a stand of old trees that would provide firewood and privacy. They'd logged eighteen kilometers.

Pretty good, actually.

'Especially,' said Nightingale, lowering himself onto a downed tree trunk, 'when you consider this is hard country. It'll level out soon. And we should be almost out of the snow.'

MacAllister also looked exhausted.

'Chiang.' Kellie said, 'let's get some wood.' She picked up a dead branch and, as if that were a signal, the ground shook. Just once, for a few seconds.

They built a fire and roasted the meat. It smelled good, not unlike venison.

'Who's going to sample it?' asked Mac.

Hutch took a piece, thinking how being a leader wasn't all it was cracked up to be. She would follow Embry's prescription and go very slowly.

'Let me cut it for you,' said Nightingale. He sliced off a narrow strip, held it so she could see it in the firelight, and surprised her by turning off his suit and taking a bite.

They watched him. 'Thanks,' said Hutch.

He shrugged, chewed it methodically, commented that it was good, and swallowed. Then he reactivated the field.

Hutch wondered why he'd done it. Nightingale did not strike her as someone who was given to the gallant gesture. She suspected he was responding on some level to MacAllister's presence. Showing him how wrong he had been.

A half hour passed. The meat looked ready. Chiang put on the coffee.

Nightingale showed no ill effect and announced that the rest of them could hang about if they liked, but that he was ready to eat. They looked at one another, killed the fields, and carved up dinner. It *was* quite good.

Conversation during meals was limited because of the low temperatures. Eating was strictly business on Deepsix, and if she lived through this, Hutch knew she would always recall these quick impersonal meals, nobody talking while they huddled as close to the fire as they could get, bolting food and coffee in the sting of cold air.

Happy days on the prairie.

They had no salt, no condiments of any kind, but that seemed only a detail.

Hutch made an announcement during the meal: 'Marcel,' she said, 'tells me that the media are only a couple of days away. They were coming to shoot the collision, but now it's all about us.'

'Of course,' said Chiang.

'Anyhow, they're asking whether they'll be able to interview us when they get here.'

MacAllister was clearly enjoying his supper. 'That should be intriguing,' he said, between bites. 'We can have an end-of-the-world party right there on Universal News, which reports only the facts. Without bias or principle.' It was a mild reference to Universal's *Without bias or distortion* credo. He looked toward the eastern sky, bright with unfamiliar constellations. It was too early yet for Morgan. 'Yes, indeed,' he said. 'If they play it right, they should be able to get their best numbers of the year. Except maybe for the World Bowl.'

'Hutch, we got a response from the Academy on your early reports at the tower. They congratulate you for your work and want you

238

to keep digging. That's the phrase they use. *Look for more evidence of the state of their science,* it says. They want you to let the other sites go because there isn't time.'

'Good,' she said. 'Tell them we'll comply.'

'They also want you to be careful. They say to avoid any hazardous situations.'

'Augie, wake up.'

Emma didn't always sleep well, and she sometimes prowled the ship at night. What she did out there he didn't know. It was even possible she ran an occasional liaison with the captain. He didn't really care all that much. As long as she was available when he needed her. But she had hold of his arm at the moment, and was dragging him out of a very sound sleep. His first thought was that the *Edward J. Zwick* had sprung a leak. 'What's wrong?' he asked, looking up at her.

She was the image of delight. 'Augie, we've gotten a *huge* break.'

He tried to imagine what it could be, but utterly failed. *In any case,* he thought, *surely it could wait until morning.*

'They've had an accident,' she said. 'Some of them are stranded down there. They're trying to find a rescue vessel and apparently not having much luck.'

That woke him up. 'What kind of accident? Was anybody killed?'

'Yep. Two or three. And you know who's among the strands? MacAllister.'

'My God. Is that *right*?'

'Absolutely.'

'How could *that* happen?'

'Don't know. They're not putting out details yet. But we've got a great story falling into our laps.' She pressed her lips against his cheek. 'I've already been in touch with them. With Clairveau. And there's no competition within light-years.' She clapped her hands and literally trembled with joy.

Canyon was still trying to grasp what she was telling him. 'They're going to get them off okay, right?'

'Hell, I don't know, Augie. Right now it's touch and go. But if we're lucky, things will stay tense for a while. At least until we get there.'

'We might have a problem,' said Beekman.

The ocean and the northern coastline were on-screen. The area looked cold and gray, and the tide was *very* far out. Marcel wasn't sure he wanted to hear what Beekman was about to tell him.

'It's like what happens,' said Beekman, 'when a tsunami is coming.'

Marcel waited impatiently. It was hard to feel any serious alarm. The coast was a long wall of high mountains. He'd been prepared to hear that there might be disturbances at sea, but the shoreline looked pretty well protected. '*Is* a tsunami coming?' he asked.

'Not exactly.' They were seated in armchairs, in Beekman's office. The project director wore a short-sleeved shirt printed with frolicking dragons that he'd bought in Hong Kong. 'It's just going to be another very high tide. The problem is that, as Morgan approaches, it's going to keep getting higher. Every day. The water's getting distorted by Morgan's gravitational pull. Mounting up. It's the first stage.'

'What's the final stage?'

'The ocean gets ripped out of its bed.'

'Gunny,' Marcel said, 'that's not going to happen tomorrow.'

Beekman nodded. 'No.'

'If it's a problem, why didn't we talk about it before?'

'Because it didn't look as if it would become a factor. Because the coastal range has the ocean effectively blocked off until you get so far east it doesn't matter anymore.'

'What's changed?'

'There are sections of the range that might not hold. That might collapse.'

'Where?'

Beekman showed him.

'When?' he asked.

'Don't know. They could stand up until the water has to come over the top. If that happens, there's nothing to worry about. Or they could give way.'

'Okay. What's the earliest it could break down?'

'We don't know that either. We don't have enough detailed information to be sure.'

'Make a guess.'

'Midnight, Tuesday. Our time.'

Marcel checked his calendars. 'That gives them eight days. *Local* days.'

'Yes.'

'They've lost a couple of days.'

'That shouldn't be a major problem for them. They still have adequate time. But keep in mind, Marcel. It's only a *guess*.'

Marcel nodded. 'I'll alert Hutch.' He felt the bulkheads closing in on him. 'Do we have any ideas for a backup plan?' he asked.

'You mean if *Tess* won't work?'

'That's right.'

He shook his head. 'Short of hoping for divine intervention, no. If *Tess* won't fly, they're dead. It's as simple as that.'

15

One never fully appreciates civilization until the lights go out.

—GREGORY MACALLISTER, *'Patriots in the Woodshed'*.
The Incomplete MacAllister

Hours to breakup (est): 210

'There's got to be a way.'

Beekman's eyes were bloodshot. 'If there is,' he said, 'I'd be grateful to know how.'

'Okay.' Marcel got up and looked down at him. 'You've been talking about the tensile strength of the stuff we cut off the assembly. How about if we removed a piece of that?'

'To do what?'

'To reach them. To give them a way off the surface.'

'Marcel, it would have to be three hundred kilometers long.'

'Gunny, we've got *four* superluminals up here to work with.'

'That's fine. You could have *forty*. So you've also got a very long shaft. What are you going to do with it?'

'Ram it down through the atmosphere. It wouldn't collapse under its own weight, would it?'

'No,' said Beekman. 'It wouldn't. But we'd have no control over it. Atmospheric forces would drive it along the ground at supersonic speed.' He smiled sadly. 'No, you wouldn't want to try to hitch a ride on something like that.'

Marcel was just tired of all the defeatism. 'Okay,' he said, 'I'll tell you what I want to happen. You've got a brain trust of major proportions scattered around this ship. Get them together, do it *now*, put everything else aside. And find a way.'

'Marcel, with any luck *Tess* will be enough to get them off.'

'There are too many things that can go wrong. And if we wait until they do, there'll be no time to come up with an alternative.' He leaned over and seized Beekman's arm. 'Consider it an intellectual challenge, if you want. But find a way.'

Chiang was still awake when Morgan appeared in the east. Surrounding stars faded in its glow, which seemed to have acquired a bluish tint. It was starkly brighter than it had been the previous evening. He could almost make out a disk.

He stood his watch under its baleful light. After Nightingale relieved him, he lay a long time watching it move through the trees. It seemed to him that he'd barely fallen asleep when Kellie roused him. 'Time to get rolling, big fella.' she said.

While they sat wearily around the campfire, breakfasting on the leftover creature meat, Hutch announced that more news had come down from *Wendy*.

'Not good. I take it,' said MacAllister.

'Not good. We've lost a day or two,' said Hutch. 'The tides are rising along the north coast. Because of Morgan. There are mountains up there, but there's a possibility the water will break through onto the plain.'

'A couple of days?' said Kellie.

'We've still got plenty of time.'

'They think if it breaks through, it'll go all the way to the tower?' asked Nightingale.

'That's what they're saying.'

'We need to hustle up,' said Chiang.

The short days were beginning to work on them and they debated whether they should try to switch back to a twenty-four-hour clock and simply ignore the rising and setting of the sun.

Embry advised it would not be a good idea, that their metabolisms would try to adjust to local conditions. 'Anyway,' she added, 'I doubt you want to be walking around down there in the dark.'

They had only about seven hours of sunlight left when they finally got moving.

'You'll come out of the snow line later today,' Marcel told them. 'Looks like relatively easy going from that point on.'

'Okay' said Hutch.

'Oh, and you've got another river to cross. A wide one this time. You'll get to it toward the end of the day.'

'Any bridges?'

'Ho, ho.'

'Seriously, can you guide us to the easiest crossing point?'

'You like wide and slow or narrow and fast?'

'We need a place where we can wade.'

'Can't tell from up here.'

'Make it wide and slow.'

Chiang didn't care for MacAllister. He treated Kellie and Hutch as if they were lackeys and gofers, persons whose sole purpose was to make the world comfortable for people like himself. He ignored Nightingale altogether. He behaved well enough toward Chiang, although there was a degree of condescension that probably was not personal but rather reflected the editor's attitude toward everyone.

Even the gas giant became a target for him. While the others thought of the approaching juggernaut with a degree of awe, MacAllister took to referring to the world by the full name of its discoverer. It became *Jerry Morgan* at first, and eventually just plain *Jerry*.

'Well, I noticed Jerry was pretty bright last night.'

And, 'I do believe Jerry's become a crescent.'

Chiang understood that the great man was frightened, maybe more so than the rest of them because he had a reputation to protect, and he was probably not sure how he'd hold up if things got worse instead of better.

The snow was thinning out, and they began one by one to discard their snowshoes.

They'd broken back out onto a broad plain. It was rolling country, marked by a few scattered trees and occasional patches of thick shrubbery. Toward midafternoon, two autumn-colored bipeds that seemed to be constructed exclusively of fangs and claws tried a coordinated attack from opposite sides. They'd been hiding behind hills and charged as the company passed. But the lasers drove them off and caused MacAllister to observe that these primitive life-forms were no match for somebody with guts and a good weapon. He looked meaningfully at Nightingale, and Hutch had to step between them again.

Tough fibrous grass pushed up through the snow, which by midday disappeared altogether. Purple and yellow shrubbery appeared, with thick stalks and wide, flat-bladed leaves that looked sharp enough to draw blood. They passed through a tree line, and the sunlight faded behind a canopy of branches and leaves. Eight-legged creatures scrambled up the trunks, and Nightingale once again regretted that there was no time for inspection.

They were small and almost invisible against the woodland background, with backs that resembled walnut shells, and triangular heads. They had antennas and beaks and mandibles that twitched constantly. He noted that, when he approached them, the antennas swung in his direction. Some hurried around to the far side of a convenient tree, out of his sight. One simply withdrew into a shell, like a turtle, and clung unmoving to thick bark. When Chiang approached, it fired black spray at him. In the direction of his eyes. It splattered against the e-suit.

Startled, Chiang fell back and went down.

'You were lucky,' said Nightingale, helping him up. 'We don't know these creatures at all. It's a good idea not to be deceived by appearances. If you see something that looks like a chipmunk, don't assume it'll *behave* like one.'

'We need to keep moving,' said Hutch. 'No time for admiring the critters.'

Some of the trees were hardwoods, very much like oak and maple. Others had soft fleshy stems and short prickly branches. Bulbous purple fruit hung from them. Hutch broke off a sample, scooped out a small piece, killed her field, and tried it. She looked pleased. 'Not bad,' she said.

But when Chiang asked to share she shook her head. 'Let's give it a while. See what happens.'

They were pushing through heavy undergrowth when Chiang almost walked off the edge of a crag. The ground simply vanished underfoot. At first he thought he was going into a hole, but the bushes opened up, and he was looking down about six meters onto a scrabble of hard rock and tough-looking greenery. MacAllister grabbed his arm and, after a nervous moment while they struggled for balance, hauled him back.

'That's two we owe you, Mac,' said Kellie. It was the first time anyone had used the shortened form of his name without derision.

The land became increasingly rough, scarred by gullies and ravines.

The earlier problem of getting MacAllister down some of the descents recurred. They tried using cable, but it was thin and smooth, hard to hold on to. And tying it around his waist and using it to lower him down an embankment offended his dignity.

Hutch looked around at the vines that snaked up tree trunks and hung out of the branches and tried to pull one loose. The vine resisted, and it took all of them to drag it out of the tree. When they had sufficient length she cut it, and MacAllister, by then covered with bruises and ready for any kind of solution, consented to use it. It worked fine. He could hang on while they lowered away, and even assist the operation. When the ground finally flattened out, in midafternoon, he threw the vine away, but Hutch retrieved it, coiled it into a loop, and draped it around one shoulder.

Chiang noticed that MacAllister was no longer volunteering to drop back in order to allow the rest of the party to move ahead more quickly. Instead, he silently endured whatever indignities he had to, and worked hard to maintain his pace.

They stopped at a pool, hidden among trees and rocks. 'What do you say,' suggested Hutch, 'we take a break and clean up a bit?'

Kellie was already pulling her blouse out away from her body. 'I'm for it,' she said. 'You guys clear out and build a fire. But guard the trail.'

'What if you get in trouble?' asked Chiang.

She laughed. 'My clothes'll be able to go for help.'

The men retreated. Hutch extracted a small piece of leftover meat and threw it into the water to see if anything would happen. When nothing did, she took up the sentry's position. Kellie shut off her field and wrapped her arms around herself for warmth. Then she took a deep breath and removed her jumpsuit. 'What've we got for pneumonia?' she asked.

'Same as usual,' Hutch smiled. 'Coffee.'

The place looked safe. Consequently, in the interests of saving time, Hutch handed her the soap and a washcloth, laid out two towels and another washcloth, put her own weapon on a rock by the water's edge, removed her gear and her clothes, and waded into the water. It was frigid.

'Nothing like a brisk dip,' Kellie said through lips that were chattering so badly she could barely get the words out.

An icy wind rippled the surface.

'Polar bear nudie club,' said Hutch.

'Water's warmer than out there, though. Once you get used to it.'

'I betcha.'

In fact it was. The water shocked her system as she waded deeper, feeling the frigid tide rise past thighs and hips to her breasts. But once in its embrace, her body adjusted. She scrunched down to keep out of the cold air.

Kellie covered herself with soap and handed it to Hutch, who quickly rubbed some onto her washcloth and began to remove the accumulated dirt and sweat of several days.

Kellie cleaned herself as best she could, and submerged. She came back up into the cold air gasping and shivering. Hutch, also half frozen, moved close to her and they embraced, sharing what body heat they could. When the joint trembling got down to a reasonable level, so that she could speak again, Hutch asked whether she was okay.

'Dandy,' Kellie said.

They retreated into shallower water, finished the job, grabbed the towels, and wiped themselves dry. Then, still naked, they put on their links and belts, reactivated the energy fields, and turned up the heat.

It was a luxurious moment. Hutch stood in the bright sunlight and clasped her arms to her breasts in an instinctive effort to absorb the warmth.

'That was really a thrill out there,' said Kellie. 'We have to do it again.'

'Bonded forever,' said Hutch.

They gazed at one another, and Hutch wasn't quite sure what had happened.

When feeling returned, they bent to the task of washing their clothes. From time to time Chiang called to ask whether they needed help. Kellie assured him they were doing fine, but Hutch could see the pleasure she was taking in the game.

When they'd finished they handed out their clothes to Chiang, and he passed blankets in to them. The clothes were hung over the fire, the women took up sentry duty in their blankets, and the men went into the pool. An hour later they were all dressed and on their way again.

Chiang was unsure what to do about Kellie. The extreme hazard in which they'd been placed had sharpened his desire for her. He had begun seriously considering making a marriage proposal. That notion would have been absurd a few days ago on *Wendy*. But now somehow it seemed like a good idea to commit himself to living his life with this extraordinary woman, and to find out whether she'd be receptive. He'd decided he wanted her, and he suspected that the opportunity would never be better.

Tonight he would ask.

It was getting dark when they filed out onto the riverbank. 'Did Marcel say *wide*?' demanded MacAllister. 'It's the *Mississippi*.'

It was broad and still and lazy in the fading light. Had it been frozen, Chiang estimated they would have needed ten minutes to walk across.

'Marcel,' said Hutch, 'does this thing by any chance go in our direction?'

'Negative. Sorry. You don't get to travel by boat.'

'How do we get across?' asked MacAllister.

It had a steady current. 'We don't swim,' said Hutch.

Nightingale nodded. 'That's a good decision for several reasons.' He pointed, and Chiang saw a pair of eyes rise out of the water and look their way.

'Alligator?' Kellie asked.

'Don't know,' said Hutch.

Nightingale repeated Hutch's test and threw a small piece of meat well out into the stream. A fin broke the surface momentarily, and then there was a brief commotion in the water.

Something in the foliage across the river screeched. A loud racket followed, more screeching, flapping of wings. A large

vulpine creature with black wings flew off, and the general stillness returned.

Chiang examined the trees. 'Anybody good at raft-
building?'

'Just tie some logs together, right?' said Kellie.

'This,' said MacAllister, 'should be a constructive experience
for us all.'

The pun provided some mock laughter.

'Let's get to it,' Hutch said. 'We'll cut the trees now, stay here
tonight, and put the raft together first thing tomorrow.'

'How'd we do today?' asked MacAllister.

'Pretty well,' said Hutch. 'Twenty kilometers.'

'Twenty?'

'Well, nineteen. But that's not bad.'

Chiang spent the evening working up his courage. After the logs
were set aside and the vines collected, Kellie sat quietly eating.
When she'd finished and buttoned up her e-suit, he saw his chance.
Get on her private channel and do the deed.

'Kellie.' His voice didn't sound right.

She turned toward him, and her features were limned in the
firelight. He watched shadows move across her face, and she
seemed more beautiful than any woman he had ever known. 'Yes,
Chiang?' she said.

He started to move toward her but caught himself and decided
it was best to stay where he was. 'I – wanted you to know I'm
in love with you.'

A long silence. The shadows moved some more.

'I've been looking for an opportunity to tell you.'

She nodded. 'I know' she said.

That threw him off-balance. 'You *know*?' He had never said
anything.

'Sure.'

He got to his feet, driven to some form of action, but he settled
for stirring the fire. 'May I ask how you feel about me?' He

251

blurted it out, and immediately knew it sounded clumsy. But there was no way to recall it.

'I like you,' she said quietly.

He waited.

She seemed lost in thought. He wondered whether she was searching her feelings, or looking for a way to let him down gently. 'I don't know.' she said. 'The circumstances we're under . . . It's hard to see clearly.'

'I understand,' he said.

'I'm not sure you do, Chiang. Everything's compressed now. I don't trust my feelings. Or yours. Everything's very emotional. Let's wait till we're back on *Wendy*, when it's not life-and-death anymore. Then if you want to take another plunge at this. I'll be happy to listen.'

Nightingale assumed guard duty. He surveyed the campsite, saw right away there were too many places where something could come up on them unseen, and decided to position himself near the riverbank, where the ground was clear. Chiang picked up the water container and went to the river's edge. MacAllister gathered some branches and started a fire. The women began trying to work out what the raft should look like.

Nightingale studied the water. It was shallow inshore, but muddy and dark. He watched Chiang make a face at it and venture out a few steps. Nightingale asked what he was doing, and Chiang explained he was after clear water. He scooped up some and it must still not have looked very good because he got rid of it and went out a bit farther.

'That's a mistake' said Nightingale. 'Forget it. We'll figure out something else.'

'It's not a—' Chiang's expression changed, and he cried out. Something yanked his feet from under him. He went down and disappeared into the current.

Nightingale whipped out the cutter, ignited it, and charged after him. He couldn't see why Chiang had fallen, but he caught a glimpse of blue-gray tendrils.

Something caught *him*, whipped around his ankles, and tried to drag him down. Then it had his arm. Nightingale sliced at the water. Mud-colored fluid spurted from somewhere.

He almost dropped the laser.

MacAllister arrived, cutter in hand, at the height of the battle. He lashed around like a wild man. The water hissed and tendrils exploded. Nightingale came loose, and then Chiang. By the time the women got there, only seconds after it had begun, it was over.

'It's okay, ladies,' said MacAllister, blowing on his cutter as if it were an old-style six-gun. 'The shooting's over.'

That night they could see Morgan's disk quite clearly. It resembled a tiny half-moon.

They assembled the raft in the morning. They lined up the logs and cut them to specification. Hutch, unsure of her engineering, required crosspieces to hold the craft together. They fashioned paddles and poles, and there was some talk about a sail, but Hutch dismissed it as time-consuming on the ground that they didn't know what they were doing.

It appeared that they were at a drinking hole. A few animals wandered close from time to time, looked curiously at the newcomers, kept their distance, dipped their snouts in the current when they could, and retreated into the forest.

The sun was overhead by the time the raft was ready. Relieved to be underway again, they climbed aboard and set off across the river.

The day was unseasonably warm. In fact, it was almost warm enough to turn off the suits. MacAllister sat down in front, made himself comfortable, and prepared to enjoy the ride.

They'd scouted out a landing spot earlier. It had a beach and no rocks that they could see and was a half kilometer downstream.

Chiang and Hutch used the poles, Kellie and Nightingale paddled, and MacAllister allowed as how he would direct. They moved easily out into the current.

Nightingale watched the banks pass by. He turned at last to Hutch. 'It was criminal of them,' he said, 'simply to abandon this world.'

'The Academy claimed limited resources.' she said.

'That was the official story. The reality is that there was a third-floor power struggle going on. The operations decision became part of a tug-of-war. The wrong side won, so we never came back.' He gazed up at the treetops. 'It never had anything to do with me, but I took the blame.'

MacAllister shielded his eyes from the sun. 'Dreary wilderness,' he said.

'You didn't know *that*, did you, MacAllister?' said Nightingale.

'Didn't know *what*?'

'That there were internal politics involved in the decision. That *I* was a scapegoat.'

MacAllister heaved a long sigh. 'Randall,' he said, 'there are *always* internal politics. I don't think anyone ever really thought *you* prevented further exploration. You simply made it easy for those who had other priorities.' He looked downriver. 'Pity we can't get all the way to the lander on this.'

Kellie was watching something behind them. Nightingale turned to look and saw a flock of birds hovering slowly in their rear, keeping pace. Not birds, he corrected himself. More like bats.

They were formed up in a V, pointed in their direction.

And they weren't bats, either. He'd been misled by the size, but they actually looked more like big dragonflies.

Dragonflies? The bodies were segmented, and as long as his forearm. They had the wingspread of pelicans. But what especially alarmed him was that they were equipped with proboscises that looked like daggers.

'Heads up,' he said.

All eyes turned to the rear.

MacAllister was getting to his feet, getting his cutter out. 'Good,' he said. 'Welcome to Deepsix, where the gnats knock you down first and *then* bite.'

'They *do* seem to be interested in us.' Hutch said.

There might be another problem: They were well toward the middle of the river, and the current was carrying them faster than anyone had anticipated. It was obvious they were going to miss their selected landing place.

The river had become too deep for the poles. Chiang and MacAllister took over the paddles and worked furiously, but they made little headway and could only watch helplessly as they floated past their beach.

The dragonflies stayed with them.

They were operating in sync, riding the wind, their wings only occasionally giving vent to a flurry of movement. 'You think they could be meat-eaters?' Hutch asked Nightingale.

'Sure,' he said. 'But it's more likely they're bloodsuckers.'

'Ugly critters.' said MacAllister.

Hutch agreed. 'If they get within range, we're going to take some of them out.'

'Maybe it's not such a bad thing,' said Chiang, 'that this world is going down the tube.'

MacAllister laughed. It was a booming sound, and it echoed off the river. 'That's not a very scientific attitude,' he said. 'But I'm with you, lad.'

'Oh, shut up, Mac,' said Nightingale. 'It's the efficiency of these creatures that makes them interesting. This is the only really old world we know of, the only one that can show us the results of six billion years of evolution. I'd kill to have some serious time here.'

'Or be killed.' MacAllister shook his head, and his eyes gleamed with good humor. 'Your basic mad scientist,' he added.

Chiang drew his paddle out of the water and laid it on the deck. 'They're getting ready.'

Nightingale saw it, too. They'd been flying in that loose V, spread out across maybe forty meters. Now they closed up, almost wingtip to wingtip.

MacAllister watched Nightingale draw his cutter. 'I'm not sure,' he said, 'that's the best weapon at the moment.' He put his own back into his pocket and hefted the paddle. 'Yeah.' He tried a practice swing. 'This should do fine.'

The dragonflies advanced steadily, approaching to within a few meters. Then they did a remarkable thing: They divided into three separate squadrons, like miniature fighter planes. One stayed aft, the others broke left and right and moved toward the beams.

Hutch held up her hand. *Wait.*

They began to close.

The boat was completely adrift now, headed downriver.

'Wait.'

The ones in the rear moved within range. Kellie and Chiang were in back, facing them.

'Not yet,' said Hutch. 'If they come at us, be careful where you fire. We don't want to take any of our own people out.'

Hutch was on the port side, MacAllister to starboard. Nightingale dropped to one knee beside Hutch. The flanking squadrons moved within range.

'On three.' she said. 'One . . .'

'You know,' said Nightingale, 'this isn't necessarily aggressive behavior.'

'Two . . .'

'As long as they don't actually attack, there's no way to know. They seem to be intelligent. They might be trying to make contact.'

MacAllister shifted his position to face the threat. 'Say hello, Randy,' he said.

'Three,' she said. 'Hit 'em.'

The ruby beams licked out.

Several of the creatures immediately spasmed and spiraled into the water, wings smoking. One landed in what appeared to be a pair of waiting jaws and was snatched beneath the surface.

The others swept in to attack. The air was filled with the beat of wings and a cacophony of clicks and squeals. One of the creatures buried its proboscis in the meaty part of Hutch's arm. MacAllister threw himself at it, knocked her down and almost into the water, but he grabbed the thing, pulled it out, and rammed it against the side of the boat. Laser beams cut the creatures out of the air. Nightingale took a position at MacAllister's back and killed two of them in a single swipe.

Mac meantime stood over the fallen Hutchins like a Praetorian, swinging his paddle, and bashing the brains out of any and all attackers. Amid all the blood, shouts, screams, and fury, and the electric hiss of the weapons, Nightingale grudgingly realized that the big dummy was emerging as the hero of the hour.

And quite suddenly it was over. The dragonflies drew off. Nightingale could count only five survivors. They lined up again, and for a moment he thought there would be a second assault. But they lifted away on the wind, wings barely moving, and turned inshore.

He looked around, assured himself that no one had been seriously injured, and listened to Hutch reassure Marcel. She was sitting on the deck of the raft, holding her injured shoulder.

'Hurts,' she said.

Marcel listened to it all and never said a word. When it was over he took a seat near one of the wallscreens where he could look down on Maleiva III's surface.

He had never felt so utterly helpless.

16

If there is one characteristic that marks all sentient creatures, it is their conviction of their own individual significance. One sees this in their insistence on leaving whatever marks they can of their passing. Thus the only race of starfaring extraterrestrials we know about distributes monuments dedicated to themselves in all sorts of unlikely places. The Noks, with their late-nineteenth-century technology, put their likeness in every park they have. Earth has its pyramids. And we pay schools and churches to name wings, awards, and parking areas after us. Every nitwit who gets promoted to supervisor thinks the rest of creation will eventually happen by and want breathlessly to know everything about him that can possibly be gathered.

—GREGORY MACALLISTER, *'The Moron in the Saddle',*
Editor at Large

Hours to breakup (est): 180

There was no single space on board *Wendy* that was large enough to accommodate everyone. So Beekman compromised by inviting a half dozen of his senior people to the project director's meeting room. Once they were assembled a technician put them on-line to the rest of the ship.

Beekman started by thanking them for coming. 'Ladies and gentlemen,' he continued. 'You're all aware of the situation on the surface. If we're fortunate, there'll be no need for an alternative course of action. But if we don't have one, and we need it, five people will die.

'We were invited to make this flight because somebody thinks we're creative. This is an opportunity to demonstrate the validity of that proposition. I've been telling the captain all along that, if the plan to retrieve and install the capacitors doesn't work, there *is* no alternative to saving the lives of our people. I'd like *you* to prove me wrong.

'I don't need to tell you that we're running out of time. And I also don't need to tell you that I personally see no way to do it. That's why we need *you*. Stretch what's possible. Devise a course of action. *Find* a solution.

'I won't waste any more of your time here. But I'll be standing by. Let me know when you have something.'

They beached the raft, limped ashore, and collapsed. Kellie got the medkit out and Nightingale set to work repairing the wounded. No toxin or biological agent could penetrate the field, so the only problem was loss of blood.

Despite the optimistic report that had gone up to *Wendy*, Nightingale alone had come away uninjured.

Fortunately, the wounds were superficial, but Kellie and MacAllister had both lost too much blood to continue.

The attackers had gotten Kellie twice in the right leg, Hutch in the shoulder. MacAllister in the neck. *That* one looked painful, but Mac just grimaced and did the kind of thing he usually did, commenting on the ancestry of the dragonflies. Chiang had taken bite wounds to the stomach and an arm.

They felt entitled to a rest and, once safely away from the river, they took it. Everyone fretted about losing time, but there was simply no help for it. Nightingale felt emotionally exhausted and would have liked to sleep, but as the only member of the group who hadn't been injured, he was assigned the watch.

They rested for four hours. Then Hutch roused them and got them on the road again.

The forest was filled with insects and blossoms and barbed bushes and creeper vines. Insects buzzed flowers, transferring pollen in the time-honored manner they'd found in every other biosphere. It was evidence once again that nature always took the simplest way. The external appearance of many of the creatures was different, but only in detail. Animals that resembled monkeys and wolves put in brief appearances. They were remarkably similar to kindred creatures elsewhere. The monkeys had long ears and hairless faces and looked very much like tiny humans. The wolves were bigger than their distant cousins, and were equipped with tusks. There was even an equine creature that came very close to qualifying as a unicorn.

The differences weren't limited to appearance. They watched a group of wolves give wide berth to a long-necked pseudo-giraffe which was munching contentedly on a tree limb and paying them no attention. Was the animal's meat toxic? Did the creature possess a long-range sting? Or perhaps skunk scent? They didn't know and there was neither time nor (except for Nightingale) inclination to linger long enough to find out.

Two more potential threats emerged. One was a python-sized serpent with green-and-gray coloring. It watched them with its black marble eyes. But it was not hungry, or it sensed that the oversized monkeys would not prove an easy quarry.

The other was a duplicate of the feline they'd seen from the tower. This one walked casually out of the shrubbery and strolled up to them as if they were old friends. It must have expected them to run. When they didn't, it hesitated momentarily, then showed them a jaw full of incisors. That was enough, and they cut it down with little trouble or regret.

Plants everywhere react to light, and a patient observer can watch them turning their petals toward the sun in its journey across the sky. There were occasional shadings here, structures, odd organs, that led Nightingale to suspect that *this* forest had *eyes*. That it was possibly aware, in some vegetative manner, of their passage. And that it followed them with a kind of divine equanimity.

In another few centuries, give or take, Maleiva and its attendant worlds would be out of the cloud and conditions would return to normal. Or they would if the land was still going to be here. The woods felt *timeless*.

He wondered if the forest, in some indefinable way, *knew* what was coming.

And whether, if it did, it *cared*?

'Hey, Hutch.' Chiang's voice. 'Look at this.'

Chiang and Kellie had gone out to gather firewood. Hutch was seated on a log, rotating her shoulder. She got up and disappeared into the woods. MacAllister, who was security, stayed nearby, but his eyes strayed toward Nightingale, and there was a weariness in them, suggesting he had little patience left for anyone's enthusiasm. They could find a brontosaurus out there, and he wasn't going to care. The only thing that mattered to him was getting home. Everything else was irrelevant.

'It's a *wall*,' said Kellie. Nightingale could see their lights moving out in the darkness.

MacAllister looked at the time, as if it had any relation to the current progress of days and nights. It was almost twelve o'clock back in orbit, but whether noon or midnight, Nightingale had no idea. Nor probably had MacAllister.

Nightingale was desperately weary. He sat with his eyes closed, letting the voices wash over him. A wall just did not seem all that significant.

There was nothing more for several minutes, although he could hear them moving around. Finally, unable to restrain his curiosity, he asked what they'd found.

'Just a wall,' said Chiang. 'Shoulder-high.'

'A building?'

'A *wall*.'

There was a brief commotion in the trees. Animals fighting over something.

'Lot of heavy growth around it,' said Kellie. 'It's been here a long time.'

Nightingale thought about getting to his feet. 'Is it stone?'

'More like bricks.'

'Anybody see the end of it?'

'Over here. It turns a corner.'

'There's a gate. With an arch.'

For several minutes they clumped around in the underbrush with no sound other than an occasional grunt. Then Chiang spoke again, excited: 'I think there's a building back there.'

They had not seen any kind of structure since leaving the tower. Nightingale gave up and reached for his staff. MacAllister saw that he was having difficulty and started over to help. 'It's okay, Gregory,' he said. 'I can manage.'

MacAllister stopped midway. 'My friends call me *Mac*.'

'I didn't know you had any friends.' He collected a lamp and turned it on.

Mac looked at him with a half smile, but there was no sign of anger.

'What kind of arch?' Nightingale asked Kellie.

'Curved. Over a pair of iron gates. Small ones. Pretty much rusted away. But there are some *symbols* carved into it. Into the arch.'

Nightingale, leaning on his staff, started for the woods. 'Do they look like the ones back at the tower?'

'Could be,' said Hutch. 'Hard to tell.'

Metal squealed. Somebody had opened the gate. 'Why don't we see what's inside?' said Chiang.

It hurt to walk. MacAllister sighed loudly. 'You ought to just take it easy. They find anything important, they'll let us know.'

'They already found something important, *Gregory*. Maybe this thing was a country estate of some sort. Who knows what's inside?'

'Why do you care? It's not your field.'

'I'd like very much to know who the original inhabitants were. Wouldn't you?'

'You want an honest answer?'

'I can guess.'

'I'm sure you can. I *know* who the original inhabitants were. They were very likely little hawk-faced guys with blowguns. They murdered one another in wars, and, judging from that tower back there, they were right out of our Middle Ages. Hutch would like to know what gods they worshiped and what their alphabet looked like. I say, who gives a damn? They were just another pack of savages.'

Nightingale arrived at the wall, and it was indeed brickwork. It was low, plain, worn, buried in shrubbery and vines. He wondered what kind of hands had constructed it.

He advanced until he'd reached the gates. They were made of iron, originally painted black, he thought, although now they were heavily corroded and it was hard to be sure. Nevertheless, one of them still moved on its hinges.

They were designed for ornamentation rather than security. Individual bars were molded in the shape of leaves and branches. The artwork seemed mundane, something Nightingale's grandmother might have appreciated. Still, it *was* decorative, and he supposed *that* told them something more about the inhabitants.

He heard MacAllister coming up behind him. He sounded like an elephant in deep grass. The light from his lamp fell across the arch.

It was curved brickwork. The symbols that Kellie had mentioned were engraved on a flat piece of stone mounted on the front. Nightingale thought it was probably the name of the estate. 'Abandon hope,' he said.

'Keep out,' offered MacAllister.

The ground was completely overgrown. If there'd ever been a trail or pathway, nothing was left of it now.

They passed through the gate and saw the others inspecting a small intact building, not much larger, Nightingale thought, than a children's playhouse. It was wheel-shaped, constructed entirely of gray stone, with a roof that angled down from a raised center.

He could see a doorway and a window. Both were thick with vegetation.

Chiang cut his way through to the entrance. He cleared away some of the shrubbery, and they filed in, under the usual low ceiling. First the women, then Chiang, and then Nightingale.

The interior consisted of a single chamber and an alcove. In both, vegetative emblems, flowers and branches and blossoms, were carved into baked clay panels that covered the walls. A stone table dominated the far end of the chamber.

The place smelled of decay. MacAllister finally squeezed through the door and squatted so he wouldn't have to stand bent over. 'It doesn't look all that old.' he said. He put one hand on the floor to steady himself.

Chiang stood by the table. 'What do you think?' he asked, pressing his fingers against it. 'Is it an *altar*?'

The other races of whom humans had knowledge had all established religions early in their history. Nightingale recalled reading Barashko's classic treatise, *Aspects of Intelligence*, in which he'd argued that certain types of iconography were wired into all of the known intelligent species. Sun-symbols and stars, for example, inevitably showed up, as did wings and blood-symbols. There was often a martyred god. And almost everyone seemed to have developed the altar. 'Yes,' Hutch said. 'I don't think there's any question that's what it is.'

It was rough-hewn, a pair of solid blocks fastened together with bolts. Hutch played her lamp on it, wiped down the surface, and studied it.

'What are you looking for?' asked Nightingale.

'Stains. Altars imply sacrifices.'

'Oh.'

'Like *here*.'

Everyone moved forward to look. Nightingale walked into a hole, but Kellie caught him before he fell. There *were* stains. 'Could be water,' he said.

Hutch scraped off a sample, bagged it, and put it in her vest.

MacAllister shifted his weight uncomfortably and looked around. He was bored.

'It's on a dais,' said Kellie. Three very small steps led up to the altar.

MacAllister stood, more or less, and walked closer. 'The chapel in the woods,' he said. 'What do you suppose became of the god-in-residence?'

Hutch flashed her light into a corner. 'Over here.' She got down on a knee, scooped at the debris and dirt, and lifted a fragment of blue stone. 'Looks like part of a statue.'

'Here's more,' said Chiang.

A score of pieces were scattered about. They set them on the altar and took pictures from a variety of angles, which would allow Bill to put them together.

'The fragments are from several distinct figures,' the AI reported back a few minutes later. *'We have one that's approximately complete.'*

'Okay,' said Hutch. 'Can we take a look?'

Marcel sent the image through Kellie's link and it blinked on. Nightingale had seen right away that the statuary had not depicted the hawk-image they'd seen back at the tower. In fact the figure that appeared could hardly have been more different: it had no feathers. It *did* have stalked eyes. A long throat. Long narrow hands ending in claws. Four digits. Eggshell skull. Ridged forehead. No ears or nostrils. Lip-less mouth. Green skin texture, if the coloring had not faded. And a blue robe.

It looked somewhat like a *cricket.*

'What happened to the hawks?' asked Nightingale.

'One or the other is probably mythical,' said Hutch.

'Which? Which is mythical and which represents the locals?'

She frowned at the image. 'I'd say the hawk is mythical.'

'Why?' asked Chiang.

'Because,' said MacAllister, 'the hawk has some grandeur. You wouldn't catch hawks imagining heroes or gods who looked like *crickets*.'

Nightingale exhaled audibly. 'Isn't that a cultural prejudice?'

'Doesn't make it any less valid. Prejudices aren't always invalid, Randy.'

The robe was cinctured down the middle, open at the breast. Its owner wore sandals, and it carried a rod whose top was broken off. A staff. The right arm was also broken, at the elbow. Had it been there, Nightingale was certain, it would have been lifted toward the sky. In prayer. In an effort to invoke divine aid. In a signal to carry on.

Among the missing pieces were an antenna, a leg, a chunk of what could only have been a thorax. But the head was intact. And it struck Nightingale that, despite MacAllister's comment, the creature *did* possess a certain dignity.

'What do you think?' asked Hutch.

The question was directed at him, but MacAllister answered it. 'It's not bad workmanship,' he said.

There was much in the image that spoke to Nightingale. The creature had endured loss and was making its appeal, or perhaps was simply resigning itself. To what? he wondered. To the common death, which is the starting point for all religions? To the everlasting cold, which had become part of the natural order?

'They would have been worth knowing,' said Hutch.

Nightingale agreed.

He was the last to leave.

They'd put a couple of the pieces into artifact bags, taken a final look around, and filed out. Hutch paused at the doorway and turned back toward him. 'Coming?' she asked.

'They've probably been dead a few centuries,' he said.

She gazed at him and seemed worried. He suspected he looked

267

pale and gray. 'There may be a few survivors left. Out in the hills somewhere.'

Nightingale nodded. 'But their civilization's gone. Everything of consequence that they ever did is lost. Every piece of knowledge. Every act of generosity or courage. Every philosophical debate. It's as if none of it ever happened.'

'Does it matter?' she asked.

He had no answer. He walked slowly out of the chapel and paused in the doorway. 'I guess not. But I'd prefer to think it's only a pile of rock and water that's going to get swallowed next week by Jerry. And not a history.'

Hutch nodded. 'I know.'

He looked at the artifact bag. 'The god. Who's here to rescue the god?'

She gazed at him and he saw a sad, pensive smile. 'We are.' she said. 'We're taking him home with us.'

'Where he'll have no believers.'

'Careful. Randy. Keep talking like that and people will think you're an archeologist.'

A few minutes later, as they walked under the arch, a temblor hit. They stopped and waited for it to pass.

Beekman appeared on-screen wearing a triumphant smile. 'We were right, Marcel,' he said. 'It's *there*.'

Marcel, wrapped in his own dark thoughts, had been staring down at the planetary surface. 'What's *where*, Gunther?'

'The skyhook base.'

'You found it!'

'Yes. It was right where we thought.'

'On the west coast.'

'Mt. Blue. There's a large structure on top. Six-sided. About two hundred meters across. It's enormous.'

'How high is it?'

'It's about six, seven stories. Looks as if it was broken off at the top.'

'And the rest of it?'

'In the ocean. It's all over the sea bottom. Hundreds of square kilometers of wreckage.' He brought up pictures.

Marcel looked at the outline of the mountaintop structure, and then at vast agglomerations of underwater debris. Some pieces even jutted above the surface.

'It's been a while since it happened' said Beekman. 'The fragments that stick up out of the water look like rocky islands.' That had in fact been the assessment during *Wendy*'s original hasty survey. 'We really don't have the right people *or* the equipment to do an analysis, but we think that if we reassembled the pieces on the bottom, we'd have a piece of the skyhook approximately a hundred kilometers high.'

'I wonder where the station itself is?' said Marcel.

Beekman shrugged. 'Who knows? We don't even know how long ago it broke up. But once we get through this, it would be worth the Academy's time to send another mission out here to look for it.'

Marcel studied the images. 'I don't understand,' he said, 'how these people could build a *skyhook*, but not leave anything in the way of a skyscraper. Or any other kind of technological artifact. Is everything buried under the glaciers?'

'Nobody has any idea,' said Beekman. 'And we have neither time nor equipment to conduct a survey. I suggest we just gather as much evidence as we can. And keep an open mind.'

'What you're telling me is that we may never get the answers to any of this.'

Beekman could not have agreed more completely. 'That's exactly right,' he said.

Marcel sighed. 'There should be *something*. Structures of some sort. I mean, you can't just have a lot of walled candlelit cities, and at the same time run equipment into orbit.' He flipped a pen across his console. 'They *did* check for that, right? The tower had no electrical capability? No real power source?'

He meant Hutch and her team. 'She was asked to look for

technology' said Beekman. 'But I think they assumed there was none. I think we *all* assumed it.'

'Well, there you go then. Maybe we were just not looking closely enough.'

'I don't think that could be. I mean, this was a *blowgun* culture.'

'Has it occurred to you,' Marcel said, 'that maybe the tower was a *museum*? Maybe *our* artifacts *were somebody else's* artifacts first.'

'That would require a fairly unlikely coincidence.'

'Gunther, when will we get back a reading on the skyhook's dates?'

'Shouldn't take long. We scanned the samples and sent the results. The Academy will have them by now. We asked for a quick turnaround, so we should get them in a few days.' He crossed his arms. 'It's really sad. I know damned well there are people back at the Academy who'd do anything to get a look at the base of the skyhook.'

Marcel said nothing.

'Maybe if the lander works okay,' Beekman suggested, 'we could ask Hutch to take a peek. Before they come back to orbit.'

'Not a chance,' said Marcel. 'If the lander works, we're bringing them home. No side stops.'

Captain Nicholson had carefully assigned full responsibility for the lander accident to Wetheral who, he'd reported, had taken the vehicle without permission. Probably, he suggested, the passengers had offered him a substantial sum for the service. He added that they were not likely to be aware that the flight was unauthorized. Because one of the passengers was the renowned editor and essayist Gregory MacAllister, he advised Corporate to find a way to overlook the incident. If he survives, Nicholson had argued, MacAllister would be a dangerous adversary should TransGalactic assume he was in some way responsible and try to take legal action against him. If he does not, there would be little advantage to pursuing him beyond the grave. Undoubtedly

Corporate could collect damages from his estate, but the cost in public relations would be enormous. Best call it an unfortunate incident.

He'd been eating a listless breakfast, trying to maintain a conversation with the frivolous guests at his table, receiving periodic updates from Clairveau. The landing party had been attacked by giant flying bugs, and they'd discovered a chapel of some sort in the forest. The important thing was that they were still on schedule to reach *Tess*. At this point, that was all that mattered.

The experience had driven a lesson home: He would never again allow himself to be talked into violating procedure. Not ever. Not for any reason. Periodically one or another of his guests jerked him back to the table with a question about the gift shop on the Starlight Deck or the collision parties planned for Saturday night. He moved his eggs around on his plate and answered as best he could.

One bad decision, allowing MacAllister to have his way, threatened to negate the solid performance of a lifetime. And it had not been his idea at all. He had in fact been pressured. Placed in a no-win situation by a pushy passenger with power and a management that wouldn't have backed him had MacAllister become offended.

It was an outrage.

His link vibrated against his wrist. He raised it casually to his ear. 'Captain,' said his officer of the deck. 'Eyes only for you. From Corporate.'

This would be management's first response to the debacle.

'Be there in a minute,' he whispered. *Please, Lord, let me survive this one time*. He drew the cloth napkin to his lips and rose, apologizing for the interruption but explaining he had to make a command decision. He smiled charmingly at the ladies, shook hands firmly with their escorts, and heard himself referred to as a *good man* as he hurried away.

He went directly to the bridge, heart pounding. The OOD, who could not have missed the gravity of the situation, greeted him with a polite nod. Nicholson returned the gesture, sat down in his chair, and directed the AI to put the message through.

FROM: DIRECTOR, OPERATIONS
TO: CAPTAIN. EVENING STAR
DTC: 11/28 1625
CONFIDENTIAL // EYES ONLY

ERIK, YOU UNDERSTAND MAJOR LIABILITY POTENTIAL HERE. DO WHATEVER YOU CAN TO EFFECT RESCUE. KEEP ADVISED. YOU MIGHT WANT TO CONTACT PRESCOTT.

BAKER

Contact Prescott.

Prescott was a law firm that specialized in defending off-world nonjurisdictional cases. They were telling him he could expect to be held accountable. That signaled the end of his career, at the very least. If they elected to prosecute, God knew what might happen to him.

He sat miserably staring at the message. And he envied MacAllister.

17

Watching Harcourt die taught me a theological lesson: Life is short; never fail to do something you really want to do simply because you're afraid of being caught.

—GREGORY MACALLISTER, 'The Last Hours of Abbey Harcourt', *Show Me the Money*

Hours to breakup (est): 153

The news that the mission had found the skyhook base didn't cheer anybody on the ground. They were far too engaged worrying about their skins.

'Pity it's not up and working,' said Chiang. 'We could use a skyhook.'

'Actually.' said Hutch, 'it *is* nearby.'

'Really? Where?'

'On the western side of the continent. It's on a mountaintop on the coast.'

'I wouldn't mind seeing it before we go,' said Nightingale.

MacAllister shook his head. Do these people never learn? 'I think,' he said, 'we should not tempt fate. Let's concentrate on getting our rear ends out of here.'

*

'There might be a way.' The grayness that had settled about Beekman had lifted slightly. Only slightly, but Marcel caught a glimpse of hope.

Marcel had been convinced by the intensity of Beekman's consistent position that no alternate method of rescue was possible. The captain had been standing on the bridge for two hours staring out at the spectacle of the approaching giant, thinking how it had all been bravado, challenge the best minds they had, come up with something, when it was quite clear there was nothing *anybody* could come up with.

Now he was confronted by this same man, gone partly mad, perhaps. Marcel did not believe him. 'How?' he asked.

'Actually, it was y*our* idea.'

'*My* idea?'

'Yes. I repeated our conversation to several of them. John thinks you might be on to something.'

'John *Drummond*?'

'Yes.'

'What am I on to?'

'Lowering a rope. Cutting off a piece of the assembly. We've been looking at the possibility of constructing a scoop.'

'Could we actually do something like that? You said it was impossible.'

'Well, we can't get it down to the ground. They're going to have to make some altitude. But if they can do *that,* if they can get *Tess* into the air, get up a bit, then yes, it might be possible.' He sat down and pushed his palms together. 'I'm not saying it'll be easy. I'm not even saying it'll be anything but a long shot. But yes, if we set things up, and we get lucky, it *might* be made to work.'

'How? What do we have to do?'

Beekman explained the idea they'd worked out. He drew diagrams and answered questions. He brought up computer images and ran schematics across the displays. 'The critical thing,' he concluded, 'is *time*. We may not have enough time for all this.'

'Then let's get started. What do you want me to do?'

'First, we need a lot of help. We need people who can go outside and *work*.'

'I can do that. So can Mira.'

'I'm not talking *two* people. I'm talking whole squadrons.'

'Okay. So we ask for volunteers. Do a little basic training.'

'This is stuff that's going to take people with some coordination. Our folks are all theorists. They'd kill themselves out there.'

'So what kind of coordinated types do we need?'

'To start with, welders.'

'Welders.'

'Right. And I have to tell you, I have no idea where we'd be able to get them.'

'Welding? How hard can it be?'

'I don't know. I've never done it.'

'It seems to me we only need one person who knows how to do it. I mean, he can teach the others.'

'So where do we find the one person?'

'Nobody here?'

'I've already looked.'

'All right. Then we go to the *Star*. There are fifteen hundred people over there. *Somebody* ought to know something about it.' He was already scratching notes. Suddenly he looked up and frowned. 'It won't work,' he said.

'Why not?'

'You're talking about a lot of e-suits. We have *four* on board. Maybe a few more on the other ships.'

'We already checked it out. Hutch was hauling a shipment of them. They're on board *Wildside*, generators, boots, everything we need.'

'Okay.' Marcel felt a fresh surge of hope. 'What about the welds? Will they actually hold? We're putting a lot of weight on them.'

Beekman nodded. 'We're confident. That's the best I can tell you. We have four ships to work with, and that's a lot of lock-down space. The material is superlight. So yes. if you ask me will it hold. I'm sure it will. If we do a good job.'

'All right. What else do we need?'

'We're still working on it.'

'Okay,' he said. 'Put together a complete list. Get it to me as soon as you have it. And. Gunther—'

'Yes?'

'Assume we're going to have to use it.'

Nicholson was loitering in the dining room with several of his passengers when his commlink vibrated. '*Command call, sir,*' said the AI's voice.

He excused himself and retreated to a private inner lounge. 'Put it through, Lori.'

Marcel Clairveau materialized. 'Erik.' he said, 'I need your help.'

'Of course. What can I do for you?'

'You're aware that we have no assurances the people on the ground will ever be able to reach orbit.'

'I understand the situation completely.' To Nicholson, facing ruin and disgrace whatever he did, it was hard to get emotionally worked up. So he had to make an effort to show that he was dismayed.

'There might be another way to go. If we have to. It would be on the desperate side, but it would be prudent for us to be prepared.' He paused, looking steadily into Nicholson's eyes. 'We'll require your assistance.'

'You know I'll do what I can.'

'Good. We need some volunteers, especially anyone with experience working in space, any engineers, anybody who has helped with large-scale construction. And a welder. Or several welders. But we have to have at least one.'

Nicholson shook his head, puzzled. 'May I ask why. Captain?'

'Some of them, the ones who are willing, will be given a couple of days' training. Then, if we need to go ahead with the alternative plan, most of them will go outside.'

'My God, Marcel.' Nicholson's pulse began to pound. 'Have you lost your mind?'

'We'll be very careful, Erik. We'll do it only as a last resort.'

'I don't care *how* careful you plan to be. I'm not going to permit *my* passengers to be sent outside. You have any idea how Corporate would react if I allowed something like that?'

'Corporate might not be too upset if you succeeded in rescuing MacAllister.'

'*No,*' he said. 'It's out of the question.'

Marcel's image gazed at him. 'You understand there'll be an investigation when it's over. I'd have no choice but to file a complaint against you.'

'File and be damned!' he said. 'I won't let you risk my passengers.'

When darkness fell *Wendy* reported that they'd covered another twenty-four kilometers. By far their best day yet. That was attributable largely to the fact that the ground had become easier, and both MacAllister and Nightingale seemed to be growing accustomed to the routine.

They stopped by a stream, caught some fish, and cooked them. MacAllister acted as taster this time. He swallowed a small piece and became almost immediately violently ill. They threw the rest back and used the last of the reddimeals.

MacAllister was still retching at midnight, when Jerry rose. (They'd all picked up his habit of referring to it by Morgan's first name. It seemed less threatening that way.) The disk was quite clear. It was in a half-moon phase.

The gas giant was well above the trees before his stomach settled down enough to let him sleep. By dawn he was back to his normal abrasive self. He refused Hutch's offer to give him a couple more hours to rest.

'No time.' he said, directing their attention toward Morgan. 'Clock's running.'

They set off at a good pace. The assorted wounds from the

battle on the river were healing. Nightingale had soaked his blisters in warm water and medications, so even he was feeling better.

The land was flat and the walking easy. During the late afternoon, they broke by the side of a stream, and Marcel told them they were within seventy-five kilometers of the lander.

Plenty of time. 'What's the northern coast look like?' Hutch asked.

'It's holding.'

'Is that good or bad?'

'It's touch-and-go,' he said. 'We think you'll be all right.'

Despite the good news, they pushed hard. Hutch shortened their breaks, and they literally ate on the march. Twice they were attacked, once by a group of *things* that looked like tumbleweeds, but which tried to sting and take down Hutch; and later, toward the end of the afternoon, by a flock of redbirds.

Nightingale recognized the redbirds as the same creatures that had overwhelmed the original expedition. This time there were fewer of them, and they were beaten off with relative ease. Kellie and Chiang were gouged during the incidents, but neither injury was severe.

Late that afternoon, they came across a field of magnificent purple blossoms. The flowers resembled giant orchids, supported by thick green stalks. They were within sixty-three kilometers of the lander, with four days remaining.

They hoped.

Nightingale looked exhausted, so Hutch decided to quit for an hour. They were, she thought, in good shape.

They'd sampled several different types of fruit by then and had found a couple they enjoyed. Mostly they were berries of a fairly tough nature, inured to the climate, but edible (and almost tasty) all the same. They located some, passed them around, and were glad to get off their feet.

Hutch wasn't hungry, and ate only enough to satisfy her conscience. Then she got up.

'Where you going?' asked Chiang.

'Washroom,' she said. 'I'll be back in a minute.'

'Wait.' Kellie jumped up. 'I'll ride shotgun.'

Hutch waved her away. The orchid patch was isolated, and beyond it they could see for a long distance. Nothing could approach unnoticed. 'It's okay. I'll yell if I need help.' She walked into the shrubbery.

After she'd finished, lured by the exquisite beauty of the giant blossoms, she took a few minutes in seclusion to enjoy the sense of well-being attendant on the forest. The day had grown uncharacteristically warm, and she liked the scent of the woods, mint and musk and pine and maybe orange. Consequently she left the e-suit off.

She approached one of the blossoms and stood before it. She stroked the petal, which was erotically soft.

Hutch regretted that these magnificent flowers were about to go extinct, and wondered whether it might be possible to rescue some pollen, take it back, and reproduce them at home. She walked from one to the next, gazing at each. At the fragile gold stamen and the long green shaft of the pistil, surging up from the receptacle. She stopped in front of one. The woods grew utterly still. She glanced around to be sure no one was watching, wondered why she cared, and stroked the pistil with her fingertips. Caressed it and felt it throb gently under her touch.

'You okay, Hutch?'

She jumped, thinking that Kellie had come up behind her, but the voice was on the link.

'I'm fine,' she said. 'Be back in a minute.'

A tide of inexpressible well-being rose through her. She took the pistil in her hands, drew it against her cheek, and luxuriated in its warmth.

The flower moved.

The soft sheaths of the petals brushed her face. She inhaled the sweet green scent, and the burden of the last few days dropped away.

She rubbed her shoulders and cheek against the blossom. Closed her eyes. Wished that she could stop time. Felt a tide of ecstasy sweep through her. She came thoroughly *alive,* rode some sort of wave, understood she was living through a moment she would remember forever.

She rocked slowly in the flower's embrace. Fondled the pistil. Felt the last of her inhibitions melt.

The blossom moved with her. Entwined her. Caressed her.

She got out of her blouse.

The outside world faded.

And she gave herself to it.

She was drowning when the voices pulled her back. But they were on the link and far away. Of no concern. She let them go.

Everything seemed far away. She drank the sensations of the moment, and laughed because there was something perverted about all this, but she couldn't quite pin it down and didn't really care. She just hoped nobody walked out of the woods and saw what she was doing.

And then she didn't care about that either.

She wasn't sure precisely when the light grew harsh, when the erotics switched off and the sheer joy vanished and she was simply looking out of a cave, as if she were buried somewhere back in her brain, unable to feel, unable to control her body. She thought she was in danger, but she couldn't rouse herself to care. Then something was tugging at her, and the voices became urgent. There was a great deal of pulling and shoving. The petals gave way to the hard earth, and she was on the ground. They were all kneeling around her and Kellie was applying ointment, telling her to keep still, assuring her she'd be okay. 'Trying to punch out a *tree?*' asked MacAllister, using the coital expression of the moment. 'I don't think I've ever seen *that* before.'

The blossom lay blackened and torn. Its fragile petals were scattered, and the pistil was broken. She was sorry for that.

'*Come on, Hutch, talk to me.*'

The other flowers swayed in sync. Or was it a breeze causing the effect?

Her neck, arms, and face burned. 'That's quite a ride,' she said. And giggled.

Kellie looked at her disapprovingly. 'At your age, you should know better.'

'It must put out an allergen,' said Nightingale. 'Apparently pretty strong stuff.'

'I guess.' Hutch still felt detached. As if she were curled up inside her brain. And she was resentful.

'I think you're a little too big for it,' Nightingale explained. 'But it was doing its damnedest when we got here.'

'Why do I hurt?' she asked.

'It tried to digest you, Hutch.'

Kellie was finished with the medication, so they activated her suit. That had the effect of getting her a supply of air with the peculiarities added by the environment filtered out. The sense that everything was funny and that they should have let her alone began to fade. She held out her arms and looked at dark patches of skin.

'Enzymes were already working when we took you out,' said Kellie.

'Psychotic flower,' she said.

Chiang laughed. 'And oversexed Earth babes.'

Her clothing was in tatters, and Nightingale produced one of the *Star* jumpsuits they'd recovered from the lander. 'It looks big, but it's the smallest we have.'

She was shivering now. And embarrassed. My God, what had she been doing when they found her? 'I can't believe that happened.' she said.

'Do you remember your first rule?' asked Nightingale.

'Yeah.' *Nobody goes off alone.*

She couldn't walk. 'Some pretty good burns there.' said Kellie. 'We'd better stop here for the night. See how you are tomorrow.'

She didn't object when they carried her back. They laid her down and built a fire. She closed her eyes and recalled an incident when she'd been about thirteen, the first time she'd allowed a boy to get inside her blouse. It had been in a utility shed out back of the house, and her mother had walked in on them. The boy had tried to brazen it out, to pretend nothing had happened, but Hutch had been humiliated, had gone to her room and thought the world was about to end, even though she'd extracted a promise that her father would not be told. This in return for a guarantee that it would not happen again. It hadn't. At least not during *that* summer.

She felt a similar level of humiliation. Lying with her eyes closed, hearing no conversation because everyone was off-channel so as not to disturb her, she listened to the fire and to the occasional sound of footsteps, and wished she could disappear somewhere. Her reputation was demolished. And with MacAllister here, of all people. He'd eventually write an account of all this, and Hutch and the blossom could expect to show up on Universal News.

Was there anybody else, she wondered, in the whole history of the species, who had tried to make it with a plant?

It was dark when she woke. The fire had died down, and she could see Kellie seated on a log nearby. The flickering light threw moving shadows across her features.

The giant blossom had shown up in her dreams, part terrifying, part exhilarating. For a while she lay quietly, thinking about it, hoping to assign the entire experience to fantasy. But it *had* happened.

She decided that she would sue the Academy when she got home.

'You awake?' Kellie asked.

'Reluctantly.'

She smiled and kept her voice low. 'Don't worry about it.' And, after a moment: 'Was it really that good?'

'How do you mean?'

'You looked as if you were having a great time.'

'Yeah. I guess I was.' She pulled herself up. 'How late is it?'

Morgan was directly overhead, getting bigger all the time. Half the giant world was in shadow.

'You're changing the subject.'

'What can I tell you, Kellie? I just lost control of everything.'

Kellie stirred the fire. Sparks rose into the night. 'A big pitcher plant. It's a strange place.'

'Yeah, it is.'

'It could have happened to either of us. But everyone understands.' She looked at Hutch's right arm. 'You should be all right in the morning.' Apparently during the encounter Hutch had succeeded in getting altogether out of her clothes. She had burns on both legs, her right arm, her pelvic area, waist, breasts, throat, and face. 'You were a mess when we brought you back here,' Kellie added with a smile.

Hutch wanted to change the subject. 'We lost a little time today.'

'Not really. We did all right. Randy was done for the day anyhow.'

Hutch stared off into the darkness. She could see the outlines of the giant blossoms against the sky. 'Randy thinks they have *eyes*' Kellie said.

She shuddered. Hutch had been assigning the experience to a simple programmed force of nature. But *eyes*. That made it personal.

'Maybe not exactly *eyes*,' she continued, 'but light receptors that are pretty sophisticated. He says he thinks the local plant life is far beyond anything we've seen elsewhere.'

Hutch didn't like being so close to them. She felt violated.

'He thinks they may even have a kind of nervous system. He's looked at a couple of the smaller ones. They don't like being uprooted or dissected.'

'How do you mean, *they don't like it?*'

'The parts move.'

'They sure do,' she said.

The *Edward J. Zwick* arrived in the Maleiva area without fanfare. Canyon looked at Morgan's World through the scopes, and at Deepsix, and felt sorry for the people trapped on the ground.

Zwick was named for a journalist who'd been killed while covering one of the numerous border wars in South America at the end of the century. Its captain was a thirty-eight-year-old former Peacekeeper named Miles Chastain. Miles was tall, lean, quiet. Something in his manner made Canyon uncomfortable. The man always seemed so serious.

He was, Canyon thought, the sort of person to have on your side if war broke out, but not someone you'd routinely invite for dinner. He had never been able to get close to the captain on the long voyage from Earth.

Emma had complained that Wilfrid, the AI, was better company. Certainly he was friendlier. Her attitude suggested the absurdity of his earlier suspicion that an affair of the heart was being conducted in the midnight corridors of the *Zwick*.

The captain spent most of his time in the cockpit or in his private quarters. He never initiated conversation unless business called for it. And once they arrived in orbit around Deepsix, there was really little for him to do except await the collision.

His commlink vibrated. It was Emma. 'August,' she said, 'I just overheard an odd conversation between Kellie Collier and Clairveau.'

'Really? What about?'

'Clairveau was wondering why they were late getting started. Kellie Collier told him that Hutchins was resting. That she'd been attacked by a *plant*.'

'By a *plant*?'

'That's what she said.'

18

Put men and women in the same room and everyone's IQ drops thirty-six points. Psychologists have recorded it, tests have shown it, studies leave no doubt. Passion doth make fools of us all.

—GREGORY MACALLISTER, *'Love and Chocolate'*,
Targets of Opportunity

Hours to breakup (est): 140

Lori's matronly image appeared on Nicholson's command screen. The AI was wearing a formal black suit with a white scarf. That was designed to impress him that the business she wished to transact was quite serious. Of course, he knew what it was.

'I think it's a mistake to refuse to help,' she said.

'My first duty is the safety of my passengers, Lori.'

'The regulations are a bit murky in this situation. In any case, one of your passengers is in extremis. *In addition, you have instructions from Corporate to cooperate with any rescue effort.'*

'That transmission won't be worth a damn if somebody volunteers and gets killed.'

'I quite agree. Captain. But I have to point out that if the current situation does not change, and Mr MacAllister loses his life, you will be in severe difficulty for having withheld assistance.'

'I know.'

'The only course that might get you through undamaged is to help where you can and hope no one is injured. If that happens . . .'

Nicholson ran his fingers through his hair. He could not see which course was safer.

'It is not my decision, Captain,' she said. 'But it is my responsibility to offer counsel. Do you wish me to contact Captain Clairveau?'

Marcel had instructed Beekman to continue working on the extraction plan. He intended to have another try at persuading Nicholson to help. But he needed to give him time to think about the decision he'd made. Time to fret.

The auxiliary screen began to blink. *CAPTAIN NICHOLSON WANTS TO SPEAK WITH YOU.*

It was quicker than he'd expected.

'We also need somebody who can rig a remote pump.'

'A remote pump?'

'Listen. Erik. I know how all this sounds. But I don't have time to go over everything at the moment. We started late and we've got a lot of ground to cover. Please just trust me for now.'

'All right, Marcel. I'll make an announcement at dinner this evening.'

'No. Not this evening. That'll be too late. Round up whatever volunteers you can get *now.* I'll want to talk to them, too. The ones who will help, and that we can use, will come over forthwith.'

'My God, Marcel, that's pressing it a bit, isn't it? Are we talking *this minute?'*

'Yes, we are.'

'At least tell me what you're planning to do?'

'*We* are going to make a skyhook, Erik.'

'Bill.'

'*Yes, Marcel.*'

'Tomorrow morning we'll take all four ships out to the assembly. Coordinate with the other AIs.'

Nicholson got on the *Star's* public address system, informed his passengers and crew that he knew everyone was aware of the difficulties that had been encountered extracting the landing party from Maleiva III, but went on to describe them anyway. 'We are still endeavoring,' he said, 'to mount a rescue.' He gazed steadily into the lens, imagining himself as an old warrior rallying the troops to victory. 'To provide insurance that we succeed,' he continued, 'we need your help.

'Let me now introduce Captain Clairveau of the *Wendy Jay*, who'll explain what we hope to be able to do. I urge you to listen carefully, and if you feel you can assist, please volunteer.

'Captain Clairveau.'

Marcel explained the general plan and made an emotional plea for passengers and crew to come forward, even those who possessed no special skills. 'We're going to have to train people, and we have only a couple of days to get it done. Most of the volunteers may be asked to go outside. That will depend on what happens on the ground.

'I'd like to underscore the fact that while going outside entails a degree of risk, it is not innately dangerous. The suits are safe. But I wanted you to know that up front. And I'd like to thank you in advance for listening.'

Within ten minutes after he signed off, Nicholson found himself awash with volunteers.

'There's one more thing, Erik.'

My God. What else could the man want?

'We both know this operation is going to require extremely

287

close coordination among the four vessels. There is simply no margin for error.'

'I understand that. What do you need?'

Marcel looked down from the overhead screen. It struck Nicholson that the man was aging before his eyes. 'During the operation, I'll want you to turn control of the *Star* over to us. We'll run everything from here.'

'I can't do that, Marcel. Even if I wanted to. I couldn't. It's against the regs.'

Marcel took a moment before responding. 'If we don't do it this way, we can't possibly succeed.'

Nicholson shook his head. 'There's no way I can comply. That's *too* much. No matter how the operation turned out, they'd hang me.'

Marcel stared at him a few moments. 'Tell you what,' he said. 'How about if we come over there? And run the operation from the *Star*?'

An hour seldom passed that Embry didn't thank her good sense for passing on Hutch's offer to go on the mission. She had mourned Toni's death, and she wished she could do something for the others. But if she'd learned anything from this experience, it was that you didn't undertake potentially lethal assignments on the fly. These things required adequate preparation and planning. The sober truth was that a few people at the Academy hadn't done their jobs, they'd tried to compensate by rushing Hutchins in, and now poor Hutch was stuck with paying the price.

During the first couple of days, before things went wrong, both she and Tom had simply been annoyed at the delay. She'd sent messages off to people at home, complaining about having to spend an extra month or so floating around in the middle of nowhere. She'd even told several of her friends that she was considering legal action against Hutchins and the Academy.

Tom had been more tolerant. He was apparently accustomed to Academy mismanagement and didn't seem to expect them to be organized. He was not at all surprised that the original survey had missed the presence of ruins on Deepsix. 'A planet's a *big* place,' he'd told her. If the civilization had been in an early stage of development when the ice age hit, as was apparently the case, there would have been few cities to find. It was no wonder, he argued, that they hadn't realized what they had. He'd have been impressed, he said, if they *had* detected it.

The turmoil on the ground was reflected in the apprehension onboard *Wildside*. Embry had experienced pangs of guilt when she realized the implication of the lost landers. She could not see how she was in any way responsible for any of this, and yet she was trying to take it on her own shoulders. Ridiculous.

She and Tom had from the beginning been sitting by the monitors listening to the conversations between the landing party and the command people on *Wendy*. When Clairveau had contacted them to let them know that a rescue vessel was on the way, she'd demanded to know how such a thing could be allowed to happen in the first place. He'd apologized, but explained that they simply could not provide for all contingencies. How could anyone have foreseen that *both* landers would be destroyed?

She might have replied that the second lander, the vehicle from the *Evening Star*, should not even have been there. It hadn't been part of what passed for Academy planning. There'd been only *one* lander really available, so the risk had been considerable right from the start.

Circumstances. It all came down to circumstances. After her conversation with the captain of the *Wendy Jay*, Tom had argued that it just wasn't always possible to eliminate the element of danger. It didn't matter, he said, what someone had done or not done twenty years earlier. The only thing that mattered was the present situation. Hutchins had been given a directive, she'd decided the payoff was worth whatever risk might be involved, and she'd consequently chosen to accept the assignment. You couldn't fault her for that.

But people had died, and more people might follow. It was

hard for Embry to accept the position that nobody was responsible. When things went wrong, in her view, someone was always responsible.

But *something* positive was coming out of the wreckage. She and Scolari, left alone and forgotten on *Wildside*, save when somebody needed medical advice, had taken comfort in each other's arms.

They listened to Canyon's periodic reports on the news link, she with contempt, Tom with his usual tolerance. 'He probably feels it just as much as we do,' he told her. 'It's just that for public consumption he has to let his feelings show. *That's* what's distasteful.'

She didn't believe it. Canyon was exploiting the disaster, profiting by it, and was probably thanking his lucky stars he'd been sent out here.

She was sitting with Tom, talking about future plans, how they would handle things when they got home. They lived on opposite sides of the North American continent, and would be forced to conduct a virtual relationship for a while. Neither was quite ready yet to make a permanent commitment. But that was not necessarily a major detriment. In an age of sophisticated technology, there was little even of an intimate nature that could not be carried out at long range.

Tom was describing how they should get together during their vacations when the monitor buzzed. Incoming.

'Put it up. Bill,' he told the AI.

Clairveau's image blinked on. He looked tired, she thought. Worn-out. 'Tom,' he said, 'I understand you have some lasers on board? Portables?'

'Yes. They have some back there somewhere.'

'Good. I need you to break them out. I'll send a shuttle for them.'

'What are you going to do?' asked Embry. 'Why do you need lasers?'

'To rescue your captain.'

'Really?' asked Tom. 'How?'

'Later. I'm on the run at the moment.'

'Do you need help?'

'By all means,' said Clairveau. 'We need all the help we can get.'

When he'd signed off, she could feel the tension in the compartment. 'Tom,' she said finally, 'you don't know anything about welding.'

'I know,' he said. 'But how hard can it be?'

'Ladies and gentlemen, this is Captain Nicholson. As you're aware, the original schedule called for us to leave our present position in two days, on Monday, and to withdraw approximately seventy million kilometers in order to be well out of the way when the collision occurs Saturday evening.

'We have, however, offered to assist in the rescue effort. That means we'll be staying in the immediate area somewhat longer. I want to stress that the *Evening Star* will at no time be at hazard. Let me repeat that, there will be absolutely no danger to this ship. We'll be away long before anyone need be concerned.

'You may wonder what part the *Evening Star* will play in rescuing the stranded scientists. We're making a detailed explanation available on the ship's net. Simply go to the Rescue site. A specially produced and embossed copy of the plan, which you may wish to keep as a souvenir of the occasion, will be distributed later today.

'We also intend to present everyone on board with a skyhook pin as a special memento.

'Ship's meals this evening will be served compliments of InterGalactic Lines. Happy hour will begin, as usual, at five. If you have any questions, my officers will be available throughout the ship.

'Thank you very much for your patience during a difficult period. Be assured we will keep you informed as matters develop.'

Within minutes after the captain's address, Marcel arrived with several people in tow. They were the team of mathematicians and physicists who were planning the backup mission. They were escorted to the temporary command center Nicholson had set up.

Nicholson sat quietly while they talked of releasing the asteroid, detaching a shaft and the net from the rest of the assembly, rotating it almost 360 degrees, and putting it on a trajectory for Deepsix. They traced the anticipated changes in stress on the shaft when the rest of the assembly was removed. They calculated how they could use four superluminals to rotate the shaft without breaking it.

The ideal length for the shaft, they determined, would be 420 kilometers. The shaft would be removed from the asteroid end, said a tall, athletic-looking man introduced as John Something-or-Other, smiling at his feeble attempt to make a joke.

When they'd finished, there were several questions. Nicholson himself asked one: 'Are we sure that a weld between the shaft, which must be made of a substance none of us has ever heard of, and the hull of a starship, will take?'

'It'll work,' said a small, waspish young man. 'We've already tried it.'

The conversation became sufficiently technical that Nicholson couldn't follow it any longer, and after a while he slipped out. They all seemed to know what they were doing. Maybe there'd be a reasonably happy ending at that. Maybe he could even emerge as a hero.

They sent a shuttle for Tom, and he hadn't been gone twenty minutes before Embry discovered she did not like being alone on *Wildside*. The ship was full of echoes and voices. Of systems clicking on and shutting off. Of the sound of warm air flowing through blowers and ducts. Of the onboard electronic systems talking incessantly to themselves. Bill the AI inquired whether she was okay, and she had to say yes or he'd want to diagnose her problem. She couldn't even ignore him because he would simply repeat the query, and he had endless patience.

It had endless patience. Best to keep the details straight.

She was not among those people who could entertain herself carrying on a conversation with an AI. Bill was, after all, only a simulation, not a *real* person. A lot of people tended to lose sight of that fact, and she'd had to refer several of them to the shrinks.

She was up front on the flight deck, seated in the pilot's chair. Deepsix lay below her, a mass of oceans and glaciers save for the narrow green-brown belt along the equator. A huge snowstorm blanketed the continent they called Northern Tempus.

None of the other three ships was in the sky. She felt utterly alone. They'd invited her to move over to *Wendy*, but she'd declined. Packing was inconvenient, and anyhow she'd have to come back here if the rescue was successful. After all, it would only be a matter of a few days.

If things went badly, on the other hand. God knew when she could expect to get home. She didn't want to seem indifferent, or cold-hearted, but she also didn't want to spend the winter out here. If Hutch and the others were lost, another long delay would be likely, lasting probably several more weeks, while a new pilot came to Maleiva to recover *Wildside*.

Her link vibrated. She was grateful for the interruption. 'Yes?' she said.

'Embry.' Marcel's image popped up on one of the auxiliary screens. 'How are you making out?'

'Okay.'

'I need a favor.'

'What can I do for you?'

'If we have to go to the backup operation, we'll need all four ships. And we have to get set up so we'll be ready to launch if needed. What I'm trying to tell you is that *Wildside* is going to be doing some maneuvering.'

'There's no pilot over here, Marcel.'

'I know. We're going to have Lori operate her.'

293

'Who's *Lori?*'

'The *Star*'s AI.'

'The *Star*'s AI? What's wrong with Bill?'

'It's a long story. I'll be happy to tell you about it when we get time,'

'Is it safe?'

'Sure. Now, can I get you to punch a code into the command console? It's right in front of the pilot's seat.'

'The black panel with the blinking lamps?'

'That's it.' He gave her a string of numbers, and she dutifully entered them. 'That allows me to talk directly with the AI,' he said. His eyes narrowed somewhat. 'Now, you're sure you're doing okay?'

'I'm fine. Captain.'

'Good. So you know: Tomorrow we're going to take *Wildside* out of orbit. You'll be going out to the skyhook assembly with the rest of us. There'll be a lot of activity when we get there, and we'll be putting some people aboard your ship. You don't have to do anything. Just sit tight. There's no danger.'

'You mean to *me*. What about Hutch? What are her chances?'

'The truth?'

'Of course.'

'I'd say the chances are decent.'

He blinked off, and she sat staring at the blank screen. Then she opened a channel to the *Evening Star*. A young, female, redheaded simulation in the ship's uniform appeared. 'Good morning,' it said. 'How may I help you?'

'When is the *Star* returning to Earth?'

'We are scheduled to depart Sunday the tenth, ma'am.' The day after the collision.

'Would it be possible to book passage?'

The simulation appeared to glance at a monitor, although Embry knew that was not necessary. 'Yes, it would,' she said. 'We have several excellent staterooms on our Festival Deck. Can I reserve one for you?'

With luck, she'd be able to bully the Academy into picking up the tab. 'How much?' she asked.

'One-ten.'

Sleep. 'I'll get back to you if I decide to do it,' she said. No need to commit now. If everything went well, and the rescue worked, she wouldn't need it. And it would be a little embarrassing to be sitting over on the *Star* when Hutch and the others came back on board.

19

There's not much to differentiate one savage from another, whether you find him in a jungle or on the streets of a modern city. They are best left to themselves, and are worth serious study only by those interested in manufacturing a better blowgun.

—GREGORY MACALLISTER, *'The Modern World'* and
'Good Luck'

Hours to breakup (est): 129
   'Evening Star How may we be of service?'
   'This is John Drummond. On the *Wendy Jay.* I wonder if you could provide thrust information for the *Star?'*
   'That would be no problem. Ship specifications are available. Please submit a transmission code.'

The electronics wizard they were looking for turned out to be little more than an adolescent. His name was Philip Zossimov. He was a product of the University of Moscow who served as a consultant to the British firm Technical Applications Ltd. He had thick brown hair, a quiet demeanor, and an expression that implied he could do anything.

Beekman explained how they planned to manage the rescue. 'But,' he said, 'we need to find a way to hold the mouth of the net open.'

Zossimov asked to see pictures of the asteroid. 'How are you arranging to get rid of it?' he asked. 'The asteroid?'

'After we cut through the net,' Beekman said, 'it will drift off on its own. We can make adjustments if it would help you in your task.'

'No,' he said. 'Go ahead as you intend. But you'll need a ring-shaped collar. I don't suppose you happen to have one?'

'No. That's why we needed you.'

'Yes. Very good. All right, we'll have to make one.' He looked around at the working staff, obviously unimpressed. 'It's a two-pan problem,' he said. 'We install the collar at the front of the net to hold it open, and then, once the lander is inside, we have to close it to make sure it *stays* inside.'

'That's correct.'

'All right. I'll want to see the specs.'

'For . . .?'

'The ships. All of them.'

'Okay,' said Beekman. 'I'll arrange it.' He directed Bill to make them available. Then he turned back to Zossimov. 'Philip,' he said, 'can you do it?'

'Oh, yes, I can do it. We'll need some parts, of course.'

'Cannibalize anything. Katie here will work with you. She's a physicist with a specialty in quantum gravity. You don't care about that. What's important is that she knows *Wendy*. Do what you have to. But make it work.'

'There's a possibility,' he said, 'we may have to shut down one of the ships.'

'You can't do that. We need all four for the maneuvers.'

'I see. What about life support?'

'We can evacuate one, if need be.'

Hutch was still showing the after effects of her bout with the blossom. They'd given her an extra hour and a half to sleep.

'We don't have that kind of time,' she complained when they finally woke her.

'Randy needed the time, too,' Kellie said. 'And this looked like a good way to provide it without laying more guilt on him for holding us up.'

They fed her a quick breakfast and got on the road.

While they walked, Hutch talked to Marcel, who seemed unduly irritable. He denied that he was feeling out of sorts, but she recognized that he was worried because they were falling behind schedule. She did what she could to allay his concerns. We're close now, she told him. There don't seem to be any problems we can't handle. Try not to worry.

He asked about the orchid. Hutch looked accusingly at Kellie.

'I provided no details.' Kellie said privately.

'Just a minor skirmish with a man-eating plant,' Hutch told him.

'A *plant*? You mean an oversize Venus flytrap? Something like that?'

'Yeah,' she said. 'That's close enough.'

When she'd signed off a few minutes later. Kellie grinned at her. 'More like a woman-eating plant.'

They'd gone only a few more steps when MacAllister got a call. Incoming visual.

'Somebody wants to talk,' he told the others.

The image took shape, projected by MacAllister's link. They were looking at a young man. Brushed-back, attractive. Lean, angular jaw. Good smile. Dark brown hair neatly cut. He wore a white pullover shirt and gray slacks, and his expression suggested he understood he was intruding but hoped no one would mind.

'August Canyon,' said MacAllister.

The visitor looked pleased. 'Good morning, Mr MacAllister. It's a pleasure to meet you, sir.' He was seated on a fabric chair, which floated a meter or so above the ground, as they walked. 'I know this is a difficult time for you. But I'm sure you're aware that the entire world is following this. I wonder if you'd care to comment for the interglobal audience?'

'About Deepsix?'

'Yes.'

'Sure. This place is a pit. And I'll admit to being scared half out of my mind.'

'Well. I'm sure you are.' He smiled pleasantly. 'But help is on the way, of course?'

'No. As I understand it, no help is available.' MacAllister was falling behind the others, so he picked up his pace a bit. Canyon, of course, stayed right with him. 'Tell me, you don't happen to have a lander on board, I don't suppose?'

'I'm afraid not. Wish we did. We thought we were just coming out here to record an astronomical event. Never occurred to anybody there might be a story on the ground, too.'

'Yes.' MacAllister looked over at Hutch. Hutch had also felt for a moment that they might have gotten lucky. But Marcel would have had the media vessel in his database, and would have known. Still, there was always human oversight. Common enough, and one hoped.

'Are we on now?' MacAllister asked. 'Is this being broadcast somewhere?'

'No,' Canyon said. 'We're recording, but we wouldn't broadcast. Not without your permission. But the public knows what's happening here. And they're concerned. Did you know that churches all over the world have been praying you'd come through this? There was a prayer meeting on the New White House lawn the other day.'

'They're praying for *me*?' MacAllister looked shocked. 'Most of them have damned me for an atheist.'

Canyon squirmed. 'Everyone wants you to come out of this. Mr MacAllister. *All* of you, that is.'

'Well, August, I have to tell you that I think that's all goosefeathers. If you follow my meaning.'

Canyon smiled. 'I don't think you realize how much interest

there *is*. Did you know that Parabola's already started making a sim?'

'Really. How does it come out?'

Canyon put an *aw shucks* expression on his well-scrubbed features. 'I guess they're waiting to see.'

Kellie made a noise deep in her throat.

'August,' MacAllister said, 'if you want to find out how we're doing, you're talking to the wrong person. Priscilla Hutchins over there is in charge. She knows more about the situation than I do.'

The image turned her way, and Hutch stepped into range of the scan so he could see her. Canyon kept her in view, but suddenly began speaking to his audience in a hushed, urgent tone. 'This is Priscilla Hutchins, who was attacked last night by a killer plant. Priscilla, I wonder if you'd care to tell us precisely what happened.'

'It grabbed me from behind,' she said.

'What kind of plant was it?'

'*Big*.' Hutch glanced over at Kellie. 'August, I don't want to seem uncooperative, but time's pressing.'

'I understand, Priscilla. And if you like, I'll get out of your way until we can find a more auspicious moment. We'd like very much to set up a live interview, though. At your convenience. If we could just sit and talk for a while. About your feelings. What it's like being on the ground under these circumstances.' He put on an expression that was intended to be sympathetic. 'Whether you're confident you'll be able to get clear before, you know—' He showed a lot of teeth, suggesting he understood that he was being insensitive to their situation, but that his job required it.

'He's a jerk,' Kellie said on a private channel. 'Don't give him anything.'

'Do what he asks,' said Nightingale, also privately. 'There's a lot in this for all of us. If we play our cards right. Why not cooperate with him?'

That had been Hutch's thought. She could end up talking to management groups for eight thousand a throw. Maybe hire a ghostwriter to do her memoirs. That wasn't bad. Her old friend

Janet Allegri had recently published *her* account of the Omega mission, *The Engines of God,* and had made very good money.

And what the hell: Canyon had to make a living. Why should she make problems for him? Moreover, it would give them all something else to think about for a while. 'Okay, August,' she said. 'We'll do it. Tonight. After dinner.'

20

That anyone could believe the human animal was designed by a divine being defies all logic. The average human is little more than an ambitious monkey. He is moronic, self-centered, cowardly, bullied by his fellows, terrified that others will see him for what he is. One can only assume his creator was in something of a hurry, or was perhaps a member of an Olympian bureaucracy. The more pious among us should pray that next time he does the job right But we might in justice concede that there is one virtue to be found in the beast: he is persistent.

—GREGORY MACALLISTER, *Bridge with the Polynesians*

Hours to breakup (est): 123

'Can we really do it?'

John Drummond nodded. He was actually on *Wendy*, virtually in the *Star* planning room. 'Marcel, it depends on the altitude they can reach with the lander.'

'How high does it have to go?'

'At least ten thousand meters. Below that, we can't hope to control events.'

Beekman indicated his agreement. 'The higher they can take the lander, the better our chances,' he said.

'We have to know in advance,' continued Drummond. 'how high they can go so we can plan the insertion.'

'We have no way to determine—'

'Marcel, it would be a *considerable* help.'

'I don't really care how much help it would be. There's no way to find out. Assume they can make ten thousand. And proceed accordingly.'

Drummond looked pained. 'You're sure? We can't have them do a test run when they get to the lander? If we knew what we were dealing with—'

'We can't do a test run because to make the test valid, she'd have to exhaust the spike. That would mean a very hard bounce going down.'

'How about a computer simulation?'

'The data stream from the lander is very likely going to be unreliable. Let's just make the assumption at ten thousand and get it done. Okay?' He was trying to keep the irritation out of his voice but not having much luck.

Drummond sighed. 'This is becoming a speculative exercise, Marcel.'

'Of course it is, John. We can do only what we can do. What about getting the shaft away from the assembly and aimed in the right direction? Can we do *that*?'

'Yes,' he said. 'We have to turn it around. I can't see that it'll be a problem. But it *will* be a delicate maneuver.

'You have only four vessels. One of them can pour it on—'

'*The Evening Star.*'

'*The Evening Star,*' said Beekman. 'But it's still only four ships trying to wrestle a four-hundred-kilometer-long shaft onto a vector. Without breaking anything. That's the real risk. Put any strain at all on the shaft and it's going to snap and that'll be the end of the project. But we can do it.'

'All right, then.' Marcel felt better than he had since the quake.

'Let's make it happen. John. I want you to help set up the time-table. We've got a couple of systems designers coming over with the people from the *Star*. Use them as you need them. Get Bill to coordinate with the AIs in the other ships.' He looked over at Beekman. 'How about our welder?'

'We've got one. Namc's Janet Hazelhurst. She spent a few years doing orbital construction until she got married. Says she knows what it's about, but it's been a while and she'll step aside if we have anybody better. She claims, though, that she can do whatever has to be done.'

'Do we have anybody better?'

'No, Captain, we do not.'

'All right. Let's hope she's a good teacher. Assign forty volunteers to her and have her show them the fine points of welding. Get them started right away.'

'Who's going to do the instruction on the e-suits?'

'Miles Chastain is on *Zwick*. He's a good man, and I'm sure he'll help. We'll get him over here right away.' Marcel checked his notes. 'Gunther, we're going to need some clips to hold the net together. Do we have a metal worker?'

They had two. One was a retiree from Hamburg, the other a Chinese entrepreneur. Marcel brought them in and explained what was needed. Could it be done?

How much time did they have?

Three days. Tops.

Yes. It should be sufficient. But they would need help. Marcel assigned them a couple of world-class physicists as gofers.

And they would need metal. Lots of metal.

That could be a problem. Starships did not carry much expendable metal.

Bill broke in: *'Captain, the people from the* Evening Star *have been assembled in the Bryant Auditorium and await your pleasure.'*

Marcel acknowledged. 'Let's go say hello to our volunteers.'

Within the hour, teams were going through *Wendy*, compartment by compartment, dismantling side panels from beds, wall sections, and anything else that was metallic. In the meantime, the retiree and the entrepreneur began to jury-rig their equipment. It was a challenge, but they would, by God, make it happen.

At about the time Beekman's bed was being taken apart, all four superluminals left orbit.

Canyon's commlink vibrated. It was Chastain. He brought the image up. The captain was seated in the cockpit. 'August,' he said, 'in case you're wondering, we're headed out to the assembly. You might be able to get some good visuals.'

'Yes,' said Canyon. 'I've done a few interviews on it. I'll tell you, Miles, I wish it had turned out to be an alien *ship*. It's a long piece of metal, but it's still just a piece of metal.'

'I know. I've also received a request from Captain Clairveau on *Wendy*. They're still working on ways to bail out their people, and they want our help. So I'm putting *Zwick* at their disposal.'

'Good.' said Canyon, thinking how well that would play. UNN to the rescue. 'But why do they need us? What do they want us to do?'

'I don't have the details.' He glanced at the time. 'There's a briefing in four minutes. I'll pipe it in. You might want to inform Emma.'

Canyon nodded. However the scenario went, it couldn't help but translate into a huge boost in the ratings. Who out there would be so jaded as not to watch?

Janet Hazelhurst took control of her volunteers in the Bryant Auditorium. They were required to sign a document holding TransGalactic harmless in the event of misadventure. When that had been accomplished, Captain Clairveau of the *Wendy Jay* talked to them about the dangers of the situation. 'We hope that you won't have to go outside,' he said. 'I want to emphasize that your training is precautionary only.'

Janet noted that some of the volunteers looked disappointed to hear it. That, she thought, was an encouraging start.

'If you do have to go out,' Clairveau continued, 'we'll do

everything possible to minimize the risk. But to be honest, it'll be in your hands. The real danger arises because of your lack of experience in what we'll be asking you to do. You'll be functioning in a zero-gee environment, and you'll be using lasers.

'The e-suit that you'll be wearing will be comfortable. It'll keep you warm, and it is almost foolproof. But it will not withstand a laser, so we'll expect you to be careful. We're going to show you how to use the lasers, how to weld, and how to do it in zero gee. And how to do it safely. You'll have an opportunity to practice under zero-gee conditions *inside* the ship. You'll do nothing for the next three days *except* practice.'

Clairveau was tall, good-looking, confident. Janet was inclined to trust him. 'As you know,' he continued, 'Morgan's World is getting close. That means there'll be some debris floating around out there. Rocks. Dust. Ice. Who knows—

'We'll have sensors on the lookout constantly. But there's no way to be absolutely safe. Consequently, if any of you want to rethink doing this, we'll understand.'

A few did.

'*I have people at home who depend on me.*'

'*I'm sorry. I wanted to help, but I didn't think it would be like this.*'

'*I have kids.*'

'*Sometimes I have a problem with heights.*'

Most stayed.

Janet was newly widowed. Not that she minded. Her ex had always been something of a bore. He'd had no imagination, had spent a lifetime watching himself portray Robin Hood and George Washington and Leonidas at Thermopylae (except that in his version the Spartans won), and his idea of a romantic evening out consisted of having dinner at the lodge with his buddies.

She'd considered not renewing every time extension came up. But she'd never taken that fatal step because her husband had loved her. He'd remained faithful, God help her, and had always remembered birthdays and anniversaries. They'd had two good children, and he had been an exemplar of a father. She could not have failed to renew without devastating him, and there was no way she could have brought herself to do that. So she'd stayed with him, bored and yearning for excitement, through all those long years.

Everyone thought they were an ideal couple. *I wish my George were more like your Will.* Will had even retained his good looks, although the smile had lost some of the old electricity. When an undetected aneurysm killed him, she'd mourned for an appropriate period, and then boarded the *Evening Star*, as she told her friends, to try to get past her loss.

Her fellow passengers knew nothing of all this. Janet had discovered that she loved her newfound freedom, and she'd been having a pretty good time.

Now she had an opportunity to call on an old skill and do something heroic.

She was charged with the responsibility to train the volunteers in welding and cutting techniques.

Marcel had sat with her, and they'd planned how they would handle the operation.

She started by asking who knew what a weld was.

She demonstrated by joining two pieces of metal. 'Simple,' she said.

She let one of the volunteers do it.

The trick to achieving a proper weld, she informed her students, was to get intimate contact between the two surfaces. Expose clean metal. Then the atoms can be joined properly. *Intimately.* It was her favorite term. When we're finished, the atoms in the two-pieces will be as close to each other as the atoms in either piece are to each other. That was the goal.

She explained proper technique, demonstrated, let them try it, and kept them at it until they could do it without thinking. They practiced cutting up shelving that was no longer in use, taking apart storage bins and slicing cabinets. Then they put everything back together.

'It's easy to do in here,' she warned them. 'When you get outside, you'll find you have a lot to think about. But the job is the same, and the technique is the same. Just do not allow yourself to be distracted.'

She had some pieces of what they all called *impossibilium*, the material from which the assembly was made. They practiced *culling* it and welding it back together. She emphasized safety, and booted three who were too casual in their approach. 'Mistakes will cost,' she told them. 'Careless will get you killed. Or will kill someone else.' And later: 'It's really not hard. But you have to keep your mind on what you're doing.'

She sent them off to dinner and brought them back for another round.

This time, when she gave them a chance to leave, everyone stayed.

They worked until almost 11:00 P.M. Then she thanked them for their attention, dismissed them, and told them they would start next day at six. 'We'll be working in our e-suits tomorrow.' she said. 'I want you to get used to them.'

Someone wanted to know whether that meant they were going outside after all.

'No,' she said. 'Not yet.' And she was pleased to hear them grumble.

The Evening Star offered a handful of compartments to Marcel's team. Unfortunately, no VIP accommodation remained available for the captain himself. Nicholson offered, in the time-honored tradition, to donate his own quarters to his visitor. Marcel, as was expected, replied that would never do, and that he would be pleased to take whatever could be had. A cot by the forward mixer, he said, would serve the purpose. He received a unit on the port side amidships that was far more comfortable, and more spacious by half, than his quarters on *Wendy*.

It was late morning when he left the welders, and he'd been up all night. He climbed out of his uniform and lay down, planning to nap for a half hour before returning to Nicholson's bridge. He'd barely closed his eyes when his link chimed.

'Marcel?' It was Abel Kinder's voice. Abel was the senior climatologist on *Wendy*. He was heading a team monitoring conditions around Deepsix for signs of planetary disintegration.

'Hello, Abel,' he said. 'What do you have?'

'Some serious storms, looks like. And an intensification of seismic activity.'

'Any of it in the tower area?'

'They're going to have some movement, but the worst of it should be northeast of them. At sea.'

'What about the storms?'

'Big ones are developing. What's happening is that the atmosphere responds to Morgan's gravitational pull just the way the oceans do. So you have big slugs of air and water moving around the planet. Everything heats up from the tidal activity. The normal scheme of things is becoming unhinged. Cold water shows up in warm latitudes, the high-pressure areas over the poles get disrupted . . .'

'Bottom line, Abel?'

'Hard to say. The weather machine is being turned to soup. Anything can happen. You'll want to warn your people to be on the lookout for hurricanes, tornadoes, God knows what. We don't have enough sensors on the ground to be able to monitor everything, so we can't even promise an advance warning.'

'Okay.'

'They're just going to have to stay loose.'

'Thanks, Abel.'

'One more thing. These storms'll be *big*. Unlike anything anybody's ever seen at home. Category seventeen stuff.'

21

*Memorials are polite fictions erected in the general pretense
that we are selfless and generous, compassionate to those in
need, brave in a just cause, faithful unto death. To establish
the absurdity of these conceits, one need only glance at the
conditions which inevitably erupt whenever police protection,
however briefly, fails.*

—GREGORY MACALLISTER, *Gone to Glory*

Hours to breakup (est): 107

They recorded eighteen kilometers before quitting for the day.
When Canyon reappeared to conduct his interview, he told them
to relax, that he'd do all the work, and that when they got home
they'd discover they were all celebrities.

It was in fact simple enough. He tossed them softballs. Were
they scared? What had they seen that most impressed them? Were
there things on Deepsix worth saving? Who was this astronomer
in the tower he'd heard about? What was the biggest surprise
they'd seen on this world?

Hutch knew what hers had been, but she talked instead about
the giant dragonflies.

He asked about their injuries. None major, said MacAllister.

311

Just a few cuts and scratches. But he admitted to having learned a bitter lesson about keeping in decent physical condition. 'You just never know,' he said, 'when you're going to be dumped into a forest on a strange world and made to walk two hundred kilometers. I recommend jogging for everyone.'

Later, when Jerry Morgan rose, it was almost the size of Earth's moon. It was, of course, still at half phase, where it would remain. The upper and lower cloud belts, somber and autumn-colored, were flecked with gold. A broad dark band lay at the equator. Hutch could pick out the altitude in the northern hemisphere where Maleiva III, Transitoria, and the tower would make their fatal plunge.

Under other circumstances, it would have been a strikingly lovely object.

NEWSLINE WITH AUGUST CANYON

'Earlier today, I spent some time with the five brave people who are stranded on Maleiva III while the giant planet named for Jeremy Morgan bears down on them. Four are scientists. The fifth is the celebrated writer and editor, Gregory MacAllister. They're trekking overland in a desperate effort to find a spacecraft left here twenty years ago. It's their only hope for getting off the surface before this world ends, which it will do in six days.

'Will they succeed? Nobody knows, of course. But we'll be talking to them in a special broadcast this evening. And after you've met them, I think you'll feel as I do, that if it can be done at all, these five people will bring it off—'

Marcel and Beekman increasingly gave way on the radio to surrogates, who kept them on course. Left to themselves, traveling through unfamiliar country, without identifiable landmarks or indeed landmarks of any kind, they'd have become hopelessly lost. There were jokes about Hutch's ability to guide them by the position of the sun, which was nil. Even at night, with clear skies and rivers of stars, she'd have been helpless. If there was a marker star, either north or south, she couldn't find it. She doubted that such a star would even be visible from the equator.

But it didn't matter. Somebody was always on the circuit. *Guide right.*

Angle left.

No. Not around the hill. Go over it.

Then, without warning. Marcel had a mission for them: 'There's something up ahead. It's not at all out of your way, and we'd like you to take a quick look.'

'What is it?'

'We don't know. A structure.'

Hutch begrudged every minute spent off-trail. She glanced at the others, soliciting opinions. They were willing to indulge a minute. But only a minute. Nightingale thought it was a good idea. So long as it was indeed nearby. 'Okay,' she said. 'We'll take a peek, let you know what it is. But then we're moving on.'

It was on the shore of a lake, tangled deep in old-growth trees and shrubbery. They could see only a few glints of metal, and were unsure it was a structure at all, so completely had the forest embraced it.

They cut down some bushes, and Hutch's first impression was that they'd found a storage dome. Until they uncovered a line of windows. Most were still intact. Kellie walked around to the rear. 'It's got a tail.' she reported.

'A tail?'

'Twin tails, in fact. It's an aircraft.'

It had a flared bottom. Symbols were stenciled on one side, so faint as to be barely noticeable. There was a windscreen up front. The vehicle was about the size of a commuter airbus. But it had no wings. Ground transportation, decided Hutch, despite the tail. Unless they had antigravity.

Judging by the trees that had engulfed it, it had been there for centuries. Hutch paced it off, and they relayed visuals back to

Wendy. Thirty-eight meters along its length, probably six in diameter. Crumpled severely to starboard, somewhat less on the port side.

Chiang climbed a tree, produced a lamp, and tried to look inside. 'Nothing.' he said. 'Get me a wet cloth.'

Kellie broke off a few flat-bladed leaves, soaked them cautiously at the edge of the lake, and handed them up. Chiang wiped the glass.

'You know,' said Kellie, 'wings or not, this thing *does* have an aerodynamic design. Look at it.'

She was right. It had flowing lines and was tapered front and rear.

'What's happening?' asked Canyon. They knew he habitually listened in on the allcom, and on conversations between the ground party and the orbiting ships.

Hutch brought him up to date. 'I'll give you the rest when we know what it is,' she said. 'If it's *anything*.'

Chiang had his lamp pressed against the glass. 'There are rows of seats inside. Little ones. They look a bit thrown about.'

'*Little* seats?' asked MacAllister. 'Same gauge as back at the tower?'

'Yes. Looks like.'

'Now *that's* really odd.'

'Why?' asked Hutch.

'Look at the door.' It was hard to see behind the tangle of growth, but it was there. Hutch saw what was odd: the door was about the right size for *her*.

It was almost at ground level, and it even had a handle, but when MacAllister tried to open it the handle broke off. So they cut a hole through it.

The interior was dark. Hutch turned on her lamp and looked at roughly thirty rows of the small seats divided by a center aisle, five on either side. Some had been torn up and lay scattered around the cabin. She saw no sign of organic remains.

The floor creaked. It was covered by a black fabric that was still reasonably intact.

The bulkheads were slightly curved. They were water-stained and, toward the front, broken open. There were scorch marks.

The cockpit supported two seats. But unlike those in the body of the craft, they were full-size, large enough to accommodate *her*. One was broken, twisted off its mount. There was also some damage to the frame that supported the windscreen. She looked down at what had once been an instrument panel.

'Crashed and abandoned,' said Kellie, behind her.

'I think so.'

'What's with the big seats?' asked MacAllister. 'Who sat in *them*?'

Nightingale swept his light from front to rear. 'It's pretty clear we have *two* separate species here,' he said.

'Hawks and crickets?' suggested Hutch. 'They're *both* real?'

'Is that possible? On the same world?'

'We have more than one intelligent species on *our* world. What I wouldn't expect to see is two *technological* species. But who knows?'

They examined a lower compartment that must have been used for cargo, but it was empty. And the power plant. It had employed liquid fuel to power a jet thrust. Air intakes. Plastic skirts around the base. Hutch got Beekman back on the circuit. 'Are we sure,' she asked, 'the locals never went high-tech?'

'That's what the Academy says.'

'Okay. When you talk to the Academy again, you can tell them there's a hovercraft down here.'

'Let's go,' said MacAllister. 'No more time to dawdle.'

Hutch stripped off a piece of a seat and put it into a sample bag. They removed a few gauges from the instrument panel and bagged those as well. None had legible symbols, but it should be possible eventually to enhance them.

Chiang took Hutch aside. 'There's something else for you to look at. Over here.' In the woods.

He'd found a black stone wall.

It was about six meters long. And engraved. It had several rows of symbols, and a likeness of the hovercraft.

Hutch could assume that the rock had once been polished, that its edges had been sharp, that the inscription had been crisp and clear. But the weather had worn it down. And the inscription ran into the ground.

She checked the time.

'It'll only take a minute,' said Chiang.

She nodded, and they dug it out while MacAllister urged them to move on. Two deeply etched parallel lines of symbols were engraved across the top, over the likeness of the wrecked vehicle. But this one was lean and powerful, undamaged, and she knew that the sculptor intended that it be perceived as hurtling through the sunlight.

Below the image of the hovercraft, two groups of characters, side by side, had been carved using block bold symbols. And beneath those two, another series, much more numerous, smaller, ten lines deep. Four across except the last line, which had only three. These might in fact have been using a different alphabet altogether. It was impossible to know because they were not block letters. Rather they had a delicate, complex character.

'What do you think?' Hutch asked. 'What's it say?'

'"Ajax Hovercraft"' said MacAllister, who was fidgeting off to one side. 'The two groups near the top constitute regional distribution centers, and these' – the smaller groups – 'are local offices.'

'Anybody else want to try?' asked Kellie.

'We really should get moving,' said MacAllister.

Nightingale joined them. 'Its proximity to the wreck,' he said, 'suggests it's a memorial.' He stared thoughtfully at it. 'These' – the lines at the top – 'are the names of the pilots. And the others are those of the passengers.'

'What about the top line?' asked Kellie.

'If it's a memorial,' said MacAllister, 'then it's a salutary phrase, *Stranger, Tell the Spartans*, something on that order.'

'So what was going on here?' asked Chiang.

'Pretty obviously a traffic accident,' said Nightingale. 'A wreck.'

'Of course. But where were they going?'

'Maybe,' said MacAllister, 'they were migrant workers of some sort. Farmhands. Indentured labor.'

'Slaves?' suggested Chiang.

Nightingale nodded. 'Maybe.'

'Do you put the names of slaves on a memorial?' Hutch shook her head. 'That doesn't sound right.'

'In human history,' said MacAllister, 'people sometimes had great affection for their slaves.' He shrugged. 'Who knows what an alien culture might be up to?'

They pressed forward late into the evening. When at last they'd made camp for the night, they did more interviews with Canyon. Chiang enjoyed the opportunity to perform on an international stage, to look heroic, to say the things that were expected of him. *We'll get home.* Smile into the scanner. *There are a lot of people rooting for us.* But every time he glanced over at Kellie he thought he detected a trace of mockery in her smile.

When he'd finished he was embarrassed.

The others were just as shameless. Nightingale's voice got deeper, MacAllister tried to suck his belly in, Kellie talked as if they didn't have a care in the world. And even Hutchins, their forthright captain, couldn't resist preening. They were for the moment famous, and it was affecting them.

Canyon talked to them individually. As he finished with them they drew around the fire and tried to pretend that nothing unusual had just happened. He was still on the circuit with Kellie, getting what he liked to call 'context'.

Chiang disliked the forest at night. There was no way to maintain security. It would have required three guards to keep the possibility of a surprise attack to a minimum.

This was their eighth night out. He thought the count was right, but everything was beginning to run together and he was no longer sure. To date, no predator had tried a night assault.

The probability, therefore, was that, if it were going to happen, it would have already occurred. Nevertheless, Chiang worried and fretted, as was his nature.

He could see Canyon's image seated on a log facing Kellie. He was asking his questions, and she listened attentively, sometimes nodding, sometimes growing thoughtful. 'Oh, yes,' she might be saying, *'we're confident we can get the lander working once we get there'* Or: *'No, we really haven't discussed that possibility. We don't expect it to happen that way'* Although there was no logical basis for jealousy, Chiang was irritated anyhow. There was something in Canyon's manner that seemed like a clumsy attempt at seduction.

In addition, Canyon couldn't hide the fact that he really had no idea what the people on the ground were feeling. And he also revealed that his primary concern in all this was to ring up high numbers back home, to please his bosses, to move up the food chain. Taking pictures of a collision between two worlds had been precisely the right assignment for him. He could have delivered himself of a few generalities. *It looks as if it's going to be an incredible smash-up,* call in, say, a couple of the astrophysicists on *Wendy* for color commentary, and it would all have worked fine.

But he just wasn't the person to talk to people in trouble.

This was Chiang's last thought. He'd been standing at the edge of the firelight, surveying the surrounding darkness, occasionally flashing his lamp into the night. And suddenly the world vanished, as if someone had folded it up and put it away.

MacAllister was also bored with Canyon. The previous night's interviews had been transmitted a few hours later to Earth. It was a long ride, even at hypercom, and they would not appear on anybody's screen for another day and a half. By then, probably, they would have found *Tess*, and the issue of survival would have been resolved. In their favor, he hoped. He imagined them spotting the abandoned spacecraft, hurrying toward it, climbing inside, pumping power into it, and flying back in the luxurious comfort of its passenger cabin to the tower. He could see them setting down and recovering the capacitors. Hutch and Kellie would install them with a minimum of fuss. Then they'd cheer as *Tess* lifted off and soared into orbit.

The trees sighed in the wind, and the fire crackled. He watched Kellie talking with Canyon, saw her pause, saw Canyon ask another question. He knew precisely what it would be.

'What are your thoughts when Morgan's World rises every night, and you see that it keeps getting bigger?' (Tonight it would, he suspected, look like a Chinese balloon.)

'Is there anything you'd like to say to the folks back home?'

Yes, thought MacAllister, *spades, there is. Life is sweet.*

The image of the newsman appeared solid, and even a trifle backwoodsy by firelight. He leaned toward Kellie, apparently listening intently, although MacAllister knew he was formulating his next question.

And in the middle of this pacific, sleepy scene, there came a sudden shriek.

Something sailed past MacAllister's head. A few days earlier he'd have sat dumbfounded, wondering what was happening. But his reflexes had improved considerably. He shouted a warning and threw himself on the ground.

Rocks whipped past them. One hit his shoulder, and another struck his skull. There were more screams, high-pitched, rather like those of angry children. He was fumbling for his cutter. Somebody's laser blazed out, and bushes erupted in fire. A tree, ripped through by a cutter beam, crashed to the ground.

A dart thunked into one of the fire logs. MacAllister saw movement in the trees; then crickets in furs charged into the camp. They were impossibly ugly savages, not at all like the robed figure who'd occupied the country chapel.

He got his weapon up just in time. Two of them were after him, with javelins. He cut them in half, the crickets and the javelins. He took out another, who was about to stab Kellie from behind. Hutch directed them to back into a tight circle, but MacAllister was too busy defending himself to try to get into a formation. Everything was utter confusion.

The crickets never stopped shrieking. Somebody cut one in two, from skull to sternum. Nightingale stepped into the middle of a charge and swung his cutter left and right. Limbs flew and the attack disintegrated. As suddenly as they'd come, the crickets broke and melted back into the forest.

Several bushes were ablaze. Something fell out of a tree and crashed beside him. It was carrying a javelin. It tried to get up and run, but MacAllister, enraged, slashed it anyhow, and the creature screamed and lay still.

Hutch and Kellie pursued the fight to the edge of the trees. Nightingale stood among those he'd killed, legs spread, cutter raised, like a modern Hector. The heroic stance was a bit much, but MacAllister was nonetheless impressed by his behavior. *Well, put a man's life on the line,* he thought, *and most of us can perform at a fairly high level.*

The attack had disintegrated, and the sounds of battle seemed to be receding. Through it all, unfazed, Canyon remained seated in his armchair. He couldn't see beyond the narrow range of the link, which had been set up on a stump. He simply kept demanding over and over to be told what was happening.

Universal News Network on the spot, thought MacAllister.

Nightingale finally explained they were being attacked.

Canyon kept talking, asking for details. Attacked by whom? Had anyone been hurt? MacAllister shut off the sound feed from the newsman and rubbed his head. It hurt, but he couldn't tell through the field whether he was bleeding. Otherwise, he thought he was okay. Couple bumps, nothing more.

Marcel was back on the circuit, asking the same questions. 'Crickets,' Kellie responded, although he couldn't see her. 'Talk in a minute.'

MacAllister was swept up in a curious combination of horror

and exhilaration. *By God, that had felt* good. *We're all savages at heart*, he thought.

Hutch came back into the camp, looked at him, and glanced around. 'Everybody okay?' she asked.

Nightingale signaled he was fine. He was shining his lamp into the trees, assuring himself they were gone. 'I guess we just met the locals.'

'How about you, Mac?'

'Alive and well,' said MacAllister. 'I don't think those little sons of bitches will be back soon.'

'Where's Chiang?' she asked.

MacAllister stared down at one of the bodies. It had sickly pale skin with a greenish tint and a hairy ridged skull. Its eyes were open, but it seemed dead.

It would have stood not quite as high as his hip. When he poked it, the creature stirred and made a sad mewling sound.

Kellie's voice broke in, subdued. 'Over here,' she said. 'I found him.'

Chiang lay still. Blood poured down inside his e-suit, leaking out of half a dozen wounds.

'Kill the suit,' said MacAllister.

'No.' Kellie had thrown herself on the ground beside him. Her voice was low and strange. 'It's all that's holding him together.'

Hutch knelt and picked up his wrist. 'Mac,' she said, 'get the medkit.'

MacAllister turned and hurried over to Hutch's backpack. 'No pulse,' Hutch said.

'He's not breathing.' Kellie's voice was thick.

Reluctantly, they punched off the suit and Hutch tried direct administration of his air supply.

Somebody must have spoken Embry's code because her voice came on the circuit. 'Don't move him,' she said.

And Marcel: 'Put out guards. They may come back.'

'I got it,' said Nightingale.

Kellie said, 'Burn anything that moves.'

'Do you have the kit yet?' Embry again.

'Mac's getting it.'

'Mac, hurry up. What's the bleeding look like? Let me see it.'

MacAllister returned with the medkit. Hutch took it and signaled for him to help Nightingale. Kellie pulled out a couple of pressure bandages and began applying them. Mac stood for a moment, staring down at Chiang. Then he turned away.

Nightingale was checking another dead attacker. MacAllister hoped Chiang's assailant was among the corpses.

They stayed together and circled the campsite. The exobiologist looked drained. MacAllister wondered for the first time whether he might have been unfair years before to Nightingale. 'You've been here before, haven't you. Randy?' he said.

'Yeah.' Nightingale made a face like someone who'd just bitten into bad fruit. 'There's a little bit of *déjà vu* about this.' He paused and took a deep breath. 'I really hate this place.'

MacAllister nodded. 'I'm sorry.' He wasn't sure what he meant by the phrase.

'Yeah. Me too.' Nightingale's features hardened. He looked as if he were going to say more. But he only shrugged and looked away.

MacAllister listened to the conversation on the allcom.

'Give him the R.O.'

'Doing it now.'

'Kellie, you need to stop the blood. Clamp down tighter.'

'It's not working, Embry.'

'Stay with it. Any pulse yet?'

'A trace.'

'Don't give up. Kellie, get a blanket or something on him.'

MacAllister looked toward the east, toward Deneb, while Chiang slipped away.

They buried him where he fell, during a ceremony at dawn. MacAllister, whose reputation ordinarily denied him the luxury of sentiment, found a stone, cut Chiang's name and dates into it, and added the comment: *DIED DEFENDING HIS FRIENDS.*

They dug the grave deep and lowered him in. Kellie wanted to conduct the ceremony, but she kept choking up, and finally she asked Hutch to finish.

He did not belong to an organized church, Kellie said, although he had a strong faith. Hutch nodded, didn't try to sort it out, and simply consigned him to the ground – she could no longer bring herself to say *earth* – observed that he had died too soon, and asked whatever god there might be, to take charge of him and to remember him.

Kellie stood paralyzed, resisting all offers of support, as they filled in the grave.

Nightingale announced that the attackers were vertebrates, but that their bones were hollow. 'Birds?' asked MacAllister.

'At one time,' he said, 'I think so.' He described filaments between arms and ribs that seemed to indicate that the species had only recently lost its flight capabilities.

They went through the creatures' garments. There were pockets, which contained fruits and nuts and a few smooth rocks. Ammunition.

'Let's get moving,' said Hutch.

'What about *these* things?' asked Nightingale. 'Shouldn't we bury them, too?'

Kellie's face hardened. 'Let their own take care of them.'

NEWSLINE WITH AUGUST CANYON

'Tonight we have bad news. An hour ago, the landing party was attacked—'

Beekman was looking out from a virtual cliff top over a turbulent ocean when Marcel arrived. Snow whipped across the crest and fell into the night, but it was a ground blizzard stirred up

323

by fierce winds, and had nothing to do with the skies, which were clear. Morgan was high overhead.

The tides on Maleiva III were, as a matter of course, gentle. There was no moon, so the only visible effects were generated by the distant sun. But tonight, with the gas giant approaching, the sea was monstrous. Huge waves pounded the cliffs on Transitoria's north coast.

'Tomorrow night,' he said, without turning toward Marcel.

Marcel sank against a bulkhead. 'My God, Gunny. That's still another day they've lost.'

'There are weaknesses in the range. Fault lines, Harry tells me. Worse than we thought. They're going to give way tomorrow night.'

'You're sure?'

'Yeah. We're sure.' He turned sad eyes toward Marcel. 'There was no way we could know—'

'It's okay. Not anybody's fault.' A cold hand gripped his spine. 'They're still thirty klicks away.'

Beekman nodded. 'I'd say they better get moving.'

22

Tides are like politics. They come and go with a great deal of fuss and noise, but inevitably they leave the beach just as they found it. On those few occasions when major change does occur, it is rarely good news.

—*Attributed to* GREGORY MACALLISTER *by Henry Kilburn, 'Gregory MacAllister: Life and Times'*

Hours to breakup (est): 78

In fact, Canyon had belatedly realized there was still another big story developing: the reaction of the people on board the other ships to the plight of the ground team.

He'd become uncomfortable interviewing Hutchins and her other trapped rabbits. It was too much like talking to dead people. So he'd switched over and done human-interest stories on the other superluminals. He'd found a young woman who'd been the traveling companion of the reporter who'd died in the *Evening Star* lander. She'd wept and struggled to hold back a case of galloping hysteria, and on the whole it had just made for a marvelous show. There were several people who'd been personally skewered or whose fondest beliefs had been shredded by MacAllister. How did they feel now that MacAllister was in danger of his life? For the record, they delivered pieties, expressing their fondest hope that he could be brought safely out. Even when the interview had formally ended, most said they wished him well, that nobody deserved what was happening to him, but something in their voices belied the sentiments. Only one, a retired politician who'd run a campaign on the need for moral reform, damned him outright. 'Nothing against the man personally,' he'd said, 'but I think it's a judgment. We'll be better off without him.'

Everyone on the *Wendy Jay* had been hit by Chiang's death. There was, he reflected, nothing like losing one of your own to bring home reality. Now they were worried about Kellie, and several of the younger males seemed stricken at the possibility of losing her, too. Her boss, Marcel Clairveau, regretted that he'd allowed her to go down to the surface. Occasionally, when he spoke of her, his voice trembled. That also made good copy.

He'd interviewed the physician left on *Wildside* about Nightingale. She expressed sorrow, of course, but it was a perfunctory response. He was quiet, she said, very reserved. Never got to know him. Canyon had done his homework and knew Nightingale's background. There was a dark irony, he thought, that every time Nightingale touched down on this world, people died.

Canyon hadn't said anything like that, at least not for public consumption. But the observation would show up in his broadcast *after* the situation had sorted itself out. He was putting a great deal of time into writing the spontaneous observations that he would make in the wake of the event.

Canyon knew the right questions to ask, and he was able to work most of his subjects up to a state of near hysteria. If Hutchins and her friends came out of this, he thought, they'd be heroes of the first order.

His own career prospects looked brighter than ever. What had begun as routine coverage of a planetary collision that was of interest primarily because the event was so rare and people liked fireworks, was instead turning into one of the human-interest stories of the decade. And it was all his.

'Marcel, you need to get some rest.' Worry lined Beekman's eyes.

'I'm all right,' Marcel said. Too many things were happening just then.

'There's no point exhausting yourself. Do that and you won't be there when we need you.' Marcel had slept only intermittently during the past few days, and it had always been a jumpy kind of rest. 'There's nothing more for you to do at the moment. Why don't you get off the bridge for a while? Go lie down.'

Marcel thought about it. The various elements of the extraction were going forward, and maybe he'd become little more than a kibitzer anyhow. 'Yeah,' he said, 'I think I will.' He propped his chin on his hands. 'Gunny, what have we overlooked?'

'We're in good shape. For the moment, there's nothing more to be done.' He folded his arms and stood waiting for Marcel to retire.

Embry was sitting up front in the pilot's seat, listening to the occasional crackle of conversation between the ground, Marcel, and Augie Canyon, who was interviewing Randy Nightingale. They sounded, she thought, in surprisingly good spirits, and she wondered how that could be.

Wildside had completed its movement, with the other three vessels, to a rendezvous near the assembly. Sitting in an empty ship while it fired thrusters and changed course had underscored her solitude. AIs were AIs and God knew she worked with them on a regular basis, as any practicing physician did. But somehow the voices that diagnosed a spinal problem or suggested a rejuvenation procedure were fundamentally different from an *intelligent* superluminal that made all its own decisions and on which she was the only passenger.

The message light blinked and an unfamiliar female face appeared on one of her screens. 'Embry?' She was wearing an Academy arm patch.

'Yes. What can I do for you?'

'Embry, my name's Katie Robinson.' Her diction was precise, and Embry wondered if she'd had theatrical experience. 'We're about to leave *Wendy*. We're coming over and will be there in a few minutes. I'd like you to pack a bag. Get all your belongings. We're going to bring you back with us.'

'May I ask why?' said Embry.

'Because we're going to remove your life support.'

They arrived within thirty minutes and went directly to work. There were eight of them. They went down into the storage bay and stripped most of the metal from the bins, containers, cabinets, storage units, and dividers. Then they came topside and went through the compartments and the common room, doing much the same sort of thing.

Katie helped her clear out her own quarters. When she was finished they repeated the process, taking most of the metal: the bed panels, the lamps, a foldout table, a built-in cabinet. They thanked her, apologized for the inconvenience, loaded everything into their shuttle, including her, and left.

The trank hadn't worked. Kellie listened to the sound of distant tides – they had finally camped near Bad News Bay – and watched Jerry Morgan, a vast swollen moon, sink toward the hills. The eastern sky had already begun to lighten. Hutch was their sentry, and her slim form leaned against a tree, just beyond the fire's glow.

She gave up finally, pulled herself into a sitting position, and wrapped her arms around her knees.

'Did you love him, Kellie?' The voice startled her. It was MacAllister. He was lying with his back to her, but he rolled over now. His face was in shadow, and she couldn't make out his expression.

'No,' she said. And, after a moment: 'I don't think so.'

'I'm sorry.' He sat up and reached for the coffeepot.

'I know,' she said. 'We're all sorry.'

328

He poured a cup and offered her some. But she declined. She didn't really want to put anything in her stomach.

'Sometimes,' he said, 'I think life is just one long series of blown opportunities.'

She nodded. 'You know what I really *hate*,' she said. 'Leaving him *here*. In this godforsaken place.'

'It's no worse than any other, Kellie. He'll never know the difference.'

She felt *empty*. 'He was a good guy,' she said, biting down a wave of anger and tears. Suddenly the grief rose in her, and she couldn't contain it. She clamped her teeth together and tried to hold on. MacAllister took her in his arms. 'Let it come,' he said.

Hutch was talking to someone. Kellie had collected herself, tamped down the storm, and was feeling drained. She poured herself some water.

Hutch stiffened. Lifted her arms in frustration. Kellie knew the gesture, and it raised the hair on her scalp.

The conversation ended, and Hutch strode swiftly into the ring of the campfire. 'Let's move, folks. We're down to our last day.' She knelt beside Nightingale and gently shook him.

'That can't be right,' said MacAllister. 'They told us we had until *tomorrow* night.'

'They've changed their minds. Come on, we have to get rolling.'

Mac needed no further prompting. He was searching for his toothbrush. 'How far do we still have to go?' he asked.

'Thirty klicks,' she said. 'Give or take.'

'In one day? We'll never make it.'

'Yeah, we will.'

'Hutch,' Mac said privately, 'it's not as if we're going to get there and you can turn the key and start the damned thing. How long's it going to take to get it up and running? Assuming we can do it at all?'

'A few hours,' she admitted.

He looked at the approaching sunrise and rubbed his feet.

'Then we have to get back to the tower and recover the capacitors. By what time?'

'Late tonight. Around midnight.'

He held out his hands helplessly. 'We need to go to Plan B.'

Nightingale was watching while he tried to pull himself together. 'What's going on?' he asked.

She explained.

'I'll be with you in a minute.' He limped down to the creek to wash his face in icy water and brush his teeth. Mac went with him.

'You okay?' she asked Kellie.

Kellie was fine. Kellie would never be better. 'You and I are going to have to do a sprint,' she said.

'I know,' said Hutch.

'We'll have to leave them.'

'Mac's already been suggesting that.'

The tides were loud in Bad News Bay. They came out onto a promontory and looked out over the water. It was a vast inland sea, the far shore lost in the distance.

'Ground gets rough to the south,' Marcel told them. 'Angle off your present course and head southwest for about a kilometer. There's a small lake. Circle the lake and keep going, same direction. It looks like easier country.'

'Okay.'

Far below, the bay was peaceful. Gulls skimmed along the surface, and Hutch saw something that looked like a large turtle basking in the rising sun.

They turned and faced each other. 'We'll wait for you here,' said Nightingale.

Hutch nodded.

Kellie was looking from one of them to the other. 'We'll be back as soon as we can.'

They had checked with Marcel. They were on high ground, and should be safe from the tides.

The four of them walked together along the rim until they found an open area that would be wide enough to set the spacecraft down. 'Since time's pressing,' Hutch said, 'we're going to go to the tower first. Then we'll be back for you.'

Kellie looked down the face of the cliff. 'Don't wander around in the dark,' she added.

'We won't.'

Mac shook himself and rubbed his spine against a tree, not unlike an elephant, Hutch thought.

'I have to tell you,' he said, 'I *love* this plan. Anything that gets me off my feet.' He extended his hand and his voice softened. Became personal. 'Good luck, ladies.'

Kellie pushed past the hand, embraced him, and planted a large wet kiss on his lips. 'You're a jerk, MacAllister,' she said. 'But you're worth saving.'

Hutch looked at Nightingale, hesitated, told herself what the hell, and repeated the ceremony.

Kellie, amused, shook her head. 'Love fest,' she said. 'Who'd've thought?'

Kellie and Hutch followed the shoreline for a time, angled away from it when Marcel told them to, and struck off again to the southwest. The land was heavily forested, marked with ravines and ridges, with rocky bluffs and narrow waterways, and with occasional mountains.

A herd of gray creatures with faces like camels and long floppy ears rumbled past in great ground-eating leaps and disappeared behind a line of hills.

Marcel sent them around a mountain and across a trail. Animal or something else? Of course, in a world in which flying creatures attacked in synchronized squadrons and hunting cats walked erect, the line between sentience and pure animal behavior had grown a bit murky.

They kept moving.

At about noon, in the middle of a forest, they came upon a

balustrade. Above it, Hutch saw a coved dome. *Two* domes. Twins.

'By God,' said Kellie. 'Look at that thing.'

The domes were connected by a cornice.

'It's a *temple*.' Hutch stopped in her tracks and stared.

It had six columns. They were fluted and supported a triangular pediment, on which a frieze had been carved. The frieze depicted two crickets, one seated in a shell of some sort, the other standing. The one in the shell was handing something, a cylinder, to the other.

No. On closer inspection Hutch saw it was a scroll.

'Lovely,' said Kellie.

Hutch was glad for the excuse to stop moving for a minute. 'It's baroque,' she said. 'Very close to eighteenth-century Parisian. Who would have thought . . .'

She could see an entrance hidden among the columns, and marble steps leading up to it. Kellie started toward them.

'No time,' said Hutch.

'There's more over here.'

A cylindrical structure was set at right angles to the temple. Pedestals projected every few meters, and a sculpted frieze circled as much of the building as she could see. It had a polyhedral roof supported by braces, and was adorned by roll molding and a small dome. The figures in the frieze seemed to show crickets in various poses, talking, reading, picking fruit from trees, playing with their young. Some were on their knees before a sun symbol.

There might have been an entire city hidden within the trees. She caught the outlines of majestic buildings, resplendent with arches and rounded windows and parabolic roofs. With galleries and buttresses and spires. And overgrown courts and abandoned fountains.

It was not a city that had ever known artificial lighting or, probably, a printing press. But it was lovely beyond any comparable complex Hutch had seen before. The detritus of centuries had blown across it, burying it, encasing it within a tangle of branches and bushes and leaves. But it nevertheless made her blood run to stand before the silent structures.

It might have been that the unearthly beauty of the place was enhanced by the encroaching forest, or by the sense of timelessness, or by its diminutive scale.

They stood entranced, relaying the visuals to *Wendy*. This time only silence came back. No one was asking them to take a moment to explore.

They spent less than two minutes at the site. Then they hurried on.

A rainstorm washed over them. Black clouds rolled in, and lightning bolts rippled down the sky.

They lost contact with Marcel for almost two hours. The rain continued steadily, then changed to sleet. Tremors periodically shook the ground, severely enough to throw both women off their feet.

'Lovely day for a stroll,' Kellie commented.

A line of trees appeared ahead. They plunged in. Something in the shrubbery went into a series of frenzied clicks. Hutch, in no mood for problems, and not wanting to give anything a clear shot at them at short range, cleared out the section with her laser. There were screeches, crashing around, animals charging off into the bush. They never got a good look at anything.

Marcel came back. 'Bad weather?'

'Electrical storms.'

'We see them. But you're doing fine. You should be there by early evening.'

'I hope so.'

'Hutch, I have another message for you from the Academy.'

'What's it say?'

He hesitated. 'It says they want you to take all precautions to avoid any further loss of life.'

'Good. Tell them I'd never have thought of it myself.'

'Hutch.'

'Tell them whatever you like. I don't really care, Marcel.'

The sun broke through. The sky cleared, and they hurried on. Something they couldn't quite make out tracked them for a while from the tops of a series of ridges. It ambled in the manner of an ape, but it apparently thought better of attempting an attack and eventually dropped out of sight.

'Scares me a little,' said Kellie.

'Why's that?'

'At home, a cougar or a tiger or a gator, if it was hungry, would go for you. Most of these critters keep their distance.'

'You're suggesting . . .'

'They're bright enough to know we're more dangerous than we look.'

By late afternoon, when the light began to change, they were out in open country again. 'Almost there,' Marcel said. 'Five klicks.'

The ground was uneven and covered with thick grass. Hutch was spent. Kellie, with her longer legs, was managing a bit better. But she, too, looked weary.

Periodically they talked to Mac and Nightingale. They were, they said, enjoying the view. There'd been a high tide at about midday, and the water had come well up the cliff face. But they believed they had a substantial safety margin. MacAllister commented that he was more comfortable than he'd been since leaving the *Star* and didn't know whether he'd ever get up on his feet again.

The sky turned purple and threatening.

'Three klicks.'

It was impossible to miss the worry in Marcel's voice.

'If you can move a little quicker, it would be a good idea.'

The splotch of light that represented the sun sank toward a line of hills. Rain began to fall.

The lander, cold and silent, stood on the banks of a river so narrow it scarcely deserved the name. It was, in fact, an idyllic scene: a line of trees, a few rocks, the river, and the dying light.

334

The trees marked the edge of the forest into which *Tess*'s crew had disappeared on that long-ago morning.

It seemed almost to be waiting for them. Hutch was pleased to see the old logo, the scroll within the orbiting star still defiantly crisp on the hatch. The lander was green and white, the colors all the Academy's vehicles had worn in the early days. And the legend ACADEMY OF SCIENCE AND TECHNOLOGY shone proudly on its hull.

They jogged across the remaining ground, not all-out because they couldn't see the holes and furrows. But Hutch remembered the voracious redbirds and glanced uneasily at the woods. 'We've got *Tess*' she told Marcel.

Marcel acknowledged, and she heard applause in the background.

Fortunately the hatch was closed. The ladder was still in place. Hutch climbed it, opened the manual control panel beside the airlock, pulled out the handle, and twisted it. The hatch clicked, and she pulled it open.

So far, so good.

They wasted no time getting through the inner door into the cabin. A layer of film and dirt covered the ports and windscreen, darkening the interior. Hutch sat down in the pilot's seat and scanned the console. Everything appeared to have been properly shut down.

In back, Kellie opened the engine panel in the deck and exposed the reactor. 'Do we know what we're doing?' she asked.

'Find the boron. I'll be right there.'

'Where are you going?'

She held up the collapsible container she'd taken from the *Star* lander. 'Down to the river to get some water. *You* look for the boron.'

Hutch wished that the pilot twenty years ago had had the foresight to land at the water's edge. The river was fifty meters away. She hurried down to it, filled the container, and dragged it back. When she got to the lander, Kellie showed her a canister.

'White powder?' she asked.

'That's it.'

'So what now?'

'We start the reactor.' A metal cylinder about the size of her arm was attached to the side of the device. The cylinder was equipped with a small crank.

'How do we do that? Is there a switch?'

'We'll have to jump-start it,' Hutch said. She shut down her e-suit and removed the Flickinger generator. 'I'll need yours, too.'

Kellie complied, turned off the power, and handed it over.

Hutch dug into her pack. 'I have a connector cable here somewhere.'

Kellie disappeared in back for a moment and returned with one. She held it up for inspection. 'Two inputs?' she asked.

'Perfect.' Hutch tied it to both generators and attached the other end to a post on the reactor. Then she detached the cylinder and poured a half cup of water into it. She turned the crank several times and reconnected the cylinder to the reactor. Then she added a spoonful of boron. 'Okay,' she said at last. 'I think we're ready to go.'

'Glad to hear it.'

'The system has a built-in Ligon roaster. All we have to do is start it.' She pressed her thumbs against the ignition switches for the Flickinger generators and pushed.

A yellow lamp on the reactor began to glow. Hutch's spirits went up a notch.

'Now what?' asked Kellie.

'Be patient. It's going to roast off a few impurities and give us enough hydrogen to run the reactor.' She closed her eyes and added, to the god within, I *hope*.

Kellie poked her. 'Hate to wake you. Hutch. But we've got a green light.'

The reactor was running on its own.

Hutch squeezed Kellie's arm, went back into the washroom, poured some river water into her hands, and washed her face. 'It has to charge,' she said. 'That's going to take a while. And there's nothing we can do to speed things up. But so far we're doing pretty well.'

She went outside, and Kellie boosted her up onto the hull. Hutch knelt beside the comm pod. The laser cut was clean, but she was able to replace damaged parts with the pieces she'd recovered from the *Star* lander. She rewired everything and, when she was satisfied it would work, climbed back down and returned to the pilot's seat.

She waited a few more minutes. Kellie paced the cabin nervously. 'We don't have a lot of time, Hutch,' she said. It was getting dark.

'I know.' Hutch propped her chin on her palm and scanned her instruments. 'All right, Collicr, if you're feeling lucky, let's see if we've got some power.' She put the vehicle into a test mode. Indicators and gauges jumped. 'That's my baby. Internal systems look good.'

'What's next?'

'Fuel.'

The rain had stopped, but the sky was still thick with clouds.

Hutch emptied the rest of the water into the fuel tank. They found a pump and hose for the tank, but the hose was only twenty meters long. 'A bit short to reach the river' said Kellie.

Hutch handed her the collapsible container. 'File a complaint when we get home.' She removed the lander's drinking water tank, which was *not* collapsible, and cradled it in her arms. 'We need a lot,' she said.

'What's the reactor actually do to the water?' Kellie asked as they hurried toward the river.

'It electrolyzes it. Separates the hydrogen and oxygen and gets rid of the oxygen.' And of course the lander would then run on the hydrogen.

They hauled water through the dark for the better part of three hours. They emptied each container into the fuel tank, hurried back to the river, refilled, and unloaded again.

When they had enough power to get some lift out of the spike, Hutch eased into her seat, murmured a prayer, and pressed a stud. Her control panel came to life, and she raised a joyous fist. 'On our way, baby,' she said.

She opened the command menu and pressed the green field marked *Tess*. Nothing happened except that the charge level dipped.

'Tess?' Hutch said. 'Are you there?'

A status line appeared on the AI monitor. It was flat.

'Looks as if *Tess* has gone to a happier world,' said Kellie.

'I'd say.'

'Try again?'

'No point. It just eats up power.' She extracted the control yoke from its bin and locked it into position.

Now she took a deep breath and started the turbines.

They sputtered, coughed, tried again, and finally staggered into life. She talked to them and coaxed them along until the power flow became smooth. 'I do believe we're in business,' she said.

'Do we have any lift?'

'Let's find out.' Hutch directed power into the spike. The gauges quivered and moved up a few notches. They were getting about twenty percent. Actually not bad, considering the age and probable condition of the capacitors. Not enough to get them into orbit, of course. Not nearly enough. But enough to get them off the ground.

Hutch opened the manual start-up compartment and activated the flight systems. Several lamps blinked on, gauges that would indicate airspeed, altitude, fuel mixture, engine temperature.

She couldn't taxi across the field and take off like twenty-first-century aircraft because she had no wheels. But the spike would get her up a couple of meters, and she could take it from there.

She drew her harness down and locked it in place. The spike activator was an illuminated gold panel. She pushed on it. Lamps changed color, and the word ENGAGED appeared on her screen.

338

Hutch felt her weight diminish somewhat. She put the thrusters into the lift mode and fired them. The vehicle *rose*.

It didn't go high. She could have jumped out without fear. *But it was sufficient unto the day.*

Kellie planted her lips on her cheek.

She maneuvered the spacecraft toward the river and brought it down on the bank. Then she shut everything off and they hustled outside.

Marcel chose that moment of absolute joy to break in. 'Bad news. The water's breaking through.'

'What are prospects?'

'It's not major yet. But it's going to get worse in a hurry.'

They attached the hose to the reactor tank, dropped the other end into the river, and started the pump. Twenty minutes later, they had full tanks.

They retrieved the pump and hose, waited patiently for another half hour while the reactor did its work. Then they lifted into the air and turned toward the northeast. Hutch raised her flaps and gunned it.

23

Despite all these years, we have not yet found anyone smarter than homo sapiens. The Noks remain caught up in their endless wars. Everyone else is dead, missing, or gone back to the woods. We are winning by default.

—GREGORY MACALLISTER, *Is Anyone Listening?*

Hours to breakup (est): 75

After Hutch and Kellie disappeared into the forest. Nightingale and MacAllister built a fire. Whatever adrenaline had been keeping MacAllister going now deserted him, and he sat almost motionless, eyes closed, propped against a tree. Nightingale had also reached the limits of his endurance, but he was frightened at the prospect of falling asleep, leaving nobody on watch.

He made coffee, drank it down, and felt marginally better.

Thank God the ordeal was almost over. This time tomorrow, if everything went well, he'd be out of it, back on *Wildside*, enjoying a hot shower, sleeping in a real bunk, ordering up whatever meals might cross his mind.

MacAllister mumbled something. His breathing fell to a regular pattern, and Nightingale listened to the wind in the trees and the hum of insects.

He looked out over the bay. Far below, large sea-colored birds flew in wide lazy circles, occasionally diving toward the water. He refilled his mug, sipped from it, put it down, dozed off, and snapped awake again when something touched his leg. It was a big bug with ten or twelve pairs of segmented legs and a vicious-looking set of claws. About the size of a lobster. He screamed, rolled away, and watched it scuttle back into the shrubbery.

Big bug. Hell of a reaction from a professional.

MacAllister never stirred.

But the incident had the effect of bringing him thoroughly awake. He talked to Hutch and Kellie, left the circuit on so he could listen in on their conversation, and occasionally traded comments with the *Wendy* mathematician who was their current contact. Then he began to sink again. 'Trouble staying awake,' he eventually told the mathematician.

'Okay.' She had a burgundy voice. 'Take off your link, set it for wide-angle visual, and let's aim it back into the woods. I'll try to keep watch for you.'

They wouldn't be able to see everything, she explained, but it would be better than nothing. He killed his field, removed the link, and set it on a rock. Then he buttoned up again.

'If we see anything,' she told him, 'I'll give a yell.'

Nightingale lay back, listening to the sullen roar of the tide. Then he closed his eyes.

He was vaguely aware of rain. Later he heard thunder. Another quake woke him briefly. And eventually he noticed that it had grown dark. MacAllister had apparently wakened long enough to throw a couple more logs on the fire. But he was fast asleep at the moment.

The tide was coming in. MacAllister sat gazing bleakly out over the bay.

'How're we doing?' Nightingale asked. 'Did they find the lander?'

'Ah.' MacAllister poured himself a fresh cup of coffee. 'You're awake.' He reached out and patted him on the shoulder, the way one might a pet collie. 'Yes,' he said, 'I'm happy to report they got there okay.' He made a second cup for Nightingale. 'Far as I can tell, they're doing fine.'

'Did they get it started?'

'Yes they did. A couple of hours ago, in fact.' Broad smile. 'They're loading up on fuel now. Randy, I do believe we're going to get away from this place with our skins after all.'

'I hope so.'

It was too cold to leave the suit off long, so Nightingale drank the coffee down and reactivated the field. That was something else he was looking forward to: being able to do basic physical maintenance without getting half-frozen.

A scuttering sound drifted up over the lip of the precipice. They looked at each other and drew their cutters from their vests. Nightingale walked to the edge and looked down. The entire face of the cliff was moving.

Coming this way.

'Heads up!' he told MacAllister.

Two pairs of jointed limbs appeared over the edge, scrabbled for a hold, and then a hardshell black creature, with somewhat the appearance of an ant about the size of a guard dog, climbed up onto flat ground. It weaved momentarily, righted itself, and clacked off past them into the dark.

But not before Nightingale had assessed it. The thing had claws like garden shears, eight thin segmented legs, and several sets of stalks.

A second one cleared the crest and lurched past them. Several more were scratching wildly for a grip on the bare rock.

Glittering and clacking, they hoisted themselves up, crossed through the firelight, and kept going.

'Mac?'

MacAllister had backed against a tree. 'Yes,' he said in a small voice. 'I'm here.'

'I think we're going to get lots of these things.' More were scrambling onto the summit. Mac's cutter flashed on.

343

Nightingale was looking frantically for a refuge. 'They're trying to get away from the rising tide.'

'What are they?'

'Big and clumsy. And dangerous.'

The numbers coming over the lip of the cliff seemed endless. 'What do we do, Randy? Get behind the fire?'

'No! That's not safe. If there's a stampede, they'll run right over it. Over *us*. Find yourself a tree.'

'I'm not sure . . .' He was gazing uncertainly at a tall hardwood. 'They're too big to climb'

'Get back of one.'

Hordes of the creatures wobbled past them. They ran in a pseudomechanical fashion, legs synchronized, mandibles pointed front as if they were expecting resistance. Those that moved too slowly or got in the way of bigger animals had their legs or antennas sheared off. One crashed into Nightingale, went down, and before it could get to its feet, was trampled. Another blundered into the fire, whistled pitifully, and ran on, trailing smoke.

When the panic was over, the dead and dying hardshells were heaped on all sides.

A straggler appeared. It was having a hard time getting onto level ground. After an interminable struggle, it succeeded, and they saw why: Two of its legs and several antennas were gone.

'What happens when they come back?' asked MacAllister.

'It won't be the same,' said Nightingale. 'It won't be a stampede.'

'That doesn't mean they won't be dangerous.'

'That's true. Also, they could be looking for a snack by then. It might be prudent to clear out of the area.'

Mac was looking both ways along the rim. 'I agree. Which direction? Back the way we came?'

'That doesn't sound like Gregory MacAllister.'

Mac laughed and shouldered his pack. 'All right then,' he said, 'onward it is.'

Both were refreshed by their long rest at the summit, and they set out at a steady pace. The arc of the gas giant was rising behind them, and the forest grew so bright they didn't need their lamps. *Not much longer.*

A fresh voice broke into his thoughts. Canyon.

'I hear things are happening, Dr Nightingale,' he said. 'I wonder if you'd care to describe them for us?'

'This is not a good time, August,' Nightingale said, and severed the connection.

'Exactly the right way to deal with the media,' said MacAllister.

'Hell, Mac, I thought *you* were the media.'

'I am indeed,' he said.

They stayed close to the rim of the escarpment. The bay spread out below them, a vast arm of the sea, smooth and hazy in Morgan's light. Along the shore, large tracts of woodland were in the water.

'Tide's come pretty far in,' said Nightingale.

It was rising visibly as they watched. 'You figure we're really high enough, Randy?'

Nightingale laughed. They were a long way up. 'I have to think that's the celebrated MacAllister wit.'

'Oh, yes. It is that.'

The forest literally went over the edge of the summit in some areas, and they were often so close to the precipice that a misstep could have ended in disaster. But occasionally the foliage opened out as much as a half kilometer. The glare of the giant planet had become so bright they were able to switch off their lamps.

MacAllister touched Nightingale's shoulder and pointed out over the water. A light was burning.

'It just came on,' he said.

And while they watched, it went off.

They peered into the semi-dark, but could make out nothing. The light came back on.

'What do you think it is?' asked MacAllister.

'Marine life.'

It went off. Nightingale lifted his lamp, pointed it out to sea, and blinked it.

The light in the water blinked back.

Mac frowned. 'I do believe somebody's saying hello.'

That hardly seemed possible. 'It's a luminous squid or something,' he said. 'We're looking at a mating call.'

'It wants to mate with *us*?'

'It wants to mate with the lamp.' Nightingale blinked again. A complicated series of longs, shorts, and mediums flashed back.

Mac got dangerously close to the edge. 'It looks like a code.'

'Did you know,' asked Nightingale, 'that some of the fireflies back home are really imitating other species of fireflies? Mimicking a desire to mate? When the recipient shows up for a big time, he gets eaten.' He narrowed his eyes, trying to pierce the darkness. It appeared to be simply a light on the surface. He imagined a hand raising a lantern from the depths.

'Can you make it out, Randy?'

'Just water.'

MacAllister blinked his light and looked expectantly seaward. There was, Nightingale thought, an element of play in his manner. He was *enjoying* this.

A reply came back, another complicated series.

'I can't tell what's doing it,' Nightingale said. 'It looks as if the light's *in* the water.' He stared at it. 'We should record it.'

MacAllister nodded. 'It almost seems like a fishing boat out there trying to talk to us.'

The ground shook. Somewhere below, a piece of rock broke off and fell down the face of the cliff into the bay.

Nightingale caught his breath, moved well back from the precipice, and waited for more shocks. When none came, he directed his scanner to record. At his signal, MacAllister blinked a couple of times, and again the lights flashed. One. Followed by two. Followed by three.

Nightingale felt a chill run down his back.

'Your squid can count,' said Mac. 'Do you think that intelligent life might have developed at sea?'

Well, it had back home. But it had taken a long time to recognize because it was nontechnological. Dolphins and whales were clever. And squids. But they didn't take to mathematics without prodding. 'It's had a long time to evolve,' Nightingale said.

Mac flashed once.

The answer came back: *Two.*

Nightingale pushed Mac's lantern down, and raised his own. He sent *Three.*

It answered: *Four.*

He looked through the glasses again. 'My God,' he said. 'We're going to come back with this story and no answers and people are going to scream.'

The ground trembled again, more intensely this time. 'Randy,' said Mac, 'this is not a good place to be right now.'

'I know.'

MacAllister took *his* shoulder. 'Come on. Before we both go into the pond.'

Nightingale nodded, pointed his lamp at the light source, and blinked again. Once. Good-bye.

The offshore light blinked back. Twice.

'They're still counting,' said Nightingale.

'How you guys doing?' Kellie's voice, sounding cheerful and relieved.

'Okay,' said Nightingale, who could not take his eyes off the bay.

'Good. I thought you'd want to know. We'll be in the air in a few minutes.'

Thank God.

'They're good babes,' MacAllister told him on the private channel.

24

Good fortune is less a product of talent or energy than it is a matter of timing. Being at the right place when the watermelon truck flips. This is how promotions happen, and how fortunes are made. Arrive at the intersection a minute behind, when the police are on the scene, and everything is undone.

—GREGORY MACALLISTER, *Lost in Babylon*

Hours to breakup (est): 63

Kellie looked down at Bad News Bay and sucked in her breath. The entire lower coastline had gone underwater, and the cliff top along which they'd walked was now not much more than a promontory.

'What do you think?' asked Hutch. She was referring to the diagnostic, and not the state of the bay.

'I don't know why the AI is disabled. Probably general degradation.'

'Okay. What else?'

'We've got problems with temp controls. Onboard communications are okay. Capacitors are at max, but we've only got twenty-one percent. That's all they'll take, apparently. Sensors are out. Forward dampers are down. We're getting a warning on the electrical system.'

Hutch made a face. 'Not *imminent* shutdown, I hope?'

'Negative.'

'Okay. When we get time I'll take a look at it. We've got plenty of spare parts on board.'

Normally, the pilot would run the diagnostic herself, but normally the AI would be operating the spacecraft. Hutch was busy.

Kellie ticked off a series of other problems, mostly minor, others potential rather than actual. 'We wouldn't want to do a lot of flying in this buggy. But it should get us to the tower.'

Hutch leveled off at two thousand meters, informed Marcel's surrogate they had no sensors, and with her help set course. The surrogate asked whether there was any chance they could ride *this* lander back to *Wendy*? As it was at the moment?

'Negative,' Hutch said. 'We can lift off and set down. We can even hover for a bit. But take it to orbit? That's not going to happen.'

Kellie took a minute to call Nightingale. 'How you guys doing?' she asked.

'Okay.'

'Good. We're overhead.' Then, to the surrogate: 'Allie, do we have time to pick up the rest of our crew?'

She nodded and throttled up. 'Negative. The plain is flooding as we speak. Lots of water.'

In the illumination cast by Jerry Morgan, the countryside was ghastly. Kellie saw the area where Chiang had died, and thought she could pick out the spot where the hovercraft was located. They soared over the dragonfly river.

Marcel came on the circuit. 'Hutch,' he said, 'there's a lot of water cascading into the valley. A *lot*. The tide keeps getting higher, and a long section of ridge has simply collapsed.'

It would continue to do so as Morgan moved across the sky. To the south, they saw roiling smoke.

350

'Volcano,' Marcel said. 'They're erupting all over the globe tonight.'

'What's the situation at the tower?'

'The water hasn't gotten there yet in any quantity. But it won't be long. Run your afterburners.'

'Afterburners,' said Hutch. 'Aye.' A joke, of course. She was already at maximum thrust.

Marcel continued: 'The tower's in a wide plain. There's a funnel of sorts that empties into it from the north. The water's coming through the funnel. When it hits the plain, it spreads out a bit. That's kept us out of the soup. But it won't contain things forever.'

'Any guesses on time?'

'How long's it going to take you to get there?'

'Twenty minutes.'

'It might be enough,' he said. 'You'll want to hit the ground running.'

'Mac.'

'Yes, Priscilla.'

'Mac, be careful. We'll be back as quickly as we can.'

'We'll be waiting.'

'You and Randy'll be okay?'

'We won't be if you don't get those batteries.'

'Capacitors, Mac.'

'Bear with me. I was never much of a technician. But by all means go get them. We'll leave a light on for you here.'

Marcel came up again. 'Hutch.' And she read everything in his voice, all the futility and despair and exasperation that had been building for days. 'You might as well break it off. Go back and—'

'What do you mean, *break it off*?'

'Just what I said. You don't have time to do this'

Kellie cut in. 'Goddammit, Marcel, we can't just *break it off*. We've got nowhere else to go here.'

'We're working on a backup plan. Forget the capacitors.'

'What's the backup plan?'

'It's complicated.'

'That's what I thought,' said Kellie. 'Give it to me in a couple of words.'

'We're going to try to take you right out of the sky.'

'You're *what*?'

'Pick you up in flight. I can't explain now.'

'I'm not surprised.'

'We're building a device that might work.'

'Marcel,' said Hutch, 'what's your level of confidence in this scheme?'

He apparently had to think about it. 'Look. Nobody's ever tried anything like this before. I can't promise success. But it's a *chancer*.'

'Right.' Kellie stared at Hutch. 'Go for the tower.'

Hutch agreed. 'I think we better get the capacitors.' She leaned forward in her chair as if she could urge the spacecraft to more acceleration.

'Hutch—' He sounded desperate.

Kellie shook her head. *Get there or nothing else matters.*

They were already at full throttle, had been since leaving the river. 'How much time do we have?' asked Kellie. 'Before the water reaches the tower?'

'The tower's getting its feet wet now.'

'How deep? How bad is it?'

'It's deep enough. You simply don't have time for this.'

'We're out over the plain,' said Hutch, 'and we don't see any water yet.'

'Take my word for it.'

'We're going to look, Marcel. We'll let you know.'

Kellie went private. 'We're not over the plain, Hutch,' she said. They were in fact passing over forest and ridges.

'We're only a couple of minutes away.' Hutch went back to Marcel. 'If it looks at all possible, we're going to try it.'

'I wish you wouldn't.'

'I wish we didn't have to. Now tell me about the water: What are we going to see? Waves? A gradual rise? What?'

'There's a wave on its way. Actually, a series of waves, running close together.'

'How far are they? From the tower? How high?'

'High enough to submerge the capacitors. They're at ground level, right?'

'Yes. On a table.'

'They're probably already in the water.'

'Any chance we can beat the waves? Any chance at all?'

'You've got about fifteen minutes.'

They were ten minutes away. Give or take. 'Okay, Marcel. All or nothing.'

'Speaking of which: You're off course. Come twelve points to port.'

Hutch moved the yoke to the left, and watched the guidance indicators. 'Okay?' she asked.

'Yeah,' he said despondently. 'Looks fine.'

Kellie listened to the steady roar of the jets and watched snow-covered ridges sweep past.

'We did a minimum charge,' Hutch told her. 'That means there's a possibility we may have to install the new capacitors before we can get off the ground. That could get interesting. You might take a look in back. Make sure we have everything close to hand in case we have to do the connections.'

'We going to do this in the backseat?'

'If things get tight, yes. We won't take time to remove the onboard capacitors. Just pull the connectors. We'll load the new ones in back as best we can, tie them in, and get the hell away. So we'll need electrical cable and wrenches ready to go.'

Kellie went back and began laying everything out.

The lander passed over the last line of hills and came out over the plain. They picked up the snow cover and the ground became ethereal, a spectral countryside of glistening trees and silver-etched shadows. Then the tones changed, and they were over water.

It looked shallow. Shin-high, knee-high. They could still see ground shrubbery. Kellie reported everything ready in the backseat.

Hutch watched the time and looked for the tower. 'Can't be far now.' And to Marcel: 'What happens if they get wet? The capacitors?'

'They aren't designed to be waterproof. Hutch. If they get wet, they will have to be dried out. Maybe they'd still be usable. I really can't say for certain, and we can't find the information in the database. But it's a circumstance we should have tried harder to avoid.'

Hutch understood what he was saying. They should have walked faster. She cut fuel and dropped close to the ground. The lander slowed. 'Kellie, keep an eye open.'

Trees and hills were creating wakes. A few animals fled before the current, and a pack of the wolflike creatures they'd seen early in their trek were moving southwest toward higher country, only their heads visible above water. They weren't going to make it.

'Hutch.' Marcel again. 'You're coming up on the tower. Three points to port, directly ahead, about two thousand meters.'

She killed the jets. The lander coasted through the silver light. 'It might be shallow enough that we can still do this,' said Kellie.

'I see it.' Hutch bent over the controls. 'I'm going to try to set down with as little help from the spike as we can manage. We want to save enough to get us out of here.'

She had no choice, however, but to use the system to stay aloft. Power levels were therefore falling. The reactor automatically shut down while they were in flight, so available power consisted of whatever had been stored in batteries or capacitors. And to save time they'd stored an absolute minimum.

Marcel's voice: 'You've got about six minutes before the ocean gets there.'

'How big's the first wave?'

'It's spreading out. Diminishing. But at the moment it's maybe ten meters.' Almost as high as the tower.

'There's our baby.' Kellie pointed. There was no sign of the chasm.

The tower rose out of the floodwaters, bleak and cold and desolate, but still standing. It seemed to Hutch almost biblical, last trace of a vanished civilization, a final defiant rocky digit raised against the unforgiving skies.

'Going down.' She lowered the treads.

'We might be okay,' said Kellie.

The lander's lights reflected off running water. Hutch went to reverse thrust, brought the vehicle almost to a standstill, and lowered it gently toward the ground.

To the north, she could make out a moving gray wall. 'Here comes the wave,' she said, activating her e-suit.

Hutch pushed the yoke forward and felt a mild jar as they touched down. Kellie opened the airlock and splashed out into the surge.

The current tried to drag her off her feet.

Hutch started out behind her, but she stopped in the airlock and watched the mountainous wave bearing down on them. Abruptly, to Kellie's dismay, she called her back. 'Forget it,' Hutch said. 'There isn't time.'

Marcel broke in. 'Let it pass,' he said. '*Then* try it.'

'No!' Kellie fought to stay on her feet. The current was moving north in the direction of the oncoming wave.

Hutch sounded cold and calm in her receiver: 'It won't do any good if we lose the lander.'

'We won't be able to find them afterward,' Kellie said. 'Dead now or dead later: What's the difference?' She was only steps away from the entrance, and she kept going.

'Won't improve things if we can't find *you* either,' Hutch said.

The wave was enormous, rising high and rising higher. A huge crest folded over and crashed down. Kellie stumbled into the tower. The capacitors lay on the worktable where they'd left them, covered by the tarp.

The water swirled around her ankles. The roar of the onrushing sea was deafening.

'Come on!' Hutch let her hear a cold flat tone. 'Kellie, I *have* to pull out.'

She actually *touched* one of the capacitors through the cloth. She couldn't leave without them. Couldn't *possibly* leave without them. Just pick the thing up and hustle back with it. But she needed Hutch. Couldn't get both of them alone.

'. . . get the lander clear.'

Kellie and the wave. It had a nice ring.

'God.'

She couldn't hope to carry it, though. Not in time—

She broke away finally and stumbled back through the muck. It was hard going, and she fell at the entrance, rolled, and came up running. Hutch stood in *Tess*'s hatch looking back past her shoulder. Looking *up*. Kellie splashed across the few meters as Hutch ducked inside. She heard the engines turn over, *felt* the shadow of the wave. The lander began to lift. The hatch was still open, but she had to jump for the ladder. She caught the bottom rung, hung on, dangled while *Tess* went up, watched the wall of water engulf the tower. It crashed over it. Submerged it. They were rising too slowly and then the vertically positioned jets cut in and they soared. She clung desperately, suddenly as heavy as a load of iron. She screamed, and the wave thundered beneath her.

The jets died, and Hutch let the lander sink a few meters. Kellie scrambled for a better grip, dragged herself up a couple more rungs, and got a foot on the ladder.

The tower was gone. She could smell seawater.

She fell in through the hatch and looked for something to throw at Hutchins, seated at the controls, not even looking back.

'You were going to leave me,' she said. 'You were actually going to leave me down there.'

'I'm responsible for two more people.' Hutch's voice simmered with anger. 'If you want to kill yourself, that's one thing. But I wasn't going to let you kill all of us.'

'We could have done it, goddam you.' She closed the hatch.

Hutch finally turned and looked at her. 'You had your hands full getting back as it was. What makes you think you could have done it carrying one of the capacitors?'

'We were too slow getting out of the lander. If we'd gone in as soon as we got here. No hesitation. Just done it—'

'We'd both be dead.'

Hutch circled around, and they flew over a sea of rampaging water. There was no sign of the tower. And a second wave was becoming visible.

They watched it in silence. It rolled in and swept past, higher than the first.

'We should have *tried*,' said Kellie.

She saw the tower, rising out of the flood, water pouring from its windows. Incredibly, it was still intact, other than a couple of pieces missing from its roof.

'Next one's three minutes away,' said Hutch.

The third wave was the giant. It kept building, and Hutch took them higher. A few trees had managed to keep their uppermost branches out of the water. But this one rolled over them and over the tower.

They waited, watching for the stone roof to reappear.

Marcel asked what had happened.

'Don't know yet,' said Hutch.

MacAllister and Nightingale also called in. 'We may have gotten here too late,' Hutch told them.

Hutch thought there was still a chance.

She engaged the jets, moved into a wide arc around the place where the tower had been, and shut down the spike, conserving energy.

'It's over,' said Kellie. Her voice shook.

'No. When the water subsides, we'll go down and look.'

But the site was now located at the bottom of a turbulent lake. The water level rose and sank as they watched. More waves thundered in. Sometimes the newly formed sea exposed large swatches of ground. But Hutch was no longer sure where the tower had even *been*.

'Hutch.' Marcel's voice. 'It should start to recede in an hour or so.'

'We've got an ocean at the moment,' she said. 'You say *recede*. Is the water going to go back out?'

'Well, not really. Some of it will. But a lot of it's going to stay right where it is. At least for the next few days.'

'Good' said Kellie. 'We don't have anything better to do. We'll just—'

'That's enough,' said Hutch. She continued to circle.

MacAllister called again. 'Listen, you did your best. Don't worry about it.'

All these people depending on her.

Kellie gave Hutch a withering look, and Hutch was getting tired of that, too.

Over the next forty-five minutes, more waves, large and small, swept through the area. Morgan moved silently across the sky into the west, enormous and bright and lovely.

At last the water began to ebb, running back the other way. A wake appeared off their starboard side. It was the tower, broken and shattered.

Cautiously, Hutch set the lander down in the retreating current and began recharging the reactor. They sat in strained silence almost an hour, until the force of the runoff had subsided. Then they climbed out into the current. The water came to their waists.

The top of the tower and the upper chambers had been ripped off. The worktable was gone, as were the capacitors. They looked carefully at the ground floor. They even took lamps and swam down the staircase to the level below. But there was nothing.

They searched the surrounding area, marking off sections and walking and swimming through them as thoroughly as they could.

Jerry set, and the sun rose.

They cannot live apart. But she is wiser than I thought. She cares for the aquarium, and feeds the fish, and keeps them alive and healthy.

25

Luck does not come out of a vacuum. It is manufactured by organization.

—GREGORY MACALLISTER, 'The Art of Julio Agostino', Editor at Large

Hours to breakup (est): 60

NEWSLINE WITH AUGUST CANYON

'The small landing party marooned on Maleiva III lost a race with the sea hours ago when the giant tides being stirred up by the approach of Morgan's World flooded extensive northern tracts of the continent everyone here calls Transitoria, and washed away two capacitors that would have lifted the stranded explorers into orbit. Nevertheless, authorities on board the Evening Star insist they have not given up.

'It's the middle of the day here, Tuesday, December 5. Inside sources expect that conditions on Maleiva III will deteriorate tomorrow, and grow much worse Thursday. They are predicting that the planet will begin to break up Thursday night. A last-ditch effort is being mounted to construct a

361

kind of sky scoop. Universal personnel will be closely involved in the attempt and I'll be back with details on a special broadcast later today.

'*This is August Canyon, in orbit around Deepsix.*'

Janet's volunteers were near the end of their third day of training when word came. They would be going outside.

Tonight.

The reaction was mixed. The news was accompanied by a sober moment while they digested the fact that the stakes, for them, had just gone up. Janet detected a trace of apprehension, now that a serious commitment had been made. But they went back to work with a will.

As to herself? She was delighted she'd come.

Chastain stopped by the Bryant Auditorium to talk to the volunteers about the Flickinger field. They were now calling themselves the Outsiders.

Only one of the thirty-odd volunteers had ever worn an e-suit before entering the training program. He reviewed how the systems worked, took questions, played a sim, and inspected harnesses. They talked about the Flickinger field, what it could do, what it could not do. He laid down some basic safety procedures, like not losing physical contact with the ship or with the alien assembly on which they'd be working.

After dinner the outsiders were called back for an evening session, during which Janet introduced Mercedes Dellamonica, Nicholson's executive officer. She was a cool, unemotional native of Mexico City. She, Marcel, and Janet accompanied the trainees outside in groups of fifteen, each taking five. They walked around on the hull, got used to conditions, got used to the systems, acquired enough skill with the communications package to get by, and received once again all the appropriate warnings, including a demonstration by Mercedes, who deliberately lost contact with the surface, floated off, and had to be rescued.

They did some zero-gee welding. Afterward they were required to give a final demonstration of their skills. When they'd finished, two more were excused.

A few tennis nets had been strung together outside, courtesy of Captain Nicholson, and those who were scheduled to work on the asteroid net got some practice climbing around on them.

At the end of the session, around eleven, they were herded into a dining room adjoining the captain's own. An assortment of snacks was served, compliments of the *Star*. Their instructors were present, and when everyone was assembled. Captains Nicholson and Clairveau filed in. Nicholson made a short speech, thanking them for their effort, and expressing his confidence that they would succeed. Afterward they were called forward individually and awarded certificates emblazoned with an image of a woman dressed apparently for an afternoon on the links, carrying a welding torch, and sitting confidently atop two of the assembly shafts.

Behind the two captains, stretched across the bulkhead, was a banner carrying the same image. Below the woman, dark green script spelled out *Evening Star*. Above was the legend *The Outsiders*.

Pindar Koliescu was delighted with himself. He'd gone outside with the rest, had handled the e-suit with aplomb, had shown a decent adroitness wielding the laser. He felt he understood enough to cut and weld with the best of them. Not bad after only three days' practice. But then he'd always been a quick study.

He was the founder of Harbinger Management Systems, which specialized in teaching people how to supervise subordinates and oversee resources. It was mundane stuff, but it was sorely needed in the commercial world of the early twenty-third century. Harbinger had made him wealthy and allowed him to indulge his principal hobby: cruising into the unknown with beautiful women.

His partner on this tour was Antonia Luciana, an exquisite

and insatiable young Roman who had kept him in quite a good mood since the start of the voyage. Antonia had tried to discourage him from joining the rescue effort, had struggled to hold back tears when he insisted, had then suggested she would have liked to go along too but doubted her ability to learn the requisite skills within the time frame. She had also admitted that the prospect of going *outside* terrified her.

In the manner of the excellent manager he was, he understood, and left her to applaud his pending heroics.

Pindar was enjoying himself thoroughly. He'd gotten caught up in the emotional swirl surrounding the rescue effort, he had come to feel a kinship with the four people on the surface, and he understood that no display of courage and skill on his part, however memorable it might be, would be satisfying unless the rescue succeeded.

The ceremony was short. 'You'll all want to get a good night's sleep,' Captain Clairveau told them at its conclusion. 'We've set up special quarters for you. I'm told you already know about that, and you know where they are. We'll escort you there anyhow when we've finished here.' He grinned. 'Consider yourselves in the military for the duration. Your morning will start early. I'd like to remind you that after you leave this room everything becomes real.'

They gave Janet the last word. She thanked her fellow Outsiders, assured them she'd be with them throughout the operation, and gave them their final instructions.

Pity. Antonia would have been thoroughly aroused by his pending exploit. Pindar consoled himself that he was making a magnanimous sacrifice and trooped off with the others.

Before bedding down for the night he called her. Her lovely image took shape and shimmered in front of him. She'd adapted her signal to present herself with precisely the degree of insubstantiality that enhanced her natural beauty. 'It's going fine,' he assured her. 'They're breaking us into groups of two and three. I've been assigned as a team leader. Can you imagine that? Me, a skyhog?'

'You *will* be careful?' said Antonia. 'I want you to come back to me.' She tried to purr, but it didn't work because she was really worried for him, and that knowledge stirred him, demonstrated it was not just his position and power that had won her over. It forced him to recognize once again that he must be an extraordinary person to command such affection from one so lovely.

'Have no fear, *Amante*,' he said. 'You just relax and enjoy the rescue.'

'Pindar.' She peered at him closely, as though to see into him. 'You're really not afraid?'

'No,' he said. 'Everything will be fine'

'Will I be able to see you?' She meant on the viewscreens.

'I'm sure you will.'

She tilted her head and smiled. 'I'll be glad when it's over.'

In the morning, they were awakened early, at about five, and marched back to the same dining room, where they received a light breakfast. Afterward he met his partner, an attractive brunette whose name was Shira DeBecque. He and Shira boarded a shuttle headed for *Wendy*. They talked over their tasks en route, and arrived on the science ship in good spirits. There they met the shuttle pilot who'd be working with them during the balance of the morning, received their schedules, and set up their gear.

Marcel could see the dismay in Ali Hamir's eyes. Ali was *Wendy*'s lead technician. He'd thought there was a decent chance to reconfigure the scanners and conduct a successful search for the capacitors. But resolution below the surface of objects smaller than a human being had not proved possible. The wave action had picked up and redeposited millions of rocks and other pieces of debris. There was no way to determine which two, if any, might be the missing units.

Marcel blamed himself for the failure at the tower. There'd been time to get to *Tess* and recover the capacitors had he not relied on the wave projections. He should have hustled them along. He should have insisted they do what they had finally done: split up and make best time for the lander. He and Hutch had discussed it, but she'd believed the danger too great to leave anyone behind. Marcel had gone along with her, reluctantly. Now he saw the magnitude of his error.

Several of Ali's people were seated in front of the operational screens, forlornly watching hundreds of markers blinking. Rubble in the muck beneath the newly created inland sea.

'Hopeless,' said Beekman.

Moose Trotter, a mathematician from the University of Toronto and, at 106, the senior member of the mission, had always seemed unfailingly optimistic. But Moose now looked like a man in pain, wandering from station to station, neglecting the work that had brought him there.

Marcel had been asked whether, if the sky-scoop initiative didn't work out, communication with the ground party should be cut off as conditions worsened. Benny Juarez, a close friend of Kellie's, thought anything less than granting the victims their privacy during their last hours, if it came to that, would be indecent.

Nicholson was getting an update from his engineer when Mercedes Dellamonica called him. 'What have you got, Meche?' he asked.

'A delegation,' she said. 'Maybe a dozen people at the moment, but it looks like more coming. They're unhappy about the rescue effort.'

The locator put her on the bridge. 'On my way,' he said. He called the kitchen and ordered several cartloads of refreshments sent up and then left the operations center and took the elevator topside. He rehearsed his comments on the way. But he was taken aback by the sheer number of angry passengers. More were trying to push into the area from outside.

The exec was standing behind a table trying to talk into a microphone. He strode through, got to Mercedes, and turned to face the crowd.

They got louder. Nicholson knew many of them. He was almost an ideal cruise-ship captain. One of his strengths was that he never forgot a name. Laramie Payton, a building contractor from the American Northwest, asked the question Nicholson knew would be at the top of the agenda: 'What's this about our being *welded* to that alien *thing*?'

'Laramie,' he said smoothly, 'I've explained all that already. There's no danger. You can rest assured I wouldn't do *anything* that would put the *Evening Star* at risk. We *will* be welded, but keep in mind this is a *very* big ship. If we need to, at any time, we'll be able to break away from the assembly as easily as you could break an egg. So you just don't have to worry about that at all.'

Hopkin McCullough, a British communications tycoon, demanded to know how he could be so sure. 'They're talking about pushing that thing down into the atmosphere. How do we know we won't go down with it?'

Nicholson raised his hands. 'We have *engines*, Hop. The fact that we're helping push isn't going to affect our ability to maneuver if we have to. It's just not a problem. Anybody else?'

He gave a few more reassurances. The donuts and coffee arrived. The disorder subsided, and the captain strolled out among his patrons, clapping some on the back, and chatting idly with others. 'I can understand why you'd be worried, Mrs Belmont,' he'd say, 'but there's really no cause for concern. We're going to rescue those people tomorrow and then we'll be on our way.'

PART THREE
Skyhook

26

There is little that is actually impossible if one is in a position to apply energy and intelligence. It is our willingness to conclude this or that cannot be done that usually defeats us. Consider for example how long the outhouse was with us.

—GREGORY MACALLISTER, *Notes from Babylon*

Hours to breakup (est): 54

NEWSLINE WITH AUGUST CANYON

'This is August Canyon reporting from Deepsix, where, as you can see, Morgan's World has become by far the dominant feature in the sky. You're looking at the gas giant as it will appear tonight over the largest continent on the planet, a place aptly named Transitoria, where the Gregory MacAllister group remain stranded.

'A last-ditch rescue effort continues today, in which Universal News will play an integral part. At this moment the science research vessel Wendy Jay is lying alongside the skyhook counterweight which scientists found here several days ago.

'To fill us in on the details of the mission, Miles Chastain, captain of the UNN starship Edward J. Zwick, *is with us, although he's actually speaking from the* Wendy Jay, *where he's advising the rescue team.*

'Captain Chastain, how precisely is this going to work?'

Miles had just completed mounting lasers in the auxiliary housings on the hulls of four of the shuttles, and was now reviewing the allocation of the shuttle fleet to the needs of the operation. They had a total of seven vehicles: three from *Wendy,* two from the *Star,* and one each from the other two ships. He was consequently feeling a bit crowded when he got on the circuit with Canyon. He delivered a few responses that might charitably have been described as curt, and excused himself. But Canyon made it work, emphasizing the point that things were accelerating, that the operation was on the move, and that there was simply no time for small talk. It was all very dramatic.

Miles had expected, as he sat down to go over mission requirements, that Canyon would be miffed. Instead, the newsman called to express his appreciation for what he called Miles's performance. 'It was superb,' he said. 'Couldn't have scripted it better.' He grinned. 'I believe, Miles, if you ever get tired of piloting, you could have a career as a journalist.'

They landed near a lake, refueled, and then hurried on to pick up MacAllister and Nightingale. It was a gloomy reunion. Hutch got a lot of commiseration. *'Nice try,'* and *'You did what you could.'* And: *'Maybe this sky scoop will work.'*

Kellie remained uncharacteristically quiet.

The reactor switched on as soon as the engines were off, and commenced recharging the various systems. Mac slipped into a seat and commented how good it was to be indoors again.

The ground shook constantly.

'After a while,' said Nightingale, 'you don't notice it.'

Morgan's wide arc was just dropping out of sight, behind the trees. The eastern sky was brightening, and the clouds had cleared off. It looked as if, finally, a sunlit day was coming. 'So what about the sky scoop?' asked Nightingale. 'What is it? Will it work? When does it happen?'

Hutch and Kellie had received more details from Beekman. But the planetologist, to use Kellie's phrase, had never learned to speak English. The description had been too technical, even for Hutch. She understood in general terms what they proposed to do, but she simply couldn't credit *impossibillum* with the capabilities they claimed for it. On the other hand, what else had they? 'They're telling us day after tomorrow. Local time.'

'*Day after tomorrow?*' Mac was horrified. 'Aren't conditions supposed to be a little rough by then?'

'It's the best they can do. Pickup will be out over the Misty Sea. During late morning.'

'Where in hell is that?' demanded Mac.

'The Misty Sea? Off the west coast. The rendezvous won't be far from here, really.'

'Bottom line,' pressed MacAllister. '*Will it work?*'

Surely Beekman's physicists knew what they were talking about. 'Yes,' Hutch said. 'I'd guess it'll be tricky. But I think we'll get clear.'

'Tricky?'

'The timing.'

'When you say you *think*,' said MacAllister, 'it doesn't give me confidence.'

'It's a long shot,' said Kellie.

MacAllister was working hard to control his voice. 'Okay,' he said. 'Now we're talking about being here a couple more days. What about this deterioration we keep hearing about? I mean, it's already a little weathery out there. How bad's it going to get? What's actually going to happen?'

'You really want the details?' asked Hutch.

'Of course.' And then Mac's voice softened. 'Please.'

Everyone turned to look at her. 'There've already been major quakes. Apparently none in this area yet. But there will be. And they'll get worse. Off the scale. We can look for chunks of land to be shoved as much as fifteen or twenty kilometers into the sky. There are going to be more volcanoes. Bigger and better. And giant storms.' She paused momentarily and let them listen to the wind. 'Higher tides than last night. *Much* higher. We'll have to find high ground somewhere. In three days, more or less, the atmosphere will get ripped away. We should be well away by then.'

'That seems like a good idea.'

'The oceans will go a few hours later.'

'The outer crust will melt. That's tidal effects and volcanic activity, as I understand it. At that point the planet will seriously begin to come apart. They're figuring midnight Thursday or maybe a little later ship time, which is coincidentally about the same time here. Approximately forty hours later, the pieces will fall into Jerry and go splash.'

'My God,' said MacAllister. 'There must be *some* way we can get off this goddam place. If the scoop doesn't work. Maybe we could get aloft, get swept off when the atmosphere goes, and *then* get picked up.'

'Not possible,' said Hutch.

'It's a *chance.*' His eyes flashed angrily. 'You sit here and keep telling us what *won't* work. What will?'

'It's *not* a chance,' said Kellie. 'Even if we did get tossed free without getting boiled, which wouldn't be very likely, there won't be anybody to pick us up.'

MacAllister's breathing was becoming labored. 'Why not?'

'Because the collision's going to put out a lot of energy. The neighborhood's going to explode like a small sun when things begin to happen. They're going to have to get the ships well clear before then.'

'Speaking of which,' added Hutch, 'we ought to head for safer ground.' She didn't like the way the area constantly bobbed and weaved.

MacAllister sighed. The endless supply of glib comments seemed finally exhausted. 'You said *Wendy*'s still looking for the capacitors. That means there's still a chance to find them, right?'

'There's a *chance*,' Hutch said.

'Maybe we should go back and look ourselves,' said Mac. 'It's not as if we have any other pressing business.' He sounded betrayed.

'We don't have working sensors,' said Hutch.

'Which means,' observed Nightingale, 'that all we could do would be to spend our last hours mucking around hip-deep in the water. You really want to do that?' He gazed at MacAllister for a long moment, and then turned back to Hutch. 'How the hell did we get into this, anyhow?'

They were casting about for someone to blame. Kellie hadn't revealed the details of their abortive attempt to retrieve the capacitors, Hutch was sure. But they felt resentful and frustrated, and they were scared. They'd certainly been listening during the salvage effort. They could not have missed Kellie's pleas. Hutch knew what that must have sounded like. Cowardly pilot blinks at the critical moment.

And she herself could not avoid thinking how easily things could have turned out differently. It had been only a matter of minutes. How many *minutes* had they squandered during the nine days of the march? If they'd left a little earlier one morning . . . Walked a bit later one night . . . Not stopped to poke into the chapel . . . If they'd left Nightingale and Mac sooner rather than later . . .

MacAllister turned a beaten gaze out the window. A wide stream gurgled past, tall green trees like nothing ever seen on Earth sparkled in the early-morning light, and a bright golden bird with red-streaked wings was walking around on the fuselage. The scene was idyllic. 'Are we sure we can't ride this thing out of here? It doesn't seem as if it would hurt to *try*.'

'We're sure. Essentially, what we've got is a rocket-assisted jet aircraft. The rockets are for maneuvering in zero gee, but they don't pack nearly enough punch to get us into orbit. We can use the spike to negate our weight, but only for a little while. A few minutes or so.'

'So if we tried it . . .?'

'We'd probably get up to twelve, thirteen thousand meters, maybe a little higher. We'd have a couple of minutes to wave, and then we'd fall back. And incidentally, if we exhausted our lift capability in the effort, we'd have no way to land.'

'I don't suppose,' Mac persisted, 'that one of the ships could come down to twelve thousand meters and pick us up?'

'No,' said Kellie. 'The superluminals can't navigate in the atmosphere.'

'Nor the shuttles?'

'Nor the shuttles.'

'So all we've got is the scoop.'

'No.' Kellie stared out at the rain. 'Hutch is right: There's not much chance of finding the capacitors. But I don't think it would hurt to look. Maybe we'll get a break.'

Hutch agreed, seeing no more useful way to spend the time, and Nightingale reversed his position and decided it was the only reasonable thing to do. Hutch engaged the spike and took off.

They sat quietly during the early minutes of the flight, as if by refusing to talk they could halt the passage of time and cling to these last hours. Nobody laughed anymore.

They were leaving the area of the bay when Hutch's commlink vibrated, Marcel calling. She put him on the allcom. 'How are you folks holding up?' He sounded artificially cheerful. Marcel was a good guy and a competent captain, but she was discovering he was the world's worst actor.

MacAllister grumbled something she couldn't make out.

'We're okay,' she said.

'I've a message for you.'

'For *me*?' asked Hutch.

'For all of you. In fact, we have a lot of messages, *thousands* of them. The whole world is following this. And wishing you well.'

'Nice to be at the center of attention,' said MacAllister.

'Of course,' he continued, 'they're all at least two days old. The people sending them don't know about . . .' – he paused, trying to find a diplomatic way to phrase it – '. . . about losing the capacitors.'

'You said there was *one* message specifically?'

'Two, actually.'

'You want to read them?'

'First one's from the General Commissioner of the World Council. She says: "*We admire your bold effort to expand the limits of human knowledge and your willingness to embrace the hazards that inevitably accompany such undertakings. Be assured that all humankind joins me in praying for your safe return.*" Signed Sanjean Romanovska.'

'Good,' said MacAllister. 'We'll all get monuments. Maybe even streets in Alexandria named after us.'

'What else have you got?' asked Hutch.

'One from Gomez. It's for you.'

'Read it,' she said.

'"*Priscilla, I need not tell you that we here at the Academy are delighted that there will apparently be a happy ending to this unfortunate incident. You had us worried for a while.*"'

'Those of us down here,' said MacAllister, 'have been worried, too.'

'What's the rest of it, Marcel?'

'It says, "*Now that you're out of danger, I want to ask you to take a look at the area designated Mt. Blue, where the base of the skyhook is reported to be located. It's essential that we know what happened on Deepsix. Where the advanced technology came from. I know it's asking a lot after what you've been through, but I know I can count on you.*" It's signed *Irene*.'

'Irene?'

'That's what it says.'

Back at the Academy, Irene Gomez could have fallen over Hutch in the corridor without knowing who she was. But it *would* be something for them to *do*. 'Give us a minute,' she told Marcel. Then she put him on hold. 'What do you think?' she asked her companions.

'This isn't brain surgery.' said MacAllister. 'We have one chance to come out of this alive: find the capacitors. Maybe my vote shouldn't count. I can't say I care much *what's* on top of Mt. Blue. I think we should be concentrating on getting out of here. I mean, hell, they want to send us on another chase. I think we've had enough.'

'Randy?'

He considered it. 'Maybe Mac's right. Maybe we *should* take a look at the tower area first. If it seems hopeless, then we could make for the mountain.'

Kellie shook her head. 'I hate to be negative, but I've been there, at the tower, and I don't think we have much chance of finding anything. Those were big waves. God knows where the capacitors are now. But, on the other hand, I *do* know we won't find them on a mountaintop.'

Hutch reopened Marcel's channel. 'We're going back to look for the capacitors.'

'Okay. I can understand that.'

'Send Irene my regrets.'

There was an awkward pause. Then Marcel reminded them there was more mail. 'The commcenter,' he said, 'has been overwhelmed with good wishes for you. For everybody.'

Hutch was impressed. Sending a hypercomm message was not inexpensive. 'Overwhelmed?'

'Thousands of them. Probably be more than that if we had a wider reception capacity. They tell us they're backed up pretty heavy at Relay. Whole classrooms of kids, in some cases.'

'I don't suppose you have any way of sorting out the personal stuff?'

'Not easily. Even by last name, I can't be sure. We have sixteen messages for *you* from people named *Hutchins*. Eighteen for Randy from assorted *Nightingales*. Ditto for everybody else.'

'All right.' said Hutch. 'Keep mine for now. Why don't you put somebody on with each of these other folks? They may have specific names they'll be looking for.' She thanked him and disconnected. Nightingale stared at her, and she could see the judgment forming. *Nobody in your entire life you want to hear from at a time like this?*

Of her immediate family, only Hutch's mother was still alive. Relations between the two had been strained for years over Hutch's failure to settle down and have a family. Like a normal young woman. Of course. Hutch wasn't that young anymore, a fact that seemed to have escaped her mother. Or added to her sense of panic. Even though she remained at the height of her physical capabilities, as people routinely did for their first century or so, she had long since discarded the happy innocence one might expect of a bride.

She'd been around long enough to know precisely what she wanted out of life. She believed weddings had to happen reasonably early if they were to have a chance of success. Mates had to grow together. She knew what she would expect of a man, and there simply was no such creature in captivity. So if she'd been stuck with being alone, and sometimes lonely, she had at least not been lonely in a marriage, which was the worst of all worlds. Anyhow, she liked her independence.

Mom had never understood. Had never wanted to understand.

Hutch sat looking at her notebook. And finally, with reluctance, opened it and tapped in a message:

Mom,
It looks as if we're down to a couple of days. Things haven't gone as well as we'd expected. But we're hopeful. You'll know how it turned out by the time you receive this.

She thought about it, wrote some more, apologized for not being the daughter her mother had wanted, explained that she'd enjoyed her life, and hoped her mother would understand that she, Priscilla, would not have had it any other way.

Having broken through the wall, she wrote to a few others, mostly people connected with the Academy.

Doesn't look promising at the moment.

They were good times.

I was thinking about you last night . . .

MacAllister looked over her shoulder and smiled. 'Be careful, Priscilla. Don't say anything you can be held to when you get home.'

There was no one with whom she could claim a romantic relationship. There'd been some men over the years, of course. One was dead. The others were happily married in suburban New Jersey or points west.

She sat quietly, trying to think what to say to old friends, and found herself regretting things not done. People for whom she had not made sufficient time. The great love that had never quite shown up. The child not borne.

Now that she faced possible termination, her life seemed curiously incomplete. She'd heard somewhere that, when death was near, one's regrets were not for one's actions, the assorted small and petty acts, the occasional immoralities, even the periodic cruelties visited on others. But rather one regretted things *not* done, adventures not undertaken, experiences left untasted, whether through some false code of morality or, more likely, shyness or fear of failure.

She smiled to herself. MacAllister had said somewhere, *through fear of getting caught.*

27

Few of the virtues are really useful. Fidelity leads to lost opportunity, truth-telling to injured feelings, charity to additional solicitations. The least productive, and possibly the most overrated, is faith. The faithful deny reason, close their minds to the evidence of their senses, and remain unfailingly optimistic in the face of disaster. They inevitably get just what they deserve.

—GREGORY MACALLISTER, *'Along for the Ride'*,
Reminiscences

Hours to breakup (est): 45

Janet Hazelhurst's people had been transported to their stations and were ready to go.

John Drummond reported that his team had worked out the details for the assembly. 'They've got it all down?' demanded Marcel. 'Every step?'

'Every step.'

'What about the rest of it?'

Beekman took him through the entire plan. The shuttles were fueled and ready. Phil Zossimov was on schedule with his collar and dividers. They were working on this, getting *that* set up. There were problems, but that was unavoidable on a jury-rigged operation this big.

'Nothing insurmountable?'

'Not so far.'

Marcel had slept a few hours, and felt better than he had in a week. But he watched Beekman suspiciously.

'What?' asked Beekman. 'What's wrong?'

'I'm waiting for you to tell me.'

'Marcel, nothing is wrong. We're doing pretty well. Better than we have a right to expect.'

They were still twenty minutes from the tower when Marcel told them *Wendy*'s search team had given up trying to find the capacitors.

'Up to us,' said Mac. 'Good thing we didn't go to Mt. Blue.'

Hutch felt better in flight, with full fuel tanks and the ground far below. Her natural optimism came back when she could throttle up. Even in these circumstances she could not escape the sense that with the jets running, anything was possible. She wondered at the recovery of her spirits and mentioned it to Mac, who suggested she was wired to assume the world was a permanent place, a view which had surely been shaken by recent events. Here among the clouds, however, they could see forever, and life did indeed seem infinite.

The day had closed in almost as soon as they'd left the ground. Hutch had gotten away from a long line of storms, and they were flying through gray, overcast skies streaked with dust. 'Volcanoes, probably,' said Nightingale.

Kellie shook her head. 'I think they'd tell us if volcanoes were going off in the neighborhood.'

Hutch wondered if that were so. Marcel might be reluctant to introduce still more bad news. In fact this had to be a nightmare for the people on *Wendy*. They might almost be wishing it were over.

There were occasional calls, from Embry, asking whether

everyone was physically okay, and could she be of assistance in any way? Guilty conscience, probably.

And from Tom Scolari, also sounding guilty, telling her he was doing everything he could to help recover them. Scolari was with the Outsiders. 'It's going to be okay,' he said. Sure. How good was he at manufacturing landers?

Kellie got calls from friends on *Wendy*. 'I wish,' she said, 'they'd just let me be. They keep telling me to hang in. What the hell else can we do?'

Mac received one from Nicholson, assuring him they were making 'every effort to extract him from his plight.' MacAllister thanked him politely and shook his head. 'How's *your* plight, Hutch? You know, I believe that's the first time I've ever actually heard a living person use that word.'

The lander flew on through the deepening morning, on this twelfth local day since their arrival on Deepsix. It now seemed to Hutch as if their departure from *Wildside* had occurred in another lifetime.

Sometimes the clouds closed in, and they could see nothing. There was no other traffic in the sky, of course, and she was confident she was above any nearby peaks, but she disliked flying blind, with neither vision nor instruments. She was dependent exclusively on guidance from *Wendy* and the satellites. To complicate matters, they lost communications with the orbiting ships for almost six minutes.

'Local interference,' their contact told them when the system came up again. 'The storm systems are starting to play hell with communications.'

Augie Canyon called, asked a few questions, and reminded them a lot of people were praying for them back home.

'Anybody here believe in life after death?' Kellie looked around at her companions.

'I do,' MacAllister said carefully.

'*You* do?' Nightingale suppressed a smile. 'You've made a career of attacking moralists and reformers, Mac. And whole sections of the country that you thought took their preachers too seriously. Which is to say that they took them at all. What are we getting here? A deathbed conversion?'

'Randy.' MacAllister's expression denied all charges. 'I'm shocked and dismayed that you would think that of me. I have only attacked people who pretend to have the answers to everything. For the very good reason that they're either imbeciles or charlatans. But that doesn't mean I've denied there's a spiritual dimension to life.'

'Really? A spiritual dimension?' Nightingale arched his eyebrows. 'Sir, what have you done with Gregory MacAllister?'

'Wait a minute,' said Kellie. 'That's a fairly sweeping statement anyhow. Are you making those charges about everyone who belongs to an established faith? What about Brother Dominic?'

Yes, thought Hutch. Brother Dominic was a modern St. Francis who'd worked forty years among the poor in east Asia. 'A fine man,' MacAllister allowed. 'I'll give you that. But I'd say he's locked into a belief system that's closed his mind.'

'You're talking about the Roman church?'

'I'm talking about any system that sets up a series of propositions that are supposed to be taken as the word from on high. Adherents get so caught up in their certainties that they miss the important things. What does Brother Dominic know about quantum mechanics?'

'What do *you* know about quantum mechanics?' demanded Hutch.

'Not much, I'll grant you. But then, I don't pretend to be pious.'

'I'm a bit slow,' said Nightingale. 'Make the connection for me.'

'Randy, doesn't it strike you that anyone truly interested in the creator, if in fact there *is* a creator, would want to take time to look at his handiwork?' He smiled benevolently at Hutch. 'Or *her* handiwork? Matter of fact, doesn't it seem likely that the creator might be a bit miffed at anybody who spends a lifetime walking around paying serious attention to church architecture and misses the stars?

'People who wear their religion on their sleeves talk a lot about going to Sunday school, reading the Bible, and doing good works. And I suppose there's no harm in that. But if I'd gone to the trouble to put all this together' – he raised his hands in the general direction of infinity – 'and people never paid any attention to it, never bothered to try to find out how the world worked, then I think I'd get annoyed.'

'I'm glad you're not running things,' said Kellie.

MacAllister agreed. 'There'd be a lot more direct action,' he assured them.

'So,' said Nightingale, unable to let it go, 'the great atheist defends theology.'

MacAllister shrugged. 'Not theology,' he said. *'Belief.'*

The conversation reminded Hutch, if she needed reminding, how frightened she was. She worried about how she'd respond if the rescue plan didn't work.

Nightingale studied her, and that dark gaze seemed to penetrate her soul. He reached over and touched her wrist. 'It's okay,' he said. 'Whatever happens, we're in it together.'

NOTEBOOKS OF RANDALL NIGHTINGALE

It's good to be in the lander. Even though it can't get us out of here, at least we've regained a sense of minimal control over what's happening. I can't explain it, but being relegated to walking around in the woods for several days left me feeling absolutely powerless. Maybe things haven't changed a whole lot, but it's nice to be able to take off, and to look down on the real estate. It makes me feel human again. On the other hand, maybe it's just a result of feeling safe from the local wildlife.

—December 5 or thereabout

Guided by *Wendy*, Hutch set down on an island to wait for the midday tide to recede. They were about fifteen klicks west of the tower.

'How long?' asked Mac.

'Make yourself comfortable,' she said. 'It'll be a few hours.'

'That's a lot of wasted time, Hutch. Why don't we just go in and get started?'

'We'd get washed away. Be patient.'

He stared out the window at the vast inland sea. 'Patience requires time, Priscilla,' he said.

'Gunther.' Janet the welder was unhappy. 'I've just been asked a question I don't know how to answer.'

'Go ahead,' said Beekman.

'All the shafts look the same. We've got teams spread out along 420 kilometers of the assembly, every eighty klicks.'

'Where the braces are,' said Beekman.

'Right. And we are going to free a single shaft and the asteroid from the rest of the construct.'

'Okay. What's the problem?'

'To do that, we have to cut the shaft free from the braces. We have five braces to deal with, plus the configuration where the assembly joins the asteroid, which is a plate. My question to you is this: We do not want to extract the central shaft because it involves too much cutting and manipulation. By far, the easiest course is to cut and remove one of the outer shafts.'

'And?'

'How can we be sure that each team works to free the same shaft? The thing's too long. The shafts are all identical. There's no way I can see to distinguish them.'

'Oh.' Beekman apparently hadn't thought about it either. 'I suppose we could send a shuttle out. Mark the damned thing.'

'You mean wait while a shuttle paints a stripe down one of them? That'll take too long. We don't have that kind of time. Or, I suspect, that much marker.'

Beekman frowned. She wondered whether other issues like this would come up, things no one had foreseen. 'What about a hammer?' she suggested.

'What would we do with a hammer?'

'Rap on the shaft. Give each team a sonocap from Medical. Let them listen for it. I'd think the vibrations would carry, even over eighty klicks.'

He made a face suggesting he didn't think much of the idea. 'I'm not versed in sonics,' he said. 'But the shafts are connected at the braces. So they'd *all* vibrate. The amplitude would be different, I suppose, but I wouldn't feel confident with that kind of approach.'

'What then?'

He took a deep breath. Exhaled.

Several members of her team were waiting below in the area they'd newly designated O Deck for the Outsiders. 'Let me get back to you.'

He was back in five minutes. 'All right,' he said. A detail of the assembly blinked onto one of her screens. 'The shafts are regularly spaced. Eight on the perimeter. Six on the inner arc. One in the center.'

The detail rotated, illustrating.

'If you look straight through it, there's only one position in which five shafts line up. We'll use one of the outer shafts from that position.'

'Which one?'

'That's easy enough. One end of the assembly is pointed directly at the center of Deepsix. Have someone stand on *top* of the assembly. The shaft at the top that matches up will be the Alpha shaft. The one we use.'

'How do we determine the *top* of the assembly?'

'Easy. Reckon from the planet. From the north pole. North is the top.'

'Are we sure everyone will be able to *find* the north pole?'

'They won't have to. Instruct the pilot to align the shuttle so that the north pole equates to topside.' His brow wrinkled. 'I can't see any reason why it won't work.'

'That's good, Gunther,' she said.

He laughed. 'That's why they pay me the big money.' He thought about it some more. 'Arrange things so all the teams make the mark at the same time. Don't forget the assembly's moving.'

Beekman had just finished describing his solution to Marcel when his screen lit up. It was Mark Bentley, a fellow planetologist whose specialty was gas-giant cores. He was currently director of Moonbase's Farside Observatory, and a longtime close friend. In his spare time, Bentley was an accomplished amateur actor.

He looked unhappy. 'I wouldn't want you to misunderstand, Gunny,' he said. 'But we're sacrificing everything we came here for.'

Beekman knew that. A substantial number of the experiments weren't even running. Specialists had been pulled off their assignments and put on the rescue operation. Worst of all, *Wendy* was on the wrong side of Deepsix, her view of developing events limited to what she could see through her satellites. The mission was turning into a fiasco. 'I know,' he said. 'What would you have me do?'

'Call it off.'

Beekman was shocked. 'What?'

'Gunny, I'd like to see those people out of there as much as anybody. But the scoop is a long shot at best.' He was quiet for a minute, apparently thinking how he was going to defend the indefensible. 'Can I be honest?'

'You always have been.'

'The chance to watch this thing close up, it's too much to let get away. Gunny, the truth is, it's *worth* a few lives, if that's what it takes.'

Beekman was surprised at his own reaction: Bentley was not necessarily wrong. From one point of view.

'Let it go,' he continued. 'You know what's going to happen: Something'll go wrong, the operation won't work, they'll all die anyhow, and we'll be left looking like idiots because we came all the way out here and got *nothing*.'

388

'Mark, what would you have me do? We can't just write them off.'

Bentley was quiet for a long minute. He knew. He understood it was not an easy decision. 'I think they've been written off. By events. Somebody needs to point that out to Marcel.'

Beckman felt a terrible weariness creeping up his insides.

'I'm not the only person here who feels this way. Gunny. It's not just me.' He held out his hands. 'Look, if there were a decent chance of getting them off, I'd say go ahead. I wouldn't be happy about it, but I'd be willing to go along with it. But this *isn't* a decent chance. It's a *gesture*. And that's *all* it is. It's being done so when we go back, Clairveau can say he did everything he could. You know as well as I do that you can't make this work.'

'I think we can,' he said.

Bentley continued as if he hadn't spoken. 'We won't have another opportunity like this. Not in our lifetimes. Maybe not in the lifetime of the species.'

Beekman didn't know what was right.

'How the hell are we going to explain this when we go home?' demanded Bentley. 'No we didn't save them, and no we didn't see the event. We were there, but we were busy.'

Beekman wondered how authority on *Wendy* ran in such a case. Beekman was the project director, charged with ensuring that they made maximum use of their time and resources to record and analyze the event. Marcel was the ship's captain.

'Talk to him. Clairveau'll listen to you.'

28

I'm always impressed when a large-scale project is successfully completed. My own research shows that, in any organization numbering more than twenty-two people, no single person can ever be found who completely understands what's going on.

—GREGORY MACALLISTER, *Gone to Glory*

Hours to breakup (est): 44

Pindar and Shira climbed into a shuttle and watched the launch doors open. Outside, a few hundred meters away, they could see the assembly. It looked like a group of unconnected narrow tubes, running absolutely parallel, stretching unbroken in both directions. 'Here we go,' said the pilot. They glided quietly forward and, to Pindar's intense excitement, moved past the enclosing bulkheads and sailed into the night.

The patch over the pilot's pocket read BOMAR. 'Klaus,' he said stiffly by way of introduction. His manner implied their presence was inconvenient. He was short and heavy-set, with a Canadian accent. Pindar thought he looked like a man who never enjoyed himself.

But the truth was Pindar barely paid any attention to the pilot.

He was captivated by the alien structure, its parallel tubes reaching toward infinity, vanishing finally in the stars.

Behind them the big luxury liner began to move. It accelerated, drew away, and its vast bulk dwindled and disappeared. It was, he knew, headed for the asteroid. Bomar advanced on the assembly, turned along its flank, braked, and coasted to a stop.

'Okay,' he said. 'You two are on.'

It was an electric moment. Pindar activated his e-suit. Bomar checked him, adjusted something on his back, and then looked at Shira. 'Looks good,' he said.

'Don't we get a go-pack?' asked Shira, eyeing the thruster harnesses stowed in the utility locker.

'Negative.' Bomar's somber features softened with amusement. 'You don't need one. Just do what you're supposed to and don't fall off.'

'Right,' said Pindar. His own voice seemed to have deepened somewhat.

Bomar opened the inner hatch. 'Keep one foot flat on the metal at all times while you're on the thing. Okay?'

'Absolutely,' said Shira.

'This is not something to smile about. Please get it right the first time. I don't want to have to do a lot of paperwork.' He exhaled and looked like a man who wasn't used to accommodating amateurs. 'They got your next of kin?'

That question had been on one of the forms. 'Yes,' said Shira.

'Keep it in mind while you're out there. All right, let's go.'

Shira and Pindar had arrived at Station One. There was no brace there, nothing to hold the shafts together. They were 320 kilometers from the asteroid, the rock that had provided the counterweight to whatever space station had once been attached. Their assignment was simply to climb on board, select the correct shaft, and mark it.

Shira was not a classic beauty. Her ears were a little big, her nose a little long, and the e-suit handicapped her by pressing her rich brown hair down against her scalp. But she was nevertheless attractive in a way he couldn't formulate. She was self-possessed, methodical, seemed quite adroit at laughing at herself. And perhaps most enchanting of all, she showed no apprehension whatever about going outside. 'Come on, Pindar,' she said, picking up her utility pack and throwing it across one shoulder. She led the way into the airlock. When the inner hatch closed she turned to him. 'I can't believe this is happening,' she said.

Pindar tried not to roll his eyes. He felt much the same way but could never have brought himself to say it.

'You ever been outside before?' she asked.

'No. Yesterday was the first time.' The training exercise. Prior to that, the opportunity had risen only once. He'd had a chance to put on an e-suit and stand on the hull of a ship in flight during an adventure tour, but he'd passed it up for an evening of poker.

The assembly stretched across the overhead monitor, its relative motion reduced to zero. Bomar had matched course, speed, and aspect.

'Opening up,' he said.

The hatch slid upward. Shira was wearing shorts and a white blouse with gold-rimmed breast pockets. She looked as if she were primed for a tennis outing.

She caught him staring. 'You're laughing,' she said.

He looked down at his own garments: tan slacks and a black pullover. He wished he'd thought to bring work clothes, something old that he wouldn't care about if he ruined. The *Star* had offered jumpsuits to the volunteers, but he hadn't been able to find one in which he felt comfortable. 'I think we're a bit overdressed for the occasion,' he said.

The assembly was almost close enough to touch.

Shira moved past him to the lip of the airlock and simply allowed her forward motion to carry her across, as she'd been taught. No jumping, no sudden exertion. She caught hold of the nearest shaft, smiled back at him, and brought her magnetic boots into contact with the next tube below.

Pindar followed, thinking how this was the first alien *anything* he'd ever touched, how he'd be telling his grand-kids about this in another half century. It was a big moment, and he was enjoying himself thoroughly.

He reached Shira's shaft and let his boots connect. 'Okay, Klaus,' he told the pilot. 'We're clear.'

'Strange feeling,' said Shira.

He looked back the way he had come and saw Morgan, a vast cobalt arc split in half by sunlight. Even though it was still at a substantial distance, he could feel its weight. Its *mass*, he recalled. Use the proper terminology.

Deepsix, floating directly ahead at the end of the assembly, was white and blue and vulnerable. Lunch, he thought. Not much more than a snack for the monster that was moving in on it.

Shira touched his arm. 'Let's find our shaft.'

The shuttle drifted alongside.

Using the spacecraft as a guide, they climbed *up*. Shira led the way. At the first two steps, she paused, looked down through the shafts, shook her head, and moved on. The third try was golden. 'Okay,' she said. She backed away to get a better look. 'This is it. No question.'

Pindar joined her, saw four shafts line up with the one he was standing on. He produced his squirt gun and splashed yellow dye on the metal. 'I dub you Alpha,' he said.

'You guys sure now?' asked Bomar.

'Of course,' Shira sounded annoyed.

Beekman was unable to make up his mind. He stood near Marcel, uncertain whether to demand that they forget this fool's errand and return to the mission they'd come there for, or inform him that there were some malcontents and not to worry, that Beekman would handle it, but that the captain should be prepared for complaints.

The hours were slipping away, and their magnificent opportunity was dwindling. Bentley and several others were watching, waiting to see whether he would act.

Lori's voice was providing periodic updates from the various teams. In addition, the conversation from the lander cabin had been put on the speaker. The AI reported that all stations on the target shaft, the one they'd designated Alpha, had been successfully marked.

Marcel looked up at him. 'So far, so good.'

'Yes.' Beekman looked directly into his eyes. 'It doesn't sound as if our ground team has much confidence in us, though.'

'I think I prefer it that way,' said Marcel, glancing around at the technicians. 'Provides extra incentive. I think everybody here would like to prove them wrong.'

Maybe not everybody. Beekman thought.

Marcel looked into his eyes and frowned. 'What is it, Gunny?'

'Nothing,' said the project director. 'Nothing that won't wait.'

Canyon recognized an emotional situation when he saw one. They were still sitting on their island as the day crept forward, waiting for the water to go down, waiting to launch an almost hopeless search for the whatzis that had been washed away.

But they didn't want to talk to him. No matter how gently he tried to frame his questions, *How does it feel to know so many people are rooting for you?*, and *If you had all this to do again, is there anything you might have done differently?*

'Nobody wants to be rude,' Hutch told him, 'but I just don't think this is a good time for an interview.'

'Okay,' he agreed. 'I understand how you feel. But if you change your mind, if anyone does, please call me. Okay?'

He was sorry about their situation. And he would have helped if he could. Sitting quietly, staring at the displays of the approaching giant, of the vast sea that surrounded the tower, he understood their frustration. He almost wished he'd followed his father's advice and gone into engineering.

He decided he'd try again when they got closer to the end. His superiors at home were pressing him to acquire what they were referring to as an exit interview with MacAllister. *'After all, he's the one everybody knows.*' But Canyon trusted his own instincts on this one. It was the two women who packed the emotional impact, who would bring tears to people's eyes around the world. Especially Hutchins. Slight of stature, quiet, almost elfin in appearance, there was much of the girl-next-door in her. And Canyon knew if he could get her to agree to talk during the final hours, as he was sure he could, he would give the public an emotional jolt like nothing anyone had ever seen before. If Hutch wouldn't cooperate, Kellie was another possibility.

As to the others, he didn't much like Nightingale, and he was afraid of MacAllister. You never quite knew what he might say.

Hutch made a premature effort to land them at the tower, but the water was too deep and the currents too swift. So she turned away and retreated to another hilltop, and they waited another forty-five minutes, watching the tide run back to the northeast.

The second effort succeeded. She got down, and they piled out into hip-deep water. First they made a careful inspection of the tower, assuring themselves that the capacitors weren't there somewhere, missed by Kellie and Hutch in the preliminary search.

Then they waded out toward the south. They'd divided the area into parcels and they tried to work within their assigned boundaries, tried to be methodical. *We'll stay on this side of a line between the tower and that tree over there.* It wasn't very efficient, but it worked to a degree. The real problem was that the search area was *immense.*

Nightingale and Mac brought with them a conviction that the units could nevertheless be found, probably because they thought this was their only decent chance at survival.

The land was not as flat as it had seemed. The depth of the water varied, up to their ankles in some places, over their heads in others. The current was strong and, in deeper areas, consistently threatened to knock them over. Hutch had arrived with no illusions about their chances. Left to herself, she'd have put all her money on the sky scoop, gone to Mt. Blue, and spent the remaining time surveying the hexagon. But she was tired, and she was not up to arguing with two males who probably already thought she'd made an inadequate effort when there had still been a chance.

She'd expected Nightingale and Mac to give up fairly quickly because of the amount of effort required to maintain the search. And the sheer size of the search area. But as the hours passed, their determination, or their desperation – it was difficult to know which – grew. They moved farther and farther south of the tower.

Kellie, who was teamed with Nightingale, seemed to have become resigned. She stayed close to her partner, worked hard, plunging her hands beneath the surface constantly to examine one suspect rock or another. But Hutch could see that she had no real hope of success, could see it in the way she paused occasionally while they rested to look out over the vast expanse of running water, sometimes gazing north, no doubt wondering whether the capacitors might somehow have gotten on the wrong side of the tower. Or were fifty kilometers away. She could hear it also in the listlessness of her voice. And who could blame her?

Once they thought they had one of them, but it turned out to be something much like a turtle shell.

When it got dark, they quit. They were exhausted, annoyed, frustrated. They were aching from pushing against the currents and constantly bending over. The knowledge that the capacitors might be within a few meters at any given time had made it impossible to give up. But fianlly they crawled back to the lander, hauled themselves into the cabin, took turns cleaning up in the washroom, and collapsed into their seats.

The water was starting to rise again anyhow. Hutch took them up.

'Can I make a suggestion?' said Marcel.

'Go ahead.'

'First, am I correct in assuming you've given up looking for the capacitors?'

Hutch glanced around. They all nodded.

'All right. I want to move you to high ground for the night.'

'Okay.'

'For the moment, there's nothing more you can do. Tomorrow, I'd like to persuade you to go to even higher ground.'

'Mt. Blue,' she said.

29

We are all afflicted with a Lone Ranger syndrome, a belief in the masked stranger who arrives well armed at dawn and settles problems in a straightforward simplistic manner. The character, whose origin stretches back to the twentieth century, owes his longevity to the fact that he connects with our most primal impulses, and represents the way we truly would be, if only we could. That we cannot, results not only from a lack of courage and ability, but also because the world is simply not built that way. When the night is dark and the storm closes in, one had best be prepared to help himself. Because as surely as the stars wheel overhead there will be no one else, masked or otherwise.

—GREGORY MACALLISTER, *Introduction to 'The Last Mythology' by Eve Shiu-Chao*

Hours to breakup (Est): 42

They locked down for the night atop a ridge in a howling blizzard not far from Bad News Bay. The ground shook constantly. Hutch slept off and on. She and Kellie both spent time listening hopefully to operational reports from the small armada overhead.

399

They heard Janet Hazelhurst issuing crisp directions to the Outsiders, who were getting ready to remove what they called the Alpha shaft from the assembly; they heard John Drummond's team working out the details of getting everything pointed in the right direction, and Abel Kinder debating the location of the pickup site with Drummond: *'It's easier to get* here, *but the weather looks doubtful, so we need to go farther north.'*

They heard Miles Chastain and the shuttle pilots planning their assignments. In the early-morning hours, Marcel came on to give them details, the coordinates and altitude and timing of the pickup. 'We've moved it slightly,' he said. 'But not by much.' Rendezvous would occur in precisely twenty-five hours and eleven minutes, mark. Three hours after sunrise day after tomorrow. 'At 10,276 meters.'

'Ten thousand two-seventy *six?*' said Hutch. 'What happens if we come in at seventy-five?'

He laughed. 'You'll be fine, but I'm serious about the precision of this. At its lowest point, we expect the center of the scoop will be at seventy-six. The mouth will be fifty-three meters in diameter. The lander, at its widest, is about fifteen meters. That means you have nineteen meters leeway on either side.'

'All right. We should be able to do that. How much time are we going to have?'

'Pinpoint. A couple of seconds. We'll have everything timed so it arrives exactly where it's supposed to, *when* it's supposed to. But it's just going to be passing through. You get one shot at it. It comes in, it goes down, it starts back up. After that it's gone.'

'Okay.'

'I'll be with you the whole way. Even if I'm not, you'll be fine.'

'Glad to hear it. I was starting to worry. Why might you *not* be?'

'There's a good probability we'll lose communications with you as the weather deteriorates. But you've got the details, and whatever else happens, you'll still be able to see the net coming in. Okay?'

'Yeah. That's good.'

They listened while Beekman and his team hammered out the method of converting the metal webbing in which the asteroid was encased into the sack that would be used to pick up the lander. *In flight.* And they heard a recording of the meeting at which the volunteers voted to call themselves the Outsiders. Marcel apparently thought the enthusiasm of their rescuers would help morale on the ground. It did.

Marcel explained that most of the volunteers were passengers from the cruise ship. A few were Kellie's colleagues from *Wendy*. Hutch's passenger Tom Scolari was among them. ('Are you serious?' she replied.) Almost none had ever been outside before.

Hutch was surprised to see Kellie surreptitiously wipe away a tear. 'They're really trying,' she commented.

Some of the Outsiders working along the assembly heard that the lander was on the circuit and could hear them. *'We're coming,'* they said. *'Hang on.'* And *'Don't worry. We'll get you out.'*

'Whatever it takes.'

Outside, the wind continued to howl, and the snow piled up. Even with the transmissions, rescue seemed impossibly far away.

They woke in late morning to clearing skies. The blizzard had blown itself out, and a heavy blanket of snow sparkled under a bright sun. They broke out the last of their stocked fruit, which consisted of almost tasteless pulp protected inside a hard shell. They talked about how good it would be to have a real breakfast again, and agreed it was time to take a look at Mt. Blue. One way or the other, this would be their last full day on Deepsix.

'What's the top of the mountain look like?' Hutch asked Marcel. 'What do we know about it?'

'Okay. You know it's been sheared off. The peak's gone. It's absolutely flat up there. Looks as if somebody took a scythe to it. But you can't see it because it's always wrapped in clouds.'

'The building's on the summit?'

'Right. It's a ruin. Several stories high. With dishes. Probably solar collectors, although God knows how it would get any energy through all those clouds.'

'Maybe they didn't used to be there,' said Nightingale.

'Probably. Anyhow it's a *big* place. The building is a hexagon, roughly two hundred meters on a side. And I should add that everybody here's convinced it was the base of the skyhook.'

'Why?' asked MacAllister.

'It's directly on the equator. And the sea to the west is full of debris.'

'The elevator,' said Hutch.

'Yes. It looks as if the elevator either broke apart or was deliberately cut. Our best guess is that it was severed at about eleven thousand meters. The upper section was dragged into space; the lower broke off the base and fell into the ocean.

'Is there a place for us to land?'

'Oh sure. No problem about that.'

Well, it was nice to have something that didn't come with a problem. 'All right,' Hutch said. 'We'll do it, Marcel. We have to stop first to pick up some food. And it would probably be a good idea to top off the tanks. Visibility up there is . . .?'

'Zero.'

'Of course. Keep in mind we have no sensors. How am I supposed to land if I can't see?'

'I'll guide you in.'

'I can't believe I've agreed to this,' said MacAllister, as she took her bearing from the superluminal and turned onto her new course.

Nightingale cleared his throat. 'It's why we're here,' he said. 'If we don't get some answers, we'll never hear the end of it.' He looked directly at Mac.

Kellie laughed, and the momentary tension fell apart.

When Beekman's people named the various continents, seas, and other physical features across Deepsix, they'd called the range along Transitoria's western coastline the Mournful Mountains. It contained several of the highest peaks on Deepsix, soaring to seven thousand meters above sea level. At sixty-six hundred, Mt. Blue was not quite the tallest, but it was one of the more picturesque. A bundle of white clouds enclosed the upper levels. Granite walls fell away at sharp angles for thousands of meters, before mutating into gradual slopes that descended into foothills and forest.

Marcel had assigned Mira Amelia to provide weather updates and tracking information to the lander. She also kept them updated on the rescue effort. Mira maintained an optimistic front without becoming annoying. Kellie commented that Mira was a good analyst and that she wouldn't sound that way unless the program was very likely to work. It was an interpretation that they all needed to hear. Even MacAllister, who was visibly shaken at the notion of flying into a midair net, seemed to take heart.

They'd been aloft an hour and a half when Mira reported that the river they were now approaching eventually passed close to Mt. Blue. 'There's some open country nearby. This would be the place to refuel. And maybe stock up.'

Hutch went down through heavy weather ('It's worse everywhere else,' said Mira) and landed in a driving rain on the south bank. The trees were loaded with fruit. They picked some pumpkin-sized delectables that they'd had before. The edible part was quite good, rather like a large dried raisin encased within a tough husk. They hurried back into the lander with them, out of the downpour. And ate up.

The simple pleasures of being alive.

They stored a hefty supply in cargo. Optimistically, Mac pointed out. Then they ran out the hose and refilled the tanks. When the job was finished they lifted off again.

Mt. Blue was on the coast. To the west, offshore, the sea had withdrawn and left a vast expanse of muddy bog.

'The water's on the other side of the world,' Mira explained. She provided a course correction and instructed Hutch to go to sixty-eight hundred meters. She also relayed pictures of the mountain, taken from satellite.

'Here's something odd,' she said. The north side was sheer precipice, from summit to ground level. A ninety-degree drop.

Nightingale stared at it. 'That almost looks artificial.'

'That's what we thought,' said Mira. 'Here's something else.' She zeroed in.

Hutch saw vertical and horizontal lines along the face of the cliff. A framework of some sort. It ran from the summit all the way to the base, at ground level.

'What is it?' asked Kellie.

'We have no idea. If you get a chance, take a look.'

Then she showed them what the scanners had seen at the mountaintop: The summit was perfectly flat. And there, in the middle, was the hexagon.

Mira enhanced the image. The structure was enormous, occupying perhaps sixty percent of the total available ground space atop the mountain. It was half-submerged in a tangle of vegetation. But they could make out windows and doorways. Hutch noted an almost classical symmetry, unlike the overblown and overdecorated styles currently favored by her own civilization. The corners were flared. Otherwise, the structure was unadorned.

The top was jagged, as if upper levels had been broken off. On average it was about six stories high, less in some places, more in others. The top – one couldn't really call it a roof since it appeared the upper level was exposed to the sky – was covered with snow.

'Here's what it looks like under the snow,' said Mira. She removed it, and they were looking down on chambers and passageways and staircases. All in a general state of collapse.

Mira sent them a reconstruction, revealing its probable appearance in its early years. The computer replaced the bushes and weeds with sculpted walkways and gravel courts, and installed gleaming windows and carved doors. The roof became an oval gridwork that rose into the clouds. It was *magnificent*.

'We think we found the missing pieces, by the way.'

'You mean the mountaintop?'

'*And* the north side of the cliff. They're a group of hills about twenty klicks east. It's all a big river valley now. Most of the granite is covered by forest.'

'So that means—'

'It came off a very long time ago. At least a thousand years. Probably a lot more.' She paused. 'Okay, if you're ready, I'm going to take you in.'

'We're ready.'

'There's plenty of room to set down,' Mira said.

'Doesn't the cloud bank ever go away?' asked MacAllister. He meant the one that shrouded the mountaintop.

'We don't have any records that go back more than a few weeks,' said Mira. 'But it's been a permanent feature during the time we've been here. Several of the other peaks in this area are the same way.'

She provided a course correction. Hutch slowed and eased into the clouds.

'Doing fine,' Mira said. 'No obstructions ahead. You're two hundred meters above the rock.'

The mist grew dark.

Hutch turned on the spike. The seat pushed up slightly against her spine. She continued to reduce airspeed, lowered her treads, and put the thrusters into vertical mode.

Snow began to fall across the windscreen, and they picked up some interference.

Mira's voice disappeared in a burst of static.

Hutch switched to another channel and recovered the transmission.

'You're now approaching the lip of the plateau,' Mira said. 'You've got plenty of clearance, so there's nothing to worry about. Give me a descent rate of five meters per second.'

Hutch complied.

Thunder rumbled below them. 'Thirty seconds to touchdown, Hutch.'

She watched them tick off on her counter, fired the thrusters, reduced airspeed to zero, and drifted in.

'Priscilla,' asked MacAllister, 'what happens if we lose radio contact?'

She was too busy to answer.

'No problem,' said Kellie after a moment. 'We just go back up. Sky's clear overhead.'

'Fifteen seconds. Go three-quarter spike.'

They dropped slowly through the mist. And touched down.

Hutch resisted the impulse to take a deep breath. She looked out through the side window but couldn't see more than a few meters into the fog. 'Mira,' she said, 'thanks.'

'My pleasure. I'll notify Marcel.'

The four superluminals, directed by the *Star*'s AI, assumed their positions along the assembly, in each case drawing up at one of the four locations marked with yellow dye, facing the asteroid. The smallest of the four, the *Zwick*, halted approximately thirty-eight kilometers from the rock. The others were spaced over the next 332 kilometers, *Wildside* second in line, followed by the *Star*, which could generate far and away the maximum thrust of the group, and finally, *Wendy*.

The positioning of the ships had been the most difficult part of the problem for John Drummond and his team. Posted in a shuttle drifting across the rocky surface of the asteroid, he went over his numbers one last time and found everything in order.

Janet Hazelhurst sat beside him to provide technical assistance to the Outsiders. And Miles Chastain, the skipper of the media ship, was in a shuttle roughly midway between the *Star* and *Wildside*, prepared to come to the assistance of anyone who got in trouble. Other shuttles were strategically placed to help. Each person who had gone outside was being tracked by one of the attending vehicles, which would immediately sound an alarm if anyone drifted away, or if any indication of distress or undue difficulty showed itself.

With so many inexperienced people trying to perform their work in a hostile environment, it seemed inevitable that someone, somewhere, would get hurt, would walk off and try to go into orbit, or would slice off somebody's foot with a cutter.

The e-suits were reliable. They would not shut off in a vacuum unless one knew a very complicated protocol. They were not subject to leaking. And they handled life support very effectively. Nevertheless, Drummond remembered his own experience outside, and he was worried.

Wildside, empty save for the onboard Outsider team and its AI, drew alongside the assembly, its nose pointed forward, and stopped where its sensors detected a yellow splotch of dye. The dye marked the site that *Wildside* would take up during the operation, and it also marked Alpha, the target shaft.

Bill rotated the vehicle until its underside snuggled within centimeters of the assembly. Its cargo airlock opened and a two-person team emerged. Wearing dark lenses, they selected an unmarked shaft and cut eight pieces from it, each about six meters long.

They returned to the *Wildside* with them. They put two inside the ship for future use and set six in place on the hull directly adjacent to the Alpha shaft. This would be, in Janet's welding terminology, their filler.

They changed the settings on their lasers, substituting a heat beam for the cutter. They turned the beams on the filler. Sparks flicked off. The metal began to glow, and then to melt. Working quickly, they welded the filler to the hull, using scoops and riggers and other makeshift tools. Under Janet's watchful eye, they combed the now-pliant metal into place, creating saddles and links in the way they'd been shown.

One of the welders, whose name was Jase Power, commented that he thought the work was pretty professional. That drew cautious agreement from Janet. 'You've got a career, Jase, if you want it. When we get home, I'll be glad to provide a recommendation.'

When they'd finished preparations to make the attachment, they retired inside the ship, and the AI withdrew to a safe distance.

'What can you see?' Marcel asked Hutch. 'What's out there?'

'Fog,' said MacAllister.

'We can't see anything from here,' said Hutch. 'The mist is too thick.' The visibility was about five meters.

'Okay. Let's talk about where you are. You already know the mountaintop is sawed off. You're on the eastern side, fifty meters from the edge. That's to your rear. I don't need to tell you not to go that way.

'One side of the hexagon looks as if it juts out a little bit over the precipice. That's on the north, where the sheer face is. Did Mira show you? Four thousand meters or so straight down. So if a floor gives way or you walk through a door without looking, you could get a god-awful surprise. I suggest you stay away altogether from the north side. Okay?'

'We'll be careful,' Hutch said.

'The structure is directly ahead of you. Just follow the lander's nose. About thirty meters.' He hesitated. 'We think we've put you down immediately outside the main entrance. Look for a set of steps. Bordered by low walls.'

Hutch acknowledged.

'Good luck,' he said. 'I'd appreciate a visual link when you have a minute. And I'll be back with you shortly.'

Hutch activated her e-suit, pinned a microscan on her vest, and turned it on. 'Anybody want to come?'

'Not me,' said MacAllister. 'I've had enough walking for this trip.' He had the grace to look embarrassed. 'This is a game for younger folks.'

Kellie volunteered, but Hutch signaled that was not a good idea. 'If you and I are both out there, and something happens, there's nobody left to fly the lander. So *you* have to stay. You can go in after I get back, if you want.'

'I guess that leaves me,' said Nightingale.

408

'Unless you'd rather not.'

'No.' Nightingale was reaching for his vest. 'To be honest, I wouldn't miss it.' He picked up one of the harnesses. 'Do we need air tanks? We're up pretty high.'

'No,' said Hutch. 'The converters'll work a little harder, but that's okay. They'll be fine.'

They took lasers, plastic bags, and notebooks, and inserted them into their vests. They picked up backpacks, into which they could put artifacts. Hutch strapped a lamp onto her wrist, spotted the rope she'd carried through the forests, and looped it over one shoulder. 'You never know,' she told Kellie.

'You look like Jack Hancock,' said Kellie, referring to the popular adventurer-archeologist of the sims.

They opened up, and Hutch looked out, saw nothing but fog, and climbed down the ladder. Nightingale adjusted the temperature in his suit and followed. Kellie asked them not to fall off the mountain. Then she shut the airlock behind them.

The cold hardscrabble ground crackled underfoot. The air was absolutely still. Snow continued to fall.

Hutch felt alone. Nightingale had never been much company, and now he rambled on about the general gloominess of the place, how difficult it was to see anything, and how easy it would be to walk into a ditch. He was right about the visibility. The mist pressed down on her, squeezed her, forced her to look inward because she could not see out.

Kellie had asked at one point whether anyone believed in an immortal soul. Certainly Hutch didn't. The world was a cold mathematical machine that produced hydrogen, stars, mosquitoes, and superluminal pilots without showing the slightest concern for any of them. But now, as she stumbled through what might be her last hours, it was painful to think that if she got unlucky she could end in the bosom of that monster in the sky, her atoms floating in gray soup for the next few billion years. *If you're there*, she murmured to no one in particular, *I'd love some help.*

'There's a wall,' said Nightingale.

'I see it.' It was flat, plain, a little more than shoulder-high. The surface was rough against her fingertips. Probably granite.

They saw the steps Marcel had described and were surprised to discover they were close to human dimensions. Beyond, Hutch could see an entrance. If there'd been doors, they were missing. The entrance and the interior were piled high with snow and earth. Tough bristly shrubbery grew on both sides of the threshold.

Nightingale took the lead. His manner suggested it would be best if he were in position to confront any potential danger. In this environment, where vision was so limited, she doubted it would matter much who was standing where. She also thought it unlikely there'd be any large predators up here, for the simple reason there was probably no prey. And she guessed Nightingale had come to the same conclusion.

They passed through the entry into a wide corridor. The walls were plain, undecorated, unmarked in any way. The ceiling was comfortably high. They switched on their lamps in an effort to dispell the general gloom. But the fog reflected the light back into their eyes, so they shut them down again.

Small animals scattered before them. It was hard to get a good look at any of them, but Hutch heard wings and saw something that looked like a white chimp. A segmented creature with a lot of legs scuttled into a side corridor.

There were rooms off either side, partially illuminated by windows. The chambers were quite large. Most could have comfortably accommodated groups of fifteen or more. They were empty of any kind of furniture. Long paneled strips overhead might have been artificial lighting devices.

'It feels as if it's been here a long time,' she told Marcel, showing him a picture.

The cross passages were equally devoid of special features.

Unlike the tower, which had seemed timeless, as if its builders had meant it for the ages, *this* structure, despite the granite, gave the impression of being a government make-do. A temporary construction.

410

They explored side corridors, passed more doorways and bare cubicles of varying sizes, filled only with whatever leaves and dirt had blown in. Most of the doors were missing. A few hung open; others were shut tight. No knobs or latches were visible. 'Electronics,' said Nightingale, examining one. 'Looks like a sensor.'

They crossed a room, passed through a door on the opposite side, and came out into a new passageway. One wall had been lined with windows, but whatever transparent material had sealed off the interior was gone, and the wind blew steadily into the building.

They went up a ramp.

Reluctantly, she began using her laser to mark the walls so they could find their way back.

They kept a channel open to Kellie and Marcel, recording their impressions, their sense of a structure that was part office building, part mall, part terminal. Commodious spaces in some areas. 'Intended for large numbers of occupants.'

'Large numbers?' asked Marcel.

'Wide corridors.'

'How many people ride on a skyhook?'

'I don't know.'

There were shelves and niches. All the surfaces were covered with thick dust, with *centuries* of accumulation, but whenever Hutch took time to wipe something clean, it looked as if it had been recently installed. Whatever it was, she decided, the construction material had resisted aging remarkably well.

They were in a passageway with a series of windows, all open to the outside.

'Hey.' Nightingale dropped to one knee. 'Look at this.'

A sign. Hung in a wall mount. But the mount was *low*, down around her hips. It contained several rows of symbols. The symbols were faded, turned to gray, but not illegible. She made sure it became part of the visual record. Then she delightedly discovered she could lift the sign off the mount. It was a plaque, and it came out whole.

'Why is it down *there*?' she asked. 'Why not put it at eye level?'

'It probably *is* at eye level,' said Nightingale. 'For the crickets.'

She studied the symbols. 'That's strange.'

'What is?'

There were six lines. The style and formation of the characters varied extensively from one to another. But within each individual row they were quite similar. Some symbols were even repeated, but only in their own line.

'I'd guess we have six alphabets,' she said.

'Is that significant?'

'What'll you bet it's the same message in six different languages?'

He shrugged. 'I don't see why that's important.'

'It's a Rosetta stone.'

'Well, maybe. But I think that's overstating the case a bit. The message is too short to qualify as a *Rosetta* stone. It probably says ONLY PASSENGERS PAST THIS POINT. Nobody's going to solve a language from *that*.'

'It's a beginning, Randy. And the fact that we can put it in context might make it easier to translate. This place was a hub, for a while. A lot of the natives came through here.'

'Going where?'

'You haven't figured it out?'

He looked at her. 'You know what was going on here? What all this was about?'

'Sure,' she said.

Hutch detected movement on the circuit and wasn't surprised to hear Marcel's voice: 'It was a rescue mission. Randy.'

Nightingale looked at her, and his brow creased.

Kellie broke in: 'When they date this place, they'll discover it's three thousand years old.'

'The ice age,' said Nightingale. '*The Quiveras Cloud*.'

'Sure.' Mac speaking now. 'Somebody tried to evacuate the locals.'

'A *whole* planetary population?'

'No,' said Hutch, 'of course not. Couldn't have. Not with one

412

skyhook. No matter how much time they had. I mean, the natives would have reproduced faster than they could be moved.'

Nightingale nodded.

'We met some of the folks that got left,' she added.

Outside, branches creaked in a sudden burst of wind.

'The *hawks* were the larger species.'

'I'd think so.'

'The rescuers.'

'Yes.'

'That's incredible. Did everybody know this except me?'

No one spoke.

She wrapped the plaque, but it was too large to put into her pack, so she hefted it under one arm.

Wall markings, most badly faded, began appearing with some regularity. She recorded what she could, started to put together a map to indicate where everything had been found, relied on her visual link to make a record of the place, and belatedly realized she hadn't been using her laser consistently and was lost. But that shouldn't be too much of a problem. They could follow the radio signals back in the correct general direction.

They walked into a bay and encountered their first furniture. Small benches, on a scale for the crickets. 'But none for the larger species,' said Nightingale.

They were a type of plastic, and they, too, seemed to have endured well.

Ramps led to both lower and higher levels. They went *down,* where they found more inscriptions, some in passageways, some on the walls of individual cubicles. These were at Hutch's eye level. Possibly a bit higher.

The offices and corridors seemed designed for the use of the hawks. The placement of inscriptions, and the size of the doors, supported that thesis.

Hutch wished the fog would go away so she could get a good look at her surroundings. 'They brought everybody cross-country, some maybe by air, certainly some by hovercraft.'

'How'd the hovercraft get up here?' The one they'd seen could never have climbed the mountain.

'That's a detail. Randy. They probably took them to an airport somewhere, and flew them up.'

'Must have been one hell of an operation. I think I'd like to meet the hawks.'

30

Life is a walk in the fog. Most people don't know that. They're fooled by the sunlight into thinking they can see what's ahead. But it's the reason they are forever getting lost or falling into ditches or committing matrimony.

—GREGORY MACALLISTER, *The Marriage Manual*

Hours to breakup (est): 33

The asteroid was almost spherical. It was somewhat more than a kilometer in diameter, contained within a metal web that was itself attached to the assembly by means of a plate.

Janet watched an Outsider team descend onto the plate and begin to cut it loose from the assembly. When they were finished, only one shaft, the Alpha, would remain attached. And only 320 kilometers of that.

John Drummond oversaw the action on a bank of screens. He was charged with monitoring all the Outsider operations: the asteroid units, the four teams that would shortly go outside on each of the ships, the five that were now being dropped along the assembly to sever the Alpha from the bands that held the structure together, and the net unit that was en route with Miles Chastain.

She didn't particularly like Drummond, who behaved as if anyone not involved in advanced mathematics was wasting her life. There was a lot of pressure on him at the moment, and she understood that, but Janet had concluded that if circumstances were normal, he'd still be a jerk.

Their pilot's name was Frank. Frank didn't care much for Drummond either, and probably for the same reasons. She could hear it in his voice, but if Drummond noticed, he paid no attention. While Janet watched their teams spread out, Frank turned in his seat and informed them that one of the *Star* shuttles would be alongside in a few minutes. That would be Miles and Phil Zossimov, who wanted to get a look at the net.

'Okay, Frank.' Drummond glanced down at his instruments. 'We'll start in three minutes.' He brought the asteroid up on his screen, rotated it, leaned forward, plumped his chin on his fist, and directed the AI to show him the proposed line where they would cut the net. The area where the plate connected to the assembly had been designated the north pole. A cursor appeared just off to one side of the plate and circled the asteroid, passing quite close to the *south* pole.

Janet looked out at the net, which was visible only when the shuttle's lights hit it the right way. Its links were narrow, no more than a finger's width, and they were closely connected, the interstices small enough that a human being could not have squeezed through.

Drummond admitted freely that, once they began cutting it, there was no way to be sure at precisely which point the asteroid would come loose. That lent a degree of uncertainty to the operation, but he seemed confident there was no possibility the rock would cause damage or threaten the team now on the far side of the plate.

She couldn't help noticing how close the shuttle was and wondered whether Drummond had considered the possibility it might come *their* way.

'Why will it go anywhere at all?' she asked him. 'What makes you think it won't stay right where it is?'

'The center of gravity will change,' he said, not entirely hiding a note of disdain. 'It'll change for both the asteroid and the assembly. So they'll both change their dynamics somewhat.'

'Can we predict what'll happen?' she asked.

'Not as precisely as I'd like. Under normal circumstances it'd be simple enough. But with the gas giant in the neighborhood, the calculations get a bit sticky.' He looked at her, apparently trying to decide whether she was frightened. 'There's really nothing to worry about, if that's what you're thinking.' He checked their position on the screens. 'Okay,' he said into a mike. 'Ready to go.'

The AI took over. It accelerated, descended closer to the surface, and aimed the lasers that Miles's team had installed. Drummond warned the people among the shafts to get behind the plate and stay there. 'Keep your heads down,' he told them. 'We're starting.'

Janet knew that he'd have preferred to have no one out on the assembly while they were releasing the rock. Especially this close. But they had to cut fifteen shafts away from the plate, and there simply wouldn't be time to get the job done unless they'd started on it as soon as they arrived.

The shuttle moved in close. Janet could have put a foot out the airlock and touched the asteroid. In its flat masculine voice, the AI informed them portentously it was about to activate the lasers.

It performed a brief countdown, and twin lances of white light sliced into the dust.

The shuttle moved slowly north to south down the face of the asteroid. It passed just wide of the south pole and started back up.

'We're getting a good cut,' said Frank. 'We should have separation in a minute or so.' Then he added, 'Uh-oh.'

Janet's heart picked up a beat.

*

417

'Everybody, heads up.' It was the voice of Frank the pilot. 'Rock swarm incoming. About thirty seconds. Get behind the plate on the assembly side.'

Tom Scolari looked over the top of the plate to see if they were visible. The action brought a cold remonstrance from Janet, and he got back down. The other members of his team were complying.

'Stay behind the plate,' warned Janet. 'They're coming in over the asteroid. Keep low, and you'll be fine.'

Something blurred past him, a quick silent shadow across the stars. And a second, little more than the whisper of his own heartbeat. It all happened so quickly he couldn't be sure. People were breathing on the circuit. Somebody made a scared noise.

He felt a vibration, and then a jolt. Out along the assembly, something flashed.

'That one hit,' Janet said.

Another tremor shook them. Scolari gazed into the eyes of the woman beside him. She looked frightened.

He waited, listening to his pulse until Frank came back up: 'That seems to be it, folks. Screen's clear.'

'Everybody okay?' asked Drummond.

There were some acknowledgments, and Janet had them respond to their names. While they did, Scolari counted bodies. All present. All moving.

They looked at one another. The woman – her name was Kit – went back to work. But from that moment, whatever nonchalance he might have possessed earlier, Scolari understood that he'd put his life at risk. He was glad not to be alone.

His instructions were simple: slice into as many of the shafts as possible. But no deeper than about halfway until the asteroid was gone. When the shuttle announced that separation was imminent, see that everyone stayed behind the plate. When it was over, when the rock had been disposed of, go back and finish the job, cut everything loose so that the Alpha shaft, the plate, and the

418

net remained one piece but had been separated from the rest of the assembly.

Scolari was the oldest member of his team. He didn't know much about the personal lives of the others, only what he'd picked up from a few dropped hints. This one was on the prowl, that one was a mother of two. But they were all excited about helping rescue the landing party. Two were visibly scared. Maybe they all were, and some just better at hiding it. God knew *he* was scared. But the adrenaline rush was high, and he felt good. Watching the dancing lights of the lasers flickering around the edges of the plate, he felt incredibly *alive*. Everyone, he thought, should have a chance to do something like this at least once in a lifetime.

Back along the assembly, toward Deepsix, lights were approaching. He recognized the triangle of lamps on the prow: It was an Academy shuttle. Though whether it was from his own ship or from *Wendy*, he had no idea.

Janet's voice broke in: 'All right, people. Everybody down. It should be any moment now.'

The glow had moved around to the other end of the plate. That meant they'd cleared the south pole and were working their way up. Janet had assured them that when the rock began to move, there was no way it could come in their direction. And he believed her, but it was easier to accept in the illuminated ready room on the ship than out here sitting behind a narrow strip of metal that was all that shielded them from the monster.

He was leaning against the plate when it shuddered.

'Asteroid's away,' said Janet.

One of the women, a middle-aged classics instructor with the unlikely name of Cleo, had backed off a bit and was gazing up. She was in tan coveralls and was wearing a blue scarf. Light from the laser fell across her features and her eyes were rising, looking at something behind him, over his shoulder. 'There it goes,' she said.

Scolari saw a black rim rolling out past one side of the

plate, moving slowly. 'And good riddance,' Cleo added, waving farewell.

The confirmation that the rock had been cut loose was the signal for Lori to move *Wildside* up close again to the Alpha shaft. It guided the ship so that the shaft did not run directly parallel to the vessel's axis, but was angled at eighteen and a fraction degrees. The *Zwick* was also being attached off center, and aimed in the opposite direction, allowing these two vessels to start the rotation that would eventually bring Alpha's forward end to bear on Deepsix. When *Wildside* was lined up. Jase Power and his crew went back outside and welded ship and shaft together.

They completed the job without incident, examined their work, decided it looked okay, and waited for Janet's verdict. She insisted on close-ups, and minutes later a shuttle moved in for a sensor inspection. She directed them to go back and reinforce a couple of areas, then gave her blessing. 'Very professional,' she said. 'Come back inside. Report when you're all in. And thanks.'

Zwick was first to check in. 'Attachment complete.' They were welded to the Alpha shaft.

Wildside followed within seconds.

'We're all set,' Janet told Drummond.

The asteroid, freed of its encumbrance, was seeking a new orbit. It would continue to circle Deepsix, at least for another day or so, until Jerry Morgan changed the deep-space geometry.

Drummond watched it go with a sense of satisfaction. It was rare, in his line of work, that he got to see so practical an application of his skills. It was true that Marcel and Beekman were technically making the decisions, but they were using Drummond's numbers. And, by God, it was a good feeling.

At the top of the assembly, the now-empty net was slowly spreading out. They had cut about three-quarters of the way around it when the asteroid came loose. Now the net trailed behind the assembly like a veil caught atop an endless stick.

Captain Nicholson announced to all vessels and shuttles that the first step had been successful, and that everything was proceeding according to schedule.

The shuttles now moved to deposit two-person Outsider teams at each of the five bands along the length of the assembly, where they would cut the Alpha shaft loose. And they placed Pindar and Shira on the assembly 420 kilometers from the plate. Here they began slicing through Alpha, to separate it from the other twenty-six-hundred-odd kilometers of its length. At the plate, Tom Scolari and his people had returned to work, striving to complete the cuts they'd begun earlier. When they were finished, there would remain as a unit only the Alpha shaft, the connecting plate, and the net.

All this activity was closely watched by Drummond and his team. His principal concern at the moment was to ensure that the separations at the various points along the shaft were made simultaneously. If they failed to do that, if one end of Alpha started to drift while another section somewhere was still secured to the assembly, it might snap.

The shuttle Scolari had seen approaching carried Miles and Philip Zossimov, whose image blinked onto Drummond's screen within seconds of the release of the asteroid. 'May we go in close to take a look?' Zossimov asked.

'Stand by. It'll be a few minutes.' Drummond opened his link to the *Star*. Marcel's carefully controlled features looked back at him.

'Right on schedule,' Drummond said. 'Be ready to go.'

At the plate, Scolari's people were three minutes away from completing their cuts. They'd stopped at that point to wait for the signal from Drummond. All along the assembly, the same kind of thing was happening: One by one, each of the five teams at the bands, and Pindar and Jane at the far end of Alpha, were reaching the three-minute mark and reporting back to Drummond, who was watching his own timepiece.

When they'd all called in, he told them to wait for his signal. He reported again to Marcel, who told him to proceed.

'Ladies and gentlemen,' he told the Outsider teams, 'cut us loose.'

Marcel and Nicholson, on the *Star* bridge, listened to the reports filtering back to Drummond.

Site Two was free.

The far end was free.

Sites One and Five.

Site Three.

Drummond queried Four.

'Just a moment, John.' Then: 'Yes—'

Aside from the rock swarm, there were two unsettling moments during the operation. One had come when the asteroid broke free. The other occurred when they finished cutting through the fifteenth shaft and the assembly separated.

Scolari had expected that the separation would be gradual. They'd cut through most of the shafts, and were working on the final three, when they simply started to snap off one by one, in precise drill, and Alpha abruptly began to float away, taking the plate and a kilometer or so of trailing net with it.

The assembly trembled, in reaction to the loss of mass. And that was it.

'Plate's free,' Drummond told Marcel.

'Everybody okay?' Janet's voice.

Scolari looked around. 'We're all here,' he said.

'Very fine,' she replied. 'Well done.'

He looked down the length of the assembly. Common sense told him that once the other fourteen shafts had been separated from the plate, they would drift apart, or drift together. Or *something*. It seemed impossible that the tubes could remain perfectly aligned with each other as they had been. He

422

understood that the other bands were still in place, holding them together. That only the Alpha shaft had been separated. But the nearest connector was eighty kilometers away. Yet they remained parallel.

He was still holding his cutter. He folded it and put it in his vest. A voice in his earphone said, 'Here comes our taxi, Tom.' It was the Academy shuttle that had brought them to the assembly two hours earlier. It came alongside, and the pilot warned them to take their time getting in. The airlock opened. They climbed inside, cycled through, and congratulated one another.

Cleo beamed at him. 'Talent I didn't know I had,' she said.

Marcel signaled Nicholson with an almost imperceptible gesture. Nicholson pushed the button. Lori's voice acknowledged: '*Activating phase two.*'

The Alpha shaft, freed from the main body of the assembly, was reduced to about thirteen percent of its former length. Lori, the controlling AI, awaited incoming results from a wide array of sensors.

When she was satisfied all was in order, and the proper moment in her internal countdown arrived, she fired maneuvering thrusters on *Zwick* and *Wildside*, orchestrated to draw Alpha clear of the assembly, to ensure that no tumble developed, and to begin the long rotation that would end with the net and plate moving toward the point out over the Misty Sea where it would, they all hoped, rendezvous in twenty hours with Hutch's lander.

She monitored progress, which was slight but satisfactory, and when conditions allowed, she fired the main engines on *Wildside*, and four minutes later, on *Zwick*. The shaft began perceptibly to rotate toward its vector.

Approximately sixteen minutes after the *Wildside* ignition, she shut off the vessel's engines, and several minutes later did the same with *Zwick*.

Now there was a quick scramble in what everyone perceived as the tightest part of the operation save the actual dip into the atmosphere.

The Outsiders on *Wildside* and *Zwick* hurried back out and released the ships from the shaft. There wasn't time to bring them back in, so they tethered down on the hulls while everyone waited. When they reported themselves secure, Lori moved the vessels cautiously to new positions along the shaft, and realigned them, bringing their axes parallel to Alpha. When that had been done, the Outsiders reattached the ships.

Meantime, the other two vessels, the *Evening Star* and *Wendy,* snuggled up against the shaft in their assigned places. More of Janet's people poured out of airlocks and secured them to the shaft.

The problem she had been waiting for developed on *Wendy.* One of the volunteers, a researcher from the science team, got ill out on the hull and brought up her lunch. The force field had no provision to handle that kind of event. It was flexible and made room, but the unfortunate woman was quickly immersed in her own ejecta. Panicked, she lost contact with the hull and drifted away from the ship.

A backup quickly replaced her and a shuttle was dispatched to do a rescue.

The replacement joined the effort almost without missing a beat.

It was a difficult maneuver because everything had to be completed within a restrictive time frame, barely two hours, or they'd lose their window. As it turned out, no one need have worried. The job was completed, and everyone, including the woman with the lunch, was back inside with eleven minutes to spare. All four vessels had been aligned directly front to rear along the shaft axis.

At Lori's signal, the four superluminals engaged their main engines and gently drew the Alpha shaft forward, beginning their long run toward the Misty Sea.

*

There were a few places where the floor had buckled or where the ceiling had caved in. They found fragments of fibrous materials in some of the cubicles off the concourse. Clothing, apparently. Small stuff.

She took samples of everything, continued to record the locations, and made voluminous notes.

A call came in from Canyon. 'Hutch,' he said, 'I'd love to do a program from inside the skyhook. If you'd be willing.' They were already broadcasting the visuals, he hoped she didn't mind, but it was a huge story back home. And everyone would like to hear her reactions.

'Give me a break, August. I can't walk around here pointing my vest at everything.'

'You don't have to. The spontaneous shots work fine. We'll use a delay, and we can reconstruct anything that we miss. You don't have to worry; we can edit out whatever might not be appropriate, whatever you want us to. It'll make a great story. And I'd be in your debt.'

'You won't see much. It's foggy.'

'I know. We *like* foggy. It's atmospheric.' He laughed at his own joke.

The Academy would love it. The romance of edge-of-the-envelope archeology. She glanced at Nightingale, who nodded his okay. 'I'll make a deal with you,' she said. 'I'll comment occasionally when I think there's something worthwhile to be said. If you can avoid asking me any questions. Just leave me alone to do my work, and I'll try to cooperate.'

'Hutch, I'd really like to do the interview.'

'I'm busy,' she said.

'Well, of course. Sure. We can do what you want. I understand entirely.'

'This is a long empty corridor,' she said. 'It's probably been like this for three thousand years.'

'*Three thousand years?* You really think it's that old?' he asked.

'Augie,' she said, 'you're incurable.'

'I'm sorry.'

'It's okay. Must be frustrating for you to be up there out of the action.'

Momentarily his tone changed. 'You know,' he said quietly, 'I'd almost accept a chance to go down there with you. It's *that* big a story.'

'Almost,' she said.

'Yeah. *Almost.*'

Curiously, she felt sorry for him.

Hutch paid particular attention to the inscriptions. The six languages were always in the same order.

In the areas behind the concourses, among the passageways and cubicles, in what they'd come to think of as back offices, they discovered a seventh alphabet. 'I've seen this before,' she said, looking at an inscription that hung at the end of a corridor, where it branched off at right angles. Two groups of characters were engraved over symbols that could only be arrows. 'They have to be *places.* Washrooms. Souvenirs here and ice cream over there. Baggage to your left.'

Nightingale tapped his lips with an index finger. 'I'll tell you where we saw it. At the hovercraft memorial.'

At that moment, somewhere ahead, they heard a click.

It was sharp and clear, and it hung in the air.

Hutch's heart stopped. Nightingale caught his breath.

'An animal,' she said.

They waited, trying to see into the fog.

There were closed doors along both sides of the passageway. As she watched, one moved. The movement was barely discernible, but it opened a finger's width. And stopped.

They drew close together for mutual support. Hutch produced her cutter. Neither spoke.

When nothing more happened, Hutch walked over to the door.

It closed, and she jumped.

It opened again.

'Maybe we ought to get out of here,' whispered Nightingale.

'Wait.' She tiptoed closer and tried to look through the opening, but as far as she could see there was nothing inside. Empty room and that was all.

She took a deep breath and tugged on the door. It opened a little wider and she let go and it swung shut. Then it opened again.

'Sensors?' asked Nightingale.

'Apparently. Still working.'

She recalled that the building seemed to be equipped with solar collectors.

The door was not quite three meters high, constructed of the same plastic material they'd seen elsewhere in the hexagon. It had no knob and no latch. But she saw a diagonal green strip that might have been the sensor. And another green strip with faded characters that might have indicated who occupied the office, or what function it had performed.

In spite of his assurances. Canyon reentered the conversation: 'Hutch, that was a riveting moment. How did you feel when you first heard the sound?'

Her next words would eventually travel around the world. She regretted having agreed to let Augie and his two billion listeners eavesdrop. She would have liked to put on a blasé exterior, to behave the way heroes are supposed to, but she couldn't recall whether she'd made frightened sounds. 'Terrified,' she said.

The door opened again.

The ground shook. Another tremor.

They walked on. The door continued to open and close, the only disruption in the general stillness.

They climbed a ramp into a compartmented section. Eight or nine rooms, several with low ceilings. There were signs at belt level and small benches and knee-high rails around the bulkheads. A cricket-sized staircase went to an upper deck.

Several rooms were fitted with lines of chairs. Very much like the hovercraft cabin. In one the gauge abruptly shifted to their own comfort level.

The complex had no egress save the way they'd come in, down the ramp and back into the concourse.

'I think we just got onto the skyhook,' said Hutch.

If so, whatever machinery might have made it work was safely concealed. 'You might be right.' He looked at the tiny handrails.

'It wasn't an advanced culture,' she said. 'How do you think the hawks were received when they arrived and told everybody they needed to get out?'

31

It's customary to argue that intelligence grants an evolutionary advantage. But where is the evidence? We are surrounded by believers in psychic healing, astrology, dreams, and drugs. Are we to accept the premise that these hordes of unfortunates descended from intelligent forebears?

I'm prepared to concede that stupidity does not help survival. One must after all understand not to poke a tiger with a stick. But intelligence leads to curiosity, and curiosity has never been a quality that helps one pour his or her genes into the pool. The truth must lie somewhere between. Whatever the reason, it is clearly mediocrity, at best, that lives and breeds.

—GREGORY MACALLISTER, *Reflections of a Barefoot Journalist*

Hours to breakup (est): 29

Several hundred people were gathered in the *Star*'s theater, where it was possible to follow the rescue effort on a dozen screens and at the same time down a few drinks with friends. Marcel had been wandering through the giant ship, trying to occupy his mind while events played out, and had stepped into the theater when Beekman called to ask where he was. Moments later they met in a small booth off the observation deck. The project director looked pale.

'What's wrong, Gunther?' he asked.

They were standing near a display exhibiting the construction of the *Evening Star*. Here was the beginning, Ordway Conover talking to engineers, explaining that he wanted the most spectacular superluminal ever built. There was the *Star* in Earth orbit when it was only a keel. Here were the electronics installations, and there the Delta deck swimming pool. And the celebrities who had come to see it off on its maiden cruise. And its first captain, Bartlett Hollinger, bearded, gray-eyed, silver-haired, looking impossibly competent, and very much like the uncle everybody remembered fondly. 'You know,' said Beekman, 'some of the people on *Wendy* think we're doing the wrong thing.'

The statement initially startled Marcel. He understood Beekman to be suggesting that the rescue effort might be going wrong somewhere, that they'd missed something fundamental, something now irreparable. 'In what way?' he asked, his voice little more than a whisper. 'What do they think we should be doing?'

'They think we're neglecting the mission.'

Marcel felt a surge of relief, and then, as Beekman's meaning became clear, of incredulity. And finally he had to choke down a rising tide of anger. 'Is that how *you* feel?'

Beekman needed a long time to answer. 'I'm not sure,' he said at last. 'We're never going to see anything like this again. Not in the lifetime of anybody here. We stand to learn more about gravity functions and planetary structure than we could pick up in a century of theorizing. Marcel, it *is* true that we're letting a priceless opportunity get away from us.'

'You want to abandon Kellie?'

'Of course not.'

'You can't have it both ways, Gunny.'

'You asked if I *wanted* to abandon her. I don't. You know that. But you and I both know that the big stick is probably not going to work. There are too many things that can go wrong. Maybe we'd do better to face that and get back to concentrating on what we came here for.'

Marcel took a deep breath. 'Gunther, let's turn this around for a minute. Make it *your* call. What do you want to do?'

'You'd abide by my decision?'

Marcel glanced up at a large framed picture of a young couple eating dinner off the promenade. Through a window, the Crab Nebula was visible. 'Yes,' he said. 'I'll abide by your decision. What do we do? Do we write Kellie off? And the others?'

Beekman looked back at Marcel, followed his gaze to the portrait, stared at it a long time. 'That's unreasonable,' he said at last.

'What is?'

'You know what I'm talking about.'

'Sure. Making the call, as opposed to criticizing.'

He made a rumbling sound in his throat. 'All right,' he said. 'Do it your way. But somewhere down the road, we're going to pay a price.'

The command crew on the bridge of the *Star* ooohed and aaahed as images of alien inscriptions and crumbling corridors and regally garbed hawks played across their screens. Lori systematically removed the fog and enhanced the pictures. Here was a series of empty cubicles along a broad concourse, there a gently curving passageway lined by doors engraved with symbols from alien alphabets. Marcel wondered whether they designated the kind of activity carried on behind the door, or whether they were the names of individuals.

Individual hawks. What had their lives been like? Did they sit around in the evening and play some sort of poker-equivalent? Did they enjoy conversation over meals? Did they have music?

He would have liked very much to be able to listen in when the decision had been taken to go to the rescue of the medieval world that was entering a dust cloud. It must have required a

431

gigantic engineering effort on the part of a species that apparently didn't even have spike technology. How many had they saved? Where had they gone?

He heard the power levels rise, felt the ship adjusting course once more.

The hexagon *was* vast. A schematic was taking shape on the main wallscreen. Human-sized cubicles in the east wing, long concourses, sections that might have been waiting or storage areas, upper levels they hadn't even gotten to. Marcel thought he saw objects on a row of shelves on the north side, but he hadn't been present when they'd passed by, had seen only the record. Hutch and Nightingale had either missed the figures or thought too little of them to waste time. He'd avoided bringing the matter up later.

'The place is a treasure trove,' said Drummond, watching from his shuttle. 'It's a pity there isn't time to get a decent look at it.'

They were lucky, Marcel reflected, that they'd seen anything. Scholars, he suspected, would be poring over the visual record for years.

Beekman appeared unexpectedly at his side. He'd been avoiding eye contact with Marcel since their conversation. 'You know,' he said, trying to pretend nothing had happened between them, 'there'll be some major changes at the top when all this gets back. Gomez will go.'

'You think so?' asked Marcel. Irene Gomez had been the Academy's director for more than ten years.

'She was part of the crowd that made the decision to pull out after the Nightingale fiasco. Now we're looking at *this*. And it's all going to be lost. This stuff's been going out from that character at Universal, what's his name?'

'Canyon.'

'Canyon. Right. They'll get it back home day after tomorrow. The board of governors will call an emergency meeting. I'll bet Gomez is gone by the end of next week. And her department heads with her.'

He looked pleased at the prospect. Marcel had no connection

with the director and had never even seen her in person. But he knew she did not command the respect or the loyalty of Academy people. Of course, he thought, neither would Beekman if it ever got out he'd wanted to abandon the ground party.

'Invaluable stuff,' Beekman said. His tone gave him away: *Even if we lose the people, maybe it will have been worth it.*

Lori's voice broke in: '*Preliminary maneuvers are complete. We are on course.*'

They found a portrait in one of the cubicles.

It was mounted on a wall, hidden behind a layer of dust, but when Hutch peeled it away and wiped a cloth over it, the images came clear.

Two of the crickets were pictured on either side of a hawk, which must have been three times their size. It was difficult to be sure about scale because the hawk was visible only from the breast up.

The crickets wore the placid expressions of philosophers. They were draped in cowls, one hooded, one bareheaded. The skulls appeared to be hairless, and she saw no indication of eyebrows. Despite the prejudice induced by her knowledge of the technological limitations of their society, Hutch read intelligence in their faces.

The otherwise fearsome appearance of the hawk was diminished by the staff it carried. Its only concession to clothing was a dark ribbon tied around one shoulder. The chest was broad, and it owned a crest that stood proudly erect. It dwarfed its companions. Yet that they *were* companions was impossible to doubt.

The thing had a predator's eyes and fangs and fur where Hutch might have expected to see feathers. She was struck by the composure manifested by the crickets, who might easily have been gobbled down by such a creature.

There was something else.

'What?' asked Nightingale.

She couldn't make up her mind about the sex of the two crickets. But the hawk? 'I think it's a female,' she said.

Nightingale sighed. 'How can you possibly tell?'

'I don't know, Randy.' She tried to analyze her reaction. 'Something in its eyes, maybe.'

Nightingale reached for the picture and was pleased to see that it lifted from its mount. It was too big to put in his pack, so he simply carried it.

They had by then mapped much of the ground level of the structure. The elevator to the orbiting station had been located on the eastern side, at the juncture of north-south and east-west concourses. The upper levels, judging by their scale, seemed to have been given over to the hawks. It seemed that the crickets used only the ground floor.

It was getting dark when they got to the north side. Here they were cautious because this was the part of the structure that, according to Marcel, jutted out over the edge of the mountain.

They came to a collapsed ramp and looked down into a lobby at another portrait. Hutch used her vine, against his protests, to descend and retrieve it. It was a full-length image of a hawk.

It had no wings.

'That figures,' said Nightingale. 'It's too big to fly.'

'Even if it had *big* wings?'

Nightingale laughed, but he kept it down. '*Really* big wings,' he said. 'Something as massive as we are, like that thing apparently was, would never be able to get off the ground under its own power.'

'Maybe it comes from a world where the gravity is light.'

They both spoke consistently in hushed voices, as if anything at normal decibels would be inappropriate. To remind them, when either got too loud, the sound echoed back.

'That's possible,' Nightingale said. 'But the gravity would have to be *very* light. And if that were the case, I don't think these creatures would have been at all comfortable on Maleiva III. No, I doubt there's anything avian about these things. I'd bet neither they nor their ancestors ever flew. The hawk resemblance simply gets us thinking that way.'

Hutch knew that Kellie would want to take a look at all this, and they'd been inside now for a long time. 'Time to start back,' she said.

Nightingale looked pained. He would have gone on forever, if he'd been permitted. 'Why don't we hold up just for a few seconds?' Off the northern concourse, twin ramps led down one level. 'Let's take a quick look downstairs, then we can go back.'

'Two minutes,' she said.

They descended and found another broad passageway whose walls were covered with inscriptions in the six languages. Sometimes, instead of just a few words, there were whole sections of twenty lines or more devoted to each group of symbols. 'This would be just what they need,' she said. 'We translated one of the languages of Quraqua with a lot less than this.' It was an exciting prospect, but the wall would have to be cleaned and restored before it would be of much use. She used the microscan to get as much as she could, knowing that they were losing most of it.

There were other inscriptions. These were short, usually only two- or three-word groups. Hutch recognized the characters from the uppermost line on the artifact they'd found at the site of the hovercraft.

She tried to imagine the concourse when it was alive.

They came to a series of wide doorways, all on the right-hand side. Each opened into a chamber about four meters wide. The rooms were devoid of any kind of furniture.

She poked her head in, saw nothing, and went to the next one.

There were eight of them, of identical dimensions. Hutch looked in each, hoping to be surprised. They had low ceilings. Designed for the crickets.

At last they stood together in the eighth room, at the end of the passageway. There were no artifacts, no inscriptions, nothing. Just bare rooms. 'Let's go,' she said.

She started out, and the room *moved*. It was a momentary quiver, as if a pulse had gone through the building.

Quake, she thought.

Something began to grind in the walls. The room *lurched*.

'Get out, Randy!' She bolted for the exit. A door was already sliding, banging, clanking down out of the overhead. Nightingale froze, and she turned back. And then it was too late. She pulled up, and her chance was gone. The door chunked to a stop, a hand's width off the floor, and then crashed down onto the dirt. It cut off the light, and Hutch found herself crouching in the dark. She turned on her wristlamp.

'This is not good,' said Nightingale.

The grinding in the walls got louder. The floor inched up. And fell back.

Mira's voice broke over the circuit: 'What happened?'

'Don't know. Stand by.'

Nightingale aimed his laser at the door and thumbed the switch. A white beam licked out, and the gray surface began to blacken. Then the floor dropped abruptly. Startled, he lost control of the laser and swept the room with it before dropping it. As designed, the thing automatically snapped off.

The room fell. Stopped. Slipped down a few meters.

'My God,' said Nightingale. 'What's going on?'

'Another elevator. A working one, looks like.'

The chamber crunched down again. Marcel was on the circuit now. 'What's happening? What's your situation?'

Canyon was still there, but aside from a word of encouragement, he kept mercifully quiet. They continued to bump, vibrate, and drop.

'On my way,' said Kellie.

'No. Stay with the lander.'

'I can't help from here.'

'I don't think there's much you can do over here either.'

Nightingale looked panicked. Probably like herself.

Something rattled beneath the floor.

The ceiling was too low for either of them to stand straight. They picked a corner of the room and retreated into it.

The grinding eased off, but the elevator continued its erratic descent. She used her laser to finish the job Nightingale had started, cutting a substantial piece out of the door. It was dark outside, and the fog was thick as ever. But the glow of her lamp revealed no wall. Instead she saw only a gridwork of struts and beams.

'What do we do?' asked Nightingale.

She widened the hole, making it big enough that they could get out if the opportunity offered. 'It'll have sharp edges, though,' she cautioned him. 'Be ready to go if we get the chance.'

The ride continued. Nightingale came over, looked out, but was careful not to get too close. There was still nothing to see except the gridwork, moving sporadically past as they continued down.

'I think we're in the basement somewhere,' she said. And then, moments later: 'I can see daylight below.'

The elevator rattled and shook, and there were squeals and shrieks in the floor and ceiling. Suddenly a void opened. The mist was gone, and they were dropping through bright day.

'Where the hell are we?' demanded Nightingale.

She looked down the side of a sheer gray wall that fell forever toward green hills. 'This is how the crickets got up to the skyhook.'

Nightingale peered out and trembled. 'You don't think we're going all the way to the bottom, do you?'

'That would be my guess. Unless their technology isn't too good. If that's the case, we might stop partway down and be expected to switch to another elevator.'

It was hard to determine whether Nightingale thought that would be good news or not. There were a few clouds below them and others out on the horizon. Nightingale steeled himself, looked down, and gasped. 'My God,' he said.

'Stay away from it.' She pulled him back.

Kellie heard it. 'I don't care what you say,' she said. 'We're going to saddle up and come over there.'

'No point. You can't reach us. Wait until we see how this plays out. I want you to be ready in case we need you in a hurry.'

'Okay.' She sighed. 'Keep the channel open.'

The banging and grinding subsided somewhat, and the ride smoothed out, became more constant, less bone-rattling, as if the machinery was becoming unlimbered.

They slowed, accelerated again, and jerked finally to a halt.

She looked down at a river valley so far below it made her head ache. They were, she realized, on the north face of the mountain, the section that appeared to have been artificially carved.

'What are we going to do?' breathed Nightingale. 'We're stuck here.'

The elevator trembled.

'Quake, I think,' she said.

'That's what we need.' He looked at her, his eyes full of fear. 'Hutch, we need help.'

'You've a talent for understatement, Randy.'

'Can you give us a description,' asked Kellie, 'of where you are?'

She told her, and added 'Pretty high up. I guess we're going to need air-to-air.'

'Okay. Sit tight. We're on our way.'

'How do you mean, "air-to-air"?' asked Nightingale privately. 'That doesn't mean what I think it does, does it?'

'Unless you want to try climbing down.' Above them she could see the framework of girders, crossbeams, and diagonals, the grid within which the elevator rode. The rear of the elevator was fitted against the face of the mountain. They were about fifty meters down. The cliff, as best she could see, was lined with shelves and outcroppings and even a few trees, but it would under no circumstances provide a means to scramble back up to safety.

'Can they really get us out of here?' asked Nightingale.

'It's lemon pie,' she said.

The comment did nothing to alleviate his state of mind. 'How?'

'Just ferry us out. Sit tight until she gets here.'

He looked down, and she watched the little color that was left drain out of his face. The elevator dropped again, slightly, probably no more than a few centimeters. He gasped and turned a terror-stricken face toward her. 'Best to stay away from it,' she said.

'What are we going to do? Jump?'

'Something like that. Randy. But you'll be tethered, so you can't fall.'

He shook his head. 'Hutch, I don't think I can do it.'

'Sure you can. No matter what, we can't stay here.'

She could see that he felt humiliated as well as frightened.

They began descending again, slowly and steadily. 'We're getting there,' he said. 'If we're patient, maybe everything'll be okay.'

She said nothing, but simply sat down and waited for the lander to appear.

'What's holding the elevator up?' Marcel asked.

'The cable, I guess,' said Hutch. She heard the welcome rumble of jets.

'That's a negative,' said Kellie. 'We do not see a cable.'

Marcel made a worried noise. 'Are you sure?'

'Yep. No cable.'

'Then,' pursued Marcel, 'it must be a different kind of system from the one we use. Maybe they don't use cables. Maybe they glide up and down some sort of magnetic rail.'

'I don't think so,' said Kellie. 'It has a cable *mount* on top.'

'You sure?' asked Hutch.

'There's a couple meters of cable dangling from it.'

32

Everybody complains about the weather, and we have the technology now to do something about it, should we choose to. But we don't. The fact is, we need bad weather. A day at the beach is much more enjoyable if we know that somebody, somewhere, is getting rained on.

—GREGORY MACALLISTER, 'Reflections', Collected
Essays

Hours to breakup (est): 27

Abel Kinder watched the numbers rippling across his screens. Off-the-chart high-pressure front moving down into the Nirvana Ocean to collide with extreme low pressure along the eastern coastline of Transitoria. Tornadoes spawning inland. Hurricanes boiling across waters normally too cold to support hurricane activity.

He punched Marcel's button.

'What do you have, Abel?' the captain asked.

'More heavy weather. When do we make the pickup?'

'Nineteen hours and change.'

'I don't suppose you can speed it up.'

'Negative. The schedule's out of our control. How heavy?'

'Extremely. I've never seen these kinds of readings before. Tell them to expect wind and rain. Especially wind.'

'How much?'

'A *lot*.'

Tom Scolari and Cleo, who had watched the asteroid rise into the night with such unabashed pleasure, were taken afterward to the *Zwick*. It was a small, boxy ship, bristling with antennas, UNIVERSAL NEWS was emblazoned on its hull.

Janet informed him that they were assigned to the onboard Outsider team. 'There's another job coming up in about seven hours. Until then, you can relax.'

They were taken in charge by a short, unobtrusive man who might have been a librarian, and a tall willowy blonde with the manner of an aristocrat pretending to be a commoner. 'Name's Jack Kingsbury,' he said. 'I'm the ship's welder.' He managed a grin.

The woman was Emma Constantine. 'It's good to have you on board,' she said, with affected interest. 'You people have been doing an extraordinary job.' She had perfect diction.

'You're the rest of the team, I assume,' Scolari said.

Emma wasn't. 'I'm August Canyon's producer.' She inspected them. 'You two have a change of clothes with you? Damn, I don't understand that. They promised they'd see that you had some fresh clothes.'

'Who promised?' asked Cleo before Scolari could react.

'My contact on *Wendy*. We wanted to do an interview. Live. But you both look a trifle mussed. Let me see if we can get something that fits.'

Marcel had lost contact with the ground party. He sat disconsolately on the *Star*'s bridge while Lori tried to raise *Tess* through the electrical storms that now blanketed the atmosphere.

The *Star*'s working spaces were far more luxurious than Marcel's cramped command area on *Wendy*. The bridge had leather panels, soft-glo lighting, full-wall flexscreens, and a captain's chair that would have looked good at the C.O. Club.

He understood why this was so: On the *Star*, the bridge was part of the tour. It was the only operational part of the great ship that the passengers actually saw, so power and opulence were *de rigueur*. Only when they commenced the final series of course adjustments would the visits be halted.

Nicholson irritated Marcel. It was hard to say why. The man was friendly enough. Having reached the decision to assist, he never failed to respond quickly and effectively to the needs of the operation. He did what he could to make Marcel and his people comfortable, and he went out of his way to tolerate Beekman, who was capable of occasional flashes of arrogance. It might have been that he tried too hard to live up to his image of what a starship captain should be. He talked as if he, Marcel, and Beekman operated on a higher plane than everyone else. He was quick to criticize, quick to suggest that the mission would have more chance of success if only they had more people on board like themselves.

He took aim particularly at the volunteers. They were *amateurs*. How could they be expected to get things right?

But the amateurs, Marcel pointed out several times, had so far done quite well.

In the short time he'd been on the *Evening Star,* Marcel had concluded that Nicholson had never learned the difference between maintaining distance between himself and his officers, and becoming aloof. The captain looked like a lonely man, and probably had no friend anywhere on the vessel.

Beekman and one of his physicists were huddled in a corner. Beekman had led the team that had analyzed course, velocity, and aspect of the Alpha shaft as it came free of the assembly. He and Drummond had calculated what was needed to turn it around and arrange for it to show up with the appropriate alignment tomorrow morning at the designated spot at the correct time on Deepsix.

There were a dozen or so visitors on the bridge, mostly overweight middle-aged couples talking about dinner or the evening's presentation in the Star Theater, which was to be a live production of Barry English's *Indigo*. Marcel had suggested canceling, because they expected to be making course adjustments through the evening, but Nicholson was afraid someone might be alarmed, or displeased, or resentful. The ship's movements were expected to be nominal. And, of course, everything would be known well in advance.

Beekman finished his conversation, excused himself, and came over. 'We're in business,' he said. 'Everything's falling into place.'

'Good.' Marcel pushed away from the console while Beekman took a seat. 'You and your people have been outstanding, Gunther.'

'Thanks. We were concerned that the rotation would put too much stress on the shaft. That it would break somewhere. Or that the welds wouldn't hold. But we seem to have gotten through okay. I *do* believe you might actually pull it off.'

'*We* might, Gunny. Or maybe *you* will. You and John and that army of part-time welders. Who'd've believed it?'

'Well, let's parcel out the credit when we have them home. There'll be a course adjustment in nine minutes. It'll be very slight. Nicholson knows.'

'You've made my day, Gunny.'

'You don't look happy. What's wrong, Marcel? The elevator thing?'

'Yes. Right now, it's scary.'

'It'll be all right. They've got Kellie to help them. Are we talking to them yet?'

'No. They're still out.'

The lander moved into position immediately in front of the elevator. Rain beat down on it, and lightning flared and boomed around them. Kellie, in the pilot's seat, was also fighting heavy winds along the face of the cliff.

'We'll have to make this fast, Hutch,' she said. 'I don't know how long I can stay here.' She was referring to the power levels needed to sustain hover mode.

'Okay,' Hutch said.

'Something else. The elevators are inside a gridwork.'

'We know.'

'Okay. Then you also know it's a Crosshatch of beams, supports, and plates. *That's* what's holding you up. There must be tracks in there, and the elevators run up and down the tracks. Everything's old and jammed up. The metal's got to be warped. So the elevator can't ride freely.'

'What are you trying to tell us, Kellie?'

'There's a clean break about fifty meters down. You get down there, and it just opens out into the great beyond. Bye-bye baby.'

'All right. It feels pretty stable now. Let's go.'

'Who's first?'

'Randy.'

Nightingale looked at her, almost pleading. His face was ashen. What did he want her to do? Leave him there?

The lander eased down until it lined up directly with the elevator. Kellie opened the hatch and MacAllister showed them a line. 'It's tied to the seat anchor, Randy,' he said.

Nightingale nodded anxiously. 'Okay.'

MacAllister stared at Hutch, across a space of only a few meters. He looked scared, too, but he was trying to appear nonchalant. How about that? The guy was a trooper after all.

The lander rose and fell, caught in an updraft. It rolled toward the elevator, then drifted away. 'Not too close,' Hutch said.

'Lot of wind here.' Kellie's voice in her earphones.

Mac coiled the rope and measured the distance. 'Ready, Hutch?'

'Yeah.'

It spun toward her. She reached for it, watched it fall short. Mac reeled it in and tried again. Still short.

'You're too far out,' he told Kellie.

Hutch heard a soft *damn*. The lander drew off, trailing line.

445

When Mac was ready she started another approach.

The lander rose on a cushion of air. It dropped suddenly and to Hutch's horror MacAllister almost fell out. Nightingale stiffened. 'Goddam downdrafts,' said Kellie.

Mac retreated from the hatch. 'You okay, Mac?' Hutch asked. 'You see what happened there?'

'I saw,' Kellie told him. 'Get a tether.'

He was gone for a few moments. Then he emerged again wearing a line tied around his ample waist. The problem, of course, was that if he *did* fall out, Kellie couldn't leave the controls to haul him back in. She'd have to go all the way to the bottom to retrieve him.

'All right,' said Mac, his voice surprisingly steady. 'Let's try it again.'

'This is a little delicate,' said Kellie. 'When you get the line, you're going to have to move fast.' Hutch understood: If the wind caught the lander in the middle of the operation, it would rip the line, and whoever happened to be attached to it, out of the elevator.

Kellie made her approach. Hutch kept her eyes on Mac, watching him gauge his distance. The line was coiled in his right hand. The lander turned sideways, sank, wobbled, came back. It climbed, getting above her.

Mac saw his chance and the line came spinning in her direction. It unraveled and it was slick from the rain, but she scooped it out of the air and held on to it.

'Okay, Randy,' she said. 'Let's move it.'

He shrank back, and she could see the struggle being fought behind his eyes.

'We don't have time to monkey around,' she told him softly. 'We stay here, we die.'

'I know.'

She waited for him.

'Hutch.' Kellie's voice. 'Let's go. I can't hold it here forever.'

'We're working on it.'

Nightingale stepped forward and closed his eyes. She coiled

446

the line around his middle, crossed it under his armpits, and secured it in front. No way he could fall out of that. But he resisted as she tried to walk him to the opening.

'Hutch,' he said, 'I can't do this.'

'It's okay, Randy. You're doing fine.'

The elevator dropped again. Banged to a stop.

'Hutch!' said Kellie.

Nightingale got to the door and looked out at the lander. Rain blew in on him.

'Don't look down,' Hutch said.

'Hurry it up,' said Kellie.

'Hutch?'

'Yes, Randy?'

'If this doesn't work—'

'It'll work'

'If it doesn't—' He was reaching for the rim of the opening, found it, gripped it. The line stretching from him to the aircraft tightened and loosened as Kellie rode the drafts along the face of the precipice.

Hutch stepped up behind him and gently peeled his fingers away. 'It *always* works,' she told him. And pushed. He went out silently, without the scream she'd expected.

He fell. It must have been a sickening few seconds, but it ended quickly when the line took hold and he rolled out in a long arc beneath the lander. Kellie pulled quickly away while he swung back and forth, clutching the line, saying *O God* over and over.

Mac began to haul him in. Hutch watched Nightingale kick frantically, and she feared he might have a heart attack. 'Relax, Randy,' she told him. 'You're okay. The hard part is over.' And she continued talking to him in the most soothing tone she could muster until Mac's hand reached down finally, seized his vest, and dragged him into the aircraft.

The lander tilted slightly and started around again. Mac reappeared in the hatch with his line. 'Okay, me proud beauty,' he said. 'You're next.'

The elevator shook. Another quake, maybe. And it started down again. She backed away from the opening and got off her feet. Rain drummed on the roof. The elevator kept dropping, and it seemed for a few seconds to be almost in free fall. Her heart came into her throat. Then metal squealed, and the elevator banged to a stop.

Kellie was calling frantically. 'I'm okay,' Hutch said.

'Maybe not.'

Hutch's heart, which was still fluttering, missed a beat. 'What's wrong?'

'I'm sinking.'

Spike depletion.

She watched the lander dropping lower. Kellie slowed the descent, hit the jets, and regained some altitude. She came around again. 'We're going to have to get it right the first time,' she said.

Mac stood in the airlock with his line. Kellie glided in overhead, killed the jets, reversed thrust, and brought the lander to a dead stop. It began to fall.

'No,' Hutch said. 'It won't work.'

It was dropping too fast. Mac looked desperately in her direction.

'I'm going to have to land and recharge,' Kellie said. 'Hutch, I'm sorry. I don't know any other way to do this.'

Hutch nodded and waved good-bye. 'Take it down. I'll be here when you come back.'

It was getting dark. Winds were high, and she had no sensors. A night rescue would be out of the question.

Kellie was fighting back rage and tears. 'You can't stay in the elevator, Hutch.'

Hutch watched the lander kick in its jets and bank away to the east. 'Is it that bad?'

'It isn't good.'

She looked out at the storm. And at the gridwork, the crossbars and diagonals and guide rails off to either side. If she could get to *them*.

A bolt of lightning exploded overhead, throwing everything into momentary relief.

The outside of the elevator was smooth, without handholds. Despite the low ceiling, the roof was out of reach. She saw no way to climb onto it, not without something to stand on.

It slipped again. Something banged hard against one of the walls.

She backed away and tried to think. It was hard, knowing what might happen at any moment, to keep her head clear.

She gathered up her vine, went back to the opening, and looked again at the roof. Then she got down on her belly, leaned out, and peered underneath. A pair of cables hung from the underside. And she saw the break, only a few meters down. A missing guide rail.

The way things were going, she had only a couple of minutes.

Hutch produced her laser, moved to one side of the doorway, and cut a hole belt high in the wall. Then a second one farther to the left at the level of her shoulders and a third one above her head directly over the first. The e-suit was supposed to protect her from extremes of heat and cold, but she wasn't sure what would happen if she put her foot on hot metal. On the other hand, she didn't have time to stand there and wait for everything to cool.

'Hutch—' Kellie's voice, broken up by the storm. '—on the ground and charging.'

'Okay.'

'Can you get out of the car?'

'I'll let you know.'

She went back to the doorway, measured distances, tried to convince herself there was no difference between what she was trying and climbing onto a garage roof, which she had done many times in her girlhood.

She leaned out and grabbed the highest of the handholds. The rain took her breath away. Even though she was protected from it by the suit, the psychological result was the same as if the field were not there. The McMurtrie Effect again.

She gathered her courage, swung out onto the face of the elevator, inserted her foot into the bottom hole, climbed quickly up, and crawled onto the roof. The cable housing was centered, and the roof angled slightly down away from it. Her first impulse was to make for the housing, to get as far from the edge as she could. But that would accomplish nothing.

She watched the network of diagonal and horizontal bars move slowly past. Move up. They were round and desperately narrow. No thicker than her wrist. What kind of building materials did these people use, anyhow?

She edged toward the gridwork, tied one end of her vine around her waist, and stepped off the roof onto a passing crossbar. The elevator kept going, and she leaned away until it was clear. Then she looped her vine around the bar, pulled it tight, and realized she'd stopped breathing. She lowered herself into a sitting position, both legs off one side of the rail although she'd have preferred to straddle because it would feel safer, but it just wasn't comfortable.

'Hutch?' Kellie's voice.

'I'm off the elevator.'

'You okay?'

'Yes. I think so.'

'Where are you?'

'Sitting on a crossbar.'

More lightning. They lost communication for a moment. When it came back, Kellie said, 'How safe are you?'

'I'm okay.'

'We'll have enough of a charge in an hour or so.'

'Don't try it. You'll get us all killed. Wait till morning.'

'Hutch—'

'Do what I'm asking you to. It's the best chance for everybody.'

The elevator was still moving steadily down. Then it stopped, and for several minutes it seemed locked in place. Finally it dropped out of the framework, out of the guide rails, and began to fall. A long time later she heard it hit the forest below.

BREAKING NEWS

'One of the two persons stranded in an elevator early this morning remains in danger . . .'

Nicholson would have preferred to be in his cabin in the Adirondacks. He wanted nothing so much as for this entire business to be over and his part in it to be forgotten. He believed he was safe. But he'd been shaken, and he hated being put into a position that required him to continue to make decisions that might backfire. He was, in fact, determined to see that nothing went wrong, that he emerged blameless from the mission. If he could accomplish that, he would consider himself very fortunate.

Secondarily, he would like to see a successful rescue. Not only because it would help his case, but because when his own immediate fears had passed, he'd begun to feel some sympathy for the four people trapped on the ground.

He was aware that his priorities, had they been known, would have reflected poorly on him. And that judgment embarrassed him, putting an even heavier load on his shoulders. But he couldn't help how he felt. He resented Marcel, not for anything *Wendy*'s captain had actually done, but because he hadn't been able to come up with a rescue plan that didn't involve additional risk for Nicholson.

There was a mild jar as the ship began the course correction. He *sensed* the mass of the object that the *Star* was hauling. Saw it in the sluggishness of the ship's responses. And that was the way of it at the moment: the *Star* was tied to this impossible alien *shaft*, much as Nicholson was tied to his decision to allow two passengers and a lander to drop out of orbit.

Power flowed through the bulkheads as the four superluminals struggled to move their burden onto the designated course. They had no serious capability for lateral maneuvering. While the ships could change their own heading through the use of strategically placed highly flexible thrusters, only the main engines had the sheer capacity to affect the Alpha shaft. That meant they could, in practical terms, only move it forward, relying on gravity fields and inertia to do the rest.

But Lori reported, well into the maneuver, that they were still on target. To Nicholson the entire operation seemed hopelessly complicated. But he had as yet no reason to believe that the plan would not work. Other than his own instincts.

The engines went neutral. Power was being applied elsewhere, by one or more of the other ships. They couldn't calibrate power levels up and down, so the computers adjusted by firing the engines of the various ships in whatever combination was necessary to achieve the desired result. It was a symphony.

One of the auxiliary screens carried a generated image of the *Evening Star*. It was in the center of a group of constellations, warm and luminous against the void. The shaft was represented by a fingernail-thin line, which extended to the edges of the display. Arrows pointed, 44 km forward to *Zwick*, and to the rear, 62 km to *Wildside*.

He refilled his coffee cup, and he saw Marcel talking earnestly with Beekman. The schedule they'd worked out told him there'd be another few hours of maneuvering. Of correcting the long rotation and nudging Alpha into its precise trajectory.

Marcel finished his conversation, looked around, and caught Nicholson's eye. 'How about some breakfast, Erik?' he suggested.

Nicholson glanced at Beekman. 'I wonder whether we shouldn't stay here. In case something happens.'

'Something's already happening,' he said. 'You know Hutch is stranded.'

'Yes. I'd heard.'

It was after 4:00 A.M. 'I don't think there's much we can do for the next few hours. Lori has all the data she needs. The Outsiders are ready to go as soon as conditions permit.'

'Suppose there's a problem?'

'If it's a little one, we can deal with it.'

'And if there's a *big* one?'

452

'It'll be over,' said Beekman matter-of-factly. 'We are past the point where we can make major adjustments.'

Maybe it was just as well to sit down with Clairveau and Beekman. If the operation succeeded, people would remember the image of the two captains and the head of the science team, putting the rescue together.

The electrical intensity of the storm showed no sign of diminishing. Rain pounded down on her, and the wind howled.

The immediate danger rose from the possibility one of the bolts would hit the grid. The e-suit would protect her from a low-level discharge, but she'd never survive a lightning strike. Fortunately, the elevator frame did not jut up into the air. It disappeared into the ruins atop the mountain. Nevertheless there was a lot of exposed metal. A bolt was inevitable.

She could see no way off the iron. The rock wall was smooth. The few bushes clinging to it would never support her. There was a tree above and not far to one side. It looked old and scrabbly, and she thought it had all it could do to hang on itself. Furthermore, it would have been a long jump, one she was pretty sure she couldn't make.

Kellie was constantly on the circuit, between bursts of interference checking on her, asking whether she was okay.

The rain battered her. The suit kept her dry, but it was hard to see.

'You're sure there's no way you can get off the iron?' Kellie asked.

Hutch shook her head wearily. They'd been over it and over it.

'That settles it.'

'No. Don't come up. Wait it out.'

'But—'

'I'll find a way to get clear. My best chance is for you to stay put.'

Another bolt exploded overhead. She jumped and would have

fallen off her perch had she not been secured. She'd almost gotten used to the constant fear, which left her feeling numb and exhausted. The tree sagged in the heavy rain.

The gridwork trembled. Quake or thunder, it no longer seemed to matter. She looked off to the east. Jerry would be rising soon, although the sky would be too heavy to allow her to see it. Thank God for small favors.

When the lander began to drop, Kellie had accelerated, gained altitude, and returned to the mountaintop, hoping that they might be able to find a way to effect a rescue from above. But the peak was still blanketed with fog, despite the heavy winds. The electrical activity had knocked out communication with *Wendy*, so there was no one to guide them in. When MacAllister urged her to try anyhow, she'd prudently pointed out that getting them all killed would do nothing whatever for Priscilla Hutchins.

Instead, she'd opted for a shelf halfway down the mountain. They could hear the ocean coming in, so she wanted to stay high.

MacAllister stared morosely out the window into the flickering darkness while rain hammered at them.

They growled at one another and complained about sitting and doing nothing. Late in the evening Mac finally fell asleep. Nightingale, having no one left to argue with, sat morosely in his chair until Kellie wondered whether he was awake. At about midnight, she lost communication altogether with Hutch.

The lightning continued through the night. She slept fitfully, and woke once to overhear a whispered conversation between her passengers. Nightingale was confessing to having delayed the rescue, was taking responsibility for Hutch's situation on his own shoulders. She could imagine what he was thinking: Priscilla had stayed behind so he could get off. Once again, a woman had rescued him at the cost of her own life. To her surprise Mac told him it could have happened to anybody.

He was hard to figure, that one. Mac characteristically turned a cynical face to the world. Yet he had urged her to try for the rescue, even when she told him it couldn't be done, not in the dark, not in this wind, that they'd only be throwing their lives away.

He'd said very little since Hutch and Nightingale had left that morning to explore the hexagon. *It must be hard on him,* she thought. *He's used to center stage. Everybody takes him seriously, hangs on his every word. He stays at the best hotels, enjoys media attention everywhere he goes. Now suddenly he's reduced to survival mode, hang on to your tether, life and death in the balance. And nobody gives a damn who he is. The only issue for the past twelve days has been: What can he do?* And the reality is, he'd been able to do more than she would have thought.

When they got home, she decided, if they got home, she was going to ask Marcel to give Mac a commendation. *That* would be something worth seeing, Gregory MacAllister showing up at the Academy to receive an award. He'd never complained, other than to yell at inanimate objects, like Jerry. He'd done everything possible within his physical limitations, and he'd not turned out to be the general pain in the rear she'd expected when they began.

'My God,' he said. The cabin brightened and darkened. Thunder ripped through the night.

'*That* one hit the elevators,' Nightingale said.

'Hutch!' Mac tapped his commlink and spoke into it. 'Priscilla. Answer up.'

It was close to dawn, five hours to rendezvous with Marcel's scoop. But there was as yet no break in the darkness. Nightingale was sitting despondently, listening to the wind. MacAllister was bunched up behind him, his teeth clenched against every lightning strike.

MacAllister had never been comfortable with the sobriquet *Hutch*. It was a warehouse worker's name, utterly inappropriate for a gallant, if foolhardy, young woman. He wondered if all these people had tin ears.

He'd begun composing a tribute to her. It would appear in *The*

Adventurers' Quarterly, the publication he'd edited for six years, and which still featured his occasional contributions.

'Anything?' he asked Kellie, who'd been trying the commlink again.

She shook her head. Just the heavy crackle of interference.

'It must be time,' said Nightingale.

'Not yet,' she said.

MacAllister went back to his project. *Priscilla was from a small town in Ohio.*

Where *was* she from? He'd have to look that up. It didn't make any difference, of course, whether it was Ohio or Scotland. Or even whether it was a small town.

Priscilla was from the lower Bronx.

It played just as well.

She worked for the Academy of Science and Technology, a pilot collecting standard pay, making the wearying runs between Earth and the dig site at Pinnacle or the black hole at Mamara.

Twenty years ago she was part of the expedition that discovered the Omega clouds, those curious constructs that erupt in waves from galactic center to attack swimming pools and twenty-story buildings. While everyone else on that mission wrote a set of memoirs, Priscilla Hutchins simply went back to piloting.

We forgot about her. And we might never have noticed who she really was. Except that eventually they sent her to Deepsix.

He made a noise in the back of his throat and scratched out *galactic center*. It sounded too much like a park.

Nightingale got up and made for the coffee dispenser. Kellie had been trying off and on to read, but he could see she was making no progress.

Mac had almost finished when she straightened up. 'Okay,' she said. 'The wind's down a bit. Everybody belt in.' It was, he thought, brighter outside, but not by much.

He heard the whine of the engines and drew his harness down over his head. Panel lights blinked on. 'Hang on,' she said, and MacAllister felt the vehicle lift into the storm. In the same instant

Kellie flicked on the running lights. They rose past walls and driving rain and writhing trees.

The lander fought its way into the sky while Nightingale tried again to raise Hutch.

Mac gazed hopefully out at the precipice. Occasionally, when the angle was right, he could see the gridwork. 'Do we know where to look?' he asked.

'She was on the far left,' said Kellie. 'At sixty-three hundred meters.'

Mac took to watching the altimeter.

In front of him, Nightingale was barely breathing.

'Elevator's gone,' Kellie said. That was no surprise.

Nightingale swept the gridwork with binoculars.

'Any sign of her?' asked Mac.

'I'll tell you if I see something,' he snapped.

Kellie stabbed at her link. 'Hutch, you out there?'

The static broke momentarily, and they heard her voice!

'—Here—'

They all tried to talk to her at once. Kellie got them quiet. 'Where are you?' she asked.

'Where you left me.' The transmission broke up. '—see your lights.'

'Okay, hang on. We'll be right there.'

'Good. I'd be grateful.'

'Hutch, what's your situation?'

'Say again?'

'What's your situation?'

'I'm okay.'

'I see her,' said Nightingale.

'Where?' Kellie asked.

'There.' He jabbed his finger.

She was dangling from one of the crosspieces. Mac took only a moment to look, then reached behind him for the cable. He looped one end around the seat anchor and pulled it tight. Nightingale opened the inner airlock.

'Don't forget yourself,' said Kellie.

He hadn't. Not after last time. He retrieved his own tether and tied himself firmly to the same base.

Kellie reminded them also to activate their e-suits. She matched air pressure. 'Ready to go,' she said.

A gust of wind hammered the lander, and Mac crashed to the floor. Nightingale helped him up.

Kellie opened the outer hatch. Wind and rain spilled into the airlock. And Mac saw why Hutchins was still alive. She'd converted her rope into a sling, looped under thighs and armpits, and lowered herself off the girder. Away from the metal.

'Hang on, Priscilla,' he told her, though he knew she could not hear him over the roar of the storm.

'Are we close enough?' asked Kellie. The lander rose and fell.

'No,' he cried. 'We're going to have to do better than this.'

'I don't know if we can.'

The cable was general-purpose lightweight stuff. Something to be used for securing cargo or possibly marking off a dig site. In this wind he wanted something more like Hutchins's heavy vine.

He missed a couple times, and then shut off his e-suit long enough to remove a shoe. He tied the cable to it and waited for the right circumstances: a drop in the wind and the lander in close. When it happened he threw the shoe and the cable. The shoe sailed over the crossbar. Hutch swung back, swung forward, grabbed the line. She hauled it down and looped it around her middle and secured it under her arms.

Mac took up the cable and got ready.

'Hurry,' Kellie pleaded, while she fought the storm and the downdrafts.

The laser appeared in Hutch's right hand. She showed the laser to them, signifying what she was about to do.

Mac glanced at the seat anchor, and tightened his grip. Nightingale, standing in the hatch, was not tethered. Mac pushed him back, out of harm's way.

Priscilla cut the vine and dropped down out of sight. The cable jerked tight. Mac held on, felt Nightingale move in behind him, and they hauled her in.

When she was safely on board, a wave of laughter engulfed them. Priscilla hugged Mac and kissed Nightingale. Kellie accelerated and shut down the spike to preserve its power supply. Then Hutch embraced her, too. They were happy, exhausted, tearful. She thanked them, wriggled out of the rope and cable, expressed her unbounded joy at being back in the lander, and hugged everybody again. She untied Mac's shoe and returned it ceremonially.

'Welcome home,' said Kellie.

Mac eased himself into his seat. 'Nice to have you back, Priscilla,' he said.

She collapsed beside him, rubbed her thighs where the vine had supported her, and closed her eyes. 'You wouldn't believe how good it is,' she said, 'to be here.'

Kellie had been climbing steadily. Suddenly they emerged above the clouds. The air was less turbulent, but Nightingale caught his breath. He was looking *up*.

Mac followed his gaze. They could see the vast arc of the onrushing planet. The entire southwestern sky quailed beneath that purple monster. They could see *into* it, into its depths. Mac felt chilled.

'What now?' he asked. 'Do we make our rendezvous?'

'Not yet,' said Hutch. 'It's too early. We've got more than four hours left.'

He grimaced and looked down at the boiling clouds. 'Do we really have to go back down there?'

Bill and Lori surprised the staff by showing up in tandem on-screen on the *Star* bridge. '*I'm pleased to announce that maneuvering is complete,*' said Lori. '*No further power applications need be made. Alpha will arrive at the designated point over the Misty Sea in the proper alignment at the specified time.*'

'*Well done,*' said Bill. He seemed quite pleased.

Kellie found high ground near the base of the mountain, and set down.

Hutch went back into the washroom. When she came out a half hour later she looked scrubbed down, and she was wrapped in a blanket, waiting for her clothes to dry. 'I hope nobody minds the informality,' she said.

'Not a bit of it,' said MacAllister, with a leer.

They passed around one of the bottles she'd salvaged from the *Star*. The wind blew, the rain fell, but for the moment at least, all was right with the world.

33

As there are some professions that demand believers in the amity of Providence, like those who work among the downtrodden, or who teach adolescents, there are others for which atheism is desirable. I am thinking particularly of pilots. When you are adrift among the clouds or the stars, you want someone in the cockpit who has as much to lose as you do if the party goes down.

—GREGORY MACALLISTER, *My Life and Loves*

Hours to breakup (est): 20

Miles Chastain returned with Phil Zossimov to the net. This time he had his gcar, a couple of assistants, and a load of material on two shuttles. Drummond waited with an Outsider team.

Miles had been piloting superluminals for almost four years, the last three for Universal News. It paid well, and equally important at this stage of his life, the job took him to places where something was usually happening. He had, for example, hauled a news team out to Nok, the only world known to have a living native civilization, just in time to see the first shots fired in the latest round of an early-twentieth-century-style war. He'd accompanied the investigators to Kruger 60 when the *Aquilar* returned

461

from the first probe across the Orion rift without its crew. He'd been the pilot when Universal did its award-winning special on the antique alien station orbiting Beta Pac III.

Now he was helping orchestrate the rescue off Deepsix. Not bad for a kid from a Baltimore row house.

He arrived within minutes after receiving the news that Alpha was on course, and no additional course changes would be needed. That meant Phil's team could begin its phase of the mission.

To release the asteroid, Drummond had cut the net almost three-quarters of the way around its circumference. The net now drifted glittering in the sunlight, two halves, partially entwined, a kind of bright tattered banner trailing from a very long post.

Their first objective was to finish what Drummond had begun: complete the cut. Get rid of one of the two halves.

Drummond's shuttle inserted itself within the drifting folds. One of his Outsiders exited the airlock and tied a cable to the half designated for disposal. He then returned inside the shuttle, which began to move away, straightening that portion of the net to prepare it for a laser cut.

Miles approached in the second vehicle and sliced through it until it was cleanly separated. Now Drummond's pilot dragged the severed portion away and released it to find its own orbit.

He returned and secured the remaining half to the shuttle. Then he gradually braked, drawing it out. When he was satisfied, he released it.

Miles moved in again.

The idea was to convert the remaining section into a sack. The part of the net attached to the plate would, when it was lowered into the atmosphere, constitute the top of the sack; the opposite end, the former south pole, would become the bottom. The task facing Miles's team was to join the severed sides near the bottom and bind them together, forming an area which would hang down toward the planetary surface, and into which, in just over six hours, the lander could descend. Or crash-land, if need be.

The shuttles took up positions on either side of the net,

approximately one hundred meters up from the 'bottom.' Miles and three of the Outsiders climbed onto it and used the shuttles to help draw the lower sections together.

The rest of the Outsider team, which totaled eight in all, joined the effort. They'd been drilled specifically for this operation, but Miles never stopped worrying. They'd practiced on the *Star*'s tennis nets, but that hadn't been the most realistic simulation.

He watched his people move out across the narrow space between the net and the airlock onto the metal links floating nearby. They connected their tethers as they'd been instructed, removed from their packs the clips which Marcia Keel had manufactured from chairs and coffee machines and cargo shelving, and began the process of binding the lower section of the net back together.

One advantage, at least: no lasers were in use. He'd hated putting lasers in the hands of the people along the assembly, and would have flat out refused to do it on the net, had he been asked. Fortunately, it wasn't necessary.

He was the only person out there with a go-pack. It was his responsibility to navigate along the edges, and to draw them close enough together that the Outsiders could connect them permanently. Only one drifted off during this phase of the operation, and Miles was quick to retrieve him.

He was uncomfortable about this aspect of the strategy. This *sack* is three-quarters of a kilometer in diameter, Marcel,' he said over a private channel. 'It wouldn't take much for it to get tangled up. Then you'd have nothing.'

'What's your suggestion?'

'I'd prefer to cut the thing down to a manageable size. Say 150 meters. Certainly no more than that.'

'How long would it take you to do it?'

He looked across the hundreds of square meters of drifting net. They'd have to go back inside, do some complicated maneuvering, do the cutting, come back out, splice it together. 'Twelve hours,' he said.

'So that shoots it, no?' He could hear Marcel's impatience. 'Do it as planned.'

The Outsiders finished, and the bottom one hundred meters were stitched together into a sack. When they'd finished, Miles's shuttle picked them up.

Now it became the Phil Zossimov Show. Phil had brought along some tubing, cut and shaped like a ring. Miles admired the young Russian. He'd made it clear an hour earlier that the thought of going outside onto the net terrified him. But he showed no sign of reluctance as he stood in front of the volunteers and activated his e-suit.

The tubing constituted most of the life-support system taken from *Wildside*. The various pieces were marked to enable the assemblers to put them together with a minimum of confusion. Under Phil's direction, they went back outside.

Above the sack they had just made, the netting was open all the way to the plate. They cut sideways across the net just above the sack, opening a large space, and secured its edges to the tubing. When the tubing was in place, Zossimov connected a pump and a sensor.

He pumped air in until it became a rigid ring-shaped collar, forming a mouth about twenty-five meters wide. This collar would hold the net open, providing entry for the lander. The sensor, made from a hatch closer on *Wildside*, would activate a valve as soon as Hutch's lander passed through. The valve would open and release the air, the collar would collapse, and the danger of the spacecraft falling back out would be all but eliminated.

The next task was to ensure that the rear of the net would not drift forward and close the sack or block the entrance.

To accomplish that they brought out a load of bars that had been manufactured from the metal taken from *Wildside*'s cargo bay, and designed with links so they could be connected to each other, end to end. There was also a supply of braces and supports.

Each bar was five meters long. (That had been the maximum

length possible to get them in and out of the shuttles.) Altogether there were forty-six.

The Outsiders used them to assemble two rails, braced with supports. They connected the rails in parallel above and on either side of the ring, front to rear in the sack. When that had been accomplished, they had a container into which the lander should be able to maneuver.

All but Phil and Miles withdrew into the shuttles. Phil set the sensor.

'You sure it'll work?' asked Miles.

'Absolutely.'

'How long will it take to close after the lander's inside?'

'It activates as soon as they pass through. I'm no physicist, so I can't tell you how fast the collar will deflate. But it shouldn't be longer than a few seconds. Especially at that altitude.'

Miles inspected the collar. 'I think we have ourselves a decent scoop.'

At about the time Miles's people were climbing onto the net, the welding teams were spreading out across the hulls of the four superluminals. Tom Scolari, Cleo, Jack Kingsbury, and an elderly man whom Scolari knew only as Chop, had responsibility for *Zwick*. The task should now be easy, because Jack and Chop had performed much the same assignment working *alone* earlier when they'd attached the starship to the Alpha shaft.

Scolari had been invited by Universal News to participate in an interview. Emma had found jumpsuits for him and Cleo, and the plan called for them to go on a live hookup when the job on the hull was finished. He was unnerved by the prospect, more frightened than he could ever have been about going outside.

It should have been easier to interview Chop and Jack, who'd been on board longer, and Scolari had wondered at first why Emma hadn't done that. But it became clear very quickly that neither of the two was very articulate. Jack responded to everything with one-word answers. And Chop scratched a lot. Scolari was concerned that they'd be resentful, but neither brought the subject up. When he told them about the pending interview, Chop had commented that he was glad they hadn't asked *him*.

Zwick was the leading vessel on the shaft, only thirty-eight kilometers from the net, which they could see shining in the sunlight. Sometimes it made Scolari think of a flag.

The shaft was currently welded to the belly of the *Zwick*. They went out through the cargo hatch on the port quarter and walked around to the underside, and it seemed as if the universe rotated as they did so, so that the hull was always down. It was an effect caused by the magnetic boots.

When they were ready, Cleo and Scolari retired to the rear, Jack and Chop went forward. They activated their lasers and began cutting the weld. Now that the shaft was safely on course, and no more corrections would be needed, they were to separate it from the ship and change its orientation. 'Be careful,' Janet reminded them from her station in Drummond's launch, which was up near the net. This was the most dangerous part of the operation for the Outsiders: cut too high, and they could slice or seriously weaken Alpha. Do that, they'd been told again and again, and repair would be impossible. The people below would die. Cut too low, and they could penetrate the ship. That indeed was not life and death. Everyone had been cleared out of areas vulnerable to puncture on all the vessels. But it would nevertheless, in Janet's dulcet admonition, have been *unprofessional*. A mess that someone else would have to clean up later.

The clear lesson: If they had to screw it up, cut low.

Getting it right wasn't all that hard, he discovered, so long as he kept his mind on what he was doing. The image of the gas giant, growing visibly larger by the hour, *did* tend to be a distraction.

They began cutting. Jack and Chop had done a good job the first time out. Their instructions had been to connect as much of the shaft as possible to the hull. They'd done that, and it required a long effort to free it. *Zwick* was by far the smallest of the

466

superluminals, but she had accepted a twenty-six-meter length of the shaft before her hull curved away.

So they worked steadily, in the shadow of the giant. Scolari had heard that almost a full kilometer had been laid on the *Star*. Getting *that* off would be a monster job, but that was where they'd concentrated the volunteers.

Janet, as usual, was watching. Occasionally she offered advice or encouragement. She let them know that *Wendy*'s crew had finished, that the people preparing the net to receive its payload were making progress. She always referred to the lander as the payload. Scolari decided she watched too many sims.

They needed an hour and a quarter to break the shaft loose, and they did it without inflicting any damage. Jack, who was the team leader, informed Janet when they were done. She acknowledged, thanked them, and directed them to retire inside the ship. 'But don't go far,' she said.

'How long?'

'About four hours.'

'We won't last that long.'

It was hard to believe the sun had been in the sky an hour and a half. The wind roared across the lander. Rain hammered down, and the water coming off the mountain had become a torrent. They huddled inside the darkened cabin while the storm raged.

'I think conditions are deteriorating,' said Mac.

Hutch nodded. 'That would be my guess. We'd better tie down if we don't want to get blown into the ocean.'

They went outside and struggled to lash the lander to the trees. The winds were approaching hurricane force. That meant flying objects, branches, rocks, and even birds that had gotten caught, became missiles.

They were all short of breath when they got back inside. They fell into their seats, feeling safer but not by much.

On the bridge of the *Star*, Nicholson and Marcel received Drummond's report. Only the giant liner itself was now still attached to Alpha.

Nicholson looked questioningly at Marcel. 'Now?' he asked.

Marcel nodded.

Nicholson addressed the AI: 'Lori, we are going to the next phase. You can turn *Zwick* around.'

'*Complying,*' said Lori.

'Lori?' said Marcel. 'Have we had any luck yet reestablishing contact with the ground party?'

'*No, Marcel. I am still trying and will inform you when I am successful.*'

He nodded, and turned his attention to *Zwick*'s status board, which was posted on one of the navigation screens. The media vessel, under Lori's direction, began to pull away from the shaft. Its thrusters would fire an orchestrated series of bursts, moving it out to one side, turning it around, and bringing it back, but facing in the opposite direction. Now, its main engines pointed toward Deepsix, it moved in once more to snuggle against Alpha.

During the course of the maneuver, word came down that the Outsiders had released the *Star*.

On board *Zwick*, Scolari and the other volunteers returned to the hull and began the cumbersome process of reattaching the shaft. Now the vessel was pointed in the opposite direction, *away* from Deepsix. Almost immediately, one of the shuttle pilots warned them of an approaching cloud.

'Cloud?' asked Scolari.

'Meteors and dust. Get back inside.'

Scolari and Cleo needed no prompting. They made for the airlock, and warned Chop and Jack not to dawdle.

A few large rocks bounced off the metal. Minutes later, when they thought it was over, one penetrated the hull, knocked out the broadcasting studio and the library, and would have killed Canyon except that he'd left moments earlier to go to the washroom.

The warning had come from Klaus Bomar, who had taken Pindar and Sharon to mark the Alpha shaft. He was, as Pindar had observed, Canadian. A Toronto native, he'd been a commercial hauler, carrying supplies to the terraformers on Quraqua; and later he'd served as a longtime instructor at the Conciliar Spaceflight Academy near Winnipeg. He'd resigned his position there two months earlier, anxious to join the superluminals that were moving out to the new frontiers.

Klaus's wife was dead, his kids were grown and gone, so he'd barely hesitated once he decided he'd had enough of classrooms. He'd signed on with TransGalactic because they paid well and the big luxury liners were visiting the places he wanted to see, black holes and star cradles and giant suns and cosmic lighthouses.

This was his first flight with TransGalactic.

He was dazzled by the ingenuity of Clairveau and Beekman, and amused at Nicholson's ability to look as if he were commanding the operation.

He'd transmitted the warning to *Zwick* and another shuttle in the path of the debris field, then turned away in an effort to get clear.

Much of the debris orbiting Morgan consisted of nothing more than dust particles too small to be tracked by sensors. As Klaus completed his turn he veered directly into a high-velocity swarm that ripped the shuttle apart before he even knew he was in trouble.

34

There is a gene we all have that when crisis comes, inevitably selects the wrong turn. It is why things run amiss, dreams remain unfulfilled, ambitions fail to materialize, life, for most of us, is simply a series of blown opportunities.

—GREGORY MACALLISTER, *Deepsix Diary*

Hours to breakup (est): 12

Hutch could have used a trank. The ones that Mac had in his pack weren't supposed to affect the user after whatever period they were set for, so theoretically they should have been safe. But she'd always tended to react badly to the damned things. And she dared not risk impairing her judgment for the final flight.

The final flight. Up or down.

She tried to push her emotions away, out to some distant boundary. She thought about what lay ahead, tried to visualize this giant net that would be dropping out of the sky.

Precision, Marcel had been saying. Everything had to be done precisely right. One chance. The net would come down and it would go up. She'd have, at best, a minute or so to find the collar and navigate into it.

The mood in the cabin was subdued. MacAllister tried to lighten

471

things a bit by proclaiming that if they came out of it alive he was going to seek out the bishop of New Jersey and submit to religious instruction.

They all laughed, but it had a hollow ring.

Periodically, without success. Hutch tried to regain contact with Marcel.

'I'll be glad,' Nightingale said, 'to get it over with. One way or the other.'

Hutch nodded as if she agreed, but she didn't. Life was sweet, and she wanted to hang on to it as long as she could. But yes, she *would* be happy to end the suspense, to fly into Marcel's celestial sack and get hauled up to safety. It was just hard to visualize something like that actually happening.

Mac broke out some fruit and nuts, but she had no appetite.

'Do you good,' MacAllister persisted.

'I doubt it.' Nevertheless, it seemed like something she should do. She selected a dark red globule that resembled and tasted like a pomegranate. Nightingale picked a few nuts and settled back to enjoy them. Mac made coffee and filled all the cups.

'We going to have any trouble getting aloft in this?' he asked, indicating the storm.

'We'll be okay.' She'd powered up to the extent possible. There was more than enough fuel in the tanks to take them out to the rendezvous. Even enough to get back, if need be. If it would matter. 'We'll do fine. As long as it doesn't get too much worse.'

They sat for a time, tasting the fruit, watching the rain.

'You guys all right?' she asked.

Nightingale nodded. 'I'm sorry about the elevator,' he said. 'I—'

'It's okay. Don't worry about it.'

Mac took a long sip of coffee. 'Confession time, I guess.'

'What've *you* got to confess, Mac?' asked Kellie.

'I . . .' He thought about it. '. . . haven't always been reasonable.'

'We know that,' said Nightingale. 'The whole world knows it.'

'I just thought I wanted to say something. I've done some damage.'

'Forget it. I'm sure nobody holds it against you.'

'That's not quite so, but it isn't the point.'

'Mac, you once said something about people who waste energy feeling sorry for themselves.'

He frowned. 'Not that I can recall. What exactly did I say?'

'"Best way to deal with a conscience is to beat it into submission so it knows who's in charge."'

'*I* said that?'

Nightingale had been looking out at the rain during the whole of this exchange. Now he turned and fixed his eyes on MacAllister. 'Not really. But it's the best I can do on short notice. Let it go, Mac. It's past.'

The lander shook as another wave rippled through the ground. MacAllister snatched his plate before it could slide off onto the deck. 'The whole world's coming apart,' he said.

Kellie adjusted her harness. 'How much longer?'

'Soon,' said Hutch.

In fact, the winds seemed to be lessening. The rain slacked off, although it never really stopped. Hutch tried the radio again.

Suddenly the sky was filled with birds. They were all of one species, black with white wing tips, big, graceful, wings spread to catch the wind. Their flight was erratic, disorganized. To a degree, they were being blown across the sky. But they fought to maintain formation. The wind died, they regrouped, and then, like a single animal, they turned north. *They know*, she thought. *They all know.*

When the bombardment had stopped, Scolari and the other Outsiders went back onto the hull and finished the welding assignment. They laid the shaft directly down the length of the ship, as they had before. The same procedure was being followed by the *Evening Star* team. On the other two vessels, the crews were reattaching the shaft at twenty-seven- and thirty-one-degree angles. That would allow *Wendy* and *Wildside*, who'd be up front during extraction, to begin the process of inserting the shaft into orbit.

Shortly after they'd begun they heard about the death of the shuttle pilot who had warned them.

Scolari and his team finished in two and a half hours and came back into the airlock. All four vessels were again locked onto Alpha, except that they now faced the opposite direction.

Although he was new to TransGalactic, Klaus Bomar had been the oldest member of the *Star*'s crew, save for the captain himself. Because he was a contemporary, Nicholson had occasionally invited him to his cabin for a drink, and had ended by becoming quite fond of him. Marcel had been wrong about Nicholson: He *did* have an onboard friend.

The news hit Nicholson hard.

One of *Wendy*'s three shuttles pulled alongside Drummond's vehicle. The airlock opened, and Drummond took on a physician: Embry Desjardain.

Drummond's assignment was to stay near the sack, and pick up the ground team after they'd been hauled clear of the atmosphere. Embry was a precaution, in case a doctor was needed.

They introduced themselves and shook hands. Then Drummond turned to Janet. 'I guess you're relieved,' he said. 'If you'd like to go back to the *Star*, your transportation's waiting.'

She declined. 'If you've no objection, I'd like to stay around for the rescue. You might be able to use some help.'

Drummond glanced at Frank, who thumbed a switch.

'Okay, Karen,' he told the other pilot, 'that's it.'

Karen blinked her lights and moved away.

'Time to go,' said Hutch. 'Let's cut ourselves loose.'

Marcel, Beekman, and Nicholson posted themselves on the *Star* bridge. They watched with satisfaction the various status reports coming in. Everything secure. Everyone on station.

All that remained now was to wait while the momentum of the *new* assembly, the alpha shaft and the four superluminals attached to it, carried the net into the atmosphere above the Misty Sea.

Nicholson had been uncustomarily quiet. Finally, he turned to Marcel and shook his hand. 'Good luck,' he said. And, repeating the gesture, 'Good luck, Gunther.'

'*Marcel.*' Lori blinked onto his screen. '*I had momentary contact with the lander, but I have lost it again.*'

'Okay. Were you able to talk to them at all?'

'*They're in the air. On their way to the rendezvous.*'

The three men nodded encouragement to each other. 'Thank God. Was Hutch with them? Who did you talk to?'

'*I talked with Captain Hutchins.*'

Marcel's eyes closed, and he breathed a prayer of thanks.

They flew through a sea of dark clouds, lightning strikes, roiling skies, and glowing red eruptions.

When finally they rose above the worst of the turmoil, Kellie succeeded in opening a channel to the *Star*.

'*Let us trust we can maintain it this time,*' said Lori. '*It's quite good to know everything is well. We've been worried. Are you on course?*'

'We are indeed,' Hutch said.

'*Just a moment, please. I'll notify Captain Clairveau.*'

Marcel showed up within seconds. 'Hutch,' he said, 'it's good to see you.'

'And you. Marcel.'

'How'd you get down off the elevator? What happened?'

'Tell you when we get there. Everything's in order here. We are approximately one hour ten minutes from rendezvous.'

'Good.'

'How are things at your end?'

She got more interference.

'. . . on schedule.' He refined the previous data, giving them the exact position where the scoop would arrive. And he transmitted some visuals. 'As you can see, the whole thing looks like

475

a sack made out of chain-link netting. Here's the opening. A nice circular front entrance. More than wide enough for you to fly through. It'll be facing east, and it's near the bottom of the sack. Once you're inside, there'll be fifty meters of empty net below you. The collar will close. Just nestle in, set down the best way you can, and leave the rest to us.'

'We will.'

'We may have some more very minor adjustments to the coordinates, depending on how the atmosphere affects the net, but don't worry about them because we'll take you every step of the way.'

'Do we have a precise time yet?' she asked.

'It'll reach its lowest point of descent in exactly seventy-four minutes and . . .' He paused. '. . . thirty seconds. Immediately after that, it'll start back up again.' Another hesitation. 'Can you make the altitude?'

'Probably. If we can't, don't wait for us.' MacAllister paled. He needed reassuring, and she nodded confidently. 'Just kidding, Mac. We'll do this with ease.

'Keep in mind,' she added, 'I have no easy way to navigate this thing. I'm not even sure which way is west anymore.'

'You're doing fine. Although I'd like you to cut your speed by about thirty klicks and come left another eight degrees.'

Hutch complied.

'That's good. I'll stay with you. How's the weather?'

'A trifle overcast.'

Hutch quietly pulled back on the yoke, relying only on the lander's aeronautical capabilities to get to ten thousand meters. She would conserve her spike until she needed it.

Marcel transmitted more images of the lower section of the net. It would be hanging almost straight down out of the sky. Facing in her direction. 'When you see it,' he explained, 'it'll be moving southwest at 180 kph. Its course will be 228 degrees – 228.7. We'll bring you in close. When I tell you, engage the spike, and just float in.'

'Marcel,' she said, 'I would not have believed this was possible.'

'With a Frenchman' – he grinned – 'everything is possible. Gravity will have hold of it by the time you get there, but we'll already be in braking mode.'

'Okay.'

'We're going to take you in just before we begin to move the shaft back out again.'

'And you say the opening's fifty-three meters across?'

'That's correct. Half a football field.'

'Can't miss,' said Hutch.

'That's what we thought.'

She said quietly, almost not wanting anybody to hear, 'I do believe we're going to pull this off.'

Nightingale looked down at the storms smeared across the sky. They were daubed with fire. Eerily lit black clouds boiled up into the higher altitudes.

He was having trouble controlling his breathing. Whatever happened, they would not be able to go back down *there*. God help him, he did not want to die out here. And he did not want the others to know how he felt. They were all scared; he realized that. But they seemed better equipped to deal with it.

Please, God, don't let me go to pieces.

Marcel's voice crackled in over the receiver, instructing Hutch to cut back speed or adjust course or go a bit higher. The voice was level and cool. Unemotional. Confident.

Easy enough for *him* to be confident. Nightingale would have given anything to be with Marcel at this moment, safely tucked away on one of the superluminals.

Hutch had said nothing about his behavior in the elevator, as far as he knew, to the others. Nor had she mentioned the incident to *him*, except to reply to his expressed regret. Yet he could read the disappointment in her eyes. The contempt. Years before, when MacAllister had held him up to worldwide ridicule, he'd been able to rationalize his behavior. Anybody could pass out under stress. He'd been injured. He'd not had much sleep during that period. He'd—

—whatever.

This time he'd failed in a more visible way. In a way he could rationalize neither to others nor to himself. When it was over, if he survived, he'd make for Scotland. And hide.

'Marcel, this is Abel. Deepsix is beginning to disintegrate.'

Marcel put the climatologist on-screen. 'How? What's going on?'

'Major rifts opening in the oceans and on two of the continents. Several volcanoes have been born on Endtime. There's a fault line east of Gloriamundi. One side of it has been shoved six thousand meters into the air. It's still coming up. There are massive quakes in both hemispheres. We've got eruptions everywhere. A couple have even shown up in the Misty Sea, not far from the lander's last position.'

'They should be safe. They're pretty high.'

'You think so? One just let go in Gloriamundi. Some of the ejecta will go into orbit.'

'Show me where they are,' he said. 'The Misty Sea volcanoes.'

Kinder was right: Two were close to the lander's flight path. But he couldn't reroute them in any significant way. Not if they were going to be in place when the net arrived. Best just to ride it out and hope.

'Thanks, Abel.'

Kinder grunted, one of those pained sounds. Then someone pressed his shoulder, handed him a note. He frowned.

'What?' asked Marcel.

'Hold on.' The climatologist looked off to one side, nodded, frowned again, talked to the individual. Marcel couldn't hear. Then he came back to the monitor. 'Northern Tempus is doing an Atlantis.'

'Sinking?'

'Yes.'

One of the screens was focused on *Wendy*'s hull. Marcel saw movement, but it happened so quickly he wasn't sure he hadn't imagined it. 'Thanks, Abel,' he said.

He was still watching the screen. A shadow passed across *Wendy*, and one of her sensors vanished. A communication pod broke open and its electronic components spilled into the void. He switched over to the AI and picked up Bill's voice in midstride: '. . . *to several forward systems. Intensity seems to be lessening* . . .' The voice failed, and the image flickered and went off. It came back, long enough for Bill to add the word *assess*; then it went down again.

Nicholson, in the command chair, took a report that communications with *Wendy* had failed.

He asked a technician whether she could restore them.

'Problem's not on this end, Captain,' she said. Another technician was running the visuals backward.

Nicholson looked at Marcel. 'What the hell's happening over there? Can you make it out?'

'More rocks, I think,' said Marcel. 'It'll get worse as Jerry gets closer.

The screen remained blank.

'What happens if we don't regain contact?'

'We don't need to. Bill knows what to do. All the AIs do. As long as there's no emergency that requires us to make adjustments.'

Canyon sat in a pose one could only describe as relaxed attention. 'So this was your first time outside a ship, Tom. Why don't you tell us what was running through your mind when you went through the airlock?'

Scolari willed himself to relax. 'Well, August, I knew it was something that had to be done. So I just made up my mind to do it.' It was a stupid response, but he had suddenly lost all capability to think. *What's my name?* 'I mean, it wasn't something we could just walk away from. It's a life-and-death situation.'

He looked over at Cleo, who was gazing innocently at the ceiling.

'And how about you, Cleo?' said Canyon. 'It must have been pretty unnerving looking down and not seeing anything.'

'Well, that's true, August. Although to be honest I never felt there was a "down." It's not like being on the side of a building.'

'I understand you got hit by a storm of meteors. How did you react to that?'

'I was scared for a minute,' she said. 'We just hid out until it was over. Didn't really see much.'

'Listen,' said Scolari, 'can I tell you something on my own?'

'Sure.'

'Everybody was scared out there today. I never knew when part of me might just disappear. You know what I mean? And even without the rocks, I don't like not having something solid underfoot. But I'm glad I did it. And I hope to God those four people come back. If they do, it'll be nice to know I had a hand in it.' He managed a smile. 'Me and Cleo and the others.'

Miles Chastain was cruising the shaft, moving deliberately from one ship to the next, inspecting the work of the Outsiders.

Maleiva III was framed against the gas giant. The continents and seas were no longer visible, and the entire globe appeared to be wrapped in a thick black pall.

He was impressed that so many had been willing to risk life and limb during the course of the operation. He'd heard about the other events, the complaints by passengers on the *Star* and by the science people on *Wendy*. He'd been through crises before, and he knew they tended to unmask people, to reveal who they really were, to bring out the best or the worst, whichever way an individual personality leaned. It was almost as if trouble stripped away the pretense of daily life, the way Jerry Morgan was stripping Maleiva.

He was somewhere between *Zwick*, his own ship, and the *Evening Star*, headed down the shaft toward the net. The actual pickup of Hutchins and her people would be made by John

480

Drummond's shuttle. Marcel wanted them out of the lander and the net as quickly as the transfer could be made. Miles's responsibility was to stand by in case of need.

He was alone. He'd returned Phil, the shuttle pilot, the assistants, and the Outsiders to the *Star* and had taken over the controls himself. He was approaching *Zwick*, which was facing him.

When the signal came, and they began to draw the shaft *out* of the atmosphere, they would be moving it into orbit. Once that had been achieved, it would become possible to retrieve the MacAllister party.

His message board lit up. Transmission from *Zwick*. Emma. Her usually sallow features blinked on-screen, but this time she was glowing. She invariably gave the impression, when she spoke to him, that she was thinking about something else, that she needed only give out instructions. That Miles himself was somehow inconsequential. Probably, he'd concluded on the way out, it resulted from dealing with too many VIPs. Everybody else became a peasant.

'Yes, Emma,' he said, 'what can I do for you?'

'Miles, where are you located now?'

'In front of you. Coming up.'

'My schedule says you're headed for the pickup.'

'More or less. I'm just going down there to be available.'

'Good. I want you to stop and collect us.'

'Why?'

'It'll only take a minute.'

'Why?' he asked again.

'Are you serious? They're about to do the rescue, or not, and you ask why we want to be there?'

He sighed. She was right, of course. 'Okay. I'll dock in about six minutes.'

'Good. And Miles, would you do something else for me?'

He waited.

'I want you to contact the other pilot, the one who's going to make the pickup. Tell him we'd like to do a broadcast as they come on board. Ask if he'll cooperate.'

481

'Why don't you do that yourself?'

'Well, pilot-to-pilot . . . You know how it is. He'll be more receptive if it comes from you. A lot of these people out here resent us. They think we're in the way. Except when they need publicity for one reason or another. I just don't want to miss this.' She was at emotional high tide. 'It's going to be the news story of the decade. Miles.'

'Emma, did you know the shuttles can't dock with each other? You'll have to go outside to make the crossing.'

'I didn't know. But that's not a problem.'

'They're going to be busy. I don't think they'll want to make time for a news team.'

'Miles.' She came down a bit from her high. 'I'd like very much for this to happen.'

Frank the pilot looked up at Drummond. 'John,' he said, 'I don't have any objection as long as they stay out of the way. How about you?'

Drummond's immediate instinct was to deny permission out of hand. But he couldn't really give a reason why except that he disliked Canyon. Nevertheless, there was plenty of room in the shuttle, and he guessed it was prudent to get on the good side of the media. 'Okay,' he said. 'Tell them what you just told me.'

Gravity had taken hold of the sack. The net gradually lengthened and began to tumble toward the troubled atmosphere. The collar was open and easy to see, and the people who'd rigged it had even managed to mark it with a system of lights. If there were no problems on board the lander, if the lander showed up at the time and place it was supposed to, the whole thing should be easy to pull off. Almost anti-climactic.

Frank disagreed. 'The collar only looks big because we're right on top of it. And we're descending at the same rate *it* is. The lander's going to be approaching at a more or less constant altitude. The net goes down and it comes up. The pilot's got to time things so she hits it at precisely the right moment. If she misses, that's the ball game.'

They rode quietly. The physician, Embry, stared moodily out the window. Janet Hazelhurst was thumbing through the onboard library, apparently just turning pages. Drummond was sipping coffee, lost in his thoughts.

'*Eighteen minutes to rendezvous,*' said the AI. '*We are on schedule.*'

The net continued to unfurl as it dropped toward the clouds. Drummond saw no tangles.

Frank slowed their descent. 'This is as low as we want to go,' he said.

Drummond nodded. 'So far, so good,' he told Marcel.

Another shuttle appeared and drew alongside. 'The media have arrived' said Frank.

Drummond activated his e-suit and went into the airlock, from which he watched two people move clumsily out of the other spacecraft. They floated across the few meters separating the shuttles, and he took each by the hand and pulled them inside.

Canyon wasn't as tall as Drummond had expected, but there was no missing that mellifluous voice. He introduced himself with quiet modesty. 'And this is Emma Constantine,' he said, 'my producer.'

'We'll want to set up here,' Emma told him, 'if that's no problem.' She indicated a section adjacent the airlock. 'We'd like to do a quick interview with you before the rescue.'

'Okay,' he said.

'August will be asking you how you plan to go about this, who'll be going out with you—'

'Wait a minute,' Drummond said. '*I'm* not going out. Frank's going to do that.'

'Oh.' She turned away from Drummond, and her eyes suggested he had just vanished from human memory. Canyon smiled at him and shrugged.

Frank saw something he didn't like on his navigation screen. 'Everybody into their seats,' he said. 'Buckle down.'

Nobody had to tell Canyon twice. He dived for the nearest chair. Emma was a little slower.

'What's wrong?' asked Drummond.

'Debris field.' As soon as his passengers were locked in he began to accelerate.

The AI was talking to Frank, but the pilot had switched the conversation over to his earphones, obviously intending to avoid alarming the passengers. *That* alarmed Drummond.

'Everybody sit tight,' said the pilot. 'Nothing to worry about.' They began to accelerate. 'They're behind us,' he explained. 'We're going to outrun them.'

'How bad is it?' asked Drummond.

Frank looked at one of the screens. 'It's a pretty big swarm. Coming fast. We wouldn't want to be there when it arrives.'

Behind Drummond, Canyon was talking into a microphone. He caught snatches of it: '. . . rescue vessel in trouble . . .' '. . . meteors . . .' '. . . harm's way . . .' Suddenly the microphone was thrust in his direction. '. . . speaking now to John Drummond, who's done most of the planning for this effort. He's an astronomer by trade—'

'A mathematician,' Drummond said.

'A mathematician. And how would you describe our situation at the moment, Dr Drummond?'

Drummond was impressed. He was speaking to an audience of probably several hundred million. Or would be when the signal reached home. *How to describe the situation?* He began to talk about the dust and debris that accumulates in a gravitational field. 'Especially one around a body this massive.' Morgan's image was on one of the monitors. He glanced at it.

Something banged off the hull. Drummond tightened up inside and became immediately concerned that the several hundred million viewers would see that he was terrified. 'Are we broadcasting pictures, too?' he asked.

Emma, seated off to one side, nodded. They were.

It seemed suddenly to be raining on the shuttle. A hard staccato rattled across the hull.

'Ladies and gentlemen,' said Canyon softly, in a voice that underscored Drummond's fears, 'you can hear what's happening.'

How big is it?' asked Marcel.

'*Big*. Thousands of kilometers across. Frank's on the forward edge of it. But he's moving pretty quick and should be clear in a few seconds. I've also sent a warning to Miles.'

'What about *Zwick*?'

Actually, he already knew the answer to that. His screens showed the swarm moving directly across the media ship's position. And, of course, unlike the shuttle, *Zwick* was unable to run.

After Emma and Canyon had left *Zwick*, the only people remaining on board were Tom Scolari, Cleo, Jack Kingsbury, and Chop. Scolari wasn't entirely comfortable being on a ship that was in effect nailed to a pole, with nobody else there. They knew that the shaft had been caught in the grip of Maleiva III's gravity well, and that it and everything attached to it was falling toward the surface.

They'd been assured there was no danger. It was a controlled fall. The AI would, at the appropriate moment, fire the engines, as would the AIs on the other three ships, and they would haul Alpha out of the well, along with the landing party.

All very simple.

Still, Scolari would have liked to see someone else on the ship, preferably someone wearing stripes on his sleeves who would know if something had gone wrong, and who'd be competent to fix things. It was why superluminals, which could be operated from the beginning to the end of a journey without human help, retained captains.

They were all in the common room. Cleo and Chop were munching on sandwiches, and Jack nursed a soft drink. Scolari would have preferred to be on the *Star*, where he'd have felt safer among the fifteen hundred tourists. Where people were actually on duty to make sure everything was okay.

They were reassuring one another when the AI broke in. 'We have a swarm of dust and pebbles approaching at high speed,' it said in its smoky female voice. 'Please retire to an acceleration station at once.'

They looked nervously at one another. 'Are we in danger?' asked Chop.

'The danger is minimal,' said the AI. 'However, in accordance with standard safety procedures, please put on an e-suit.'

Acceleration stations consisted of bunks installed throughout the ship. There was a rack of six against one bulkhead in the common room. They collected e-harnesses and breathers from the emergency panel and strapped them on. Then they activated the fields.

'It thinks a meteor might come through the hull,' said Cleo, looking scared.

Scolari put on his most reassuring manner. 'It's just a precaution.'

Chop's eyes moved nervously around the interior. Kingsbury clapped a hand on Scolari's shoulder. 'When this is done, lad, I'd like to buy everyone a drink.'

They climbed in, and the restraints settled over them.

'Make mine Hebert's,' he said.

'I'll inform you,' said the AI, 'when the emergency has passed.' There was, he told himself, really no reason to be alarmed.

'I wonder how far away they are,' said Chop. 'The rocks.'

A new voice spoke in his earphones: 'This is Captain Claireveau. Your AI has just informed me that you folks are alone on Zwick. Are you okay?'

'Jack Kingsbury here. We're fine, Captain. I wonder if you can tell us what's happening?'

Before he could answer, there was a hammerblow forward, the ship shuddered, and Scolari's earphones clicked. The sound of the carrier wave changed.

'Captain,' said Scolari, 'are you still there?'

There was another clang. It echoed through the chamber.

The transmission died.

An automated voice said, '*Fourteen minutes.*'

'*We've reestablished communications with* Wendy,' Lori told he bridge. 'Zwick *is still down.*'

Marcel was studying the situation screen, which depicted the debris field as a blinking yellow glow. Some of the rocks were entering the atmosphere. But it appeared that the worst would be over in another couple of minutes.

'Lori,' Marcel said, 'do we have a picture of them anywhere? Of *Zwick?*'

'*No. Only vehicle close enough is* Miles, *but he doesn't have an angle. I'll let you know as soon as we get something.*'

The comm board lit up. 'Captain Clairveau.' It was Drummond.

'Go ahead, John.'

'Bad news . . .'

Marcel held his breath. Drummond was still speaking, so it couldn't be *too* bad. 'What is it?'

'Transmitting visual.'

An auxiliary screen lit up and Marcel found himself looking at the net. The bottom of the net.

The *sack*.

Except that the sack wasn't there anymore.

Where the net should have flared out to provide a haven for the lander, where the collar should have lighted the way, everything simply hung down toward the clouds, limp and dead.

'What happened?'

'Don't know. Marcel. It must have been hit.'

He *willed* the image away.

'Must have been a strike directly on the collar,' said Drummond. 'Or the supports. Everything collapsed.'

'*Thirteen minutes,*' said the voice.

The AI warned Scolari and the others that *Zwick* was about to fire its engines. The process of slowing and eventually reversing Alpha's descent phase had begun.

It also informed them that communications with the other vessels had been reestablished.

35

Survival in a crisis is often a matter of sheer good fortune. The good fortune may consist of the timely arrival of a platoon of Peacekeepers, of having a power source unexpectedly kick in, of sitting in the correct part of the aircraft. Most frequently, it is being with the right people.

—GREGORY MACALLISTER, *Spiritual Guidance for Tentmakers*

Hours to breakup (est): 10

'. . . not an unbeatable problem . . .' Marcel's image seemed to lose definition on screen. He was still talking, but Hutch was no longer hearing him.

'. . . can still maybe ease your way in . . .'

She stared straight ahead, through the windscreen, into the ashen sky that went on forever. Off to her right, a huge pall of smoke trailed upward. A volcano, they were telling her. Behind her, somebody moved. But no one spoke.

'. . . bad luck, but we'll just have to work around it . . .' She clung to the yoke as though it could save her. Move it forward, drop the flaps, the lander angled down. Nice, dependable physics.

'. . . still manage . . .'

She killed the sound, left him mouthing the words, staring at her with empty eyes. Curiously, she felt sorry for him. He had gone far beyond what anybody could have expected, and it had simply blown up at the last second.

A meteor strike. How could they have been so unlucky?

'What now?' asked MacAllister.

She could barely hear him.

'My God,' breathed Nightingale.

'How about nosing our way in?' said Kellie. 'We know there's an opening. All we have to do is find it.'

'Yeah.' Nightingale reached forward and squeezed her shoulder. 'It doesn't sound all that hard.'

She brought Marcel back. 'You said the collar's collapsed. But it had lights. Can you still light it up?'

'Negative,' he said. 'There's no response from it.'

'If we can find the collar, what's to stop us from just pushing our way in?'

'Not a thing. It's not exactly what we'd planned, but you might be able to do it. If it's not too badly tangled. It's hard to tell what the precise conditions are.'

Might. If.

'Hell, Marcel, the plans are by the board.' She stared at her instruments. 'I hate to put it to you in these terms, but we don't have any place to land.'

'I know.'

'Am I still on course?'

'Yes, Hutch. Dead on.'

Unhappy choice of phrase. She saw him cringe, realizing what he'd said, wishing he could recall it. *There it is,'* said Kellie.

It was a long filmy garment descending out of the sky. She watched it come down, saw the winds sucking at it, twisting it, pushing it first one way and then another. That surprised her, at this altitude, and she grasped finally how light the construction material really was.

But the whole thing had collapsed. It wasn't just the ring. The support rails, which actually separated back from front and the sides from each other and consequently *made* the sack, were down, too. She could see them caught up in the linkage. One fell away as she watched. She tracked it down into the clouds below.

There was no sack to ease into.

'What are we going to do?' asked Nightingale, unable to keep the terror out of his voice. 'What in God's name are we going to do?'

She would at that moment have taken pleasure in throwing him out of the spacecraft.

'You're coming in too fast,' said Marcel. 'Cut back ten klicks. No, twelve. Cut back twelve.'

She eased off. And tried simultaneously to slow her heartbeat.

'Six minutes,' Marcel told her. 'It'll still be in the descent phase. At the very end. Just before it starts up again. You'll have not quite ninety seconds to get on board. Then the net will start back up.'

'Can you give us a little more time?'

'Unfortunately not. If we try to do that, we'll lose control of the shaft. Won't be able to pull it out at all.' He looked as if he felt additional justification was necessary. 'Hutch, if we don't retract it on schedule, it'll go into the ocean.'

She studied the sequence Marcel had given her. At the moment, two of the four superluminals were using their main engines to brake the descent. Over the next few minutes, that application of power would slow Alpha, bringing it briefly to a halt. Then it would start *up*.

She knew approximately where the opening should be, but she couldn't see it, could see only a jumbled mass of chain linkage. 'Anybody see the collar? Marcel, is it facing us? Is it still on the east?'

'I can't tell. Hutch. Your picture is better than ours. The atmosphere's been raising hell with the scopes.'

'I can't see anything,' said Kellie. 'It's a tangle.'

'What do you think?' asked Marcel. 'Can you do it?'

'It isn't going to work,' said Kellie. 'It's too screwed up. You won't be able to push into that.'

'I agree,' said Hutch.

'Hutch.' Mac's voice went high. 'We don't have anything else.'

'Maybe we have.' She took a deep breath. 'Okay. Everybody relax. And here's what we're going to do.'

Kellie's dark eyes met hers, and a message passed between them, a question. Hutch nodded.

Kellie opened the storage cabinets and started pulling out air tanks. She handed one to Nightingale.

'What's this for?' he asked, looking genuinely puzzled.

'Everybody into your e-suit,' said Hutch.

'Why?' demanded Mac.

Hutch's voice was level. 'We're going to abandon ship.'

'Hutch,' said Marcel, 'slow down. Cut back six klicks.'

Hutch complied. Her adrenaline was pumping, and she was trying to rush things. 'How many tethers do we have?' she asked Kellie.

Kellie rummaged around in the cabinets. Hutch heard one of the e-suits activate. Nightingale's.

'Two,' said Kellie. She gave them to Mac and Nightingale, and showed them how to use the clips. 'Just hook it on the web, and it'll lock.'

'Hutch,' said Nightingale. 'Are you telling me we're going *outside*? We're going to *jump*?'

She nodded. 'I can put you right next to the net, Randy. You can walk over.'

'My God,' he said.

Hutch turned back to Marcel. 'How thick are the links in the net?'

'Narrow. Think of your index finger. Why do you ask?'

'I wanted to be sure our tethering clips would work. We're going to bail out.'

'What? You can't do that, Hutch.'

'Why not? Listen, it's our best chance, and I don't have time to argue.'

Kellie cut two more pieces of cable and handed one to Hutch. Hutch pulled on her air tanks and activated her e-suit.

'Yours and Hutch's don't have clips,' said Mac.

'We'll do fine,' Hutch told him. 'Now listen: When we get there, I'm going to lay this thing directly alongside. We're going to match its rate of descent, so the only thing you're going to have to do is lean out and grab hold. And climb on.'

Nightingale had gone chalk white.

'It'll work, Randy. No reason it won't. Once you're across, clip yourself on. Okay? It'll *look* scary, but you'll be safe. When you're there, and tethered, you can relax and enjoy the ride.'

She wanted to tell Nightingale they were going to be cutting things close, that there'd be no time to freeze in the airlock. But she restrained herself, knowing she might only cause the logjam she feared.

Kellie looked steadily at her. 'Why don't you let me take the controls?'

Hutch shook her head. 'Thanks,' she said. 'I got it.'

'I'll toss you for it.'

'It's okay.'

'Wait a minute,' said Nightingale. 'What's going on?' 'There won't be anybody to hold it steady for *her*' said Kellie.

'I'll get out,' said Hutch.

Kellie persisted. 'Maybe we should go back to trying to find the collar.'

'Won't work. Forget it. I'll manage.'

They were in close. They came out of a cloud bank and saw sunlight. The net hung out of the sky, directly in front of them.

Kellie was right, of course. The spike would hold the lander at a constant altitude, but the net was moving. Once Hutch let go of the controls, the net and the lander would separate very quickly. She could expect to get to the airlock and find the net thirty meters away.

Well, there was no help for it.

Damn.

'What about the wind?' asked Nightingale.

'No problem at this altitude.'

He was looking at her desperately. Poor son of a bitch was terrified. She tried to give him an encouraging smile. But there was no time to talk things over. She reduced the air pressure in the cabin to duplicate conditions outside. Then she opened the inner airlock hatch. 'Mac,' she said, 'you first. Go when I tell you.'

MacAllister nodded. 'Thanks, Hutch,' he said. And then he gazed wistfully at her. 'Thanks for everything.' He walked into the lock, and the outer hatch opened.

Never look down.

The net was hopelessly snarled.

'Wait till I tell you, Mac.' She moved closer, felt the links brush the hull. Be careful: She didn't want to get tangled. 'Okay, Mac. Go.'

MacAllister hesitated, and she caught her breath. *Please, Lord, not another one.*

Then he was gone. Hutch pulled quickly away to give him room, to reduce the possibility of hitting him or the net with the spacecraft.

Kellie was leaning out, looking off to one side. 'He's okay,' she said. 'He's on.'

'Kellie, you're next. Wait for the signal.' This way, if Nightingale panicked, he'd kill only himself.

Kellie leaned close to her in passing. 'Love you. Hutch,' she said.

Hutch nodded. 'You too.'

Kellie got into the airlock.

Nightingale was pulling more cable out of the locker. She wanted to ask what he was doing, but she was busy with other things.

Hutch brought the lander back in close. 'When I tell you,' she said.

Kellie waited, muscles tensed.

'*Now. Do it.*'

Kellie stepped out into the sky. Hutch pulled away again. 'Okay.' Kellie's voice rang on the circuit. 'I'm on board.'

Two for two.

The net's rate of descent was slowing. Hutch matched it and moved in again. 'Your turn. Randy,' she said.

He stood looking at her. 'How are you going to get out?'

'I'll get out.'

'*How?*'

The net stopped, paused, and began to rise. Hutch adjusted the lander's buoyancy, pushed into the linkage.

'Go,' she said.

He was standing immediately behind her.

'Not without you.' His voice sounded odd.

'Randy, I can't hold it here forever.'

He leaned down, showed her the piece of cable he'd just taken from the cabinet, and began to loop it around her waist.

'What are you doing?' she demanded.

The cable was about forty meters long. He hurried to the airlock and she saw that he'd tied the other end around his own middle. 'After I'm out,' he said, 'count to *one,* and come.'

'Randy, this is crazy. If I don't get clear—'

'We both go. Up or down together.'

The net was rising more quickly, accelerating, but she stayed with it. It clinked against the hull.

Hutch might have untied the tether. *But it gave her a chance.* Hell, it gave her a *good* chance. 'Okay, Randy,' she said. 'Go!'

He disappeared into the airlock, and then he was gone. She veered off, giving him room, listening for him to tell her he was okay. But he was breathing too hard to speak, or maybe his vocal cords were frozen and the cable between them was snaking out of the cabin. *I hope you're hooked to something, buddy.* She let go the yoke, leaped full tilt across the deck, and dived through the airlock, scooping the tether as she went so it wouldn't become tangled with the lander. The net was already out of reach, rising and drifting away.

Nightingale would almost have preferred to stay in the cabin, with its comforting bulkheads and its seats, to go down with it, rather than throw himself into the sky.

There had been a moment, when he was tying himself and Hutch together, that he'd thought he was really looking for an excuse to avoid the jump. And maybe that's what it had been. Maybe he'd hoped she would refuse his help, and he could then have simply, magnanimously, stayed with her, shielded from that terrible hatch.

But she'd trusted him, and that trust had fueled his determination not to humiliate himself again. The net had been within easy reach. He had simply taken it, gathered it into his arms, and *dragged* himself from the spacecraft. Then he was alone and the lander was veering away and he was hanging on, his eyes shut.

The net was rippling and moving. Nightingale clung to it, stood on it, felt its folds all around him, made himself part of it. He got his eyes open. The lander looked very far away, and the line that connected him to Hutchins lengthened until he feared he would be torn from his perch. *Where was she?*

Connect the tether.

He had to let go with one hand to do that. Impossible.

He concentrated on the links, on the smooth burnished surface of the chain, on the way they were fastened. On getting secured to the net before Hutch came out of the airlock.

On anything other than the open void that yawned all around him.

He pried a hand loose, gathered up the tether, which dangled from his vest, and hooked it to a link. Pulled on it. Felt it lock down.

The net was moving up, accelerating. He was getting heavier. Below him, Hutch came out of the lander, tumbling.

He lost sight of her. Loose cable spilled into the sky, and he slid both arms into the links, grabbed hold of Hutch's line, which was tied securely around his middle, and braced himself. 'I've got you,' he told her.

The jolt ripped the cable out of his hands and yanked hard at his midsection. It dragged the loop down past his beltline to his knees, tore his feet off the cable, and for a terrifying moment he thought they were both going to take the plunge. But his tether held. He grabbed frantically for her line and clung to it with one hand and to the net with the other.

Someone was asking whether he was okay. Hutch's line was slipping away, and he gathered his nerve and let go of the net to get a better grip. He looked down at her swinging gently back and forth above the cloud tops.

He was afraid his own tether would part under the strain.

'Hutch?' he cried. 'You okay?'

No answer.

She'd become an anchor, a deadweight, and he couldn't hold on, couldn't hold on. He squeezed his eyes shut, and his shoulders began to hurt.

He tried to pull up, tried to figure out a way to fasten her to the net, but he couldn't let go with either hand, or he'd lose her.

Kellie was asking for a goddam status report. 'Hanging by my fingernails,' he told her.

'Don't let go,' said Mac. Good old Mac, always full of obvious advice.

His arms and shoulders began to ache. 'Hutch? Help me.'

Stupid thing to say. She was swinging back and forth, God knows how far below the bottom of the net, and she obviously couldn't help *herself*.

Why didn't she answer? Was she dead? Killed in the fall? How far had she fallen anyhow? He tried to calculate, to give his mind something else to concentrate on.

'I can't hold her much longer,' he screamed at the circuit, at anyone who was listening. He was bent over and she weighed too much and he couldn't get her line up any higher. 'Please help.'

Marcel came on. 'Randy, don't let go.'

'How much longer?' he demanded. 'How much longer do I have to hang on?'

'Until you're in orbit,' he said. 'Fourteen minutes.'

His spirit sagged. *Never happen. Not close.* Fourteen minutes. *I might as well drop her now.*

Hutch had gotten the breath knocked out of her when she fell. She'd heard the voices on her circuit but they'd been distant and unintelligible until that last.

'Randy, don't let go.'

'How much longer?'

She looked up at the line, arcing overhead for what seemed an interminable length, up to the net. Up to Nightingale, twisted and hanging on. Reflexively she thought about trying to climb it, to get to safety, but it was a *long* way. She couldn't manage it under these circumstances, and she didn't want to put additional pressure on Nightingale,

'I'm okay, Randy,' she told him.

'Hutch!' He sounded so desperate. 'Can you climb up?'

'I don't think so.'

'Try.'

'Not a good idea,' she said.

'All right.' He sounded so tired. So *scared*.

'Don't let go, Randy.'

'I won't, Hutch. God help me, I won't.'

'It's because we're lifting you out,' Marcel told him. 'Hang on.'

'What do you think I'm trying to do?' He delivered a string of epithets, howling curses at tethers and landers and starship captains.

'Randy.' Marcel's voice, cutting through his rage.

'Yeah? Goddam, yes, what do you want?'

'We're going to try something.'

Oh God, he wanted to let go.

'Thirty seconds,' said Marcel. 'Just hold her for thirty seconds more.'

His arms and back were on fire.

'She's going to get heavier,' Marcel continued. 'But only for thirty seconds. Hang on that long, and it'll be okay.'

'Why? What?'

'On a five count. One.'

'For God's sake, do it.'

He waited. And abruptly the net jerked up. The line tore at him. Tore the flesh off his hands. Cut to bone.

He whimpered. He screamed.

He hated Hutchins. Hated her. Hated her.

Let go.

Please God let go.

The line curved away from him, disappearing under the net.

Won't.

Voice in his head or on the circuit telling him to hang on.

Any moment now.

We're almost there.

Won't.

Won't pass out. Won't let go.

Mac's voice, but the words unintelligible.

Not this time.

Not this time.

And suddenly the weight vanished. For a terrible moment he thought she was gone. But *he* floated free. Weightless. Zero gee.

He still held on.

'Randy.' Marcel now. 'You have about forty seconds. Tie her to the net. Tight. Because it's coming back. The weight's coming back.'

His fingers ached. They refused to open.

'Randy?' Kellie now. 'You okay?'

'I'm here.'

'Do what they tell you.'

'Half a minute, Randy. Get it done.' Marcel sounded desperate.

There was no *down* anymore. He drifted peacefully through the sky, waiting for the agony in his hands and shoulders to subside.

'Randy.' Hutch's voice sounded small and far away. 'Do it, Randy.'

Yes. He pulled slowly, painfully on her line. Hauled it in. Looped it through the net. And tied it. Knotted it. Square knot. Never come loose.

Not in a million years.

They were moving again, rising, the weight flowing back. 'It's okay,' he said. 'I've got her.'

He hurt. Everything he had hurt.

But a joy unlike anything he'd ever known before washed through him.

36

Most of us sleepwalk through our lives. We take all its glories, its wine, food, love, and friendship, its sunsets and its stars, its poetry and fireplaces and laughter, for granted. We forget that experience is not, or should not be, a casual encounter, but rather an embrace. Consequently, for too many of us, when we come to the end, we wonder where the years have gone. And we suspect we have not lived.

—GREGORY MACALLISTER, *Deepsix Diary*

'Hey!' Mac sounded frantic. 'What just happened?'

'They went to zero gee,' said Kellie. 'To give Randy a chance to get himself together.'

'How'd they do *that*?'

'You understand they were never trying to pull the net straight out of the atmosphere, right? You understand that?'

'Not really. But go ahead.'

'They had to angle the extraction, to get us into orbit. That neutralizes gravity and allows them to pick us up. They were probably turning into a parabola right from the start. What they must have done was to pick up the pace. Remember how heavy you got?'

'I have a vague recollection, yes.'

'That gains time. Then they cut the engines. In all four ships.'

'What's that do?'

'The whole system begins to drop back. It puts us in free fall.'

'Did we want that?'

'Zero gee, Mac. It makes everything weightless. Until they restart the engines, which of course they had to do pronto. But it gave Randy time to get Hutch aboard.'

'I'll be damned.'

'Probably that, too.'

One of the shuttles moved in just ahead of the *Star* and used a laser to cut through the Alpha shaft. This divided the system into two sections. The *Star* and *Zwick* remained attached to the trailing portion, whose length was reduced to a more manageable eighty kilometers; the other two vessels remained connected to the balance, which was over two hundred kilometers long, and which they could not hope to control. But other shuttles rendezvoused fore and aft to set *Wendy* and *Wildside* free, leaving the separated pieces spinning off into the dark.

The *Star* and *Zwick*, carrying what remained of the shaft, the net, and its four passengers, continued maneuvering cautiously toward orbit.

Hutch was still trailing behind the linkage. 'Randy,' she was saying, 'you did a helluva job.'

Nicholson came on the circuit to inquire after the welfare of his passenger Mr MacAllister. And belatedly of the others. Whoever they might be, thought Kellie. The *Star* was planning a celebration in their honor.

Canyon showed up, *en virtuo*, to inform Kellie she was on live, and to ask if she was all right.

'Pretty good,' Kellie told him. He tried to conduct an interview, and she answered a few questions, then pleaded exhaustion. 'Mac would enjoy talking to you,' she added.

When at last they achieved orbit, they didn't need anyone to let them know. Their weight simply melted away. This time for good.

Marcel, sounding as cool and collected as he had through most of the crisis, congratulated them on their good fortune. 'I thought,' he said, 'you might like to hear what's going on in the main dining room.'

They listened to the sound of cheers.

The sky was black. Not the smoky debris-ridden sky of the dying world below, but the pure diamond-studded sky that one sees from a superluminal.

Nightingale, still cautiously hanging on to the net, gave Hutch a nervous little wave, as if he didn't want to show too much emotion.

She was drifting toward him. 'Hi, Hutch,' he said. 'I didn't freeze.'

No, you didn't, she thought. And she said: 'You were outstanding, Randy.'

'Welcome to the accommodations, Hutch,' said Kellie.

And Mac: 'Nice to have you aboard. Next lime you'll want to reserve a better seat.'

Lights moved among the stars.

'You all right?' asked Nightingale. He reached for her, and she felt a sharp pain in her left shoulder when she responded. But what the hell.

'I'm fine,' she said.

'I'd never have dropped you.' Nightingale's voice sounded strange.

She nodded yes. She knew.

'I'd never have let you go. Not ever.'

She took his head in her hands, gazed at him a long time, and kissed him. Deep and long. Right through the Flickinger field.

'There they are.' Embry pointed at the screen and Frank enhanced the picture. They were still far away, but she could make out

Hutch, even amid the tangles. One of the others, Kellie probably, waved.

Frank set course and reported to Marcel that he was about to pick up the survivors.

Embry had already been on the circuit with them. 'Be especially careful with Hutchins,' she said. 'I think she's got a problem.'

'Okay, Doc,' said Frank. 'We'll be careful.'

They closed on the net.

'Get Hutchins first. Just pull up alongside her. I'll bring her in.'

'You need help?' asked Frank.

'It wouldn't hurt.'

The situation demanded a human pilot, so Frank looked around for a volunteer. He'd gotten the impression, from bits and pieces of things said, and from nonverbal clues, that Drummond didn't like the idea of going outside. Janet Hazelhurst caught his eyes and eased out of her chair. 'Just tell me what to do,' she said.

Drummond tried to look as if he'd been about to offer, but had been too late.

Hutch watched the lights coming. It was okay to relax. She closed her eyes and floated. The shuttle came alongside, and she could hear voices on the circuit. Somebody was cutting through the tether, taking her off the net.

The pain in her shoulder got worse. Now that she was safe.

Hatches closed somewhere. More lights appeared. Bright and then dim. Lowered voices. Pressure on the injured shoulder. Restraints. A sense of well-being flooding through her.

Somebody was telling her it was over, she was okay, nothing to worry about.

'Good,' she said, not sure to whom she was speaking.

'You look all right. Skipper.'

Skipper? She opened her eyes and tried to pierce the haze. Embry.

'Hello, Embry. Nice to see you again.' Randy was still there.

off to the side, staying close. Then he became indistinct, as did Embry, the restraints, the voices, and the lights.

From Nicholson's bridge, Marcel directed the fleet of shuttles. They deployed near the *Star* and *Zwick* and cut them free of the shaft. At Beekman's suggestion, they salvaged six samples, each four meters long. Five were intended for research, and one would go on display at the Academy. At Nicholson's request a smaller piece was picked up and earmarked for exhibition on the *Star*.

Another shuttle approached the connecting plate and separated it from the net and from the stump of the Alpha shaft. It hovered momentarily while its occupants inspected the symbols engraved across its face. Then they cut it neatly into two pieces of equal size. Shortly thereafter, *Wendy* approached and took both pieces into her cargo hold.

The remaining fragments of Alpha, and the net, floated away into the dark.

Because time was pressing, no immediate attempt was made to return the captains to their respective ships. Miles, in fact, was retained as acting captain on *Wendy*. Hutch, of course, was in no condition to be sent back to *Wildside*. Guided from the bridge of the *Star*, the shuttles were taken into whichever bays were convenient, and, with little more than a day remaining before the collision, the fleet began to withdraw.

By then conditions on the planetary surface had become so turbulent that the orbiting vehicles were themselves at hazard. Marcel guessed that much of the data coming in from the probes had been lost after *Wendy*'s communications went down. This assumption was confirmed by Miles. 'They are not a happy group over here,' he said.

Beekman sympathized. 'You can't really blame them. Some of them have been preparing twenty years for this mission, and they lost a substantial piece of it.' He gazed steadily at the banks of screens, which displayed views of the impending collision, taken from an array of satellites.

Marcel really didn't give a damn. He'd been through too much over the two weeks. He was tired and irritable, but they'd gotten Kellie and the others back, and that was all he cared about. Chiang Harmon had died down there. One of Hutch's people had died, one of Nicholson's passengers, and one of his crew. One of Nicholson's pilots had died during the rescue. In the face of that, it was hard to work up too much regret that they had lost some details on the formation of high-pressure fronts during a planetary traffic accident. 'We'll do better next time.'

Beekman pursed his lips and looked thoughtful. 'There'll be no next time. Probably not in the life span of the species.'

Too bad, thought Marcel. But he didn't say anything.

It seemed as if the entire atmosphere of Deepsix had become one massive electrical storm. Blizzards swept the equatorial area, and giant hurricanes roared across the Coraggio and the Nirvana. A mountainous tide soared thousands of meters above nominal sea level. The range along the northern coast of Transitoria, which had held back the tides so long, vanished beneath the waters.

The worlds moved inexorably toward each other. But it was a mismatch, thought Hutch, a pebble falling into a pond.

She watched from her bed in the *Star*'s dispensary. She'd required minor surgery for a torn muscle and a broken rib, and they didn't want her moving around for a bit. With his hands wrapped Randy sat off to one side, wearing a shoulder brace. Mac was off somewhere giving an interview; and Kellie was down getting some goodies at the snack bar.

Hutch's link chimed. Canyon's voice: 'Hutch, I'll be down to see you later. Meantime, I thought you'd like to know we're a big hit back home. They're a couple days behind, of course. Last we heard, the whole world was listening while the tide broke through and got the whatchamacallits. They think you don't have a chance now. Wait till they see the finish. You guys will be celebrities when you get back.'

'Nice to hear,' grumbled Nightingale.

'Anyhow, our numbers are through the roof.'

'Sounds as if you'll do pretty well yourself, Augie,' said Hutch.

'Well, I can't see that it'll hurt my career any.' His eyes literally *flashed*. 'Wait until they get to the lander!'

'Yeah,' said Nightingale. 'That sure was a hoot.'

Canyon kept going: 'Incidentally, you folks have acquired a sobriquet back home.'

'I'm not sure I want to hear what it is,' Hutch said.

'The Maleiva Four.'

'By God,' said Nightingale, 'who thought that up? Magnificent, August. My compliments to the cliché unit.'

When he was gone, she looked at Nightingale severely. 'You were awfully hard on him. He means well.'

'Yep. But he'd have been happier if we'd fallen off the goddam thing.'

'Why do you think that?'

'Better story.'

Mac came into the room, carrying flowers, which had been grown in the *Star* nurseries. He beamed down at Hutch and held them out to her. 'You look good enough to have for lunch,' he said.

She accepted a kiss and smelled the bouquet. They were yellow roses. 'Gorgeous. Thanks, Mac.'

'For the Golden Girl.' He gazed at her. 'What are they saying? The medical people?'

'They'll let me up tomorrow.' She turned her attention back to Nightingale. '*You*,' she said, 'should ease up. Let people do their jobs and don't be such a crank.'

'I enjoy being a crank.'

Roiling clouds of immense proportions billowed out of Maleiva III's atmosphere. Fireballs erupted and fell back. And erupted again. The entire black atmosphere seemed to be expanding, fountaining into the sky, a burning river beginning to flow toward the placid disk of the gas giant.

'Here it comes,' said Mac.

Nightingale nodded. 'Everything that's loose anywhere on Deepsix is being ripped out now and sent elsewhere.' His voice was quiet. Resigned.

Mac shifted in his chair. 'There's no point getting sentimental over a piece of real estate,' he said.

Nightingale stared straight ahead. 'I was thinking about the lights.'

'The lights?' Hutch's brow furrowed.

'I don't think we told you. Forgot in all the rushing around. At Bad News Bay. We saw something out in the water. Signaled back and forth.'

'A boat?'

'Don't know what it was.'

Steam was pouring off Deepsix. Fire and lightning swirled across the vast expanse of its clouds.

Kellie came back with donuts and coffee.

MacAllister was still there a half hour later when Marcel, Nicholson, and Beekman came by to see how she was doing. Hutch thought all three looked tired, happy, relieved. They shook hands all around. 'We're glad to have you back,' Marcel said. 'Things looked a little doubtful there for a while.'

'Did they *really*?' asked Mac. 'I thought we had it under control all the way.'

Nicholson beamed at him. 'We're planning a little celebration tomorrow,' he said. Hutch caught the flavor of the remark, that dinner with the two captains was an Event, and that they should all feel appropriately honored. But he was trying to do the right thing. And what the hell, it was a small enough failing.

'I'd be delighted to attend,' said Mac.

'As would I.' Hutch gave him a warm smile.

Marcel introduced Beekman as the manager of the rescue operation. 'Saved your life,' he added.

Hutch wasn't sure what he meant. 'You mean *all* our lives.'

'Yours, specifically. Gunther came up with the zero-gee maneuver.'

Tom Scolari called, and his image formed at the foot of her bed. He was wearing dark slacks and a white shirt open to his navel. Sending somebody a message, looked like. 'Glad you came through it okay,' he said. 'We were worried.'

'Where are you now, Tom?'

'On *Zwick*.'

'Good. Did you get interviewed?'

'I don't think there's anybody out here who hasn't had a chance to talk on UNN. Listen' – his eyes found hers, and glanced over at Mac – 'you guys put on one hell of a show.'

'Thanks. We had a lot of help. Not to mention your own. I understand you're a pretty good welder.'

'I'll never be without work again.'

'Next time you tell me not to do something,' she added, 'I'll try to take you more seriously.'

He grinned and blew her a kiss. 'I doubt it.'

She woke up in the middle of the night and noticed they were no longer accelerating.

It was, finally, over.

Epilogue

Cataclysms too vast to be defined as quakes threw forests and mountain ranges skyward, as much as twenty thousand meters, where they were caught between competing gravity wells, and eventually swept off. Tidal effects literally ripped Maleiva III apart. The swirl of gas and debris surrounding the world had become so thick that it blinded the opticals. The placid snow-covered plains around the tower, the baroque temple that had seemed almost Parisian, the lights at Bad News Bay, the memorial and the hexagon, all disintegrated in the general ruin.

Wherever fractures or faults existed, the rock was shredded, torn free, and hurled upward. The planet bled lava. The mantle disintegrated, exposing the core. Energy release was so titanic that it could not be viewed directly. Scientists on board *Wendy*, finally able to concentrate on the event they'd come to see, cheered and began to think about future papers.

Shortly before the collision, Maleiva III exploded and burned like a small nova. Then the light dimmed, and it dissolved into a series of individual embers curving through the night, falling finally into Morgan's cobalt gulfs, where they left bruises.

Within hours, the shower of debris was gone from the sky, and only the bruises remained to mark the incident. Meantime, Morgan would continue on its way, barely affected by the encounter. Its orbit would not change appreciably. Its massive gravity would eventually scramble a few moons elsewhere in the system. But that was a couple of centuries away.

Hutch had assumed the dinner was to be in honor of the Maleiva Four. At first it seemed that way. They were introduced to the crowded main dining hall individually, applauded, and seated at the captain's table. Everyone wanted to shake their hands, wish them well, get their autographs.

They were invited to make speeches. ('But we'd appreciate it if you kept your remarks to five minutes.' When Nightingale ran over, Nicholson took to glancing ostentatiously at the time.) And everyone got a picture taken with one or another of the rescuees.

There were also pictures from the adventure itself, and hundreds of these were put forward to be signed. Some were of the Astronomer's Tower (which no one was any longer calling Burbage Point), others were from the interviews on the ground conducted by August Canyon, still others of the long empty corridors in the hexagon atop Mt. Blue. Here was Nightingale seated beside a campfire early in the trek, and Hutch hanging from the net as seen through the telescopes on the rescue shuttle. There was Gregory MacAllister shaking hands with well-wishers on their arrival at the *Star*. Someone had gotten a portrait of Kellie posed against a sky overwhelmed by Morgan's World. She looked beautiful and defiant, and it rapidly became the favorite of the evening. Eventually, it would become the jacket for *Deepsix Diary* MacAllister's best-selling account of the episode.

Despite all this, the evening belonged, not to the Four, but to their rescuers. The three captains, Marcel, Nicholson, and Miles Chastain, took round after round of applause. Beekman and his team were credited with working out the general strategy. John Drummond, who did much of the orbital calculations, took a bow. And the cheers for Janet Hazelhurst were deafening.

The Outsiders were invited to stand, while the band played a few bars from a military anthem. The shuttle pilots were introduced. And Abel Kinder, who was credited with keeping the weather sufficiently calm until the rescue could be effected. Phil Zossimov, who developed the collar and the support rails that would have made things so much easier. Had they, as he commented wryly, only had an opportunity to work.

And there was finally a moment to remember those whose lives had been lost. Cole Wetherai, pilot of the *Star* lander. Klaus Bomar, the shuttle pilot. *Star* passenger Casey Hayes, who, as MacAllister pointed out, had died trying to salvage one of the landers. Chiang Harmon of the science research team. And Toni Hamner, who would not have been there at all, said Hutch, except that she stayed with a friend.

They set up a buffet. The ship's best wines were uncorked. And Captain Nicholson announced that TransGalactic would pick up the tab. Passengers and guests were responsible only for whatever gratuities they might choose to leave.

Late in the evening, Hutch found herself alone on the dance floor with Marcel. When she'd arrived, fourteen standard days before (had it really been so recently?), he'd been only a colleague, an occasional voice in the cockpit, a person she'd seen at a seminar or two. Now she thought of him as the Gallant Frenchman. 'I've got some news for you,' the Gallant Frenchman said. 'We got the results back on the scan of the shaft. It's three thousand years old.'

She was in his arms, in the exotic style of the time. Everybody's arms felt good, his and Mac's and Kellie's and Tom Scolari's and Randy Nightingale's. Especially Randy Nightingale's, the man who would not let go.

Three thousand years. 'So we were right.'

'I'd say so. It was a rescue mission. The hawks were doing what they could to get a nontechnical people out of harm's way. Or at least to give their species a chance to survive elsewhere.'

513

'Where, I wonder?'

Marcel placed his lips against her cheek. 'Who knows? Maybe one day we'll find them.'

Hutch recalled the predator appearance of the hawks. 'They did not look friendly.'

'No. I thought not either.' Her lips found his. 'Shows you how looks can deceive.'

There was, inevitably, a sim. Hutch was played by Ivy Kramer, an actress of truly magnificent proportions. Mac appeared in a cameo, not as himself, but as Beekman. The drama portrayed Erik Nicholson as the true hero of the rescue. This interpretation of events might have been influenced by the fact that the production company was owned by the same multinational as TransGalactic.

It introduced persons on board the *Star* who tried actively to sabotage the effort for murky reasons never quite made clear, and it depicted the crew of the *Boardman* striving heroically to retrieve their lost lander so they could come to the rescue. Hutch and Nightingale were tracked relentlessly through the hexagon by a shape-changing *thing*.

There were books, other than Mac's. Action figures appeared and sold briskly. All four survivors were subjected to extensive interviews, and Kellie eventually became the official representative for Warburton, a company that manufactured sports equipment. E-cards featuring her with a set of golf clubs have since become a collector's item.

An effort was made to get Nightingale to run for governor of Georgia, but he declined. His onetime wife, the daughter of a retired Academy director, made several unsuccessful attempts to renew their relationship.

Mac continued to write scathing commentary on assorted hypocrisies in high places and low, without which hypocrisies, he cheerfully conceded, civilized life would be impossible.

Hutch remained in the service of the Academy.

They all profited from the action toys, from the games, from various kinds of sports clothes, and also from the sale of a line of Deepsix Four (the name change to *Deepsix* had been urged by the action toy company) long-stem glassware, which inevitably featured a female figure dangling from a tether that disappeared into a cloud – an artistic embellishment – and the motto, *Nunquam dimitte.* Never Let Go.

Never Let Go.

It is now the official motto of at least three specialized military forces in Germany, China, and Brazil.

They named a high school in New York Park South for Kellie, a mall in Toronto for Hutch, and a Lisbon zoo for Nightingale. There is now a Colt Wetherai Memorial Library off Fulham Palace Road in London, and a Toni Hamner Science Museum in Hamburg. The Winnipeg space flight school in which Klaus Bomar used to teach now has a wing named for him. Mac received no such accolades, although he claimed that the local bishop had wanted to put his name on the new Correlates Religious Studies Center in Des Moines.

Awards were passed to almost everyone involved in the rescue. The most heavily recognized was Erik Nicholson, widely credited with persisting during the darkest hours of the effort. Beekman received the Conciliar Award for Science, usually reserved for those instances when humanitarian applications of a breakthrough can be shown. Marcel was given a formal commendation from the Academy and became a figure of interest to the corporate world. Within a year, he'd been offered, and had accepted, a director's post with TransGalactic. He's now a vice president, makes more money than he ever dreamed possible, and talks a lot about the good old days. When he's pressed, he admits to being bored.

Kellie, Hutch, Randy, and Mac continue to get together whenever occasion permits. They are frequently joined by

Marcel, and occasionally by Janet Hazelhurst, the world's most famous welder, and by one or another of their rescuers. Last year they took eleven members of the Outsiders to dinner at Iceman's in Philadelphia.

Iceman's is more than simply the finest restaurant in the Delaware Valley. It's also on the ground floor.

Afterword

Let me stipulate that, while the questions raised concerning the failure of the Athena Boardman to come to the assistance of the vessels at Maleiva III were legitimate, they were not initiated by me, as has been charged by officials at Kosmik, Inc. In fact, they grew out of a reaction to the sim, which portrayed the Boardman captain in heroic terms. This in turn sparked an investigation, originally for the implied purpose of handing out awards. My only connection with the proceedings arose from the fact that I happened to be one of the persons left to do as best we could when Boardman went missing in action.

The problem for Kosmik quickly became one of potential liability, and they consequently reacted to the initial inquiry by doing what large corporations always do: First they stonewalled, and then when they realized that wouldn't work, they found a mechanic at the Wheel and blamed the incident on him, citing failure to inspect a faulty RX-17 black box that rendered the launcher unstable. They gave him a formal letter of reprimand, fired him, and released his name to the media.

This was too much for Eliot Penkavic, the ship's captain, who called a press conference, admitted to lying about the incident, and blamed the entire unhappy episode on Ian Helm, Kosmik's new director of operations at the Quraqua terraforming unit.

Helm has denied everything, and Penkavic now faces prosecution.

But company spokesmen have had a difficult time explaining just what Penkavic hoped to gain by failing to assist when it was clearly in his power to do so, or why he had agreed to come to the rescue, then apparently changed his mind.

To get a clearer picture of what must actually have transpired one has only to ask the basic question any policeman asks when faced with conflicting stories: Who stood to profit? The pilot to whom it made no difference whatever whether he went to Maleiva III or to Quraqua? Or the company big shot anxious to get to his new position with a shipload of time-sensitive personnel and supplies?

As I write this, Penkavic's trial is less than a week away. I am pleased to report that, since the arrival on the case of Archie Stoddard, the lawyer hired by this publishing house and best-known for securing substantial judgments against corporate scofflaws, rumors have begun to circulate that the so-called in-house investigation by Kosmik has taken on new life. And that Helm may be thrown to the wolves to head off the legal action that would clearly follow a finding of not guilty in the Penkavic case.

The Engines of God

Jack McDevitt

The Academy Series – Book One

Two hundred years ago, humans made a stunning discovery in the far reaches of the solar system: a huge statue of an alien creature, with an inscription that defied all efforts at translation.

Now, as faster-than-light drive opens the stars to exploration, humans are finding other relics of the race they call the Monument-Makers – each different, and each heartbreakingly beautiful. But except for a set of footprints on Jupiter's moon Iapetus, there is no trace of the enigmatic race that has left them behind.

Then a team of scientists working on a dead world discover an ominous new image of the Monument-Makers. Somehow it all fits with other lost civilizations and possibly with Earth's own future. And distant past. But Earth itself is on the brink of ecological disaster – there is no time to search for answers. Even to a question that may hold the key to survival for the entire human race.

Praise for Jack McDevitt:

'The logical heir to Isaac Asimov and Arthur C. Clarke'   *Stephen King*

'Another highly intelligent, absorbing portrayal of the far future from a leading creator of such tales'   *Booklist*

'Combines hard science fiction with mystery and adventure in a wild tour of the distant future. Stellar plotting, engaging characters, and a mastery of storytelling'   *Library Journal* (starred review)

978 1 4722 0319 9

headline